Twayne's United States Classics Series

SYLVIA E. BOWMAN, Editor

Indiana University

THE BRAVO

THE BRAVO

by JAMES FENIMORE COOPER

Edited for the Modern Reader by
Donald A. Ringe
UNIVERSITY OF KENTUCKY

COLLEGE & UNIVERSITY PRESS · *Publishers*
NEW HAVEN, CONN.

INTRODUCTION

Writing in *Maule's Curse* (1938) in an essay that is perhaps the best brief treatment of James Fenimore Cooper as a literary artist, Yvor Winters recommends *The Bravo*—along with the Leatherstocking tales and the first two Littlepage novels—as "indispensable" to the student of American literature (p. 49). Winters makes a good case for his opinion. Although he rightly concedes the sentimental style of the tale to be an obvious flaw, he argues convincingly that this defect does not seriously detract from the book's main virtues: the "subtleties of perception" that can be discerned in this as in any other consistently maintained style, and the important social theme in terms of which the details of the action take on a truly "dramatic significance" (pp. 33-34). Nor are these the only merits that he finds in the book. He praises the "profundity of conception of *The Bravo*" as far beyond the powers of comprehension or creation of a man like Poe (p. 117), and he sees in the depiction of the corrupt and corrupting Venetian senators "a moral portrait worthy of Hawthorne" (p. 34). Cooper is placed in excellent company here—better company certainly than many critics are willing to allow him—but Winters is essentially right in his estimate. The book does deserve to be better known.

Other critics have also found much to praise in *The Bravo*. Robert E. Spiller, for example, in *Fenimore Cooper: Critic of His Times* (1931), not only describes the book as "one of the best of Cooper's romances" (p. 218), but also considers it the first of his works in which the "moral purpose" determines "the pattern of the plot structure and the entire motivation of the story" (p. 258). James Grossman, moreover, in *James Fenimore Cooper* (1949), observes the success with which Cooper creates in the impersonal machine of the Venetian government a "dramatic character" that dominates the tale, and he sees in the dénouement of the story—the beheading of Jacopo, the Bravo— a "brilliant reversal" of the apparent course of the plot that "stuns us into enlightenment" (pp. 78-79). With a single incident, Cooper brings the whole meaning of the book into sharp focus in a perfect union of action and theme. Marius Bewley, too, in *The Eccentric Design* (1959), praises *The Bravo* for the "strict economy" with which it develops its "central theme," for the color and splendor of its romantic descriptions, and for the brilliant analysis of the character of the ruling class (pp. 59, 63-64). None of these critics, perhaps, would insist upon the absolute success of the tale as a work of literary art, but all make abundantly clear that *The Bravo* has much to recommend it to the discerning modern reader.

Yet for all its obvious merits, *The Bravo* has never been widely known. Although it seems to have been well received by the reading public when it was published late in 1831, it has never found the audience of such works as *The Spy, The Pilot*, and the Leatherstocking tales. At first the reception was friendly. Cooper's American publishers wrote him in March, 1832, that Americans liked the book "very well," [1] and as Dorothy Waples has shown in *The Whig Myth of James Fenimore Cooper* (1938), the notices of the book that first appeared in American newspapers and magazines seem to establish the fact that "*The Bravo* was accepted as a good piece of fiction and as an obviously republican work" (pp. 87-88). Because it affirms such strong republican principles, however, the book soon became entangled in political controversy and suffered attacks both here and abroad from which its reputation has never fully recovered. Critical opinion in France, for example, divided along political lines: the book was attacked by conservatives, who naturally opposed its liberal political principles, and was praised by those who accepted them (Waples, pp. 85-86). These reactions were to be expected, for the basic ideas expressed in the book had an obvious application to French politics that was apparent to both the conservative forces and their republican opponents.

Cooper, moreover, had openly identified himself with the republican side on a specific political issue. Out of friendship for Lafayette, Cooper, who lived in Europe from 1826 to 1833, had allowed himself in 1831-32 to be drawn into a French domestic controversy, in which he attempted to demonstrate that republics are not more expensive than monarchies. Since the view

---

1 *The Letters and Journals of James Fenimore Cooper,* ed. by James Franklin Beard (Cambridge, Mass., 1960), II, 151. Hereafter abbreviated as *L&J*.

he expressed directly opposed the contention of Louis Philippe's conservative supporters, Cooper's part in the Finance Controversy was bound to bring him under attack by the conservative faction. To Cooper's mind, this was no more than natural. What surprised—and pained—him was that American journals did not give him the support to which his affirmation of republican principles entitled him (Waples, p. 86). Instead, Cooper soon found his book under attack at home in the Whig press. In June, 1832, the *New York American*, a journal that had already noticed *The Bravo* favorably, published an extremely unfriendly review of the book signed by "Cassio." This review misrepresents the book so grossly that the attack seems to have been deliberate. Dorothy Waples believes that it may have been politically inspired (pp. 90-91).

Be that as it may, some of Cooper's friends thought that agents of the French government lay behind the "Cassio" review, and Samuel F. B. Morse, in particular, set out to discover the identity of the reviewer. Actually, "Cassio" turned out to be an American, Edward S. Gould, who wrote for a number of different journals, but Cooper, too, became convinced of the foreign origin of the "Cassio" review, and he stressed this point in his own replies on the subject. Meanwhile, the controversy over *The Bravo* and Cooper's activities in Europe became deeply involved with politics so that subsequent attacks on Cooper and *The Bravo* in the Whig press had little if anything to do with the literary merits of the tale. Cooper's defense of his views and his book in *A Letter to His Countrymen* (1834) only added fuel to the flames. In it, among other things, he defends himself against the reviewers; criticizes the American people for falling under the influence of foreign opinion; and makes a plea for American intellectual independence. This reply only provoked the Whigs to further personal attacks that, in one form or another, were to continue for many years.

All of the bitter controversy surrounding *The Bravo* has surely had its effect upon the reputation of the tale. As Miss Waples has shown, the consistent attacks in the Whig press created a warped image of Cooper the man that persisted for over a century, and the repeated denunciations of his European tales have certainly contributed to the general neglect into which they have fallen. To be sure, William Cullen Bryant, in his Memorial Address on Cooper (1852), assigned *The Bravo* a

7

"high rank among his works," [2] but Bryant was a friend—and the Democratic editor of the *New York Evening Post*—who could be counted upon to agree with the theme of the book and to defend it. Thomas R. Lounsbury, however, in his *James Fenimore Cooper* (1883), while recognizing that the book had never been fairly criticized, disapproved in general of the novel of explicit purpose, and found little to praise in *The Bravo* (pp. 108-111). Only during the last few decades, therefore, has the book been seriously judged on its merits alone. Now at last, we may hope, *The Bravo* can be read for its true importance as a significant intellectual document and valued work of art.

I

The Bravo is a thesis novel. We know from Cooper's writings in the preface and elsewhere that he deliberately intended to develop a political and social theme for the edification and enlightenment as well as the pleasure of his countrymen. By the time he conceived the story—during a short stay in Venice in the spring of 1830—he had already spent four years in Europe, had lived both in England and on the continent, and had pondered much on the political and social differences between Europe and the United States. He came to believe that an American could not really know his own country's institutions if he did not have a knowledge of Europe, for it is only by comparison that one can appreciate the true advantages that he enjoys (*L&J*, I, 411). Too many Americans, he knew, were not aware of European reality and were far too ready to look to European institutions for analogies and precedents rather than to launch out on their own and act in accordance with superior American principles. Aristocratic England, in particular, could provide no suitable model for Americans to follow.[3] In writing *The Bravo*, therefore, Cooper was, in part, directing his attack against the British aristocrats, and, as James F. Beard has observed, against "the pattern of British oligarchy which the Doctrinaires were seeking to impose on France" (*L&J*, II, 4).

---

2 Most easily found in *Prose Writings* (New York, 1884), I, 316.

3 *A Letter to His Countrymen*, reprinted in part in Robert E. Spiller, *James Fenimore Cooper: Representative Selections* (New York, 1936), pp. 170-181, 293-295. See pp. 174, 179. Hereafter, page references to the *Letter* are to these selections, abbreviated *RS*.

That Cooper had also another purpose in mind has been advanced by other critics. Russell Kirk, writing in *College English* (1946), believes that Cooper presented "the failings of European systems" to warn Americans that their institutions, too, could be destroyed (VII, 199), a belief that is shared by Marius Bewley, who contends that Cooper wrote *The Bravo* to warn his countrymen that a commercial oligarchy, using republican institutions to mask its activities, might gain control of the American government (p. 58). That Cooper was correct in his analysis, moreover, has been suggested by Yvor Winters, who observes that just such an aristocracy of wealth was developing in the United States within a decade of Cooper's death, that within twenty years it had, for all practical purposes, effectively nullified the legal government during the Grant administration (p. 26). The problem that Cooper treats in *The Bravo*, therefore, is both a significant and a continuing one, for it remains very much alive a century and more after his death. Stated simply, it is the question of how the modern state shall be governed.

Cooper believed that many people misunderstood the fundamental issue. They thought that the contest lay between monarchy and democracy, whereas he observed that monarchy as a ruling principle was dead, except insofar as it was maintained, as in England, to cloak the real power in the hands of the aristocracy.[4] The true conflict lay, therefore, between the aristocrats and the democrats, between those who would place power in the hands of an élite, either hereditary or financial, and those who would entrust it to the mass of the people themselves. Political terminology had confused the issue. The word "republic" can be used to describe a variety of different political states. It can be applied, for example, both to the United States of America and to Venice as it had existed through the eighteenth century. A republic, as Cooper wrote in *The American Democrat* (1838), could be either aristocratic or democratic. The only quality that distinguishes it from a monarchy is that in the one the rights of the monarch, in the other the rights of the community, prevail (*AD*, pp. 13-15). A republic, however, may have either a large or a small base (*AD*, p. 65). If the base is

---

4 *RS*, p. 293. For Cooper's discussion of the power of the British aristocracy, see *RS*, pp. 176-177. See also James Fenimore Cooper, *The American Democrat*, with an introductory note by Robert E. Spiller (New York, 1956), pp. 10-12. Hereafter abbreviated as *AD*.

9

small and powerful enough to control the machinery of government, the forms of a republic, as Grossman has noted (p. 76),
can be used to hide an aristocratic reality as effectively as can
those of a monarchy.

In Cooper's view, this danger was especially to be avoided,
for he believed that the purely aristocratic form of government
is among the worst known. Cooper, of course, was not unaware
of the advantages of aristocratic states, for he knew that they
are run with energy and efficiency by men who favor the culti-
vation of the civilizing graces of society in their patronage of
knowledge and the arts (*AD*, pp. 57-59). He was well aware,
too, that the educated and wealthy classes are better able to come
to intelligent decisions in public affairs than is the uninformed
mass of the people, for their wealth, leisure, and education afford
them the means for "observation and comparison" and for judging "more accurately of men and measures" (*AD*, p. 50). Cooper
was thus entirely familiar with the line of argument so frequently put forth by those in favor of rule by the qualified
few. He also believed, however, that although these men should
use their advantages for proper ends, in practice they do not.
When power is possessed by only the few, they use it to their
own advantage (*AD*, p. 51).

Cooper goes on to say, moreover, that aristocracies, like corporations, are irresponsible, soulless bodies, which, because of
"human selfishness," are generally "administered in the interests
of the few." Because the controlling element, at least in modern
aristocracies, is that of property, they are open to the most
corrupting influence that affects the actions of men, an influence, that, when united with "political patronage and power,"
leads, he argues, to social corruption (*AD*, pp. 64-65). By 1838,
Cooper had already depicted in a number of books the abuses he
saw in aristocratic societies. In addition to *The Bravo*, where his
attack is most successful, he had written *The Headsman* (1833)
to illustrate the hardships of the worthy commoner in an aristocratic state, and *The Monikins* (1835) to satirize the stake in
society theory—and British aristocracy—through the characters
of John Goldencalf and the Lords of Leaphigh. Cooper was
thus always the loyal democrat who saw in a politically powerful
and self-perpetuating élite a dangerous threat to a free society.

Cooper was not so partisan a democrat, however, as to fail
to see the abuses of the democratic system. Always the keen

10

observer of men and manners, he knew that democracy, too, could be far from perfect. He recognized most clearly, as he wrote in *The American Democrat*, the tendency to mediocrity among the citizens of a democratic society because all things gravitate toward a common average. He realized, too, that a serious danger in democracies is the substitution of public opinion for law; that the tyranny of the majority can be a severe one; that public opinion is sometimes misled by unscrupulous men for improper ends; that men are disposed to defer to the popular will, even when it is wrong (*AD*, pp. 66-71). Cooper criticized abuses wherever he found them; and, after his return from Europe in 1833, he attacked those he saw in American society as vigorously as he had the quite different ones he had found in Europe. In his treatment of the citizens of Leaplow (the United States) in *The Monikins* and in his picture of American society in *Homeward Bound* and *Home as Found* (1838), he is merciless in his satire on American demagogues and leveling democrats. This attack, which he continued during the middle 1840's in his anti-rent trilogy, the Littlepage novels (1845-46), earned him, ironically, the name of "aristocrat."

It is a mistake, however, to read these later works as a sign of Cooper's withdrawal into conservatism from the liberal stand he had taken in *The Bravo*. To do so is to misunderstand all of these books and the basic point that Cooper repeatedly stresses. Part of the trouble comes once again from terminology: this time the word "aristocrat." Edward and John Effingham in *Homeward Bound* and *Home as Found* and the Littlepage heroes in the anti-rent novels are the type of men that Americans are likely to call aristocratic: they are educated gentlemen with tastes and manners far above the average. But this is not what Cooper means by the term. To be sure, they are gentlemen, but they differ from the kind of aristocrat he had always attacked in that they do not have exclusive political power. Cooper reserved the word "aristocrat" to mean one of a small group who hold the political power in a country (*AD*, pp. 92-93). Since power in the United States is in the possession of the many, these men could not be called true aristocrats. Indeed, if there is danger to American institutions, it comes more likely, he believed, not from these educated gentlemen, but from the leveling democrats and demagogues who would subvert principle for personal gain, and from the new commercial class, similar in

11

some ways to the Venetian senators, that he foresaw was on the rise.[5]

The Bravo is thus a significant book, not only for the study of Cooper's thought, but also for the light it throws upon some fundamental questions of democracy. Cooper perceived that the forms of a republic could easily be used to cloak almost any kind of tyrannous authority. He believed, therefore, that in the affairs of the world, one must always probe the externals of things to the reality that lies beneath, lest one be deceived by a shadow. We of the twentieth century who know that the forms of democracy represent quite different realities on each side of the Iron Curtain can appreciate the clearness of Cooper's vision and the soundness of his political analysis. We know, moreover, that even in our society, power can gravitate into the hands of a financial class, as it did in the Grant administration, though the forms of the republic remain unchanged. The danger, indeed, is always a potential one in a commercial or industrial society. The Bravo remains, therefore, a significant political novel, one whose central issue is as important today as it was when the book first appeared over a century ago.

II

The significance of The Bravo as an intellectual document, however, must not be allowed to obscure its literary value. It is something more than the distinguished statement of a politically liberal point of view: it is a highly successful work of fiction that has both an important place in literary history and inherent value as a work of art. Its historical significance can be readily demonstrated. Part derives from Cooper's convincing depiction of the operations of the Venetian state, a picture of society, which, in Bewley's opinion, bears a certain affinity to "the sinister atmosphere of Kafka's The Castle or Orwell's 1984" (p. 58). In the operations of an impersonal power that pries relentlessly into the lives and thoughts of the people, Cooper has presented a political order that is frighteningly contemporary and has done it with a skill that reminds one of Orwell's work. Indeed, the beheading of Jacopo certainly compares with the grim fate of

---

5 For Cooper's criticism of both the demagogues and the commercial class, see AD, pp. 96-98, 166-167.

12

Winston Smith at the end of *1984* as an effective means for bringing into sharp focus the entire meaning of the book. *The Bravo* deserves recognition, therefore, as one of the first of a group of modern novels that depicts with convincing horror the plight of the individual before the power of what we would call the totalitarian state.

More important, however, from the point of view of American literature is the significance of *The Bravo* as an early attempt to treat the International Theme, the confrontation of American ideas and attitudes by those of Europe, that Henry James was later to treat so well. To be sure, *The Bravo* only foreshadows the basic elements in the theme and exhibits little of the complexity that we associate with James' later treatments of the subject. Yet the basic impulse that impelled James moved Cooper too. Conscious of the fact that many Americans were unaware of the realities of aristocratic societies, Cooper set out in his European tales to bring "American opinion . . . to bear on European facts" so that Americans might understand the workings of exclusive political systems (*RS*, p. 293). This is not to say, of course, that Cooper was narrowly provincial in his attitude. He was surely as much at home with European culture and social form as James was later to become; and, during his stay in Europe, he was accepted as a gentleman. But although he perceived much of value in European life, he was equally clearsighted in his penetration to the unpleasant reality that so often lay beneath the surface.

Cooper, of course, was not so successful as James in presenting his version of the theme. Because of the time and place he chose for the setting of the tale—Venice in the early eighteenth century (*L & J*, II, 42)—he could not include an American character to react to the European scene. Instead, as Grossman has shown, Cooper himself assumes the role of American observer (p. 78), and this, to the modern taste, will likely be considered a flaw. The tension between the views and attitudes of Europe and America is by no means so well maintained in Cooper's tale as it is in those by James, and *The Bravo* lacks the subtlety we have come to expect in the development of the theme. To say this, however, is only to point out that more than a generation lies between *The Bravo* and James' treatment of the theme, that Cooper's novel exhibits the weakness of the pioneer effort in a type of fiction that was to be refined to a high degree by a

13

consummate artist. We must remember too that a different sensibility is at work in *The Bravo*, one less closely attuned to the modern taste than that of his great successor. Despite these facts, however, we can still turn to *The Bravo* for the light it sheds on the development of a theme that has remained an important one in the history of American literature.

To insist upon the historical importance of *The Bravo*, however, is to do an injustice to the book. It can stand upon its own merits as a serious work of art. Cooper himself has left us a full statement of the care with which he constructed the novel. In his defense of the book in *A Letter to His Countrymen* (1834), following the attacks upon it in the Whig press, Cooper clearly states that he intended to show the "ruthless movement" of an aristocratic system by illustrating its influence upon those who live under its power (*RS*, pp. 293-294). This object, he goes on to say, "was not to be attained by an essay, or a commentary." Rather, he preferred to use the fictional method, whereby the theme is "to be inferred from the events" (*RS*, p. 294). To this end, he imagined the various elements in the tale, laying special stress on the subplot and the character of Jacopo Frontoni. The theme, however, was not to be revealed in this element alone, but "was enlarged upon in different ways" (*RS*, p. 295), so that the interplay of the various characters in action should reveal the novel's meaning.

A careful examination of the book in terms of this intention should go a long way toward silencing once and for all the old and often repeated fable that Cooper was only a gifted amateur, a hasty—and careless—writer. In *The Bravo*, Cooper was a serious and conscious artist, as careful in developing most of the details of his work as he was in constructing its overall plan. A romantic realist who prided himself on the accuracy of his maritime novels and who sometimes took great pains to make his physical descriptions exact, Cooper took care to render his scene with due respect to time and place as "to preserve a verisimilitude to received facts" and to maintain the illusion of the tale (*RS*, p. 294). Cooper had himself lived briefly in Venice and was familiar with the Comte Daru's *Histoire de la République de Venise*, which gave him the basic idea of the subplot, the plight of Jacopo that leads him to assume the character of a Bravo (*RS*, pp. 294-295). But like most romantic artists, Cooper includes the realistic details not for themselves alone, but for what they contribute to his overall meaning. Cooper is accurate, for example, in his description of the silence of Venice, but the reader must look beyond the detail to perceive its significance.

For setting in Cooper, as in much romantic art, serves a thematic function. The sea in his maritime novels, as Joseph Conrad observed in *Notes on Life and Letters* (1925), so "interpenetrates with life" as to become itself a factor in the action (p. 55); the forest in the Leatherstocking tales is not merely a backdrop, but an essential element both in the actions of the individual novels and in the development of the series as a whole.[6] So it is also with the setting of *The Bravo*. The modern reader of Cooper must put aside his preconceptions of what a novel should do and approach the work with an open mind. If he reads carefully—and Cooper gives us sufficient clues concerning what he is about—he will soon perceive the important function that the setting of Venice, its architecture and its ceremonies, serves in the story. The setting is rich in detail, but it is not so much its accuracy as its suggestiveness that is important in the development of the theme. The reader, therefore, should not dismiss the setting as mere romantic trappings. Rather, he should try to perceive the thematic function that the carefully drawn and lighted scenes are intended to serve.

Once the function of the physical setting is understood, the meaning of the action should become clear. We must always remember, however, that, as Bewley has shown, action in Cooper's best work—thrilling, indeed, even melodramatic, as it can sometimes be—is not included for itself alone, but serves an important thematic purpose (pp. 73-74). The theme is revealed through the actions of the various characters seen in terms of the physical environment in which they move. The union of setting, characters, and action in a coherent whole that yields a significant theme is fundamental to Cooper's art. Failure to perceive the function of these basic elements, therefore, will lead inevitably to a misunderstanding both of the theme itself and of his artistic accomplishment. Thus, the reader of *The Bravo* should not seek the niceties of style nor the psychological probing of character that we value in later novelists. These are not Cooper's virtues. Rather, the highly evocative descriptions and well-paced

---

6 Cf. James Franklin Beard, "Cooper and His Artistic Contemporaries," *James Fenimore Cooper: A Re-Appraisal* (Cooperstown, N.Y., 1954), p. 124.

narrative passages provide the means through which James Fenimore Cooper, a serious romantic artist, managed to create an intellectually significant and artistically sound novel.

III

A word should be said about the text. It is based upon that of the first American edition, published in two volumes in Philadelphia in November, 1831. It does not attempt, however, a completely literal reproduction of that edition. The aim has been to provide a good text for the modern reader. For this reason, I have corrected obvious errors in spelling, and have made certain mechanical changes. Where Cooper is reasonably consistent in capitalization and spelling, I have retained his practice. Where there is no consistency in the mechanics (and some words in the text appear in two or three different forms), I have normalized to modern usage. I have also modernized the spelling of hyphenated and other compound words.

Punctuation presented a more difficult problem. In the original edition, the punctuation is sometimes illogical and inconsistent; occasionally it even obscures the sense. Semi-colons and commas are used indiscriminately between direct quotations and the identification of the speaker; and commas frequently appear illogically and inconsistently between restrictive modifiers and the words modified, between subject and verb, and in other unexpected places. For this edition, therefore, I have silently made a number of changes, deleting many unnecessary commas, and, in general, normalizing the punctuation to modern practice. I have added and removed quotation marks as necessary, and I have in a very few instances added commas for the sense.

Finally, I would like to thank Miss Harriet C. Jameson, Rare Book Librarian at the University of Michigan Library, for making available for reproduction the library's copy of the first American edition of *The Bravo*, and Miss Isabelle F. Grant, Rare Book Room Librarian at the University of Illinois Library for answering questions about the edition of *The Bravo* that Cooper prepared for Bentley's Standard Novels (London, 1834).

Ann Arbor, Michigan   Donald A. Ringe
January, 1963

PREFACE

It is to be regretted the world does not discriminate more
justly in its use of political terms. Governments are usually called
either monarchies or republics. The former class embraces equally those institutions in which the sovereign is worshipped as a
god, and those in which he performs the humble office of a
mannikin. In the latter we find aristocracies and democracies
blended in the same generic appellation. The consequence of a
generalization so wide is an utter confusion on the subject of
the polity of states.

The author has endeavored to give his countrymen, in this
book, a picture of the social system of one of the *soi-disant* republics of the other hemisphere. There has been no attempt to
portray historical characters, only too fictitious in their graver
dress, but simply to set forth the familiar operations of Venetian
policy. For the justification of his likeness, after allowing for the
defects of execution, he refers to the well-known work of M.
Daru.

A history of the progress of political liberty, written purely
in the interests of humanity, is still a desideratum in literature.
In nations which have made a false commencement, it would be
found that the citizen, or rather the subject, has extorted immunity after immunity, as his growing intelligence and importance have both instructed and required him to defend those
particular rights which were necessary to his well-being. A
certain accumulation of these immunities constitutes, with a
solitary and recent exception in Switzerland, the essence of European liberty, even at this hour. It is scarcely necessary to tell
the reader that this freedom, be it more or less, depends on a
principle entirely different from our own. Here the immunities
do not proceed from, but they are granted to, the government,
being, in other words, concessions of natural rights made by the
people to the state for the benefits of social protection. So long
as this vital difference exists between ourselves and other nations,
it will be vain to think of finding analogies in their institutions.

17

It is true that, in an age like this, public opinion is itself a charter, and that the most despotic government which exists within the pale of Christendom must, in some degree, respect its influence. The mildest and justest governments in Europe are, at this moment, theoretically despotisms. The characters of both prince and people enter largely into the consideration of so extraordinary results, and it should never be forgotten that, though the character of the latter be sufficiently secure, that of the former is liable to change. But, admitting every benefit which can possibly flow from a just administration, with wise and humane princes, a government which is not properly based on the people possesses an unavoidable and oppressive evil of the first magnitude, in the necessity of supporting itself by physical force and onerous impositions, against the natural action of the majority.

Were we to characterize a republic, we should say it was a state in which power, both theoretically and practically, is derived from the nation, with a constant responsibility of the agents of the public to the people: a responsibility that is neither to be evaded nor denied. That such a system is better on a large than on a small scale, though contrary to brilliant theories which have been written to uphold different institutions, must be evident on the smallest reflection, since the danger of all popular governments is from popular mistakes, and a people of diversified interests and extended territorial possessions are much less likely to be the subjects of sinister passions, than the inhabitants of a single town or county. If to this definition we should add, as an infallible test of the genus, that a true republic is a government of which all others are jealous and vituperative, on the instinct of self-preservation, we believe there would be no mistaking the class. How far Venice would have been obnoxious to this proof, the reader is left to judge for himself.

THE BRAVO

CHAPTER I

"I stood in Venice on the Bridge of Sighs,
A palace and a prison on each hand;
I saw from out the wave her structures rise,
As from the stroke of the enchanter's wand:
A thousand years their cloudy wings expand
Around me, and a dying glory smiles
O'er the far times, when many a subject land
Look'd to the winged lions' marble piles,
Where Venice sate in state, throned on her hundred isles."

BYRON

THE SUN had disappeared behind the summits of the Tyrolean Alps, and the moon was already risen above the low barrier of the Lido. Hundreds of pedestrians were pouring out of the narrow streets of Venice into the square of St. Mark, like water gushing through some strait aqueduct, into a broad and bubbling basin. Gallant cavalieri and grave cittadini; soldiers of Dalmatia, and seamen of the galleys; dames of the city, and females of lighter manners; jewellers of the Rialto, and traders from the Levant; Jew, Turk, and Christian; traveller, adventurer, podesta, valet, avvocato and gondolier, held their way alike to the common centre of amusement. The hurried air and careless eye; the measured step and jealous glance; the jest and laugh; the song of the cantatrice, and the melody of the flute; the grimace of the buffoon, and the tragic frown of the improvisatore; the pyramid of the grotesque, the compelled and melancholy smile of the harpist, cries of water sellers, cowls of monks, plumage of warriors, hum of voices, and the universal movement and bustle, added to the more permanent objects of the place, rendered the scene the most remarkable of Christendom.

On the very confines of that line which separates western

19

from eastern Europe, and in constant communication with the latter, Venice possessed a greater admixture of character and costume, than any other of the numerous ports of that region. A portion of this peculiarity is still to be observed, under the fallen fortunes of the place; but at the period of our tale, the city of the isles, though no longer mistress of the Mediterranean, nor even of the Adriatic, was still rich and powerful. Her influence was felt in the councils of the civilized world, and her commerce, though waning, was yet sufficient to uphold the vast possessions of those families whose ancestors had become rich in the day of her prosperity. Men lived among her islands in that state of incipient lethargy which marks the progress of a downward course, whether the decline be of a moral or of a physical decay.

At the hour we have named, the vast parallelogram of the piazza was filling fast, the cafés and casinos within the porticoes, which surround three of its sides, being already thronged with company. While all beneath the arches was gay and brilliant with the flare of torch and lamp, the noble range of edifices called the Procuratories, the massive pile of the Ducal Palace, the most ancient Christian church, the granite columns of the piazzetta, the triumphal masts of the great square, and the giddy tower of the campanile, were slumbering in the more mellow glow of the moon.

Facing the wide area of the great square stood the quaint and venerable cathedral of San Marco. A temple of trophies, and one equally proclaiming the prowess and the piety of its founders, this remarkable structure presided over the other fixtures of the place, like a monument of the republic's antiquity and greatness. Its Saracenic architecture, the rows of precious but useless little columns that load its front, the low Asiatic domes, which rest upon its walls in the repose of a thousand years, the rude and gaudy mosaics, and above all the captured horses of Corinth, which start from out the sombre mass in the glory of Grecian art, received from the solemn and appropriate light, a character of melancholy and mystery that well comported with the thick recollections which crowd the mind as the eye gazes at this rare relic of the past.

As fit companions to this edifice, the other peculiar ornaments of the place stood at hand. The base of the campanile lay in shadow, but a hundred feet of its gray summit received the full rays of the moon along its eastern face. The masts destined to bear the conquered ensigns of Candia, Constantinople, and the Morea, cut the air by its side, in dark and fairy lines, while at the extremity of the smaller square, and near the margin of the sea, the forms of the winged lion* and the patron saint of the city,** each on his column of African granite, were distinctly traced against the background of the azure sky.

It was near the base of the former of these massive blocks of stone, that one stood who seemed to gaze at the animated and striking scene with the listlessness and indifference of satiety. A multitude, some in masks and others careless of being known, had poured along the quay into the piazzetta, on their way to the principal square, while this individual had scarce turned a glance aside, or changed a limb in weariness. His attitude was that of patient, practised, and obedient waiting on another's pleasure. With folded arms, a body poised on one leg, and a vacant though good-humored eye, he appeared to attend some beck of authority ere he quitted the spot. A silken jacket, in whose tissue flowers of the gayest colors were interwoven, the falling collar of scarlet, the bright velvet cap with armorial bearings embroidered on its front, proclaimed him to be a gondolier in private service.

Wearied at length with the antics of a distant group of tumblers, whose pile of human bodies had for a time arrested his look, this individual turned away, and faced the light air from the water. Recognition and pleasure shot into his countenance, and in a moment his arms were interlocked with those of a swarthy mariner, who wore the loose attire and Phrygian cap of men of his calling. The gondolier was the first to speak, the words flowing from him in the soft accents of his native islands.

"Is it thou, Stefano! They said thou hadst fallen into the grip of the devils of Barbary, and that thou wast planting flowers for an infidel with thy hands, and watering them with thy tears!"

The answer was in the harsher dialect of Calabria, and it was given with the rough familiarity of a seaman.

"*La Bella Sorrentina* is no housekeeper of a curato!*** She is not a damsel to take a siesta with a Tunisian rover prowling about in her neighborhood. Hadst ever been beyond the Lido,

---

* Symbol of St. Mark, patron saint of Venice.—Editor.
** St. Theodore, an earlier patron.—Editor.
*** Curate, priest.—Editor.

thou wouldst have known the difference between chasing the felucca* and catching her."

"Kneel down, and thank San Teodoro for his care. There was much praying on thy decks that hour, caro Stefano, though none is bolder among the mountains of Calàbria when thy felucca is once safely drawn upon the beach!"

The mariner cast a half-comic, half-serious glance upward at the image of the patron saint, ere he replied.

"There was more need of the wings of thy lion than of the favor of thy saint. I never come further north for aid than San Gennaro, even when it blows a hurricane."

"So much the worse for thee, caro, since the good bishop is better at stopping the lava than at quieting the winds. But there was danger, then, of losing the felucca and her brave people among the Turks?"

"There was, in truth, a Tunis man prowling about, between Stromboli and Sicily; but, Ali di San Michele! he might better have chased the cloud above the volcano, than run after the felucca in a sirocco!"

"Thou wast chickenhearted, Stefano?"

"I!—I was more like thy lion, here, with some small additions of chains and muzzles."

"As was seen by thy felucca's speed?"

"Cospetto! I wished myself a knight of San Giovanni a thousand times during the chase, and *La Bella Sorrentina* a brave Maltese galley, if it were only for the cause of Christian honor! The miscreant hung upon my quarter for the better part of three glasses; so near, that I could tell which of the knaves wore dirty cloth in his turban, and which clean. It was a sore sight to a Christian, [Gino]**, to see the right thus borne upon by an infidel."

"And thy feet warmed with the thought of the bastinado, caro mio?"

"I have run too often barefoot over our Calabrian mountains, to tingle at the sole with every fancy of that sort."

"Every man has his weak spot, and I know thine to be dread of a Turk's arm. Thy native hills have their soft as well as their hard ground, but it is said the Tunisian chooses a board knotty

---

* Narrow, fast boat rigged with a triangular sail; used chiefly by Arabs and in Mediterranean.—Editor.

** The first edition reads "Stefano."—Editor.

as his own heart, when he amuses himself with the wailings of a Christian."

"Well, the happiest of us all must take such as fortune brings. If my soles are to be shod with blows, the honest priest of Sant' Agata will be cheated of a penitent. I have bargained with the good curato, that all such accidental calamities shall go in the general account of penance. But how fares the world of Venice?—and what dost thou among the canals at this season, to keep the flowers of thy jacket from wilting?"

"Today as yesterday, and tomorrow will be as today. I row the gondola from the Rialto to the Giudecca; from San Giorgio to San Marco; from San Marco to the Lido, and from the Lido home. There are no Tunis men by the way, to chill the heart or warm the feet."

"Enough of friendship. And is there nothing stirring in the republic?—no young noble drowned, nor any Jew hanged?"

"Nothing of that much interest—except the calamity which befell Pietro. Thou rememberest Pierello? he who crossed into Dalmatia with thee once, as a supernumerary, the time he was suspected of having aided the young Frenchman in running away with a senator's daughter?"

"Do I remember the last famine? The rogue did nothing but eat maccaroni, and swallow the lachrymae christi which the Dalmatian count had on freight."

"Poverino! His gondola has been run down by an Ancona man, who passed over the boat, as if it were a senator stepping on a fly."

"So much for little fish coming into deep water."

"The honest fellow was crossing the Giudecca, with a stranger who had occasion to say his prayers at the Redentore, when the brig hit him in the canopy, and broke up the gondola as if it had been a bubble left by the Bucentaur." *

"The padrone** should have been too generous to complain of Pietro's clumsiness, since it met with its own punishment."

"Madre di Dio! He went to sea that hour, or he might be feeding the fishes of the Lagunes! There is not a gondolier in Venice who did not feel the wrong at his heart; and we know how to obtain justice for an insult, as well as our masters."

---

* The barge of state used in the ceremony of the marriage to the Adriatic. See Chapter VIII.—Editor

** The master of a small vessel in the Mediterranean.—Editor

"Well, a gondola is mortal, as well as a felucca, and both have their time; better die by the prow of a brig, than fall into the grip of a Turk.—How is thy young master, Gino? and is he likely to obtain his claims of the senate?"

"He cools himself in the Giudecca in the morning; and if thou would'st know what he does at evening, thou hast only to look among the nobles in the Broglio."

As the gondolier spoke, he glanced an eye aside, at a group of patrician rank, who paced the gloomy arcades which supported the superior walls of the doge's palace, a spot sacred, at times, to the uses of the privileged.

"I am no stranger to the habit thy Venetian nobles have of coming to that low colonnade at this hour, but I never before heard of their preferring the waters of the Giudecca for their baths."

"Were even the doge to throw himself out of a gondola, he must sink or swim, like a meaner Christian."

"Acqua dell' Adriatico! Was the young duca going to the Redentore, too, to say his prayers?"

"He was coming back after having—but what matters it in what canal a young noble sighs away the night! We happened to be near when the Ancona man performed his feat: while Giorgio and I were boiling with rage at the awkwardness of the stranger, my master, who never had much taste or knowledge in gondolas, went into the water to save the young lady from sharing the fate of her uncle."

"Diavolo! This is the first syllable thou hast uttered concerning any young lady, or of the death of her uncle!"

"Thou wert thinking of thy Tunis man, and hast forgotten. I must have told thee how near the beautiful signora was to sharing the fate of the gondola, and how the loss of the Roman marchese weighs, in addition, on the soul of the padrone."

"Santo Padre! That a Christian should die the death of a hunted dog by the carelessness of a gondolier!"

"It may have been lucky for the Ancona man that it so fell out, for they say the Roman was one of influence enough to make a senator cross the Bridge of Sighs, at need."

"The devil take all careless watermen, say I!— And what became of the awkward rogue?"

"I tell thee he went outside the Lido, that very hour, or—"

"Pietrello?"

"He was brought up by the oar of Giorgio, for both of us were active in saving the cushions and other valuables."

"Could'st thou do nothing for the poor Roman? Ill luck may follow that brig on account of his death!"

"Ill luck follow her, say I, till she lays her bones on some rock that is harder than the heart of her padrone. As for the stranger, we could do no more than offer up a prayer to San Teodoro, since he never rose after the blow. But what has brought thee to Venice, caro mio? for thy ill-fortune with the oranges, in the last voyage, caused thee to denounce the place."

The Calabrian laid a finger on one cheek, and drew the skin down, in a manner to give a droll expression to his dark, comic eye, while the whole of his really fine Grecian face was charged with an expression of coarse humor.

"Look you, Gino—thy master sometimes calls for his gondola between sunset and morning?"

"An owl is not more wakeful than he has been of late. This head of mine has not been on a pillow before the sun has come above the Lido, since the snows melted from Monselice."

"And when the sun of thy master's countenance sets in his own palazzo, thou hastenest off to the bridge of the Rialto, among the jewellers and butchers, to proclaim the manner in which he passed the night?"

"Diamine! 'Twould be the last night I served the Duca di Sant' Agata, were my tongue so limber! The gondolier and the confessor are the two privy councillors of a noble, Master Stefano, with this small difference—that the last only knows what the sinner wishes to reveal, while the first sometimes knows more. I can find a safer, if not a more honest employment, than to be running about with my master's secrets in the air."

"And I am wiser than to let every Jew broker in San Marco, here, have a peep into my charter party."

"Nay, old acquaintance, there is some difference between our occupations, after all. A padrone of a felucca cannot, in justice, be compared to the most confidential gondolier of a Neapolitan duke who has an unsettled right to be admitted to the Council of Three Hundred." *

"Just the difference between smooth water and rough—you ruffle the surface of a canal with a lazy oar, while˜I run the

_____

* Cooper explains the function of the various councils of Venice in Chapter XI.—Editor.

channel of Piombino in a mistral, shoot the Faro of Messina in a white squall, double Santa Maria de Leuca in a breathing levanter, and come skimming up the Adriatic before a sirocco that is hot enough to cook my maccaroni, and which sets the whole sea boiling worse than the caldrons of Scylla."

"Hist!" eagerly interrupted the gondolier, who had indulged, with Italian humor, in the controversy for pre-eminence, though without any real feeling; "here comes one who may think, else, we shall have need of his hand to settle the dispute—Eccolo!"

The Calabrian recoiled apace, in silence, and stood regarding the individual who had caused this hurried remark, with a gloomy but steady air. The stranger moved slowly past. His years were under thirty, though the calm gravity of his countenance imparted to it a character of more mature age. The cheeks were bloodless, but they betrayed rather the pallid hue of mental than of bodily disease. The perfect condition of the physical man was sufficiently exhibited in the muscular fullness of a body which, though light and active, gave every indication of strength. His step was firm, assured, and even; his carriage erect and easy, and his whole mien was strongly characterized by a self-possession that could scarcely escape observation. And yet his attire was that of an inferior class. A doublet of common velvet, a dark Montero cap, such as was then much used in the southern countries of Europe, with other vestments of a similar fashion, composed his dress. The face was melancholy rather than sombre, and its perfect repose accorded well with the striking calmness of the body. The lineaments of the former, however, were bold and even noble, exhibiting that strong and manly outline which is so characteristic of the finer class of the Italian countenance. Out of this striking array of features gleamed an eye that was full of brilliancy, meaning, and passion.

As the stranger passed, his glittering organs rolled over the persons of the gondolier and his companion, but the look, though searching, was entirely without interest. 'Twas the wandering but wary glance which men who have much reason to distrust habitually cast on a multitude. It turned, with the same jealous keenness, on the face of the next it encountered, and by the time the steady and well-balanced form was lost in the crowd, that quick and glowing eye had gleamed, in the same rapid and uneasy manner, on twenty others.

Neither the gondolier nor the mariner of Calabria spoke, until their riveted gazes after the retiring figure became useless.

Then the former simply ejaculated, with a strong respiration—
"Jacopo!"

His companion raised three of his fingers, with an occult meaning, towards the palace of the doges.

"Do they let him take the air, even in San Marco?" he asked, in unfeigned surprise.

"It is not easy, caro amico, to make water run up stream, or to stop the downward current. It is said that most of the senators would sooner lose their hopes of the horned bonnet,* than lose him. Jacopo! He knows more family secrets than the good priore of San Marco himself, and he, poor man, is half his time in the confessional."

"Ay, they are afraid to put him in an iron jacket, lest awkward secrets should be squeezed out."

"Corpo di Bacco! there would be little peace in Venice, if the Council of Three should take it into their heads to loosen the tongue of yonder man in that rude manner."

"But they say, Gino, that thy Council of Three has a fashion of feeding the fishes of the Lagunes which might throw the suspicion of his death on some unhappy Ancona man, were the body ever to come up again."

"Well, no need of bawling it aloud, as if thou wert hailing a Sicilian through thy trumpet, though the fact should be so. To say the truth, there are few men in business who are thought to have more custom than he who has just gone up the piazzetta."

"Two sequins!" rejoined the Calabrian, enforcing his meaning by a significant grimace.

"Santa Madonna! Thou forgettest, Stefano, that not even the confessor has any trouble with a job in which he has been employed. Not a caratano less than a hundred will buy a stroke of his art. Your blows, for two sequins, leave a man leisure to tell tales, or even to say his prayers half the time."

"Jacopo!" ejaculated the other, with an emphasis which seemed to be a sort of summing up of all his aversion and horror.

The gondolier shrugged his shoulders, with quite as much meaning as a man born on the shores of the Baltic could have conveyed by words; but he, too, appeared to think the matter exhausted.

"Stefano Milano," he added, after a moment of pause, "there

---

* A kind of peaked biretta worn by the doge.—Editor.

are things in Venice which he who would eat his maccaroni in peace would do well to forget. Let thy errand in port be what it may, thou art in good season to witness the regatta which will be given by the state, itself, tomorrow."

"Hast thou an oar for that race?"

"Giorgio's, or mine, under the patronage of San Teodoro. The prize will be a silver gondola to him who is lucky or skilful enough to win; and then we shall have the nuptials with the Adriatic." *

"Thy nobles had best woo the bride well, for there are heretics who lay claim to her good will. I met a rover of strange rig and miraculous fleetness, in rounding the headlands of Otranto, who seemed to have half a mind to follow the felucca in her path towards the Lagunes."

"Did the sight warm thee at the soles of thy feet, [Stefano] ** dear?"

"There was not a turbaned head on his deck, but every sea cap set upon a well-covered poll and a shorn chin. Thy Bucentaur is no longer the bravest craft that floats between Dalmatia and the islands, though her gilding may glitter brightest. There are men beyond the pillars of Hercules who are not satisfied with doing all that can be done on their own coasts, but who are pretending to do much of that which can be done on ours."

"The republic is a little aged, caro, and years need rest. The joints of the Bucentaur are racked by time and many voyages to the Lido. I have heard my master say that the leap of the winged lion is not as far as it was, even in his young days."

"Don Camillo has the reputation of talking boldly of the foundation of this city of piles, when he has the roof of old Sant' Agata safely over his head. Were he to speak more reverently of the horned bonnet, and of the Council of Three, his pretensions to succeed to the rights of his forefathers might seem juster in the eyes of his judges. But distance is a great mellower of colors, and softener of fears. My own opinion of the speed of the felucca, and of the merits of a Turk, undergo changes of this sort between port and the open sea; and I have known thee, good Gino, [to] forget San Teodoro, and bawl as lustily to San Gen-

---

* An inconsistency; in Chapter VIII, the prize is an "oar of gold," and the race follows the nuptials.—Editor.

** The first edition reads "Gino."—Editor.

naro, when at Naples, as if thou really fancied thyself in danger from the mountain."

"One must speak to those at hand, in order to be quickest heard," rejoined the gondolier, casting a glance that was partly humorous, and not without superstition, upwards at the image which crowned the granite column against whose pedestal he still leaned. "A truth which warns us to be prudent, for yonder Jew cast a look this way, as if he felt a conscientious scruple in letting any irreverend remark of ours go without reporting. The bearded old rogue is said to have other dealings with the Three Hundred besides asking for the moneys he has lent to their sons. And so, Stefano, thou thinkest the republic will never plant another mast of triumph in San Marco, or bring more trophies to the venerable church?"

"Napoli herself, with her constant change of masters, is as likely to do a great act on the sea, as thy winged beast, just now! Thou art well enough to row a gondola in the canals, Gino, or to follow thy master to his Calabrian castle; but if thou would'st know what passes in the wide world, thou must be content to listen to mariners of the long course. The day of San Marco has gone by, and that of the heretics more north has come."

"Thou hast been much, of late, among the lying Genoese, Stefano, that thou comest hither with these idle tales of what a heretic can do. Genova la Superba! What has a city of walls to compare with one of canals and islands, like this?—and what has that Apennine republic performed, to be put in comparison with the great deeds of the Queen of the Adriatic? Thou forgettest that Venezia has been—"

"Zitto, zitto! that *has* been, caro mio, is a great word with all Italy. Thou art as proud of the past as a Roman of the Trastevere."

"And the Roman of the Trastevere is right. Is it nothing, Stefano Milano, to be descended from a great and victorious people?"

"It is better, Gino Monaldi, to be one of a people which is great and victorious just now. The enjoyment of the past is like the pleasure of the fool who dreams of the wine he drank yesterday."

"This is well for a Neapolitan, whose country never was a nation," returned the gondolier, angrily. "I have heard Don

29

Camillo, who is one educated as well as born in the land, often say that half of the people of Europe have ridden the horse of Sicily, and used the legs of thy Napoli, except those who had the best right to the services of both."

"Even so; and yet the figs are as sweet as ever, and the beccafichi* as tender! The ashes of the volcano cover all!"

"Gino," said a voice of authority, near the gondolier.

"Signore."

He who interrupted the dialogue pointed to the boat, without saying more.

"A rivederti," hastily muttered the gondolier. His friend squeezed his hand in perfect amity—for, in truth, they were countrymen by birth, though chance had trained the former on the canals—and, at the next instant, Gino was arranging the cushions for his master, having first aroused his subordinate brother of the oar from a profound sleep.

---

* Warblers (lit. fig pickers), birds considered a delicacy by Italians.— Editor.

CHAPTER II

"Hast ever swam in a gondola at Venice?"
SHAKESPEARE

WHEN Don Camillo Monforte entered the gondola, he did not take his seat in the pavilion. With an arm leaning on the top of the canopy, and his cloak thrown loosely over one shoulder, the young noble stood, in a musing attitude, until his dexterous servitors had extricated the boat from the little fleet which crowded the quay, and had urged it into open water. This duty performed, Gino touched his scarlet cap, and looked at his master, as if to inquire the direction in which they were to proceed. He was answered by a silent gesture that indicated the route of the Great Canal.

"Thou hast an ambition, Gino, to show thy skill in the regatta?" Don Camillo observed, when they had made a little progress. "The motive merits success. Thou wast speaking to a stranger, when I summoned thee to the gondola?"

"I was asking the news of our Calabrian hills from one who has come into port with his felucca; though the man took the name of San Gennaro to witness that his former luckless voyage should be the last."

"How does he call his felucca, and what is the name of the padrone?"

"*La Bella Sorrentina*, commanded by a certain Stefano Milano, son of an ancient servant of Sant' Agata. The bark is none of the worst for speed, and it has some reputation for beauty. It ought to be of happy fortune, too, for the good curato recommended it, with many a devout prayer, to the Virgin and to San Francesco."

The noble appeared to lend more attention to the discourse, which, until now, on his part, had been commenced in the listless manner with which a superior encourages an indulged dependant.

"*La Bella Sorrentina!* Have I not reason to know the bark?"

"Nothing more true, Signore. Her padrone has relations at

31

Sant' Agata, as I have told your eccellenza, and his vessel has lain on the beach, near the castle, many a bleak winter."

"What brings him to Venice?"

"That is what I would give my newest jacket of your eccellenza's colors to know, Signore. I have as little wish to inquire into other people's affairs as anyone, and I very well know that discretion is the chief virtue of a gondolier. I ventured, however, a deadly hint concerning his errand, such as ancient neighborhood would warrant, but he was as cautious of his answers as if he were freighted with the confessions of fifty Christians. Now, if your eccellenza should see fit to give me authority to question him, in your name, the deuce is in't if, between respect for his lord, and good management, we could not draw something more than a false bill of lading from him."

"Thou wilt take thy choice of my gondolas for the regatta, Gino," observed the Duke of Sant' Agata, entering the pavilion, and throwing himself on the glossy black leathern cushions, without adverting to the suggestion of his servant.

The gondola continued its noiseless course, with the sprite-like movement peculiar to that description of boat. Gino, who, as superior over his fellow, stood perched on the little arched deck in the stern, pushed his oar with accustomed readiness and skill, now causing the light vessel to sheer to the right, and now to the left, as it glided among the multitude of crafts, of all sizes and uses, which it met in its passage. Palace after palace had been passed, and more than one of the principal canals, which diverged towards the different spectacles, or the other places of resort frequented by his master, were left behind, without Don Camillo giving any new direction. At length the boat arrived opposite to a building which seemed to excite more than common expectation. Giorgio worked his oar with a single hand, looking over his shoulder at Gino, and Gino permitted his blade fairly to trail on the water. Both seemed to await new orders, manifesting something like that species of instinctive sympathy with him they served which a long practised horse is apt to show when he draws near a gate that is seldom passed unvisited by his driver.

The edifice which caused this hesitation in the two gondoliers was one of those residences of Venice which are quite as remarkable for their external riches and ornaments, as for their singular situation amid the waters. A massive rustic basement of marble was seated as solidly in the element, as if it grew from a living rock, while story was seemingly raised on story, in the wanton observance of the most capricious rules of meretricious architecture, until the pile reached an altitude that is little known, except in the dwellings of princes. Colonnades, medallions, and massive cornices overhung the canal, as if the art of man had taken pride in loading the superstructure in a manner to mock the unstable element which concealed its base. A flight of steps, on which each gentle undulation produced by the passage of the barge washed a wave, conducted to a vast vestibule, that answered many of the purposes of a court. Two or three gondolas were moored near, but the absence of their people showed they were for the use of those who dwelt within. The boats were protected from rough collision with the passing craft by piles driven obliquely into the bottom. Similar spars, with painted and ornamented heads, that sometimes bore the colors and arms of the proprietor, formed a sort of little haven for the gondolas of the household before the door of every dwelling of mark.

"Where is it the pleasure of your eccellenza to be rowed?" asked Gino, when he found his sympathetic delay had produced no order.

"To the palazzo."

Giorgio threw a glance of surprise back at his comrade, but the obedient gondola shot by the gloomy, though rich abode, as if the little bark had suddenly obeyed an inward impulse. In a moment more, it whirled aside, and the hollow sound, caused by the plash of water between high walls, announced its entrance into a narrower canal. With shortened oars, the men still urged the boat ahead, now turning short into some new channel, now glancing beneath a low bridge, and now uttering, in the sweet shrill tones of the country and their craft, the well-known warning to those who were darting in an opposite direction. A backstroke of Gino's oar, however, soon brought the side of the arrested boat to a flight of steps.

"Thou wilt follow me," said Don Camillo, as he placed his foot, with the customary caution, on the moist stone, and laid a hand on the shoulder of Gino; "I have need of thee."

Neither the vestibule, nor the entrance, nor the other visible accessories of the dwelling, were so indicative of luxury and wealth as that of the palace on the Great Canal. Still, they were all such as denoted the residence of a noble of consideration.

33

"Thou wilt do wisely, Gino, to trust thy fortunes to the new gondola," said the master, as he mounted the heavy stone stairs, to an upper floor, pointing as he spoke to a new and beautiful boat, which lay in a corner of the large vestibule, as carriages are seen standing in the courts of houses built on more solid ground. "He who would find favor with Jupiter must put his own shoulder to the wheel, thou knowest, my friend."

The eye of Gino brightened, and he was voluble in his expression of thanks. They had ascended to the first floor, and were already deep in a suite of gloomy apartments, before the gratitude and professional pride of the gondolier were exhausted.

"Aided by a powerful arm and a fleet gondola, thy chance will be as good as another's, Gino," said Don Camillo, closing the door of his cabinet on his servant; "at present, thou mayest give some proof of zeal in my service in another manner. Is the face of a man called Jacopo Frontoni known to thee?"

"Eccellenza!" exclaimed the gondolier, gasping for breath.

"I ask thee if thou knowest the countenance of one named Frontoni?"

"His countenance, Signore!"

"By what else would'st thou distinguish a man?"

"A man, Signor Don Camillo!"

"Art thou mocking thy master, Gino? I have asked thee if thou art acquainted with the person of a certain Jacopo Frontoni, a dweller here in Venice?"

"Eccellenza, yes."

"He I mean has been long remarked by the misfortunes of his family, the father being now in exile on the Dalmatian coast, or elsewhere."

"Eccellenza, yes."

"There are many of the name of Frontoni, and it is important that thou should'st not mistake the man. Jacopo, of that family, is a youth of some five-and-twenty, of an active frame and melancholy visage, and of less vivacity of temperament than is wont at his years."

"Eccellenza, yes."

"One who resorts but little with his fellows, and who is rather noted for the silence and industry with which he attends to his concerns, than for any of the usual pleasantries and trifling of men of his cast. A certain Jacopo Frontoni that hath his abode somewhere near the arsenal?"

"Cospetto! Signor Duca, the man is as well known to us

gondoliers as the bridge of the Rialto! Your eccellenza has no need to trouble yourself to describe him."

Don Camillo Monforte was searching among the papers of a secretary. He raised his eyes in some little amazement, at the sally of his dependant, and then he quietly resumed his occupation.

"If thou knowest the man, it is enough."

"Eccellenza, yes. And what is your pleasure with this accursed Jacopo?"

The Duke of Sant' Agata seemed to recollect himself. He replaced the papers which had been deranged, and he closed the secretary.

"Gino," he said, in a tone of confidence and amity, "thou wert born on my estates, though so long trained here to the oar in Venice, and thou hast passed thy life in my service."

"Eccellenza, yes."

"It is my desire that thou should'st end thy days where they began. I have had much confidence in thy discretion, hitherto, and I have satisfaction in saying it has never failed thee, notwithstanding thou hast necessarily been a witness of some exploits of youth which might have drawn embarrassment on thy master were thy tongue less disposed to silence."

"Eccellenza, yes."

Don Camillo smiled; but the gleam of humor gave way to a look of grave and anxious thought.

"As thou knowest the person of him I have named, our affair is simple. Take this packet," he continued, placing a sealed letter of more than usual size into the hand of the gondolier, and drawing from his finger a signet ring, "with this token of thy authority. Within that arch of the doge's palace which leads to the canal of San Marco, beneath the Bridge of Sighs, thou wilt find Jacopo. Give him the packet; and should he demand it, withhold not the ring. Wait his bidding, and return with the answer."

Gino received this commission with profound respect, but with an awe he could not conceal. Habitual deference to his master appeared to struggle with deep distaste for the office he was required to perform; and there was even some manifestation of a more principled reluctance in his hesitating yet humble manner. If Don Camillo noted the air and countenance of his menial at all, he effectually concealed it.

"At the arched passage of the palace, beneath the Bridge of

Sighs," he coolly added; "and let thy arrival there be timed, as near as may be, to the first hour of the night."

"I would, Signore, that you had been pleased to command Giorgio and me to row you to Padua!"

"The way is long. Why this sudden wish to weary thyself?"

"Because there is no doge's palace, nor any Bridge of Sighs, nor any dog of Jacopo Frontoni, among the meadows."

"Thou hast little relish for this duty; but thou must know that what the master commands, it is the duty of a faithful follower to perform. Thou wert born my vassal, Gino Monaldi, and though trained from boyhood in this occupation of a gondolier, thou art properly a being of my fiefs in Napoli."

"St. Gennaro make me grateful for the honor, Signore! But there is not a water seller in the streets of Venice, nor a mariner on her canals, who does not wish this Jacopo anywhere but in the bosom of Abraham. He is the terror of every young lover, and of all the urgent creditors on the islands."

"Thou seest, silly babbler, there is one of the former, at least, who does not hold him in dread. Thou wilt seek him beneath the Bridge of Sighs, and, showing the signet, deliver the package according to my instructions."

"It is certain loss of character to be seen speaking with the miscreant! So lately as yesterday, I heard Annina, the pretty daughter of the old wine seller on the Lido, declare, that to be seen once in company with Jacopo Frontoni was as bad as to be caught twice bringing old rope from the arsenal, as befell Roderigo, her mother's cousin."

"Thy distinctions savor of the morals of the Lido. Remember to exhibit the ring, lest he distrust thy errand."

"Could not your eccellenza set me about clipping the wings of the lion, or painting a better picture than Tiziano di Vecelli? I have a mortal dislike even to pass the mere compliments of the day with one of your cutthroats. Were any of our gondoliers to see me in discourse with the man, it might exceed your eccellenza's influence to get me a place in the regatta."

"If he detain thee, Gino, thou wilt wait his pleasure; and if he dismiss thee at once, return hither with all expedition, that I may know the result."

"I very well know, Signor Don Camillo, that the honor of a noble is more tender of reproach than that of his followers, and that the stain upon the silken robe of a senator is seen farther than the spot upon a velvet jacket. If anyone unworthy of your eccellenza's notice has dared to offend, here are Giorgio and I, ready, at any time, to show how deeply we can feel an indignity which touches our master's credit; but a hireling of two, or ten, or even of a hundred sequins!"

"I thank thee for the hint, Gino. Go thou and sleep in thy gondola, and bid Giorgio come into my cabinet."

"Signore!"

"Art thou resolute to do none of my biddings?"

"Is it your eccellenza's pleasure that I go to the Bridge of Sighs by the footways of the streets, or by the canals?"

"There may be need of a gondola—thou wilt go with the oar."

"A tumbler shall not have time to turn round before the answer of Jacopo shall be here."

With this sudden change of purpose, the gondolier quitted the room; for the reluctance of Gino disappeared the moment he found the confidential duty assigned him by his master was likely to be performed by another. Descending rapidly, by a secret stairs, instead of entering the vestibule, where half a dozen menials of different employments were in waiting, he passed by one of the narrow corridors of the palace into an inner court, and thence by a low and unimportant gate into an obscure alley, which communicated with the nearest street.

Though the age is one of so great activity and intelligence, and the Atlantic is no longer a barrier even to the ordinary amusements of life, a great majority of Americans have never had an opportunity of personally examining the remarkable features of a region of which the town that Gino now threaded with so much diligence is not the least worthy of observation. Those who have been so fortunate as to have visited Italy, therefore, will excuse us if we make a brief, but what we believe useful, digression, for the benefit of those who have not had that advantage.

The city of Venice stands on a cluster of low, sandy islands. It is probable that the country which lies nearest to the gulf, if not the whole of the immense plain of Lombardy itself, is of alluvial formation. Whatever may have been the origin of that wide and fertile kingdom, the causes which have given to the Lagunes their existence, and to Venice its unique and picturesque foundation, are too apparent to be mistaken. Several torrents,

37

which flow from the valleys of the Alps, pour their tribute into the Adriatic at this point. Their waters come charged with the débris of the mountains, pulverized nearly to their original elements. Released from the violence of the stream, these particles have necessarily been deposited in the gulf at the spot where they have first become subjected to the power of the sea. Under the influence of counteracting currents, eddies, and waves, the sands have been thrown into submarine piles, until some of the banks have arisen above the surface, forming islands, whose elevation has been gradually augmented by the decay of vegetation. A glance at the map will show that, while the Gulf of Venice is not literally, it is, practically, considered with reference to the effect produced by the southeast wind called the sirocco, at the head of the Adriatic. This accidental circumstance is probably the reason why the Lagunes have a more determined character at the mouths of the minor streams that empty themselves here, than at the mouths of most of the other rivers which equally flow from the Alps or the Apennines, into the same shallow sea.

The natural consequence of a current of a river meeting the waters of any broad basin, and where there is no base of rock, is the formation, at or near the spot where the opposing actions are neutralized, of a bank, which is technically called a bar. The coast of the Union furnishes constant evidence of the truth of this theory, every river having its bar, with channels that are often shifted, or cleared, by the freshets, the gales, or the tides. The constant and powerful operation of the southeastern winds on one side, with the periodical increase of the Alpine streams on the other, have converted this bar at the entrance of the Venetian Lagunes, into a succession of long, low, sandy islands, which extend in a direct line, nearly across the mouth of the gulf. The waters of the rivers have necessarily cut a few channels for their passage, or what is now a lagune would long since have become a lake. Another thousand years may so far change the character of this extraordinary estuary, as to convert the channels of the bay into rivers, and the muddy banks into marshes and meadows, resembling those that are now seen for so many leagues inland.

The low margin of sand that, in truth, gives all its maritime security to the port of Venice and the Lagunes is called the Lido di Palestrino. It has been artificially connected and secured, in many places, and the wall of the Lido (literally the beach), though incomplete, like most of the great and vaunted works of the other hemisphere, and more particularly of Italy, ranks with the mole of Ancona, and the sea-wall of Cherbourg. The hundred little islands which now contain the ruins of what, during the Middle Ages, was the mart of the Mediterranean, are grouped together within cannon shot of the natural barrier. Art has united with nature to turn the whole to good account; and, apart from the influence of moral causes, the rivalry of a neighboring town, which has been fostered by political care, and the gradual filling up of the waters, by the constant deposit of the streams, it would be difficult to imagine a more commodious, or a safer haven when entered, than that which Venice affords, even to this hour.

As all the deeper channels of the Lagunes have been preserved, the city is intersected, in every direction, by passages which, from their appearance, are called canals, but which, in truth, are no more than so many small natural branches of the sea. On the margin of these passages, the walls of the dwellings arise literally from out of the water, since economy of room has caused their owners to extend their possessions to the very verge of the channel, in the manner that quays and wharfs are pushed into the streams in our own country. In many instances the islands themselves were no more than banks which were periodically bare, and on all, the use of piles has been necessary to support the superincumbent loads of palaces, churches, and public monuments, under which, in the course of ages, the humble spits of sand have been made to groan.

The great frequency of the canals, and perhaps some attention to economy of labor, has given to by far the greater part of the buildings the facility of an approach by water. But, while nearly every dwelling has one of its fronts on a canal, there are always communications by the rear with the interior passages of the town. It is a fault in most descriptions, that while the stranger hears so much of the canals of Venice, but little is said of her streets: still, narrow, paved, commodious, and noiseless passages, of this description, intersect all the islands, which communicate with each other by means of a countless number of bridges. Though the hoof of a horse, or the rumbling of a wheel is never heard in these strait avenues, they are of great resort for all the purposes of ordinary intercourse.

Gino issued into one of these thoroughfares, when he quitted the private passage which communicated with the palace of his master. He threaded the throng by which it was crowded with a dexterity that resembled the windings of an eel among the weeds of the Lagunes. To the numerous greetings of his fellows, he replied only by nods; nor did he once arrest his footsteps, until they had led him through the door of a low and dark dwelling that stood in a quarter of the place which was inhabited by people of an inferior condition. Groping his way among casks, cordage, and rubbish of all descriptions, the gondolier succeeded in finding an inner and retired door that opened into a small room, whose only light came from a species of well that descended between the walls of the adjacent houses and that in which he was.

"Blessed St. Anne! Is it thou, Gino Monaldi!" exclaimed a smart Venetian grisette, whose tones and manner betrayed as much of coquetry as of surprise. "On foot, and by the secret door; is this an hour to come on any of thy errands?"

"Truly, Annina, it is not the season for affairs with thy father, and it is something early for a visit to thee. But there is less time for words than for action, just now. For the sake of San Teodoro, and that of a constant and silly young man who, if not thy slave, is at least thy dog, bring forth the jacket I wore when we went together to see the merrymaking at Fusina."

"I know nothing of thy errand, Gino, nor of thy reason for wishing to change thy master's livery for the dress of a common boatman. Thou art far more comely with those silken flowers, than in this faded velveteen; and if I have ever said aught in commendation of its appearance, it was because we were bent on merrymaking, and being one of the party, it would have been churlish to have withheld a word of praise to a companion who, as thou knowest, does not dislike a civil speech in his own praise."

"Zitto, zitto! here is no merrymaking and companions, but a matter of gravity, and one that must be performed offhand. The jacket, if thou lovest me!"

Annina, who had not neglected essentials while she moralized on motives, threw the garment on a stool that stood within reach of the gondolier's hand, as he made this strong appeal, in a way to show that she was not to be surprised out of a confession of this sort, even in the most unguarded moment.

"If I love thee, truly! Thou hast the jacket, Gino, and thou mayest search in its pockets for an answer to thy letter, for which I do not thank thee for having got the duca's secretary to indite. A maiden should be discreet in affairs of this sort, for one never knows but he may make a confidant of a rival."

"Every word of it as true as if the devil himself had done the office for me, girl," muttered Gino, uncasing himself from his flowery vestment, and as rapidly assuming the plainer garment he had sought. "The cap, Annina, and the mask?"

"One who wears so false a face, in common, has little need of a bit of silk to conceal his countenance," she answered, throwing him, notwithstanding, both the articles he required.

"This is well—Father Battista himself, who boasts he can tell a sinner from a penitent merely by the savor of his presence, would never suspect a servitor of Don Camillo Monforte in this dress! Cospetto! but I have half a mind to visit that knave of a Jew who has got thy golden chain in pledge, and give him a hint of what may be the consequences, should he insist on demanding double the rate of interest we agreed on."

" 'Twould be Christian justice! But what would become of thy matter of gravity the while, Gino, and of thy haste to enter on its performance?"

"Thou sayest truly, girl. Duty, above all other things; though to frighten a grasping Hebrew may be as much of a duty as other matters. Are all thy father's gondolas in the water?"

"How else could he be gone to the Lido, and my brother Luigi to Fusina, and the two serving men on the usual business to the islands, or how else should I be alone?"

"Diavolo! is there no boat in the canal?"

"Thou art in unwonted haste, Gino, now thou hast a mask and a jacket of velvet! I know not that I should suffer one to enter my father's house, when I am in it alone, and take such disguises to go abroad, at this hour. Thou wilt tell me thy errand, that I may judge of the propriety of what I do."

"Better ask the Three Hundred to open the leaves of their book of doom! Give me the key of the outer door, girl, that I may go my way."

"Not till I know whether this business is likely to draw down upon my father the displeasure of the senate. Thou knowest, Gino, that I am—"

"Diamine! There goes the clock of San Marco, and I tarry past my hour. If I am too late, the fault will rest with thee!"

41

"'Twill not be the first of thy oversights which it has been my business to excuse. Here thou art, and here shalt thou remain, until I know the errand which calls for a mask and jacket, and all about this matter of gravity."

"This is talking like a jealous wife, instead of a reasonable girl, Annina. I have told thee that I am on business of the last importance, and that delay may bring heavy calamities."

"On whom?—What is thy business? Why art thou, whom in general it is necessary to warn from this house by words many times repeated, now in such a haste to leave it?"

"Have I not told thee, girl, 'tis an errand of great concern to six noble families, and if I fail to be in season, there may be a strife—ay, between the Florentine and the republic!"

"Thou hast said nothing of the sort, nor do I put faith in thy being an ambassador of San Marco. Speak truth for once, Gino Monaldi, or lay aside the mask and jacket, and take up thy flowers of Sant' Agata."

"Well, then, as we are friends, and I have faith in thy discretion, Annina, thou shalt know the truth to the extremity, for I find the bell has only tolled the quarters, which leaves me yet a moment for confidence."

"Thou lookest at the wall, Gino, and art consulting thy wits for some plausible lie!"

"I look at the wall because conscience tells me that too much weakness for thee is about to draw me astray from duty. What thou takest for deceit is only shame and modesty."

"Of that we shall judge, when the tale is told."

"Then listen. Thou hast heard of the affair between my master and the niece of the Roman marchese, who was drowned in the Giudecca, by the carelessness of an Ancona man, who passed over the gondola of Pietro as if his felucca had been a galley of state?"

"Who has been upon the Lido, the month past, without hearing the tale repeated, with every variation of a gondolier's anger?"

"Well, the matter is likely to come to a conclusion this night; my master is about to do, as I fear, a very foolish thing!"

"He will be married?"

"Or worse;—I am sent, in all haste and secrecy, in search of a priest."

Annina manifested strong interest in the fiction of the gondolier. Either from a distrustful temperament, long habit, or great familiarity with the character of her companion, however, she did not listen to his explanation without betraying some doubts of its truth.

"This will be a sudden bridal feast!" she said, after a moment of pause.—"'Tis well that few are invited, or its savor might be spoiled by the Three Hundred! To what convent art thou sent?"

"My errand is not particular. The first that may be found, provided he be a Franciscan, and a priest likely to have bowels for lovers in haste."

"Don Camillo Monforte, the heir of an ancient and great line, does not wive with so little caution. Thy false tongue has been trying to deceive me, Gino; but long use should have taught thee the folly of the effort. Unless thou sayest truth, not only shalt thou not go to thy errand, but here art thou prisoner at my pleasure."

"I may have told thee what I expect will shortly happen, rather than what has happened. But Don Camillo keeps me so much upon the water of late, that I do little beside dream, when not at the oar."

"It is vain to attempt deceiving me, Gino, for thine eye speaketh truth, let thy tongue and brains wander where they will. Drink of this cup, and disburthen thy conscience, like a man."

"I would that thy father would make the acquaintance of Stefano Milano!" resumed the gondolier, taking a long breath, after a still longer draught. "'Tis a padrone of Calabria, who oftentimes brings into the port excellent liquors of his country, and who would pass a cask of the red lachrymae christi through the Broglio itself, and not a noble of them all should see it. The man is here at present, and, if thou wilt, he shall not be long without coming into terms with thee for a few skins."

"I doubt if he have better liquors than this which hath ripened upon the sands of the Lido. Take another draught, for the second taste is thought to be better than the first."

"If the wine improve in this manner, thy father should be heavyhearted at the sight of the lees. 'Twould be no more than charity to bring him and Stefano acquainted."

"Why not do it, immediately? His felucca is in the port, thou sayest, and thou canst lead him hither by the secret door and the lanes."

"Thou forgettest my errand. Don Camillo is not used to be served the second. Cospetto! 'Twere a pity that any other got the liquor which I am certain the Calabrian has in secret."

"This errand can be no matter of a moment, like that of being sure of wine of the quality thou namest; or, if it be, thou canst first dispatch thy master's business, and then to the port, in quest of Stefano. That the purchase may not fail, I will take a mask and be thy companion, to see the Calabrian. Thou knowest my father hath much confidence in my judgment in matters like this."

While Gino stood half stupefied, and half delighted at this proposition, the ready and wily Annina made some slight change in her outer garments, placed a silken mask before her face, applied a key to the door, and beckoned to the gondolier to follow.

The canal with which the dwelling of the wine dealer communicated was narrow, gloomy, and little frequented. A gondola of the plainest description was fastened near, and the girl entered it, without appearing to think any further arrangement necessary. The servant of Don Camillo hesitated a single instant, but having seen that his half-meditated project of escaping by the use of another boat could not be accomplished for want of means, he took his wonted place in the stern, and began to ply the oar with mechanical readiness.

CHAPTER III

"What well-appointed leader fronts us here?"
King Henry VI

THE presence of Annina was a grave embarrassment to Gino. He had his secret wishes and limited ambition, like other men, and among the strongest of the former was the desire to stand well in the favor of the wine seller's daughter. But the artful girl, in catering to his palate with a liquor that was scarcely less celebrated among people of his class for its strength than its flavor, had caused a momentary confusion in the brain of Gino that required time to disperse. The boat was in the Grand Canal, and far on its way to the place of its destination before this happy purification of the intellects of the gondolier had been sufficiently effected. By that time, however, the exercise of rowing, the fresh air of the evening, and the sight of so many accustomed objects, restored his faculties to the necessary degree of coolness and forethought. As the boat approached the end of the canal, he began to cast his eyes about him in quest of the well-known felucca of the Calabrian.

Though the glory of Venice had departed, the trade of the city was not then at its present low ebb. The port was still crowded with vessels from many distant havens, and the flags of most of the maritime states of Europe were seen, at intervals, within the barrier of the Lido. The moon was now sufficiently high to cast its soft light on the whole of the glittering basin, and a forest, composed of lateen yards,* of the slender masts of polaccas,** and of the more massive and heavy hamper of regularly rigged ships, was to be seen rising above the tranquil element.

"Thou art no judge of a vessel's beauty, Annina," said the gondolier, who was deeply housed in the pavilion of the boat, "else should I tell thee to look at this stranger from Candia.

---

* Spars for lateen sails, triangular sails much used in the Mediterranean.—Editor.
** Polacres, Mediterranean vessels, usually square rigged.—Editor.

'Tis said that a fairer model has never entered within the Lido than that same Greek!"

"Our errand is not with the Candian trader, Gino; therefore, ply thy oar, for time presses."

"There's plenty of rough Greek wine in his hold; but, as thou sayest, we have naught with him. Yon tall ship, which is moored without the smaller craft of our seas, is the vessel of a Lutheran, from the islands of Inghilterra. 'Twas a sad day for the republic, girl, when it first permitted the stranger to come into the waters of the Adriatic!"

"Is it certain, Gino, that the arm of St. Mark was strong enough to keep him out?"

"Body of Diana! I would rather thou didst not ask that question in a place where so many gondolas are in motion! Here are Ragusans, Maltese, Sicilians, and Tuscans, without number; and a little fleet of French lie near each other, there, at the entrance of the Giudecca. They are a people who get together, afloat or ashore, for the benefit of the tongue. Here we are, at the end of our journey."

The oar of Gino gave a backward sweep, and the gondola was at rest, by the side of a felucca.

"A happy night to the *Bella Sorrentina* and her worthy padrone!" was the greeting of the gondolier, as he put his foot on the deck of the vessel. "Is the honest Stefano Milano on board the swift felucca?"

The Calabrian was not slow to answer; and in a few moments the padrone and his two visitors were in close and secret conference.

"I have brought one, here, who will be likely to put good Venetian sequins into thy pocket, caro," observed the gondolier, when the preliminaries of discourse had been properly observed. "She is the daughter of a most conscientious wine dealer, who is quite as ready at transplanting your Sicilian grapes into the islands, as he is willing and able to pay for them."

"And one, no doubt, as handsome as she is ready," said the mariner, with blunt gallantry, "were the black cloud but fairly driven from before her face."

"A mask is of little consequence in a bargain, provided the money be forthcoming. We are always in the Carnival at Venice; and he who would buy, or he who would sell, has the same right to hide his face as to hide his thoughts. What hast thou in

46

the way of forbidden liquors, Stefano, that my companion may not lose the night in idle words?"

"Per Diana! Master Gino, thou puttest thy questions with little ceremony. The hold of the felucca is empty, as thou mayest see by stepping to the hatches; and as for any liquor, we are perishing for a drop to warm the blood."

"And so far from coming to seek it here," said Annina, "we should have done better to have gone into the cathedral, and said an Ave, for thy safe voyage home. And now that our wit is spent, we will quit thee, friend Stefano, for some other less skilful in answers."

"Cospetto! thou knowest not what thou sayest," whispered Gino, when he found that the wary Annina was not disposed to remain. "The man never enters the meanest creek in Italy, without having something useful secreted in the felucca, on his own account. One purchase of him would settle the question between the quality of thy father's wines and those of Battista. There is not a gondolier in Venice but will resort to thy shop, if the intercourse with this fellow can be fairly settled."

Annina hesitated; long practised in the small, but secret, and exceedingly hazardous commerce which her father, notwithstanding the vigilance and severity of the Venetian police, had thus far successfully driven, she neither liked to risk an exposure of her views to an utter stranger, nor to abandon a bargain that promised to be lucrative. That Gino trifled with her, as to his true errand, needed no confirmation, since a servant of the Duke of Sant' Agata was not likely to need a disguise to search a priest; but she knew his zeal for her personal welfare too well to distrust his faith in a matter that concerned her own safety.

"If thou distrust that any here are the spies of the authorities," she observed to the padrone, with a manner that readily betrayed her wishes, "it will be in Gino's power to undeceive thee.—Thou wilt testify, Gino, that I am not to be suspected of treachery in an affair like this."

"Leave me to put a word into the private ear of the Calabrian," said the gondolier, significantly.— "Stefano Milano, if thou love me," he continued, when they were a little apart, "keep the girl in parley, and treat with her, fairly, for thy adventure."

"Shall I sell the vintage of Don Camillo, or that of the Viceroy of Sicily, caro? There is as much wine of each on board the *Bella Sorrentina*, as would float the fleet of the republic."

47

"If, in truth, thou art dry, then feign that thou hast it, and differ in thy prices. Entertain her, but a minute, with fair words, while I can get, unseen, into my gondola; and then, for the sake of an old and tried friend, put her tenderly on the quay, in the best manner thou art able."

"I begin to see into the nature of the trade," returned the pliant padrone, placing a finger on the side of his nose. "I will discourse the woman by the hour, about the flavor of the liquor, of if thou wilt, of her own beauty; but to squeeze a drop of anything better than the water of the Lagunes out of the ribs of the felucca would be a miracle worthy of San Teodoro."

"There is but little need to touch on aught but the quality of thy wine. The girl is not like most of her sex, and she takes sudden offence when there is question of her appearance. Indeed, the mask she wears is as much to hide a face that has little to tempt the eye, as from any wish at concealment."

"Since Gino has entered frankly into the matter," resumed the quick-witted Calabrian, cheerfully, and with an air of sudden confidence, to the expectant Annina, "I begin to see more probability of our understanding each other's meaning. Deign, bella donna, to go into my poor cabin, where we will speak more at our ease, and something more to our mutual profit, and mutual security."

Annina was not without secret doubts, but she suffered the padrone to lead her to the stairs of the cabin, as if she were disposed to descend. Her back was no sooner turned, than Gino slid into the gondola, which one shove of his vigorous arm sent far beyond the leap of man. The action was sudden, rapid, and noiseless; but the jealous eye of Annina detected the escape of the gondolier, though not in time to prevent it. Without betraying uneasiness, she submitted to be led below, as if the whole were done by previous concert.

"Gino has said that you have a boat which will do the friendly office to put me on the quay, when our conference is over," she remarked, with a presence of mind that luckily met the expedient of her late companion.

"The felucca itself should do that much, were there want of other means," gallantly returned the mariner when they disappeared in the cabin.

Free to discharge his duty, Gino now plied his task with redoubled zeal. The light boat glided among the vessels, inclining, by the skilful management of his single oar, in a manner to avoid all collision, until it entered the narrow canal which separates the palace of the doge from the more beautiful and classic structure that contains the prisons of the republic. The bridge which continues the communication of the quays was first passed, and then he was stealing beneath that far-famed arch which supports a covered gallery leading from the upper story of the palace into that of the prisons, and which, from its being appropriated to the passage of the accused from their cells to the presence of their judges, has been so poetically, and, it may be added, so pathetically called the Bridge of Sighs.

The oar of Gino now relaxed its efforts, and the gondola approached a flight of steps, over which, as usual, the water cast its little waves. Stepping on the lowest flag, he thrust a small iron spike, to which a cord was attached, into a crevice between two of the stones, and left his boat to the security of this characteristic fastening. When this little precaution was observed, the gondolier passed up lightly beneath the massive arch of the water gate of the palace, and entered its large but gloomy court.

At that hour, and with the temptation of the gay scene which offered in the adjoining square, the place was nearly deserted. A single female water carrier was at the well, waiting for the element to filter into its basin, in order to fill her buckets, while her ear listened in dull attention to the hum of the moving crowd without. A halberdier paced the open gallery at the head of the Giant's Stairs, and, here and there, the footfall of other sentinels might be heard among the hollow and ponderous arches of the long corridors. No light was shed from the windows; but the entire building presented a fit emblem of that mysterious power which was known to preside over the fortunes of Venice and her citizens. Ere Gino trusted himself without the shadow of the passage by which he had entered, two or three curious faces had appeared at the opposite entrance of the court, where they paused a moment to gaze at the melancholy and imposing air of the dreaded palace, before they vanished in the throng which trifled in the immediate proximity of that secret and ruthless tribunal, as man riots in security even on the verge of an endless and unforeseen future.

Disappointed in his expectation of meeting him he sought

on the instant, the gondolier advanced, and taking courage by the possibility of his escaping altogether from the interview, he ventured to furnish audible evidence of his presence by a loud hem. At that instant a figure glided into the court from the side of the quay, and walked swiftly towards its centre. The heart of Gino beat violently, but he mustered resolution to meet the stranger. As they drew near each other, it became evident, by the light of the moon, which penetrated even to that gloomy spot, that the latter was also masked.

"San Teodoro and San Marco have you in mind!" commenced the gondolier. "If I mistake not, you are the man I am sent to meet."

The stranger started, and first manifesting an intention to pass on quickly, he suddenly arrested the movement to reply.

"This may be so, or not. Unmask, that I may judge by thy countenance if what thou sayest be true."

"By your good leave, most worthy and honorable Signore, and if it be equally agreeable to you and my master, I would choose to keep off the evening air by this bit of pasteboard and silk."

"Here are none to betray thee, wert thou naked as at thy birth. Unless certain of thy character, in what manner may I confide in thy honesty?"

"I have no distrust of the virtues of an undisguised face, Signore, and therefore do I invite you, yourself, to exhibit what nature has done for you in the way of features, that I, who am to make the confidence, be sure it be to the right person."

"This is well, and gives assurance of thy prudence. I may not unmask, however; and as there seemeth little probability of our coming to an understanding, I will go my way. A most happy night to thee."

"Cospetto!—Signore, you are far too quick in your ideas and movements for one little used to negotiations of this sort. Here is a ring whose signet may help us to understand each other."

The stranger took the jewel, and holding the stone in a manner to receive the light of the moon, he started in a manner to betray both surprise and pleasure.

"This is the falcon crest of the Neapolitan—he that is the lord of Sant' Agata!"

"And of many other fiefs, good Signore, to say nothing of

50

the honors he claims in Venice. Am I right in supposing my errand with you?"

"Thou hast found one whose present business has no other object than Don Camillo Monforte. But thy errand was not solely to exhibit the signet?"

"So little so, that I have a packet here which waits only for a certainty of the person with whom I speak, to be placed into his hands."

The stranger mused a moment; then glancing a look about him, he answered hurriedly—

"This is no place to unmask, friend, even though we only wear our disguises in pleasantry. Tarry here, and at my return I will conduct thee to a more fitting spot."

The words were scarcely uttered when Gino found himself standing in the middle of the court alone. The masked stranger had passed swiftly on, and was at the bottom of the Giant's Stairs, ere the gondolier had time for reflection. He ascended with a light and rapid step, and without regarding the halberdier, he approached the first of three or four orifices which opened into the wall of the palace, and which, from the heads of the animal being carved in relief around them, had become famous as the receptacles of secret accusations, under the name of the Lions' Mouths. Something he dropped into the grinning aperture of the marble, though what, the distance and the obscurity of the gallery prevented Gino from perceiving; and then his form was seen gliding like a phantom down the flight of massive steps.

Gino had retired towards the arch of the water gate, in expectation that the stranger would rejoin him within its shadows; but, to his great alarm, he saw the form darting through the outer portal of the palace into the square of St. Mark. It was not a moment ere Gino, breathless with haste, was in chase. On reaching the bright and gay scene of the piazza, which contrasted with the gloomy court he had just quitted, like morning with night, he saw the utter fruitlessness of further pursuit. Frightened at the loss of his master's signet, however, the indiscreet but well-intentioned gondolier rushed into the crowd, and tried in vain to select the delinquent from among a thousand masks.

"Harkee, Signore," uttered the half-distracted gondolier to one who, having first examined his person with distrust, evidently betrayed a wish to avoid him; "if thou hast sufficiently pleased thy finger with my master's signet, the occasion offers to return it."

"I know thee not," returned a voice in which Gino's ear could detect no familiar sound.

"It may not be well to trifle with the displeasure of a noble as powerful as him you know," he whispered at the elbow of another who had come under his suspicions. "The signet, if thou pleasest, and the affair need go no further."

"He who would meddle in it, with or without that gage, would do well to pause."

The gondolier again turned away disappointed.

"The ring is not suited to thy masquerade, friend of mine," he essayed with a third; "and it would be wise not to trouble the podesta about such a trifle."

"Then name it not, lest he hear thee." The answer proved, like all the others, unsatisfactory and bootless.

Gino now ceased to question any; but he threaded the throng with an active and eager eye. Fifty times was he tempted to speak, but as often did some difference in stature or dress, some laugh, or trifle uttered in levity, warn him of his mistake. He penetrated to the very head of the piazza, and, returning by the opposite side, he found his way through the throng of the porticoes, looking into every coffeehouse, and examining each figure that floated by, until he again issued into the piazzetta, without success. A slight jerk at the elbow of his jacket arrested his steps, and he turned to look at the person who had detained him. A female attired like a contadina addressed him in the feigned voice common to all.

"Whither so fast, and what hast thou lost in this merry crowd? If a heart, 'twill be wise to use diligence, for many here may be willing to wear the jewel!"

"Corpo di Bacco!" exclaimed the disappointed gondolier; "any who find such a bauble of mine under foot are welcome to their luck! Hast thou seen a domino of a size like that of any other man, with a gait that might pass for the step of a senator, padre, or Jew, and a mask that looks as much like a thousand of these in the square as one side of the campanile is like the other?"

"Thy picture is so well drawn, that one cannot fail to know the original. He stands beside thee."

52

Gino wheeled suddenly, and saw that a grinning harlequin was playing his antics in the place where he had expected to find the stranger.

"And thy eyes, bella contadina, are as dull as a mole's."

He ceased speaking, for, deceived in his person, she who had saluted him was no longer visible. In this manner did the disappointed gondolier thread his way toward the water, now answering to the boisterous salute of some clown, and now repelling the advances of females less disguised than the pretended contadina, until he gained a space near the quays where there was more room for observation. Here he paused, undetermined whether to return and confess his indiscretion to his master, or whether he should make still another effort to regain the ring which had been so sillily lost. The vacant space between the two granite columns was left to the quiet possession of himself and one other, who stood near the base of that which sustained the Lion of St. Mark, as motionless as if he too were merely a form of stone. Two or three stragglers, either led by idle curiosity, or expecting to meet one appointed to await their coming, drew near this immovable man, but all glided away, as if there were repulsion in his marble-like countenance. Gino had witnessed several instances of this evident dislike to remain near the unknown figure, ere he felt induced to cross the space between them in order to inquire into its cause. A slow movement, at the sound of his footsteps, brought the rays of the moon full upon the calm countenance and searching eye of the very man he sought.

The first impulse of the gondolier, like that of all the others he had seen approach the spot, was to retreat; but the recollection of his errand and his loss came in season to prevent such an exhibition of his disgust and alarm. Still he did not speak; but he met the riveted gaze of the Bravo with a look that denoted, equally, confusion of intellect and a half-settled purpose.

"Would'st thou aught with me?" demanded Jacopo, when the gaze of each had continued beyond the term of accidental glances.

"My master's signet?"

"I know thee not."

"That image of San Teodoro could testify that this is holy truth, if it would but speak! I have not the honor of your friendship, Signor Jacopo; but one may have affairs even with a

53

stranger. If you met a peaceable and innocent gondolier, in the court of the palace, since the clock of the piazza told the last quarter, and got from him a ring, which can be of but little use to any but its rightful owner, one so generous will not hesitate to return it."

"Dost thou take me for a jeweller of the Rialto, that thou speakest to me of rings?"

"I take you for one well known and much valued by many of name and quality, here in Venice, as witness my errand from my own master."

"Remove thy mask. Men of fair dealing need not hide the features which nature has given them."

"You speak nothing but truths, Signor Frontoni, which is little remarkable, considering thy opportunities of looking into the motives of men. There is little in my face to pay you for the trouble of casting a glance at it. I would as lief do as others in this gay season, if it be equally agreeable to you."

"Do as thou wilt; but I pray thee to give me the same permission."

"There are few so bold as to dispute thy pleasure, Signore."

"It is, to be alone."

"Cospetto! There is not a man in Venice who would more gladly consult it, if my master's errand were fairly done!" muttered Gino, between his teeth.—"I have, here, a packet which it is my duty to put into your hands, Signore, and into those of no other."

"I know thee not—thou hast a name?"

"Not in the sense in which you speak, Signore. As to that sort of reputation, I am as nameless as a foundling."

"If thy master is of no more note than thyself, the packet may be returned."

"There are few within the dominions of St. Mark of better lineage, or of fairer hopes, than the Duke of Sant' Agata."

The cold expression of the Bravo's countenance changed.

"If thou comest from Don Camillo Monforte, why dost thou hesitate to proclaim it?—Where are his requests?"

"I know not whether it is his pleasure, or that of another, which this paper contains, but such as it is, Signor Jacopo, my duty commands me to deliver it to thee."

The packet was received calmly, though the organ which glanced at its seal and its superscription gleamed with an expres-

54

sion which the credulous gondolier fancied to resemble that of the tiger at the sight of blood.

"Thou said'st something of a ring. Dost thou bear thy master's signet? I am much accustomed to see pledges, ere I give faith."

"Blessed San Teodoro grant that I did! Were it as heavy as a skin of wine, I would willingly bear the load; but one that I mistook for you, Master Jacopo, has it on his own light finger, I fear."

"This is an affair that thou wilt settle with thy master," returned the Bravo, coldly, again examining the impression of the seal.

"If you are acquainted with the writing of my master," hurriedly remarked Gino, who trembled for the fate of the packet, "you will see his skill in the turn of those letters. There are few nobles in Venice, or indeed in the Sicilies, who have a more scholarly hand with a quill than Don Camillo Monforte; I could not do the thing half so well myself."

"I am no clerk," observed the Bravo, without betraying shame at the confession. "The art of deciphering a scroll, like this, was never taught me. If thou art so expert in the skill of a penman, tell me the name the packet bears."

" 'Twould little become me to breathe a syllable concerning any of my master's secrets," returned the gondolier, drawing himself up in sudden reserve. "It is enough that he bid me deliver the letter; after which I should think it presumption even to whisper more."

The dark eye of the Bravo was seen rolling over the person of his companion, by the light of the moon, in a manner that caused the blood of the latter to steal towards his heart.

"I bid thee read to me aloud the name the paper bears," said Jacopo, sternly. "Here is none but the lion and the saint above our heads to listen."

"Just San Marco! who can tell what ear is open, or what ear is shut in Venice? If you please, Signor Frontoni, we will postpone the examination to a more suitable occasion."

"Friend, I do not play the fool! The name, or show me some gage that thou art sent by him thou hast named, else take back the packet; 'tis no affair for my hand."

"Reflect a single moment on the consequences, Signor Jacopo, before you come to a determination so hasty."

"I know no consequences which can befall a man who refuses to receive a message like this."

"Per Diana! Signore, the duca will not be likely to leave me an ear to hear the good advice of Father Battista."

"Then will the duca save the public executioner some trouble."

As he spoke, the Bravo cast the packet at the feet of the gondolier, and began to walk calmly up the piazzetta. Gino seized the letter, and, with his brain in a whirl, with the effort to recall some one of his master's acquaintances to whom he would be likely to address an epistle on such an occasion, he followed.

"I wonder, Signor Jacopo, that a man of your sagacity has not remembered that a packet to be delivered to himself should bear his own name."

The Bravo took the paper, and held the superscription again to the light.

"That is not so. Though unlearned, necessity has taught me to know when I am meant."

"Diamine! That is just my own case, Signore. Were the letter for me, now, the old should not know its young quicker than I would come at the truth."

"Then thou canst not read?"

"I never pretended to the art. The little said was merely about writing. Learning, as you well understand, Master Jacopo, is divided into reading, writing, and figures; and a man may well understand one, without knowing a word of the others. It is not absolutely necessary to be a bishop to have a shaved head, or a Jew to wear a beard."

"Thou would'st have done better to have said this at once; go, I will think of the matter."

Gino gladly turned away, but he had not left the other many paces, before he saw a female form gliding behind the pedestal of one of the granite columns. Moving swiftly in a direction to uncover this seeming spy, he saw at once that Annina had been a witness of his interview with the Bravo.

CHAPTER IV

"'Twill make me think
The world is full of rubs, and that my fortune
Runs 'gainst the bias."
Richard the Second

THOUGH Venice at that hour was so gay in her squares, the rest of the town was silent as the grave. A city in which the hoof of horse or the rolling of wheels is never heard necessarily possesses a character of its own; but the peculiar form of the government, and the long training of the people in habits of caution, weighed on the spirits of the gay. There were times and places, it is true, when the buoyancy of youthful blood, and the levity of the thoughtless, found occasion for their display; nor were they rare; but when men found themselves removed from the temptation, and perhaps from the support of society, they appeared to imbibe the character of their sombre city.

Such was the state of most of the town, while the scene described in the previous chapter was exhibited in the lively piazza of San Marco. The moon had risen so high that its light fell between the range of walls, here and there touching the surface of the water, to which it imparted a quivering brightness, while the domes and towers rested beneath its light in a solemn but grand repose. Occasionally the front of a palace received the rays on its heavy cornices and labored columns, the gloomy stillness of the interior of the edifice furnishing, in every such instance, a striking contrast to the richness and architectural beauty without. Our narrative now leads us to one of these patrician abodes of the first class.

A heavy magnificence pervaded the style of the dwelling. The vestibule was vast, vaulted, and massive. The stairs, rich in marbles, heavy and grand. The apartments were imposing in their gildings and sculpture, while the walls sustained countless works on which the highest geniuses of Italy had lavishly diffused their power. Among these relics of an age more happy in this respect than that of which we write, the connoisseur would

57

readily have known the pencils of Titian, Paul Veronese, and Tintoretto—the three great names in which the subjects of St. Mark so justly prided themselves. Among these works of the higher masters were mingled others by the pencils of Bellino, and Montegna, and Palma Vecchio—artists who were secondary only to the more renowned colorists of the Venetian school. Vast sheets of mirrors lined the walls, wherever the still more precious paintings had no place; while the ordinary hangings of velvet and silk became objects of secondary admiration, in a scene of nearly royal magnificence. The cool and beautiful floors, made of a composition in which all the prized marbles of Italy and of the East, polished to the last degree of art, were curiously embedded, formed a suitable finish to a style so gorgeous, and in which luxury and taste were blended in equal profusion.

The building, which, on two of its sides, literally rose from out the water, was, as usual, erected around a dark court. Following its different faces, the eye might penetrate, by many a door, open at that hour for the passage of the air from off the sea, through long suites of rooms, furnished and fitted in the manner described, all lighted by shaded lamps that spread a soft and gentle glow around. Passing, without notice, ranges of reception and sleeping rooms—the latter of a magnificence to mock the ordinary wants of the body—we shall at once introduce the reader into the part of the palace where the business of the tale conducts us.

At the angle of the dwelling, on the side of the smaller of the two canals, and most remote from the principal water avenue of the city on which the edifice fronted, there was a suite of apartments, which, while it exhibited the same style of luxury and magnificence as those first mentioned in its general character, discovered greater attention in its details to the wants of ordinary life. The hangings were of the richest velvets or of glossy silks, the mirrors were large and of exquisite truth, the floors of the same gay and pleasing colors, and the walls were adorned with their appropriate works of art. But the whole was softened down to a picture of domestic comfort. The tapestries and curtains hung in careless folds, the beds admitted of sleep, and the pictures were delicate copies by the pencil of some youthful amateur, whose leisure had been exercised in this gentle and feminine employment.

The fair being herself, whose early instruction had given birth to so many skilful imitations of the divine expression of Raphael, or to the vivid tints of Titian, was at that hour in her privacy, discoursing with her ghostly adviser, and one of her own sex who had long discharged the joint trusts of instructor and parent. The years of the lady of the palace were so tender that, in a more northern region, she would scarcely have been deemed past the period of childhood, though, in her native land, the justness and maturity of her form, and the expression of a dark, eloquent eye, indicated both the growth and the intelligence of womanhood.

"For this good counsel, I thank you, my father; and my excellent Donna Florinda will thank you still more, for your opinions are so like her own, that I sometimes admire at the secret means by which experience enables the wise and the good to think so much alike, on a matter of so little personal interest."

A slight but furtive smile struggled around the mortified mouth of the Carmelite, as he listened to the naïve observation of his ingenuous pupil.

"Thou wilt learn, my child," he answered, "as time heaps wisdom on thy head, that it is in concerns which touch our passions and interests least, we are most apt to decide with discretion and impartiality. Though Donna Florinda is not yet past the age when the heart is finally subdued, and there is still so much to bind her to the world, she will assure thee of this truth, or I greatly mistake the excellence of that mind which hath, hitherto, led her so far blameless in this erring pilgrimage to which we are all doomed."

Though the cowl was over the head of the speaker, who was evidently preparing to depart, and his deeply seated eye never varied from its friendly look at the fair face of her he instructed, the blood stole into the pale cheeks of the maternal companion, and her whole countenance betrayed some such reflection of feeling at his praise, as a wintry sky exhibits at a sudden gleam from the setting sun.

"I trust that Violetta does not now hear this for the first time," observed Donna Florinda, in a voice so meek and tremulous, as to be observed.

"Little that can be profitably told one of my inexperience has been left untaught," quickly answered the pupil, unconscious herself that she reached her hand towards that of her constant

59

monitor, though too intent on her object, to change her look from the features of the Carmelite. "But why this desire in the senate to dispose of a girl who would be satisfied to live forever, as she is now, happy in her youth, and contented with the privacy which becomes her sex?"

"The relentless years will not stay their advance, that even one innocent as thou, may never know the unhappiness and trials of a more mature age. This life is one of imperious and, oftentimes, of tyrannical duties. Thou art not ignorant of the policy that rules a state which hath made its name so illustrious by high deeds in arms, its riches, and its widely spread influence. There is a law in Venice which commandeth that none claiming an interest in its affairs shall so bind himself to the stranger, as to endanger the devotion all owe to the republic. Thus may not the patrician of St. Mark be a lord in other lands, nor may the heiress of a name, great and valued as thine, be given in marriage to any of note in a foreign state without counsel and consent from those who are appointed to watch over the interests of all."

"Had Providence cast my lot in an humbler class, this would not have been. Methinks it ill comports with the happiness of woman to be the especial care of the Council of Ten!"

"There is indiscretion and, I lament to say, impiety in thy words. Our duty bids us submit to earthly laws, and more than duty, reverence teaches us not to repine at the will of Providence. But I do not see the weight of this grievance against which thou murmurest, daughter. Thou art youthful, wealthy beyond the indulgence of all healthful desires, of a lineage to excite an unwholesome worldly pride, and fair enough to render thee the most dangerous of thine own enemies—and thou repinest at a lot to which all of thy sex and station are, of necessity, subject!"

"For the offence against Providence I am already a penitent," returned the Donna Violetta. "But surely it would be less embarrassing to a girl of sixteen were the fathers of the state so much occupied with more weighty affairs, as to forget her birth and years, and haply her wealth?"

"There would be little merit in being content with a world fashioned after our own caprices, though it may be questioned if we should be happier, by having all things as we desire, than by being compelled to submit to them as they are. The interest taken by the republic in thy particular welfare, daughter, is the price thou payest for the ease and magnificence with which thou art encircled. One more obscure, and less endowed by fortune, might have greater freedom of will, but it would be accompanied by none of the pomp which adorns the dwelling of thy fathers."

"I would there were less of luxury and more of liberty within its walls."

"Time will enable thee to see differently. At thy age all is viewed in colors of gold, or life is rendered bootless, because we are thwarted in our ill-digested wishes. I deny not, however, that thy fortune is tempered by some peculiar passages. Venice is ruled by a policy that is often calculating, and haply some deem it remorseless." Though the voice of the Carmelite had fallen, he paused and glanced an uneasy look from beneath his cowl, ere he continued. "The caution of the senate teaches it to preclude, as far as in it lies, the union of interests that may not only oppose each other, but which may endanger those of the state. Thus, as I have said, none of senatorial rank may hold lands without the limits of the republic, nor may any of account connect themselves, by the ties of marriage, with strangers of dangerous influence, without the consent and supervision of the republic. The latter is thy situation, for of the several foreign lords who seek thy hand, the council see none to whom the favor may be extended, without the apprehension of creating an influence here, in the centre of the canals, which ought not to be given to a stranger. Don Camillo Monforte, the cavalier to whom thou art indebted for thy life, and of whom thou hast so lately spoken with gratitude, has far more cause to complain of these hard decrees, than thou mayest have, in any reason."

" 'Twould make my griefs still heavier, did I know that one who has shown so much courage in my behalf has equal reason to feel their justice," returned Violetta, quickly. "What is the affair that, so fortunately for me, hath brought the lord of Sant' Agata to Venice, if a grateful girl may, without indiscretion, inquire?"

"Thy interest in his behalf is both natural and commendable," answered the Carmelite, with a simplicity which did more credit to his cowl than to his observation. "He is young, and, doubtless, he is tempted by the gifts of fortune, and the passions of his years, to divers acts of weakness. Remember him, daughter, in thy prayers, that part of the debt of gratitude may be repaid. His worldly interest here is one of general notoriety, and I can ascribe thy ignorance of it only to a retired manner of life."

"My charge hath other matters to occupy her thoughts than the concerns of a young stranger who cometh to Venice for affairs," mildly observed Donna Florinda.

"But if I am to remember him in my prayers, father, it might enlighten my petition to know in what the young noble is most wanting."

"I would have thee remember his spiritual necessities only. He wanteth, of a truth, little in temporalities that the world can offer, though the desires of life often lead him who hath most in quest of more. It would seem that an ancestor of Don Camillo was anciently a senator of Venice, when the death of a relation brought many Calabrian seigniories into his possession. The younger of his sons, by an especial decree which favored a family that had well served the state, took these estates, while the elder transmitted the senatorial rank and the Venetian fortunes to his posterity. Time hath extinguished the elder branch; and Don Camillo hath for years besieged the council to be restored to those rights which his predecessor renounced."

"Can they refuse him?"

"His demand involves a departure from established laws. Were he to renounce the Calabrian lordships, the Neapolitan might lose more than he would gain; and to keep both is to infringe a law that is rarely suffered to be dormant. I know little, daughter, of the interests of life; but there are enemies of the republic who say that its servitude is not easy, and that it seldom bestows favors of this sort without seeking an ample equivalent."

"Is this as it should be? If Don Camillo Monforte has claims in Venice, whether it be to palaces on the canals, or to lands on the main; to honors in the state, or voice in the senate; justice should be rendered without delay, lest it be said the republic vaunts more of the sacred quality than it practises."

"Thou speakest as a guileless nature prompts. It is the frailty of man, my daughter, to separate his public acts from the fearful responsibility of his private deeds; as if God, in endowing his being with reason and the glorious hopes of Christianity, had also endowed him with two souls, of which only one was to be cared for."

"Are there not those, father, who believe that, while the evil we commit as individuals is visited on our own persons, that which is done by states falls on the nation?"

"The pride of human reason has invented divers subtleties to satisfy its own longings, but it can never feed itself on a delusion more fatal than this! The crime which involves others in its guilt, or consequences, is doubly a crime, and though it be a property of sin to entail its own punishment, even in our present life, he trusts to a vain hope who thinks the magnitude of the offence will ever be its apology. The chief security of our nature is to remove it beyond temptation, and he is safest from the allurements of the world who is farthest removed from its vices. Though I would wish justice done to the noble Neapolitan, it may be for his everlasting peace that the additional wealth he seeks should be withheld."

"I am unwilling to believe, father, that a cavalier who has shown himself so ready to assist the distressed will easily abuse the gifts of fortune."

The Carmelite fastened an uneasy look on the bright features of the young Venetian. Parental solicitude and prophetic foresight were in his glance, but the expression was relieved by the charity of a chastened spirit.

"Gratitude to the preserver of thy life becomes thy station and sex; it is a duty. Cherish the feeling, for it is akin to the holy obligation of man to his Creator."

"Is it enough to feel grateful?" demanded Violetta. "One of my name and alliances might do more. We can move the patricians of my family, in behalf of the stranger, that his protracted suit may come to a more speedy end."

"Daughter, beware; the intercession of one in whom St. Mark feels so lively an interest may raise up enemies to Don Camillo, instead of friends."

Donna Violetta was silent, while the monk and Donna Florinda both regarded her with affectionate concern. The former then adjusted his cowl, and prepared to depart. The noble maiden approached the Carmelite, and looking into his face with ingenuous confidence, and habitual reverence, she besought his blessing. When the solemn and customary office was performed, the monk turned towards the companion of his spiritual charge. Donna Florinda permitted the silk on which her needle had been busy to fall into her lap, and she sat in meek silence, while the

63

Carmelite raised his open palms towards her bended head. His lips moved, but the words of benediction were inaudible. Had the ardent being, intrusted to their joint care, been less occupied with her own feelings, or more practised in the interests of that world into which she was about to enter, it is probable she would have detected some evidence of that deep, but smothered sympathy which so often betrayed itself, in the silent intelligence of her ghostly father and her female mentor.

"Thou wilt not forget us, father?" said Violetta, with winning earnestness. "An orphan girl, in whose fate the sages of the republic so seriously busy themselves, has need of every friend in whom she can confide."

"Blessed be thy intercessor," said the monk, "and the peace of the innocent be with thee."

Once more he waved his hand, and, turning, he slowly quitted the room. The eye of Donna Florinda followed the white robes of the Carmelite while they were visible; and when it fell again upon the silk, it was for a moment closed, as if looking at the movements of the rebuked spirit within. The young mistress of the palace summoned a menial, and bade him do honor to her confessor, by seeing him to his gondola. She then moved to the open balcony. A long pause succeeded: it was such a silence, breathing, thoughtful, and luxurious with the repose of Italy, as suited the city and the hour. Suddenly, Violetta receded from the open window, and withdrew a step, in alarm.

"Is there a boat beneath?" demanded her companion, whose glance was unavoidably attracted to the movement.

"The water was never more quiet. But thou hearest those strains of the hautboys?"

"Are they so rare on the canals, that they drive thee from the balcony?"

"There are cavaliers beneath the windows of the Mentoni palace; doubtless, they compliment our friend, Olivia."

"Even that gallantry is common. Thou knowest that Olivia is shortly to be united to her kinsman, and he takes the usual means to show his admiration."

"Dost thou not find this public announcement of a passion painful? Were I to be wooed, I could wish it might only be to my own ear!"

"That is an unhappy sentiment for one whose hand is in the gift of the senate! I fear that a maiden of thy rank must be content to hear her beauty extolled and her merits sung, if not exaggerated, even by hirelings beneath a balcony."

"I would that they were done!" exclaimed Violetta, stopping her ears. "None know the excellence of our friend better than I; but this open exposure of thoughts that ought to be so private must wound her."

"Thou mayest go again into the balcony; the music ceases."

"There are gondoliers singing near the Rialto: these are sounds I love! Sweet in themselves, they do no violence to our sacred feelings. Art thou for the water tonight, my Florinda?"

"Whither would'st thou?"

"I know not—but the evening is brilliant, and I pine to mingle with the splendor and pleasure without."

"While thousands on the canals pine to mingle with the splendor and pleasure within!—Thus is it ever with life: that which is possessed is little valued, and that which we have not is without price."

"I owe my duty to my guardian," said Violetta; "we will row to his palace."

Though Donna Florinda had uttered so grave a moral, she spoke without severity. Casting aside her work, she prepared to gratify the desire of her charge. It was the usual hour for the high in rank and the secluded to go abroad; and neither Venice, with its gay throngs, nor Italy, with its soft climate, ever offered greater temptation to seek the open air.

The groom of the chambers was called, the gondoliers were summoned, and the ladies, cloaking and taking their masks, were quickly in the boat.

CHAPTER V

"If your master
Would have a queen his beggar, you must tell him
That majesty, to keep decorum, must
No less beg than a kingdom."
Antony and Cleopatra

THE silent movement of the hearse-like gondola soon brought the fair Venetian and her female mentor to the water gate of the noble who had been intrusted, by the senate, with the especial guardianship of the person of the heiress. It was a residence of more than common gloom, possessing all the solemn but stately magnificence which then characterized the private dwellings of the patricians in that city of riches and pride. Its magnitude and architecture, though rather less imposing than those which distinguished the palace of the Donna Violetta, placed it among the private edifices of the first order, and all its external decorations showed it to be the habitation of one of high importance. Within, the noiseless steps and the air of silent distrust among the domestics, added to the gloomy grandeur of the apartments, rendered the abode no bad type of the republic itself.

As neither of his present visitors was a stranger beneath the roof of the Signor Gradenigo—for so the proprietor of the palace was called—they ascended its massive stairs, without pausing to consider any of those novelties of construction that would attract the eye of one unaccustomed to such a dwelling. The rank and the known consequence of the Donna Violetta assured her of a ready reception; and while she was ushered to the suite of rooms above, by a crowd of bowing menials, one had gone, with becoming speed, to announce her approach to his master. When in the antechamber, however, the ward stopped, declining to proceed any further, in deference to the convenience and privacy of her guardian. The delay was short; for no sooner was the old senator apprized of her presence, than he hastened from his closet to do her honor, with a zeal that did credit to his fitness for the trust he filled. The countenance of the old patrician—a face in which thought and care had drawn as many lines as time—lighted with unequivocal satisfaction as he pressed forward to receive his beautiful ward. To her half-uttered apologies for the intrusion, he would not listen; but as he led her within, he gallantly professed his pleasure at being honored with her visits even at moments that, to her scrupulous delicacy, might appear the most ill-timed.

"Thou canst never come amiss, child as thou art of my ancient friend, and the especial care of the state!" he added. "The gates of the Gradenigo palace would open of themselves, at the latest period of the night, to receive such a guest. Besides, the hour is most suited to the convenience of one of thy quality who would breathe the fresh evening air on the canals. Were I to limit thee to hours and minutes, some truant wish of the moment—some innocent caprice of thy sex and years, might go ungratified.—Ah! Donna Florinda, we may well pray that all our affection—not to call it weakness—for this persuasive girl, shall not in the end lead to her own disadvantage!"

"For the indulgence of both, I am grateful," returned Violetta; "I only fear to urge my little requests at moments when your precious time is more worthily occupied in behalf of the state."

"Thou overratest my consequence. I sometimes visit the Council of Three Hundred; but my years and infirmities preclude me now from serving the republic as I could wish.—Praise be to St. Mark, our patron! its affairs are not unprosperous for our declining fortunes. We have dealt bravely with the infidel of late; the treaty with the emperor is not to our wrong; and the anger of the church, for the late seeming breach of confidence on our part, has been diverted. We owe something in the latter affair to a young Neapolitan who sojourns here at Venice, and who is not without interest at the Holy See, by reason of his uncle, the Cardinal Secretary. Much good is done by the influence of friends, properly employed. 'Tis the secret of our success in the actual condition of Venice; for that which power cannot achieve must be trusted to favor and a wise moderation."

"Your declarations encourage me to become, once more, a suitor; for I will confess that, in addition to the desire of doing you honor, I have come, equally with the wish, to urge your great influence, in behalf of an earnest suit I have."

"What now! Our young charge, Donna Florinda, has inherited, with the fortunes of her family, its ancient habits of patronage and protection! But we will not discourage the feeling, for it has a worthy origin, and, used with discretion, it fortifies the noble and powerful in their stations."

"And may we not say," mildly observed Donna Florinda, "that when the affluent and happy employ themselves with the cares of the less fortunate, they not only discharge a duty, but they cultivate a wholesome and useful state of mind?"

"Doubt it not. Nothing can be more useful than to give each class in society a proper sense of its obligations, and a just sentiment of its duties. These are opinions I greatly approve, and which I desire my ward may thoroughly understand."

"She is happy in possessing instructors so able and so willing to teach all she should know," rejoined Violetta. "With this admission, may I ask the Signor Gradenigo to give ear to my petition?"

"Thy little requests are ever welcome. I would merely observe, that generous and ardent temperaments sometimes regard a distant object so steadily, as to overlook others that are not only nearer, and perhaps of still more urgent importance, but more attainable. In doing a benefit to one, we should be wary not to do injury to many. The relative of some one of thy household may have thoughtlessly enlisted for the wars?"

"Should it be so, I trust the recruit will have the manhood not to quit his colors."

"Thy nurse, who is one little likely to forget the service she did thy infancy, urges the claim of some kinsman, to an employment in the customs?"

"I believe all of that family are long since placed," said Violetta laughing, "unless we might establish the good mother herself in some station of honor. I have naught to ask in their behalf."

"She who hath reared thee, to this goodly and healthful beauty, would prefer a well-supported suit, but still is she better, as she is, indolent, and, I fear, pampered by thy liberality. Thy private purse is drained by demands on thy charity;—or, perhaps, the waywardness of a female taste hath cost thee dear, of late?"

68

"Neither.—I have little need of gold, for one of my years cannot properly maintain the magnificence of her condition. I come, guardian, with a far graver solicitation than any of these."

"I hope none in thy favor have been indiscreet of speech!" exclaimed the Signor Gradenigo, casting a hasty and suspicious look at his ward.

"If any have been so thoughtless, let them abide the punishment of their fault."

"I commend thy justice. In this age of novel opinions, innovations of all descriptions cannot be too severely checked. Were the senate to shut its ears to all the wild theories that are uttered by the unthinking and vain, their language would soon penetrate to the ill-regulated minds of the ignorant and idle. Ask me, if thou wilt, for purses in scores, but do not move me to forgetfulness of the guilt of the disturber of the public peace!"

"Not a sequin.—My errand is of nobler quality."

"Speak without riddle, that I may know its object."

Now that nothing stood between her wish to speak, and her own manner of making known the request, Donna Violetta appeared to shrink from expressing it. Her color went and came, and she sought support from the eye of her attentive and wondering companion. As the latter was ignorant of her intention, however, she could do no more than encourage the suppli- cant, by such an expression of sympathy as woman rarely refuses to her sex, in any trial that involves their peculiar and distinc- tive feelings. Violetta struggled with her diffidence, and then laughing at her own want of self-possession, she continued—

"You know, Signor Gradenigo," she said, with a loftiness that was not less puzzling, though far more intelligible, than the agitation which, a moment before, had embarrassed her manner, "that I am the last of a line, eminent for centuries, in the state of Venice."

"So sayeth our history."

"That I bear a name long known, and which it becomes me to shield from all imputation of discredit, in my own person."

"This is so true, that it scarce needed so clear an exposure," drily returned the senator.

"And that, though thus gifted by the accidents of fortune and birth, I have received a boon that remains still unrequited, in a manner to do no honor to the house of Tiepolo."

"This becometh serious! Donna Florinda, our ward is more

earnest than intelligible, and I must ask an explanation at your hands. It becometh her not to receive boons of this nature from any."

"Though unprepared for this request," mildly replied the companion, "I think she speaks of the boon of life."

The Signor Gradenigo's countenance assumed a dark expression.

"I understand you," he said, coldly. "It is true that the Neapolitan was ready to rescue thee, when the calamity befell thy uncle of Florence, but Don Camillo Monforte is not a common diver of the Lido, to be rewarded like him who finds a bauble dropped from a gondola. Thou hast thanked the cavalier; I trust that a noble maiden can do no more, in a case like this."

"That I have thanked him, and thanked him from my soul, is true!" fervently exclaimed Violetta. "When I forget the service, Maria Santissima, and the good saints, forget me!"

"I doubt, Signora Florinda, that your charge hath spent more hours among the light works of her late father's library, and less time with her missal, than becomes her birth?"

The eye of Violetta kindled, and she folded an arm around the form of her shrinking companion, who drew down her veil at this reproof, though she forbore to answer.

"Signor Gradenigo," said the young heiress, "I may have done discredit to my instructors, but if the pupil has been idle, the fault should not be visited on the innocent. It is some evidence that the commands of Holy Church have not been neglected, that I now come to entreat favor in behalf of one to whom I owe my life. Don Camillo Monforte has long pursued, without success, a claim so just, that were there no other motive to concede it, the character of Venice should teach the senators the danger of delay."

"My ward has spent her leisure with the doctors of Padua! The republic hath its laws, and none who have right of their side appeal to them in vain. Thy gratitude is not to be censured; it is rather worthy of thy origin and hopes; still, Donna Violetta, we should remember how difficult it is to winnow the truth from the chaff of imposition and legal subtlety, and, most of all, should a judge be certain, before he gives his decree, that, in confirming the claims of one applicant, he does not defeat those of another."

"They tamper with his rights! Being born in a foreign realm, he is required to renounce more in the land of the stranger, than

70

he will gain within the limits of the republic. He wastes life and youth in pursuing a phantom! You are of weight in the senate, my guardian, and were you to lend him the support of your powerful voice and great instruction, a wronged noble would have justice, and Venice, though she might lose a trifle from her stores, would better deserve the character of which she is so jealous."

"Thou art a persuasive advocate, and I will think of what thou urgest," said the Signor Gradenigo, changing the frown which had been gathering about his brow to a look of indulgence, with a facility that betrayed much practice in adapting the expression of his features to his policy. "I ought only to hearken to the Neapolitan, in my public character of a judge; but his service to thee, and my weakness in thy behalf, extorts that thou would'st have."

Donna Violetta received the promise, with a bright and guileless smile. She kissed the hand he extended, as a pledge of his faith, with a fervor that gave her attentive guardian serious uneasiness.

"Thou art too winning, even to be resisted by one wearied with rebutting plausible pretensions," he added. "The young and the generous, Donna Florinda, believe all to be as their own wishes and simplicity would have them. As for this right of Don Camillo—but no matter—thou wilt have it so, and it shall be examined with that blindness which is said to be the failing of justice."

"I have understood the metaphor to mean blind to favor, but not insensible to the right."

"I fear that is a sense which might defeat our hopes—but we will look into it. My son has been mindful of his duty and respect of late, Donna Violetta, as I would have him? The boy wants little urging, I know, to lead him to do honor to my ward, and the fairest of Venice. Thou wilt receive him with friendship, for the love thou bearest his father?"

Donna Violetta curtsied, but it was with womanly reserve.

"The door of my palace is never shut on the Signor Giacomo, on all proper occasions," she said, coldly. "Signore, the son of my guardian could hardly be other than an honored visitor."

"I would have the boy attentive—and even more, I would have him prove some little of that great esteem,—but we live in a jealous city, Donna Florinda, and one in which prudence is a

71

virtue of the highest price. If the youth is less urgent than I could wish, believe me, it is from the apprehension of giving premature alarm to those who interest themselves in the fortunes of our charge."

Both the ladies bowed, and by the manner in which they drew their cloaks about them, they made evident their wish to retire. Donna Violetta craved a blessing, and after the usual compliments, and a short dialogue of courtesy, she and her companion withdrew to their boat.

The Signor Gradenigo paced the room, in which he had received his ward, for several minutes in silence. Not a sound of any sort was audible throughout the whole of the vast abode, the stillness and cautious tread of those within, answering to the quiet town without; but a young man, in whose countenance and air were to be seen most of the usual signs of a well-bred profligacy, sauntering along the suite of chambers, at length caught the eye of the senator, who beckoned him to approach.

"Thou art unhappy, as of wont, Giacomo," he said, in a tone between paternal indulgence and reproach. "The Donna Violetta has, but a minute since, departed, and thou wert absent. Some unworthy intrigue with the daughter of a jeweller, or some more injurious bargain of thy hopes, with the father, hath occupied the time that might have been devoted more honorably, and to far better profit."

"You do me little justice," returned the youth. "Neither Jew, nor Jewess, hath this day greeted my eye."

"The calendar should mark the time, for its singularity! I would know, Giacomo, if thou turnest to a right advantage the occasion of my guardianship, and if thou thinkest, with sufficient gravity, of the importance of what I urge?"

"Doubt it not, father. He who hath so much suffered for the want of that which the Donna Violetta possesses in so great profusion, needeth little prompting on such a subject. By refusing to supply my wants, you have made certain of my consent. There is not a fool in Venice who sighs more loudly beneath his mistress's window, than I utter my pathetic wishes to the lady—when there is opportunity, and I am in the humor."

"Thou knowest the danger of alarming the senate?"

"Fear me not. My progress is by secret and gradual means. Neither my countenance nor my mind is unused to a mask,—thanks to necessity! My spirits have been too buoyant not to have made me acquainted with duplicity!"

"Thou speakest, ungrateful boy, as if I denied thy youth the usual indulgences of thy years and rank. It is thy excesses, and not thy spirits, I would check. But I would not, now, harden thee with reproof. Giacomo, thou hast a rival in the stranger. His act in the Giudecca has won upon the fancy of the girl, and like all of generous and ardent natures, ignorant as she is of his merits, she supplies his character with all necessary qualities by her own ingenuity."

"I would she did the same by me!"

"With thee, sirrah, my ward might be required to forget, rather than invent. Hast thou bethought thee of turning the eyes of the council on the danger which besets their heiress?"

"I have."

"And the means?"

"The plainest and the most certain—the Lion's Mouth."

"Ha!—that, indeed, is a bold adventure."

"And, like all bold adventures, it is the more likely to succeed. For once Fortune hath not been a niggard with me.—I have given them the Neapolitan's signet by way of proof."

"Giacomo! dost thou know the hazard of thy temerity? I hope there is no clue left in the handwriting, or by any other means taken to obtain the ring?"

"Father, though I may have overlooked thy instruction in less weighty matters, not an admonition which touches the policy of Venice hath been forgotten. The Neapolitan stands accused, and if thy council is faithful, he will be a suspected, if not a banished, man."

"That the Council of Three will perform its trust is beyond dispute. I would I were as certain that thy indiscreet zeal may not lead to some unpleasant exposure!"

The shameless son stared at the father a moment in doubt, and then he passed into the more private parts of the palace, like one too much accustomed to double-dealing, to lend it a second, or a serious thought. The senator remained. His silent walk was now manifestly disturbed by great uneasiness; and he frequently passed a hand across his brow, as if he mused in pain. While thus occupied, a figure stole through the long suite of antechambers, and stopped near the door of the room he occupied. The intruder was aged; his face was tawny by exposure, and his hair thinned and whitened by time. His dress was that of a fisherman, being both scanty and of the meanest materials. Still there was a naturally noble and frank intelligence in his

73

bold eye and prominent features, while the bare arms and naked legs exhibited a muscle and proportion which proved that nature was rather at a stand than in the decline. He had been many moments dangling his cap, in habitual but unembarrassed respect, before his presence was observed.

"Ha! thou here, Antonio!" exclaimed the senator, when their eyes met. "Why this visit?"

"Signore, my heart is heavy."

"Hath the calendar no saint—the fisherman no patron? I suppose the sirocco hath been tossing the waters of the bay, and thy nets are empty.—Hold! thou art my foster brother, and thou must not want."

The fisherman drew back with dignity, refusing the gift simply, but decidedly, by the act.

"Signore, we have lived from childhood to old age since we drew our milk from the same breast; in all that time, have you ever known me a beggar?"

"Thou art not wont to ask these boons, Antonio, it is true; but age conquers our pride with our strength. If it be not sequins that thou seekest, what would'st thou?"

"There are other wants than those of the body, Signore, and other sufferings beside hunger."

The countenance of the senator lowered. He cast a sharp glance at his foster brother, and ere he answered he closed the door which communicated with the outer chamber.

"Thy words forebode disaffection, as of wont. Thou art accustomed to comment on measures and interests that are beyond thy limited reason, and thou knowest that thy opinions have already drawn displeasure on thee. The ignorant and the low are, to the state, as children, whose duty it is to obey, and not to cavil.—Thy errand?"

"I am not the man you think me, Signore. I am used to poverty and want, and little satisfies my wishes. The senate is my master, and as such I honor it; but a fisherman hath his feelings as well as the doge!"

"Again!—These feelings of thine, Antonio, are most exacting. Thou namest them on all occasions, as if they were the engrossing concerns of life."

"Signore, are they not to me? Though I think mostly of my own concerns, still I can have a thought for the distress of those I honor. When the beautiful and youthful lady, your eccellenza's

74

daughter, was called away to the company of the saints, I felt the blow as if it had been the death of my own child; and it has pleased God, as you very well know, Signore, not to leave me unacquainted with the anguish of such a loss."

"Thou art a good fellow, Antonio," returned the senator, covertly removing the moisture from his eyes; "an honest and a proud man, for thy condition!"

"She from whom we both drew our first nourishment, Signore, often told me that, next to my own kin, it was my duty to love the noble race she had helped to support. I make no merit of natural feeling, which is a gift from Heaven, and the greater is the reason that the state should not deal lightly with such affections."

"Once more the state!—Name thy errand."

"Your eccellenza knows the history of my humble life. I need not tell you, Signore, of the sons which God, by the intercession of the Virgin and blessed St. Anthony, was pleased to bestow on me, or of the manner in which He hath seen proper to take them, one by one, away."

"Thou hast known sorrow, poor Antonio; I well remember thou hast suffered, too."

"Signore, I have. The deaths of five manly and honest sons is a blow to bring a groan from a rock. But I have known how to bless God, and be thankful!"

"Worthy fisherman, the doge himself might envy this resignation. It is often easier to endure the loss than the life of a child, Antonio!"

"Signore, no boy of mine ever caused me grief, but the hour in which he died. And even then," the old man turned aside, to conceal the working of his features—"I struggled to remember, from how much pain, and toil, and suffering they were removed, to enjoy a more blessed state."

The lip of the Signor Gradenigo quivered, and he moved to and fro with a quicker step.

"I think, Antonio," he said, "I think, honest Antonio, I had masses said for the souls of them all?"

"Signore, you had; St. Anthony remember the kindness in your own extremity! I was wrong in saying that the youths never gave me sorrow but in dying, for there is a pain the rich cannot know, in being too poor to buy a prayer for a dead child!"

"Wilt thou have more masses? Son of thine shall never want a voice with the saints, for the ease of his soul!"

"I thank you, eccellenza, but I have faith in what has been done, and, more than all, in the mercy of God. My errand now is in behalf of the living."

The sympathy of the senator was suddenly checked, and he already listened with a doubting and suspicious air.

"Thy errand?" he simply repeated.

"Is to beg your interest, Signore, to obtain the release of my grandson from the galleys. They have seized the lad in his fourteenth year, and condemned him to the wars with the infidels, without thought of his tender years, without thought of evil example, without thought of my age and loneliness, and without justice; for his father died in the last battle given to the Turk."

As he ceased, the fisherman riveted his look on the marble countenance of his auditor, wistfully endeavoring to trace the effect of his words. But all there was cold, unanswering, and void of human sympathy. The soulless, practised, and specious reasoning of the state had long since deadened all feeling in the senator on any subject that touched an interest so vital as the maritime power of the republic. He saw the hazard of innovation in the slightest approach to interests so delicate, and his mind was drilled by policy into an apathy that no charity could disturb, when there was question of the right of St. Mark to the services of his people.

"I would thou hadst come to beg masses, or gold, or aught but this, Antonio!" he answered, after a moment of delay. "Thou hast had the company of the boy, if I remember, from his birth, already?"

"Signore, I have had that satisfaction, for he was an orphan born; and I would wish to have it until the child is fit to go into the world, armed with an honesty and faith that shall keep him from harm. Were my own brave son here, he would ask no other fortune for the lad, than such counsel and aid as a poor man has a right to bestow on his own flesh and blood."

"He fareth no worse than others; and thou knowest that the republic hath need of every arm."

"Eccellenza, I saw the Signor Giacomo land from his gondola, as I entered the palace."

"Out upon thee, fellow! Dost thou make no distinction

76

between the son of a fisherman, one trained to the oar and toil, and the heir of an ancient house? Go to, presuming man, and remember thy condition, and the difference that God hath made between our children."

"Mine never gave me sorrow but the hour in which they died," said the fisherman, uttering a severe but mild reproof.

The Signor Gradenigo felt the sting of this retort, which in no degree aided the cause of his indiscreet foster brother. After pacing the room in agitation for some time, he so far conquered his resentment, as to answer more mildly, as became his rank.

"Antonio," he said, "thy disposition and boldness are not strangers to me—If thou would'st have masses for the dead, or gold for the living, they are thine; but in asking for my interest with the general of the galleys, thou askest that which, at a moment so critical, could not be yielded to the son of the doge, were the doge—"

"A fisherman," continued Antonio, observing that he hesitated—"Signore, adieu; I would not part in anger with my foster brother, and I pray the saints to bless you and your house. May you never know the grief of losing a child by a fate far worse than death—that of destruction by vice."

As Antonio ceased, he made his reverence and departed by the way he had entered. He retired unnoticed, for the senator averted his eyes, with a secret consciousness of the force of what the other, in his simplicity, had uttered; and it was some time before the latter knew he was alone. Another step, however, soon diverted his attention. The door reopened, and a menial appeared. He announced that one without sought a private audience.

"Let him enter," answered the ready senator, smoothing his features to the customary cautious and distrustful expression.

The servant withdrew, when one masked, and wearing a cloak, quickly entered the room. When the latter instrument of disguise was thrown upon an arm, and the visor was removed, the form and face of the dreaded Jacopo became visible.

CHAPTER VI

"Caesar himself has work, and our oppression
Exceeds what we expected."
SHAKESPEARE

"Didst thou note him that left me?" eagerly demanded the Signor Gradenigo.

"I did."

"Enough so to recognize form and countenance?"

" 'Twas a fisherman of the Lagunes, named Antonio."

The senator dropped the extended limb, and regarded the Bravo with a look in which surprise and admiration were equally blended. He resumed his course up and down the room, while his companion stood waiting his pleasure, in an attitude so calm as to be dignified. A few minutes were wasted in this abstraction.

"Thou art quick of sight, Jacopo!" continued the patrician, breaking the pause—"Hast thou had dealings with the man?"

"Never."

"Thou art certain it is—"

"Your eccellenza's foster brother."

"I did not inquire into thy knowledge of his infancy and origin, but of his present state," returned the Signor Gradenigo, turning away to conceal his countenance from the glowing eye of Jacopo—"Has he been named to thee by any in authority?"

"He has not—my mission does not lie with fishermen."

"Duty may lead us into still humbler society, young man. They who are charged with the grievous burthen of the state must not consider the quality of the load they carry. In what manner hath this Antonio come to thy knowledge?"

"I have known him as one esteemed by his fellows—a man skilful in his craft, and long practised in the mystery of the Lagunes."

"He is a defrauder of the revenue, thou would'st be understood to say?"

"I would not. He toils too late and early to have other means of support than labor."

"Thou knowest, Jacopo, the severity of our laws in matters that concern the public moneys?"

"I know that the judgment of St. Mark, Signore, is never light when its own interest is touched."

"Thou art not required to utter opinions beyond the present question. This man hath a habit of courting the good will of his associates, and of making his voice heard concerning affairs of which none but his superiors may discreetly judge."

"Signore, he is old, and the tongue grows loose with years."

"This is not the character of Antonio. Nature hath not treated him unkindly; had his birth and education been equal to his mind, the senate might have been glad to listen—as it is, I fear he speaks in a sense to endanger his own interests."

"Surely, if he speaks to offend the ear of St. Mark."

There was a quick suspicious glance from the senator to the Bravo, as if to read the true meaning of the latter's words. Finding, however, the same expression of self-possession in the quiet features he scrutinized, the latter continued as if distrust had not been awakened.

"If, as thou sayest, he so speaks as to injure the republic, his years have not brought discretion. I love the man, Jacopo, for it is usual to regard, with some partiality, those who have drawn nourishment from the same breast with ourselves."

"Signore, it is."

"And feeling this weakness in his favor, I would have him admonished to be prudent. Thou art acquainted, doubtless, with his opinions concerning the recent necessity of the state to command the services of all the youths on the Lagunes in her fleets?"

"I know that the press has taken from him the boy who toiled in his company."

"To toil honorably, and perhaps gainfully, in behalf of the republic!"

"Signore, perhaps!"

"Thou art brief in thy speech tonight, Jacopo!—But if thou knowest the fisherman, give him counsel of discretion. St. Mark will not tolerate such free opinions of his wisdom. This is the third occasion in which there has been need to repress that fisherman's speech; for the paternal care of the senate cannot see discontent planted in the bosom of a class it is their duty and pleasure to render happy. Seek opportunities to let him hear this wholesome truth, for, in good sooth, I would not willingly see a misfortune light upon the head of a son of my ancient nurse, and that, too, in the decline of his days."

The Bravo bent his body in acquiescence, while the Signor Gradenigo paced the room in a manner to show that he really felt concern.

"Thou hast had advice of the judgment, in the matter of the Genoese?" resumed the latter, when another pause had given time to change the current of his thoughts. "The sentence of the tribunals has been prompt, and, though there is much assumption of a dislike between the two republics, the world can now see how sternly justice is consulted on our isles. I hear the Genoese will have ample amends, and that certain of our own citizens will be mulcted of much money."

"I have heard the same since the sun set, in the piazzetta, Signore!"

"And do men converse of our impartiality, and more than all of our promptitude? Bethink thee, Jacopo, 'tis but a se'nnight since the claim was preferred to the senate's equity!"

"None dispute the promptitude with which the republic visits offences."

"Nor the justice, I trust also, good Jacopo. There is a beauty and a harmony in the manner in which the social machine rolls on its course, under such a system, that should secure men's applause! Justice administers to the wants of society, and checks the passions with a force as silent and dignified, as if her decrees came from a higher volition. I often compare the quiet march of the state, contrasted with the troubled movements of some other of our Italian sisters, to the difference between the clatter of a clamorous town, and the stillness of our own noiseless canals. Then the uprightness of the late decree is in the mouths of the maskers tonight?"

"Signore, the Venetians are bold when there is an opportunity to praise their masters."

"Dost thou think thus, Jacopo? To me they have ever seemed more prone to vent their seditious discontent. But 'tis the nature of man to be niggardly of praise and lavish of censure. This decree of the tribunal must not be suffered to die, with the mere justice of the case. Our friends should dwell on it, openly, in the cafés, and at the Lido. They will have no cause to fear, should they give their tongues a little latitude. A just government hath no jealousy of comment."

"True, Signore."

"I look to thee and thy fellows to see that the affair be not too quickly forgotten. The contemplation of acts such as this will quicken the dormant seeds of virtue in the public mind. He who has examples of equity incessantly before his eyes will come at last to love the quality. The Genoese, I trust, will depart satisfied?"

"Doubt it not, Signore; he has all that can content a sufferer; his own with usury, and revenge of him who did the wrong."

"Such is the decree—ample restoration and the chastening hand of punishment. Few states would thus render a judgment against itself, Jacopo!"

"Is the state answerable for the deed of the merchant, Signore?"

"Through its citizen. He who inflicts punishment on his own members is a sufferer, surely. No one can part with his own flesh without pain; is not this true, fellow?"

"There are nerves that are delicate to the touch, Signore, and an eye or a tooth is precious; but the paring of a nail, or the fall of the beard, is little heeded."

"One who did not know thee, Jacopo, would imagine thee in the interest of the emperor! The sparrow does not fall in Venice without the loss touching the parental feelings of the senate. Well, is there further rumor among the Jews of a decrease of gold? Sequins are not so abundant as of wont, and the chicanery of that race lends itself to the scarcity, in the hope of larger profits."

"I have seen faces on the Rialto, of late, Signore, that look empty purses. The Christian seems anxious, and in want, while the unbelievers wear their gaberdines with a looser air than is usual."

"This hath been expected. Doth report openly name any of the Israelites who are in the custom of lending, on usury, to the young nobles?"

"All who have to lend may be accounted of the class; the whole synagogue, rabbis, and all, are of a mind, when there is question of a Christian's purse."

"Thou likest not the Hebrew, Jacopo; but he is of good service in the republic's straits. We count all friends who are

81

ready with their gold at need. Still the young hopes of Venice must not be left to waste their substance in unwary bargains with the gainful race, and should'st thou hear of any of mark who are thought to be too deeply in their clutches, thou wilt do wisely to let the same be known, with little delay, to the guardians of the public weal. We must deal tenderly with those who prop the state, but we must also deal discreetly with those who will shortly compose it. Hast thou aught to say in the matter?"

"I have heard men speak of Signor Giacomo as paying dearest for their favors."

"Gesu Maria! my son and heir! Dost thou not deceive me, man, to gratify thine own displeasure against the Hebrews?"

"I have no other malice against the race, Signore, than the wholesome disrelish of a Christian. Thus much I hope may be permitted to a believer, but beyond that, in reason, I carry hatred to no man. It is well known that your heir is disposing freely of his hopes, and at prices that lower expectations might command."

"This is a weighty concern! The boy must be speedily admonished of the consequences, and care must be had for his future discretion. The Hebrew shall be punished, and as a solemn warning to the whole tribe, the debt confiscated to the benefit of the borrower. With such an example before their eyes, the knaves will be less ready with their sequins. Holy St. Theodore! 'twere self-destruction to suffer one of such promise to be lost for the want of prudent forethought. I will charge myself with the matter, as an especial duty, and the senate shall have no cause to say that its interests have been neglected. Hast thou had applications of late, in thy character of avenger of private wrongs?"

"None of note—there is one that seeks me earnestly, though I am not yet wholly the master of his wishes."

"Thy office is of much delicacy and trust, and, as thou art well assured, the reward is weighty and sure." The eyes of the Bravo kindled with an expression which caused his companion to pause. But observing that the repose, for which the features of Jacopo were so remarkable, again presided over his pallid face, he continued, as if there had been no interruption; "I repeat, the bounty and clemency of the state will not be forgotten. If its justice is stern and infallible, its forgiveness is cordial, and its favors ample. Of these facts I have taken much pains to assure thee, Jacopo.—Blessed St. Mark! that one of the scions of thy great stock should waste his substance for the benefit of a race of unbelievers! But thou hast not named him who seeks thee with this earnestness?"

"As I have yet to learn his errand, before I go further, Signore, it may be well to know more of his wishes."

"This reserve is uncalled for. Thou art not to distrust the prudence of the republic's ministers, and I should be sorry were the inquisitors to get an unfavorable opinion of thy zeal. The individual must be denounced."

"I denounce him not. The most that I can say is that he hath a desire to deal privately with one with whom it is almost criminal to deal at all."

"The prevention of crime is better than its punishment, and such is the true object of all government. Thou wilt not withhold the name of thy correspondent?"

"It is a noble Neapolitan, who hath long sojourned in Venice, on matters touching a great succession, and some right, even, to the senate's dignity."

"Ha! Don Camillo Monforte! Am I right, sirrah?"

"Signore, the same!"

The pause which followed was only broken by the clock of the great square striking eleven, or the fourth hour of the night, as it is termed, by the usage of Italy. The senator started, consulted a timepiece in his own apartment, and again addressed his companion.

"This is well," he said; "thy faith and punctuality shall be remembered. Look to the fisherman Antonio; the murmurs of the old man must not be permitted to awaken discontent for a cause so trifling as this transfer of his descendant from a gondola to a galley; and most of all, keep thy ears attentive to any rumors on the Rialto. The glory and credit of a patrician name must not be weakened by the errors of boyhood. As to this stranger—quickly, thy mask and cloak—depart as if thou wert merely a friend bent on some of the idle pleasantries of the hour."

The Bravo resumed his disguise with the readiness of one long practised in its use, but with a composure that was not so easily disconcerted as that of the more sensitive senator. The latter did not speak again, though he hurried Jacopo from his presence by an impatient movement of the hand.

When the door was closed and the Signor Gradenigo was again alone, he once more consulted the timepiece, passed his hand slowly and thoughtfully across his brow, and resumed his walk. For nearly an hour this exercise, or nervous sympathy of the body with a mind that was possibly overworked, continued without any interruption from without. Then came a gentle tap at the door, and at the usual bidding, one entered, closely masked, like him who had departed, as was so much the usage of that city, in the age of which we write. A glance at the figure of his guest seemed to apprize the senator of his character, for the reception, while it was distinguished by the quaint courtesy of the age, was that of one expected.

"I am honored in the visit of Don Camillo Monforte," said the host, while the individual named laid aside his cloak and silken visor; "though the lateness of the hour had given me reason to apprehend that some casualty had interfered between me and the pleasure."

"A thousand excuses, noble senator, but the coolness of the canals, and the gaiety of the square, together with some apprehension of intruding prematurely on time so precious, has, I fear, kept me out of season. But I trust to the known goodness of the Signor Gradenigo for my apology."

"The punctuality of the great lords of Lower Italy is not their greatest merit," the Signor Gradenigo drily answered. "The young esteem life so endless that they take little heed of the minutes that escape them; while we, whom age begins to menace, think chiefly of repairing the omissions of youth. In this manner, Signor Duca, does man sin and repent daily, until the opportunities of doing either are imperceptibly lost. But we will not be more prodigal of the moments than there is need—are we to hope for better views in the Spaniard?"

"I have neglected little that can move the mind of a reasonable man, and I have, in particular, laid before him the advantage of conciliating the senate's esteem."

"Therein have you done wisely, Signore, both as respects his interests and your own. The senate is a liberal paymaster to him who serves it well, and a fearful enemy to those who do harm to the state. I hope the matter of the succession draws near a conclusion?"

"I wish it were possible to say it did. I urge the tribunal in all proper assiduity, omitting no duty of personal respect, nor of private solicitation. Padua has not a doctor more learned than he who presents my right to their wisdom, and yet the affair lingers like life in the hectic. If I have not shown myself a worthy son of St. Mark in this affair with the Spaniard, it is more from the want of a habit of managing political interests than from any want of zeal."

"The scales of justice must be nicely balanced to hang so long, without determining to one side or the other! You will have need of further assiduity, Don Camillo, and of great discretion in disposing the minds of the patricians in your favor. It will be well to make your attachment to the state be observed by further service near the ambassador. You are known to have his esteem, and counsel coming from such a quarter will enter deeply into his mind. It should also quicken the exertions of so benevolent and generous a young spirit, to know that in serving his country, he also aids the cause of humanity."

Don Camillo did not appear to be strongly impressed with the justice of the latter remark. He bowed, however, in courtesy to his companion's opinion.

"It is pleasant, Signore, to be thus persuaded," he answered; "my kinsman of Castile is a man to hear reason, let it come from what quarter it may. Though he meets my arguments with some allusions to the declining power of the republic, I do not see less of deep respect for the influence of a state that hath long made itself remarkable by its energy and will."

"Venice is no longer what the city of the isles hath been, Signor Duca; still is she not powerless. The wings of our lion are a little clipped, but his leap is still far, and his teeth dangerous. If the new-made prince would have his ducal coronet sit easily on his brow, he would do well to secure the esteem of his nearest neighbors."

"This is obviously true, and little that my influence can do toward effecting the object shall be wanting. And now, may I entreat of your friendship, advice as to the manner of further urging my own long-neglected claims?"

"You will do well, Don Camillo, to remind the senators of your presence, by frequent observance of the courtesies due to their rank and yours."

"This do I never neglect, as seemly both in my station and my object."

"The judges should not be forgotten, young man, for it is wise to remember that justice hath ever an ear for solicitation."

"None can be more assiduous in the duty, nor is it common

to see a suppliant so mindful of those whom he troubleth, by more substantial proofs of respect."

"But chiefly should you be particular to earn the senate's esteem. No act of service to the state is overlooked by that body, and the smallest good deed finds its way into the recesses of the two councils."

"Would I could have communication with those reverend fathers! I think the justice of my claim would speedily work out its own right."

"That were impossible!" gravely returned the senator. "Those august bodies are secret, that their majesty may not be tarnished by communication with vulgar interests. They rule like the unseen influence of mind over matter, and form, as it were, the soul of the state, whose seat, like that of reason, remains a problem exceeding human penetration."

"I express the desire, rather as a wish than with any hope of its being granted," returned the Duke of St. Agata, resuming his cloak and mask, neither of which had been entirely laid aside. "Adieu, noble Signore; I shall not cease to move the Castilian with frequent advice, and, in return, I commit my affair to the justice of the patricians, and your own good friendship."

Signor Gradenigo bowed his guest through all the rooms of the long suite but the last, where he committed him to the care of the groom of his chambers.

"The youth must be stirred to greater industry in this matter, by clogging the wheels of the law. He that would ask favors of St. Mark must first earn them by showing zealous dispositions in his behalf."

Such were the reflections of the Signor Gradenigo, as he slowly returned towards his closet, after a ceremonious leave-taking with his guest, in the outer apartment. Closing the door, he commenced pacing the small apartment, with the step and eye of a man who again mused with some anxiety. After a minute of profound stillness, a door, concealed by the hangings of the room, was cautiously opened, and the face of still another visitor appeared.

"Enter!" said the senator, betraying no surprise at the apparition; "the hour is past, and I wait for thee."

The flowing dress, the gray and venerable beard, the noble outline of features, the quick, greedy, and suspicious eye, with an expression of countenance that was, perhaps, equally marked by worldly sagacity, and feelings often rudely rebuked, proclaimed a Hebrew of the Rialto.

"Enter, Hosea, and unburthen thyself," continued the senator, like one prepared for some habitual communication. "Is there aught new that touches the public weal?"

"Blessed is the people over whom there is so fatherly a care! Can there be good or evil to the citizen of the republic, noble Signore, without the bowels of the senate moving, as the parent yearneth over its young? Happy is the country in which men of reverend years and whitened heads watch, until night draws toward the day, and weariness is forgotten in the desire to do good, and to honor the state!"

"Thy mind partaketh of the eastern imagery of the country of thy fathers, good Hosea, and thou art apt to forget that thou art not yet watching on the steps of the temple. What of interest hath the day brought forth?"

"Say rather the night, Signore, for little worthy of your ear hath happened, save a matter of some trifling import, which hath grown out of the movements of the evening."

"Have there been stilettoes busy on the bridge?—ha!—or do the people joy less than common in their levities?"

"None have died wrongfully, and the square is gay as the fragrant vineyards of Engedi. Holy Abraham! what a place is Venice for its pleasures, and how the hearts of old and young revel in their merriment! It is almost sufficient to fix the font in the synagogue, to witness so joyous a dispensation in behalf of the people of these islands! I had not hoped for the honor of an interview tonight, Signore, and I had prayed, before laying my head upon the pillow, when one charged by the council brought to me a jewel, with an order to decipher the arms and other symbols of its owner. 'Tis a ring, with the usual marks which accompany private confidences."

"Thou hast the signet?" said the noble, stretching out an arm.

"It is here, and a goodly stone it is; a turquoise of price."

"Whence came it—and why is it sent to thee?"

"It came, Signore, as I gather more through hints and intimations of the messenger than by his words, from a place resembling that which the righteous Daniel escaped, in virtue of his godliness and birth."

"Thou meanest the Lion's Mouth?"

"So say our ancient books, Signore, in reference to the prophet, and so would the council's agent seem to intimate, in reference to the ring."

"Here is naught but a crest with the equestrian helmet—comes it of any in Venice?"

"The upright Solomon guide the judgment of his servant in a matter of this delicacy! The jewel is of rare beauty, such as few possess but those who have gold in store for other purposes. Do but regard the soft lustre in this light, noble Signore, and remark the pleasing colors that rise by the change of view!"

"Ay—'tis well—but who claimeth the bearings?"

"It is wonderful to contemplate how great a value may lie concealed in so small a compass! I have known sequins of full weight and heavy amount given for baubles less precious."

"Wilt thou never forget thy stall and the wayfarers of the Rialto? I bid thee name him who beareth these symbols as marks of his family and rank."

"Noble Signore, I obey. The crest is of the family of Monforte, the last senator of which died some fifteen years since."

"And his jewels?"

"They have passed, with other movables of which the state taketh no account, into the keeping of his kinsman and successor—if it be the senate's pleasure that there shall be a successor to that ancient name—Don Camillo of St. Agata. The wealthy Neapolitan, who now urges his rights here in Venice, is the present owner of this precious stone."

"Give me the ring; this must be looked to—hast thou more to say?"

"Nothing, Signore—unless to petition, if there is to be any condemnation and sale of the jewel, that it may first be offered to an ancient servitor of the republic who hath much reason to regret that his age hath been less prosperous than his youth."

"Thou shalt not be forgotten. I hear it said, Hosea, that divers of our young nobles frequent thy Hebrew shops with intent to borrow gold, which, lavished in present prodigality, is to be bitterly repaid at a later day by self-denial, and such embarrassments as suit not the heirs of noble names. Take heed of this matter—for if the displeasure of the council should alight on any of thy race, there would be long and serious accounts to settle! Hast thou had employment of late with other signets, besides this of the Neapolitan?"

88

"Unless in the vulgar way of our daily occupation, none of note, illustrious Signore."

"Regard this," continued the Signor Gradenigo, first searching in a secret drawer, whence he drew a small bit of paper to which a morsel of wax adhered; "canst thou form any conjecture, by the impression, concerning him who used that seal?"

The jeweller took the paper and held it towards the light, while his glittering eyes intently examined the conceit.

"This would surpass the wisdom of the son of David!" he said, after a long and seemingly a fruitless examination; "here is naught but some fanciful device of gallantry, such as the light-hearted cavaliers of the city are fond of using, when they tempt the weaker sex with fair words and seductive vanities."

"It is a heart pierced with the dart of love, and a motto of '*pensa al cuore trafitto d'amore*.' " *

"Naught else, as my eyes do their duty. I should think there was but very little meant by those words, Signore!"

"That as may be. Thou hast never sold a jewel with that conceit?"

"Just Samuel! We dispose of them daily, to Christians of both sexes and all ages. I know no device of greater frequency, whereby I conceive there is much commerce in this light fidelity."

"He who used it did well in concealing his thoughts beneath so general a dress! There will be a reward of a hundred sequins to him who traces the owner."

Hosea was about to return the seal as beyond his knowledge, when this remark fell casually from the lips of the Signor Gradenigo. In a moment his eyes were fortified with a glass of microscopic power, and the paper was again before the lamp.

"I disposed of a cornelian of no great price, which bore this conceit, to the wife of the emperor's ambassador, but conceiving there was no more in the purchase than some waywardness of fancy, I took no precaution to note the stone. A gentleman in the family of the Legate of Ravenna, also, trafficked with me for an amethyst of the same design, but with him, neither, did I hold it important to be particular. Ha! here is a private mark that in truth seemeth to be of my own hand!"

"Dost thou find a clue? What is the sign of which thou speakest?"

---

* Think of the heart transfixed with love.—Editor.

89

"Naught, noble senator, but a slur in a letter, which would not be apt to catch the eye of an over-credulous maiden."

"And thou parted with the seal to—?"

Hosea hesitated, for he foresaw some danger of losing his reward, by a too-hasty communication of the truth.

"If it be important that the fact be known, Signore," he said, "I will consult my books. In a matter of this gravity, the senate should not be misled."

"Thou sayest well. The affair is grave, and the reward a sufficient pledge that we so esteem it."

"Something was said, illustrious Signore, of a hundred sequins; but my mind taketh little heed of such particulars, when the good of Venice is in question."

"A hundred is the sum I promised."

"I parted with a signet ring, bearing some such design, to a female in the service of the nuncio's first gentleman. But this seal cannot come of that, since a woman of her station—"

"Art sure?" eagerly interrupted the Signor Gradenigo.

Hosea looked earnestly at his companion; and reading in his eye and countenance that the clue was agreeable, he answered promptly,—

"As that I live under the law of Moses! The bauble had been long on hand without an offer, and I abandoned it to the uses of my money."

"The sequins are thine, excellent Jew! This clears the mystery of every doubt. Go; thou shalt have thy reward; and if thou hast any particulars in thy secret register, let me be quickly possessed of them. Go to, good Hosea, and be punctual as of wont. I tire of these constant exercises of the spirit!"

The Hebrew, exulting in his success, now took his leave, with a manner in which habitual cupidity and subdued policy completely mastered every other feeling. He disappeared by the passage through which he had entered.

It seemed, by the manner of the Signor Gradenigo, that the receptions for that evening had now ended. He carefully examined the locks of several secret drawers in his cabinet, extinguished the lights, closed and secured the doors, and quitted the place. For some time longer, however, he paced one of the principal rooms of the outer suite, until the usual hour having arrived, he sought his rest, and the palace was closed for the night.

The reader will have gained some insight into the character

90

of the individual who was the chief actor in the foregoing scenes. The Signor Gradenigo was born with all the sympathies and natural kindliness of other men, but accident, and an education which had received a strong bias from the institutions of the self-styled republic, had made him the creature of a conventional policy. To him Venice seemed a free state, because he partook so largely of the benefits of her social system; and, though shrewd and practised in most of the affairs of the world, his faculties, on the subject of the political ethics of his country, were possessed of a rare and accommodating dullness. A senator, he stood in relation to the state as a director of a moneyed institution is proverbially placed in respect to his corporation; an agent of its collective measures, removed from the responsibilities of the man. He could reason warmly, if not acutely, concerning the principles of government, and it would be difficult, even in this money-getting age, to find a more zealous convert to the opinion that property was not a subordinate, but the absorbing interest of civilized life. He would talk ably of character, and honor, and virtue, and religion, and the rights of persons; but when called upon to act in their behalf, there was in his mind a tendency to blend them all with worldly policy, that proved as unerring as the gravitation of matter to the earth's centre. As a Venetian, he was equally opposed to the domination of one, or of the whole; being, as respects the first, a furious republican, and, in reference to the last, leaning to that singular sophism which calls the dominion of the majority the rule of many tyrants! In short, he was an aristocrat; and no man had more industriously or more successfully persuaded himself into the belief of all the dogmas that were favorable to his caste. He was a powerful advocate of vested rights, for their possession was advantageous to himself; he was sensitively alive to innovations on usages and to vicissitudes in the histories of families, for calculation had substituted taste for principles; nor was he backward, on occasion, in defending his opinions by analogies drawn from the decrees of Providence. With a philosophy that seemed to satisfy himself, he contended that, as God had established orders throughout His own creation, in a descending chain from angels to men, it was safe to follow an example which emanated from a wisdom that was infinite. Nothing could be more sound than the basis of his theory, though its application had the capital error of believing there was any imitation of nature in an endeavor to supplant it.

CHAPTER VII

"The moon went down; and nothing now was seen
Save where the lamp of a Madonna shone
Faintly."

ROGERS

JUST as the secret audiences of the Palazzo Gradenigo were ended, the great square of St. Mark began to lose a portion of its gaiety. The cafés were now occupied by parties who had the means, and were in the humor, to put their indulgences to more substantial proof than the passing gibe or idle laugh; while those who were reluctantly compelled to turn their thoughts from the levities of the moment to the cares of the morrow were departing in crowds to humble roofs and hard pillows. There remained one of the latter class, however, who continued to occupy a spot near the junction of the two squares, as motionless as if his naked feet grew to the stone on which he stood. It was Antonio.

The position of the fisherman brought the whole of his muscular form and bronzed features beneath the rays of the moon. The dark, anxious, and stern eyes were fixed upon the mild orb, as if their owner sought to penetrate into another world, in quest of that peace which he had never known in this. There was suffering in the expression of the weather-worn face; but it was the suffering of one whose native sensibilities had been a little deadened by too much familiarity with the lot of the feeble. To one who considered life and humanity in any other than their familiar and vulgar aspects, he would have presented a touching picture of a noble nature, enduring with pride, blunted by habit; while to him who regards the accidental dispositions of society as paramount laws, he might have presented the image of dogged turbulence and discontent, healthfully repressed by the hand of power. A heavy sigh struggled from the chest of the old man, and, stroking down the few hairs which time had left him, he lifted his cap from the pavement, and prepared to move.

"Thou art late from thy bed, Antonio," said a voice at his

92

elbow. "The triglie* must be of good price, or of great plenty, that one of thy trade can spare time to air himself in the piazza at this hour. Thou hearest, the clock is telling the fifth hour of the night."

The fisherman bent his head aside, and regarded the figure of his masked companion, for a moment, with indifference, betraying neither curiosity nor feeling at his address.

"Since thou knowest me," he answered, "it is probable thou knowest that in quitting this place, I shall go to an empty dwelling. Since thou knowest me so well, thou should'st also know my wrongs."

"Who hath injured thee, worthy fisherman, that thou speakest so boldly beneath the very windows of the doge?"

"The state."

"This is hardy language for the ear of St. Mark! Were it too loudly spoken, yonder lion might growl.—Of what dost thou accuse the republic?"

"Lead me to them that sent thee, and I will spare the trouble of a go-between. I am ready to tell my wrongs to the doge, on his throne; for what can one, poor and old as I, dread from their anger?"

"Thou believest me sent to betray thee?"

"Thou knowest thine own errand."

The other removed his mask, and turned his face towards the moon.

"Jacopo! exclaimed the fisherman, gazing at the expressive Italian features; "one of thy character can have no errand with me."

A flush that was visible even in that light passed athwart the countenance of the Bravo; but he stilled every other exhibition of feeling.

"Thou art wrong. My errand is with thee."

"Does the senate think a fisherman of the Lagunes of sufficient importance to be struck by a stiletto? Do thy work, then!" he added, glancing at his brown and naked bosom; "there is nothing to prevent thee!"

"Antonio, thou dost me wrong. The senate has no such purpose. But I have heard that thou hast reason for discontent, and that thou speakest openly, on the Lido and among the

---

* Mullets.—Editor.

93

islands, of affairs that the patricians like not to be stirred among men of your class. I come, as a friend, to warn thee of the consequences of such indiscretion, rather than as one to harm thee."

"Thou art sent to say this?"

"Old man, age should teach thy tongue moderation. What will avail vain complaints against the republic, or what canst thou hope for, as their fruits, but evil to thyself, and evil to the child that thou lovest?"

"I know not—but when the heart is sore, the tongue will speak. They have taken away my boy, and they have left little behind that I value. The life they threaten is too short to be cared for."

"Thou should'st temper thy regrets with wisdom. The Signor Gradenigo has long been friendly to thee, and I have heard that thy mother nursed him. Try his ears with prayers, but cease to anger the republic with complaints."

Antonio looked wistfully at his companion, but when he had ceased, he shook his head mournfully, as if to express the hopelessness of relief from that quarter.

"I have told him all that a man, born and nursed on the Lagunes, can find words to say. He is a senator, Jacopo; and he thinks not of suffering he does not feel."

"Art thou not wrong, old man, to accuse him who hath been born in affluence, of hardness of heart, merely that he doth not feel the misery thou would'st avoid, too, were it in thy power? Thou hast thy gondola and nets, with health and the cunning of thy art, and in that art thou happier than he who hath neither—would'st thou forget thy skill, and share thy little stock with the beggar of San Marco, that your fortunes might be equal?"

"There may be truth in what thou sayest of our labor and our means, but when it comes to our young, nature is the same in both. I see no reason why the son of the patrician should go free, and the child of the fisherman be sold to blood. Have not the senators enough of happiness, in their riches and greatness, that they rob me of my son?"

"Thou knowest, Antonio, the state must be served, and were its officers to go into the palaces in quest of hardy mariners for the fleet, would they, think you, find them that would honor the winged lion, in the hour of his need? Thy old arm is muscular, and thy leg steady on the water, and they seek those who, like thee, have been trained to the seas."

"Thou should'st have said, also, and thy old breast is scarred. Before thy birth, Jacopo, I went against the infidel, and my blood was shed, like water, for the state. But they have forgotten it, while there are rich marbles raised in the churches, which speak of what the nobles did, who came unharmed from the same wars."

"I have heard my father say as much," returned the Bravo, gloomily, and speaking in an altered voice. "He, too, bled in that war; but that is forgotten."

The fisherman glanced a look around, and perceiving that several groups were conversing near in the square, he signed to his companion to follow him, and walked towards the quays.

"Thy father," he said, as they moved slowly on together, "was my comrade and my friend. I am old, Jacopo, and poor; my days are passed in toil on the Lagunes, and my nights in gaining strength to meet the labor of the morrow; but it hath grieved me to hear that the son of one I much loved, and with whom I have so often shared good and evil, fair and foul, hath taken to a life like that which men say is thine. The gold that is the price of blood was never yet blessed to him that gave, or him that received."

The Bravo listened in silence, though his companion, who, at another moment, and under other emotions, would have avoided him as one shrinks from contagion, saw, on looking mournfully up into his face, that the muscles were slightly agitated, and that a paleness crossed his cheeks, which the light of the moon rendered ghastly.

"Thou hast suffered poverty to tempt thee into grievous sin, Jacopo; but it is never too late to call on the saints for aid, and to lay aside the stiletto! It is not profitable for a man to be known in Venice as thy fellow, but the friend of thy father will not abandon one who shows a penitent spirit. Lay aside thy stiletto, and come with me to the Lagunes. Thou wilt find labor less burdensome than guilt, and though thou never canst be to me like the boy they have taken, for he was innocent as the lamb! thou wilt still be the son of an ancient comrade, and a stricken spirit. Come with me then to the Lagunes, for poverty and misery like mine cannot meet with more contempt, even for being thy companion."

95

"What is it men say, that thou treatest me thus?" demanded Jacopo, in a low, struggling voice.

"I would they said untruth! But few die by violence, in Venice, that thy name is not uttered."

"And would they suffer one thus marked to go openly on the canals, or to be at large in the great square of San Marco?"

"We never know the reasons of the senate. Some say thy time is not yet come, while others think thou art too powerful for judgment."

"Thou dost equal credit to the justice and the activity of the inquisition. But should I go with thee tonight, wilt thou be more discreet in speech, among thy fellows of the Lido, and the islands?"

"When the heart hath its load, the tongue will strive to lighten it. I would do anything to turn the child of my friend from his evil ways, but forget my own. Thou art used to deal with the patricians, Jacopo; would there be possibility for one, clad in this dress, and with a face blackened by the sun, to come to speak with the doge?"

"There is no lack of seeming justice in Venice, Antonio; the want is in the substance. I doubt not thou would'st be heard."

"Then will I wait, here, upon the stones of the square, until he comes forth for the pomp of tomorrow, and try to move his heart to justice. He is old, like myself, and he hath bled too, for the state, and what is more, he is a father."

"So is the Signor Gradenigo."

"Thou doubtest his pity—ha?"

"Thou canst but try. The doge of Venice will hearken to a petition from the meanest citizen. I think," added Jacopo, speaking so low as to be scarcely audible, "he would listen even to me."

"Though I am not able to put my prayer in such speech as becometh the ear of a great prince, he shall hear the truth from a wronged man. They call him the chosen of the state, and such a one should gladly listen to justice. This is a hard bed, Jacopo," continued the fisherman, seating himself at the foot of the column of St. Theodore, "but I have slept on colder and as hard, when there was less reason to do it—a happy night."

The Bravo lingered a minute near the old man, who folded his arms on his naked breast, which was fanned by the sea breeze, and disposed of his person to take his rest in the square, a practice not unusual among men of his class; but when he found that Antonio was inclined to be alone, he moved on, leaving the fisherman to himself.

The night was now getting to be advanced, and few of the revellers remained in the areas of the two squares. Jacopo cast a glance around, and noting the hour and the situation of the place, he proceeded to the edge of the quay. The public gondoliers had left their boats moored, as usual, at this spot, and a profound stillness reigned over the whole bay. The water was scarce darkened by the air, which rather breathed upon than ruffled its surface, and no sound of oar was audible amid the forest of picturesque and classical spars which crowded the view between the piazzetta and the Giudecca. The Bravo hesitated, cast another wary glance around him, settled his mask, undid the slight fastenings of a boat, and presently he was gliding away into the centre of the basin.

"Who cometh?" demanded one who seemingly stood at watch, in a felucca anchored a little apart from all others.

"One expected," was the answer.

"Roderigo?"

"The same."

"Thou art late," said the mariner of Calabria, as Jacopo stepped upon the low deck of the *Bella Sorrentina*. "My people have long been below, and I have dreamt thrice of shipwreck, and twice of a heavy sirocco, since thou hast been expected."

"Thou hast had more time to wrong the customs. Is the felucca ready for her work?"

"As for the customs, there is little chance of gain in this greedy city. The senators secure all profits to themselves and their friends, while we of the barks are tied down to low freights and hard bargains. I have sent a dozen casks of lachrymae christi up the canals since the maskers came abroad, and beyond that I have not occasion. There is enough left for thy comfort, at need. Wilt drink?"

"I am sworn to sobriety. Is thy vessel ready, as wont, for the errand?"

"Is the senate as ready with its money? This is the fourth of my voyages in their service; and they have only to look into their own secrets to know the manner in which the work hath been done."

"They are content, and thou hast been well rewarded."

97

"Say it not. I have gained more gold by one lucky shipment of fruits from the isles, than by all their night work. Would those who employ me give a little especial traffic on the entrance of the felucca, there might be advantage in the trade."

"There is nothing which St. Mark visits with a heavier punishment than frauds on his receipts. Have a care with thy wines, or thou wilt lose not only thy bark and thy voyage, but thy liberty!"

"This is just the ground of my complaint, Signor Roderigo. Rogue and no rogue is the republic's motto. Here, they are as close in justice as a father amid his children; and there, it is better that what is done should be done at midnight. I like not the contradiction, for just as my hopes are a little raised, by what I have witnessed, perhaps a little too near, they are all blown to the winds, by such a frown as San Gennaro himself might cast upon a sinner."

"Remember thou art not in thy wide Mediterranean, but on a canal of Venice. This language might be unsafe, were it heard by less friendly ears."

"I thank thee for thy care, though the sight of yonder old palace is as good a hint to the loose tongue, as the sight of a gibbet, on the seashore, to a pirate. I met an ancient fellow in the piazzetta, about the time the maskers came in, and we had some words on this matter. By his tally, every second man in Venice is well paid for reporting what the others say and do. 'Tis a pity, with all their seeming love of justice, good Roderigo, that the senate should let divers knaves go at large; men whose very faces cause the stones to redden with anger and shame!"

"I did not know that any such were openly seen in Venice; what is secretly done may be favored for a time, through difficulty of proof, but—"

"Cospetto! They tell me the councils have a short manner of making a sinner give up his misdeeds. Now, here is the miscreant Jacopo.—What aileth thee, man? The anchor on which thou leanest is not heated."

"Nor is it of feathers; one's bones may ache from its touch without offence, I hope."

"The iron is of Elba—and was forged in a volcano. This Jacopo is one that should not go at large in an honest city, and yet is he seen pacing the square with as much ease as a noble in the Broglio!"

"I know him not."

"Not to know the boldest hand and surest stiletto in Venice, honest Roderigo, is to thy praise. But he is well marked among us of the port, and we never see the man but we begin to think of our sins, and of penances forgotten. I marvel much that the inquisitors do not give him to the devil, on some public ceremony, for the benefit of small offenders!"

"Are his deeds so notorious that they might pronounce on his fate without proof?"

"Go, ask that question in the streets! Not a Christian loses his life in Venice without warning, and the number is not few, to say nothing of those who die with state fevers, but men see the work of his sure hand in the blow. Signor Roderigo, your canals are convenient graves for sudden deaths!"

"Methinks there is contradiction in this. Thou speakest of proofs of the hand that gave it, in the manner of the blow, and then thou callest in the aid of the canals to cover the whole deed. Truly, there is some wrong done this Jacopo, who is, haply, a man slandered."

"I have heard of slandering a priest, for they are Christians, bound to keep good names for the church's honor, but to utter an injury against a Bravo would a little exceed the tongue of an avvocato. What mattereth it whether the hand be a shade deeper in color or not, when blood is on it."

"Thou sayest truly," answered the pretended Roderigo, drawing a heavy breath. "It mattereth little, indeed, to him condemned, whether the sentence cometh of one, or of many crimes."

"Dost know, friend Roderigo, that this very argument hath made me less scrupulous concerning the freight I am called on to carry, in this secret trade of ours? Thou art fairly in the senate's business, worthy Stefano, I say to myself, and therefore the less reason that thou should'st be particular in the quality of the merchandise. That Jacopo hath an eye and a scowl that would betray him, were he chosen to the chair of St. Peter! But doff thy mask, Signor Roderigo, that the sea air may cool thy cheek; 'tis time there should no longer be this suspicion between old and tried friends."

"My duty to those that send me forbids the liberty, else would I gladly stand face to face with thee, Master Stefano."

"Well, notwithstanding thy caution, cunning Signore, I

99

would hazard ten of the sequins thou art to pay to me, that I will go, on the morrow, into the crowd of San Marco, and challenge thee, openly, by name, among a thousand. Thou mayest as well unmask, for I tell thee thou art as well known to me as the lateen yards of my felucca."

"The less need to uncover. There are certain signs, no doubt, by which men who meet so often should be known to each other."

"Thou hast a goodly countenance, Signore, and the less need to hide it. I have noted thee among the revellers, when thou hast thought thyself unseen, and I will say of thee this much, without wish to gain aught in our bargain, one of appearance fair as thine, Signor Roderigo, had better be seen openly than go thus forever behind a cloud."

"My answer hath been made. What the state wills cannot be overlooked; but since I see thou knowest me, take heed not to betray thy knowledge."

"Thou would'st not be more safe with thy confessor. Diamine! I am not a man to gad about among the water sellers, with a secret at the top of my voice; but thou didst leer aside when I winked at thee dancing among the maskers on the quay. Is it not so, Roderigo?"

"There is more cleverness in thee, Master Stefano, than I had thought; though thy readiness with the felucca is no secret."

"There are two things, Signor Roderigo, on which I value myself, but always, I hope, with Christian moderation. As a mariner of the coast, in mistral or sirocco, levanter or zephyr, few can claim more practice; and for knowing an acquaintance in a carnival, I believe the father of evil himself could not be so disguised that eye of mine should not see his foot! For anticipating a gale, or looking behind a mask, Signor Roderigo, I know not my own equal among men of small learning."

"These faculties are great gifts in one who liveth by the sea and a critical trade."

"Here came one Gino, a gondolier of Don Camillo Monforte, and an ancient fellow of mine, aboard the felucca, attended by a woman in mask. He threw off the girl dexterously enough, and, as he thought, among strangers; but I knew her at a glance for the daughter of a wine seller who had already tasted lachrymae christi of mine. The woman was angered at the trick, but making the best of luck, we drove a bargain for the few casks which lay beneath the ballast, while Gino did his master's business in San Marco."

"And what that business was thou didst not learn, good Stefano?"

"How should I, Master Roderigo, when the gondolier scarce left time for greeting; but Annina—"

"Annina!"

"The same. Thou knowest Annina, old Tommaso's daughter; for she danced in the very set in which I detected thy countenance! I would not speak thus of the girl, but that I know thou art not backward to receive liquors that do not visit the custom-house, thyself."

"For that, fear nothing. I have sworn to thee that no secret of this nature shall pass my lips. But this Annina is a girl of quick wit and much boldness."

"Between ourselves, Signor Roderigo, it is not easy to tell who is in the senate's pay, here in Venice, or who is not. I have sometimes fancied, by thy manner of starting, and the tones of thy voice, that thou wert, thyself, no less than the lieutenant-general of the galleys, a little disguised."

"And this with thy knowledge of men!"

"If faith were always equal, where would be its merit? Thou hast never been hotly chased by an infidel, Master Roderigo, or thou would'st know how the mind of man can change from hope to fear, from the big voice to the humble prayer! I remember once, in the confusion and hurry of baffling winds and whistling shot, having always turbans before the eye, and the bastinado in mind, to have beseeched St. Stefano in some such voice as one would use to a dog, and to have bullied the men with the whine of a young kitten. Corpo di Bacco! One hath need of experience in these affairs, Signor Roderigo, to know even his own merits."

"I believe thee. But who is this Gino, of whom thou hast spoken, and what has his occupation, as a gondolier, to do with one known in thy youth in Calabria?"

"Therein lie matters exceeding my knowledge. His master, and I may say, my master, for I was born on his estates, is the young Duca di Sant' Agata,—the same that pushes his fortunes with the senate, in a claim to the riches and honors of the last Monforte that sat in thy councils. The debate hath so long endured, that the lad hath made himself a gondolier, by sheer shoving an oar between his master's palace and those of the nobles he moves with interest—at least such is Gino's own history of his education."

"I know the man. He wears the colors of him he serves. Is he of quick wit?"

"Signor Roderigo, all who come of Calabria cannot boast that advantage. We are no more than our neighbors, and there are exceptions in all communities, as in all families. Gino is ready enough with his oar, and as good a youth, in his way, as need be. But as to looking into things beyond their surface, why we should not expect the delicacy of a beccafico in a goose. Nature makes men, though kings make nobles.—Gino is a gondolier."

"And of good skill?"

"I say nothing of his arm, or his leg, both of which are well enough in their places; but when it comes to knowing men and things—poor Gino is but a gondolier! The lad hath a most excellent heart, and is never backward to serve a friend. I love him, but thou would'st not have me say more than the truth will warrant."

"Well, keep thy felucca in readiness, for we know not the moment it may be needed."

"Thou hast only to bring thy freight, Signore, to have the bargain fulfilled."

"Adieu.—I would recommend to thee, to keep apart from all other trades, and to see that the revelries of tomorrow do not debauch thy people."

"God speed thee, Signor Roderigo.—Naught shall be wanting."

The Bravo stepped into his gondola, which glided from the felucca's side with a facility which showed that an arm skilled in its use held the oar. He waved his hand in adieu to Stefano, and then the boat disappeared among the hulls that crowded the port.

For a few minutes the padrone of the *Bella Sorrentina* continued to pace her decks, snuffing the fresh breeze that came in over the Lido, and then he sought his rest. By this time, the dark, silent gondolas, which had been floating by hundreds through the basin, were all gone. The sound of music was heard no longer on the canals, and Venice, at all times noiseless, and peculiar, seemed to sleep the sleep of the dead.

CHAPTER VIII

"The fisher came
From his green islet, bringing o'er the waves
His wife and little one; the husbandman
From the firm land, with many a friar and nun,
And village maiden, her first flight from home,
Crowding the common ferry."

ROGERS

A BRIGHTER day than that which succeeded the night last mentioned never dawned upon the massive domes, the gorgeous palaces, and the glittering canals of Venice. The sun had not been
long above the level of the Lido, before the strains of horns
and trumpets arose from the square of St. Mark. They were
answered, in full echoes, from the distant arsenal. A thousand
gondolas glided from the canals, stealing in every direction across
the port, the Giudecca, and the various outer channels of the
place, while the well-known routes from Fusina and the neighboring isles were dotted with endless lines of boats, urging their
way towards the capital.

The citizens began to assemble early, in their holiday attire,
while thousands of contadini landed at the different bridges,
clad in the gay costumes of the main. Before the day had far
advanced, all the avenues of the great square were again
thronged, and by the time the bells of the venerable cathedral
had finished a peal of high rejoicing, St. Mark's again teemed
with its gay multitude. Few appeared in masks, but pleasure
seemed to lighten every eye, while the frank and unconcealed
countenance willingly courted the observation and sympathy of
its neighbors. In short, Venice and her people were seen in all
the gaiety and carelessness of a favorite Italian festa. The banners of the conquered nations flapped heavily on the triumphal
masts, each church tower hung out its image of the winged
lion, and every palace was rich in its hangings of tapestry and
silk, floating from balcony and window.

In the midst of this exhilarating and bright spectacle was heard the din of a hundred thousand voices. Above the constant hum, there arose, from time to time, the blasts of trumpets and the symphonies of rich music. Here the improvisatore, secretly employed by a politic and mysterious government, recounted, with a rapid utterance, and in language suited to the popular ear, at the foot of the spars which upheld the conquered banners of Candia, Crete, and the Morea, the ancient triumphs of the republic; while there, a ballad singer chanted to the greedy crowd the glory and justice of San Marco. Shouts of approbation succeeded each happy allusion to the national renown, and bravos, loud and oft-repeated, were the reward of the agents of the police, whenever they most administered to the self-delusion and vanity of their audience.

In the meantime, gondolas rich in carvings and gildings, and containing females renowned for grace and beauty, began to cluster in hundreds around the port. A general movement had already taken place among the shipping, and a wide and clear channel was opened from the quay at the foot of the piazzetta to the distant bank which shut out the waves of the Adriatic. Near this watery path, boats of all sizes and descriptions, filled with the curious and observant, were fast collecting.

The crowd thickened as the day drew in, all the vast plains of the Padovano appearing to have given up their people to swell the numbers of those that rejoiced. A few timid and irresolute maskers now began to appear in the throng, stealing a momentary pleasure under the favor of that privileged disguise, from out of the seclusion and monotony of their cloisters. Next came the rich marine equipages of the accredited agents of foreign states, and then, amid the sound of clarions and the cries of the populace, the Bucentaur rowed out of the channel of the arsenal, and came sweeping to her station at the quay of St. Mark.

These preliminaries, which occupied some hours, being observed, the javelin men, and others employed about the person of the head of the republic, were seen opening an avenue through the throng. After which, the rich strains of a hundred instruments proclaimed the approach of the doge.

We shall not detain the narrative to describe the pomp in which a luxurious and affluent aristocracy that in general held itself aloof from familiar intercourse with those it ruled, displayed its magnificence to the eyes of the multitude on an occasion of popular rejoicing. Long lines of senators, dressed in their robes of office, and attended by crowds of liveried followers, came from under the galleries of the palace, and descended by the Giant's Stairway into the sombre court. Thence, the whole issued into the piazzetta in order, and proceeded to their several stations on the canopied deck of the well-known bark. Each patrician had his allotted place, and before the rear of the cortège had yet quitted the quay, there was a long and imposing row of grave legislators seated in the established order of their precedency. The ambassadors, the high dignitaries of the state, and the aged man who had been chosen to bear the empty honors of sovereignty, still remained on the land, waiting, with the quiet of trained docility, the moment to embark. At this moment, a man of an embrowned visage, legs bare to the knee, and breast open to the breeze, rushed through the guards, and knelt on the stones of the quay, at his feet.

"Justice!—great Prince!" cried the bold stranger; "justice and mercy! Listen to one who has bled for St. Mark, and who hath his scars for his witnesses."

"Justice and mercy are not always companions," calmly observed he who wore the horned bonnet, motioning to his officious attendants to let the intruder stay.

"Mighty Prince! I come for the last."

"Who and what art thou?"

"A fisherman of the Lagunes. One named Antonio, who seeketh the liberty of the prop of his years—a glorious boy that force and the policy of the state have torn from me."

"This should not be! Violence is not the attribute of justice—but the youth hath offended the laws, and he suffereth for his crimes?"

"He is guilty, excellent and most serene Highness, of youth, and health, and strength, with some skill in the craft of the mariner. They have taken him, without warning or consent, for the service of the galleys, and have left me in my age, alone."

The expression of pity which had taken possession of the venerable features of the prince changed instantly to a look of uneasiness and distrust. The eye which just before had melted with compassion became cold and set in its meaning, and signing to his guards, he bowed with dignity to the attentive and curious auditors among the foreign agents to proceed.

105

"Bear him away," said an officer, who took his master's meaning from the glance; "the ceremonies may not be retarded for a prayer so idle."

Antonio offered no resistance, but yielding to the pressure of those around him, he sunk back meekly among the crowd, disappointment and sorrow giving place, for an instant, to an awe and an admiration of the gorgeous spectacle, that were perhaps in some degree inseparable from his condition and habits. In a few moments, the slight interruption produced by this short scene was forgotten in the higher interest of the occasion.

When the ducal party had taken their places, and an admiral of reputation was in possession of the helm, the vast and gorgeous bark, with its gilded galleries thronged with attendants, swept away from the quay with a grand and stately movement. Its departure was the signal for a new burst of trumpets and clarions, and for fresh acclamations from the people. The latter rushed to the edge of the water, and by the time the Bucentaur had reached the middle of the port, the stream was black with the gondolas that followed in her train. In this manner did the gay and shouting cortège sweep on, some darting ahead of the principal bark, and some clinging, like smaller fish swimming around the leviathan, as near to her sides as the fall of the ponderous oars would allow. As each effort of the crew sent the galley farther from the land, the living train seemed to extend itself by some secret principle of expansion; nor was the chain of its apparent connexion entirely broken, until the Bucentaur had passed the island, long famous for its convent of religious Armenians. Here the movement became slower, in order to permit the thousand gondolas to approach, and then the whole moved forward in nearly one solid phalanx to the landing of the Lido.

The marriage of the Adriatic, as the ceremony was quaintly termed, has been too often described to need a repetition here. Our business is rather with incidents of a private and personal nature than with descriptions of public events, and we shall pass over all that has no immediate connexion with the interest of the tale.

When the Bucentaur became stationary, a space around her stern was cleared, and the doge appeared in a rich gallery, so constructed as to exhibit the action to all in sight. He held a ring, glittering with precious stones, on high, and, pronouncing the words of betrothal, he dropped it upon the bosom of his fancied spouse. Shouts arose, trumpets blew their blasts, and each lady waved her handkerchief in felicitation of the happy union. In the midst of the fracas—which was greatly heightened by the roar of cannon on board the cruisers in the channel, and from the guns in the arsenal—a boat glided into the open space beneath the gallery of the Bucentaur. The movement of the arm which directed the light gondola was dexterous and still strong, though the hairs of him who held the oar were thin and white. A suppliant eye was cast up at the happy faces that adorned the state of the prince, and then the look was changed intently to the water. A small fisherman's buoy fell from the boat, which glided away so soon, that, amid the animation and uproar of that moment, the action was scarce heeded by the excited throng.

The aquatic procession now returned towards the city, the multitude rending the air with shouts at the happy termination of a ceremony to which time and the sanction of the sovereign pontiff had given a species of sanctity that was somewhat increased by superstition. It is true that a few among the Venetians themselves regarded these famous nuptials of the Adriatic with indifference; and that several of the ministers of the northern and more maritime states, who were witnesses on the occasion, had scarcely concealed, as they cast glances of intelligence and pride among themselves, their smiles. Still, such was the influence of habit, for so much does even arrogant assumption, when long and perseveringly maintained, count among men, that neither the increasing feebleness of the republic, nor the known superiority of other powers on the very element which this pageant was intended to represent as the peculiar property of St. Mark, could yet cover the lofty pretension with the ridicule it merited. Time has since taught the world that Venice continued this idle deception for ages after both reason and modesty should have dictated its discontinuance; but, at the period of which we write, that ambitious, crapulous, and factitious state was rather beginning to feel the symptomatic evidence of its fading circumstances, than to be fully conscious of the swift progress of a downward course. In this manner do communities, like individuals, draw near their dissolution, inattentive to the symptoms of decay, until they are overtaken with that fate which finally overwhelms empires and their power in the common lot of man.

The Bucentaur did not return directly to the quay to disburthen itself of its grave and dignified load. The gaudy galley anchored in the centre of the port, and opposite to the wide mouth of the Great Canal. Officers had been busy, throughout the morning, in causing all the shipping and heavy boats, of which hundreds lay in that principal artery of the city, to remove from the centre of the passage, and heralds now summoned the citizens to witness the regatta, with which the public ceremonies of the day were to terminate.

Venice, from her peculiar formation and the vast number of her watermen, had long been celebrated for this species of amusement. Families were known and celebrated in her traditions for dexterous skill with the oar, as they were known in Rome for feats of a far less useful and of a more barbarous nature. It was usual to select from these races of watermen the most vigorous and skilful; and, after invoking the aid of patron saints, and arousing their pride and recollections by songs that recounted the feats of their ancestors, to start them for the goal with every incitement that pride and the love of victory could awaken.

Most of these ancient usages were still observed. As soon as the Bucentaur was in its station, some thirty or forty gondoliers were brought forth, clad in their gayest habiliments, and surrounded and supported by crowds of anxious friends and relatives. The intended competitors were expected to sustain the long-established reputations of their several names, and they were admonished of the disgrace of defeat. They were cheered by the men, and stimulated by the smiles and tears of the other sex. The rewards were recalled to their minds; they were fortified by prayers to the saints; and then they were dismissed, amid the cries and the wishes of the multitude, to seek their allotted places beneath the stern of the galley of state.

It has already been mentioned in these pages, that the city of Venice is divided into two nearly equal parts by a channel much broader than that of the ordinary passages of the town. This dividing artery, from its superior size and depth, and its greater importance, is called the Grand Canal. Its course is not unlike that of an undulating line, which greatly increases its length. As it is much used by the larger boats of the bay—being, in fact, a sort of secondary port—and [as] its width is so considerable, it has throughout the whole distance but one bridge—the celebrated Rialto. The regatta was to be held on this canal, which offered the requisites of length and space, and which, as it was lined with most of the palaces of the principal senators, afforded all the facilities necessary for viewing the struggle.

In passing from one end of this long course to the other, the men destined for the race were not permitted to make any exertion. Their eyes roamed over the gorgeous hangings which, as is still wont throughout Italy on all days of festa, floated from every window, and on groups of females in rich attire, brilliant with the peculiar charms of the famed Venetian beauty, that clustered in the balconies. Those who were domestics rose and answered to the encouraging signals thrown from above, as they passed the palaces of their masters; while those who were water-men of the public endeavored to gather hope among the sym-pathizing faces of the multitude.

At length every formality had been duly observed, and the competitors assumed their places. The gondolas were much larger than those commonly used, and each was manned by three watermen in the centre, directed by a fourth, who, stand-ing on the little deck in the stern, steered, while he aided to impel the boat. There were light, low staffs in the bows with flags that bore the distinguishing colors of several noble families of the republic, or which had such other simple devices as had been suggested by the fancies of those to whom they belonged. A few flourishes of the oars, resembling the preparatory move-ments which the master of fence makes ere he begins to push and parry, were given; a whirling of the boats, like the pranc-ing of curbed racers, succeeded; and then at the report of a gun, the whole darted away as if the gondolas were impelled by volition. The start was followed by a shout which passed swiftly along the canal, and an eager agitation of heads that went from balcony to balcony, till the sympathetic movement was com-municated to the grave load under which the Bucentaur labored.

For a few minutes the difference in force and skill was not very obvious. Each gondola glided along the element, appar-ently with that ease with which a light-winged swallow skims the lake, and with no visible advantage to any one of the ten. Then, as more art in him who steered, or greater powers of endurance in those who rowed, or some of the latent properties of the boat itself, came into service, the cluster of little barks, which had come off like a closely united flock of birds taking flight together in alarm, began to open, till they formed a long and vacillating line, in the centre of the passage. The whole train shot beneath the bridge, so near each other as to render it still doubtful which was to conquer, and the exciting strife came more in view of the principal personages of the city.

But here those radical qualities which insure success in efforts of this nature manifested themselves. The weaker began to yield, the train to lengthen, and hopes and fears to increase, until those in the front presented the exhilarating spectacle of success, while those behind offered the still more noble sight of men struggling without hope. Gradually the distances between the boats increased, while that between them and the goal grew rapidly less, until three of those in advance came in, like glancing arrows, beneath the stern of the Bucentaur with scarce a length between them. The prize was won, the conquerors were rewarded, and the artillery gave forth the usual signals of rejoicing. Music answered to the roar of cannon and the peals of bells, while sympathy with success, that predominant and so often dangerous principle of our nature, drew shouts even from the disappointed.

The clamor ceased, and a herald proclaimed aloud the commencement of a new and a different struggle. The last, and what might be termed the national race, had been limited by an ancient usage to the known and recognized gondoliers of Venice. The prize had been awarded by the state, and the whole affair had somewhat of an official and political character. It was now announced, however, that a race was to be run in which the reward was open to all competitors, without question as to their origin, or as to their ordinary occupations. An oar of gold, to which was attached a chain of the same precious metal, was exhibited as the boon of the doge to him who showed most dexterity and strength in this new struggle; while a similar ornament of silver was to be the portion of him who showed the second-best dexterity and bottom. A mimic boat, of less precious metal, was the third prize. The gondolas were to be the usual light vehicles of the canals, and as the object was to display the peculiar skill of that city of islands, but one oarsman was allowed to each, on whom would necessarily fall the whole duty of guiding, while he impelled his little bark. Any of those who had been engaged in the previous trial were admitted to this; and all desirous of taking part in the new struggle were commanded to come beneath the stern of the Bucentaur, within a prescribed number of minutes, that note might be had of their wishes. As notice of this arrangement had been previously given, the interval between the two races was not long.

The first who came out of the crowd of boats, which environed the vacant place that had been left for the competitors, was a gondolier of the public landing, well known for his skill with the oar, and his song on the canal.

"How art thou called, and in whose name dost thou put thy chance?" demanded the herald of this aquatic course.

"All know me for Bartolomeo, one who lives between the piazzetta and the Lido, and, like a loyal Venetian, I trust in San Teodoro."

"Thou art well protected; take thy place, and await thy fortune."

The conscious waterman swept the water with a back stroke of his blade, and the light gondola whirled away into the centre of the vacant spot, like a swan giving a sudden glance aside.

"And who art thou?" demanded the official of the next that came.

"Enrico, a gondolier of Fusina. I come to try my oar with the braggarts of the canals."

"In whom is thy trust?"

"Sant' Antonio di Padua."

"Thou wilt need his aid, though we commend thy spirit. Enter, and take place."—"And who art thou?" he continued, to another, when the second had imitated the easy skill of the first.

"I am called Gino of Calabria, a gondolier in private service."

"What noble retaineth thee?"

"The illustrious and most excellent Don Camillo Monforte, Duca and Lord of Sant' Agata in Napoli, and of right a senator in Venice."

"Thou should'st have come of Padua, friend, by thy knowledge of the laws! Dost thou trust in him thou servest for the victory?"

There was a movement among the senators at the answer of Gino; and the half-terrified varlet thought he perceived frowns gathering on more than one brow. He looked around in quest of him whose greatness he had vaunted, as if he sought succor.

"Wilt thou name thy support in this great trial of force?" resumed the herald.

111

"My master," uttered the terrified Gino, "St. Januarius, and St. Mark."

"Thou art well defended. Should the two latter fail thee, thou mayest surely count on the first!"

"Signor Monforte has an illustrious name, and he is welcome to our Venetian sports," observed the doge, slightly bending his head towards the young Calabrian noble, who stood at no great distance, in a gondola of state, regarding the scene with a deeply interested countenance. This cautious interruption of the pleasantries of the official was acknowledged by a low reverence, and the matter proceeded.

"Take thy station, Gino of Calabria, and a happy fortune be thine," said the latter; then turning to another, he asked in surprise—"Why art thou here?"

"I come to try my gondola's swiftness."

"Thou art old, and unequal to this struggle; husband thy strength for daily toil. An ill-advised ambition hath put thee on this useless trial."

The new aspirant had forced a common fisherman's gondola, of no bad shape, and of sufficient lightness, but which bore about it all the vulgar signs of its daily uses, beneath the gallery of the Bucentaur. He received the reproof meekly, and was about to turn his boat aside, though with a sorrowing and mortified eye, when a sign from the doge arrested his arm.

"Question him, as of wont," said the prince.

"How art thou named?" continued the reluctant official, who, like all of subordinate condition, had far more jealousy of the dignity of the sports he directed, than his superior.

"I am known as Antonio, a fisherman of the Lagunes."

"Thou art old!"

"Signore, none know it better than I. It is sixty summers since I first threw net, or line, into the water."

"Nor art thou clad, as befitteth one who cometh before the state of Venice in a regatta."

"I am here in the best that I have. Let them who would do the nobles greater honor come in better."

"Thy limbs are uncovered—thy bosom bare—thy sinews feeble—go to; thou art ill advised to interrupt the pleasures of the nobles by this levity."

Again Antonio would have shrunk from the ten thousand eyes that shone upon him, when the calm voice of the doge once more came to his aid.

"The struggle is open to all," said the sovereign; "still I would advise the poor and aged man to take counsel; give him silver, for want urges him to this hopeless trial."

"Thou hearest; alms are offered thee; but give place to those who are stronger, and more seemly, for the sport."

"I will obey, as is the duty of one born and accustomed to poverty. They said the race was open to all, and I crave the pardon of the nobles, since I meant to do them no dishonor."

"Justice in the palace, and justice on the canals," hastily observed the prince. "If he will continue, it is his right. It is the pride of St. Mark that his balances are held with an even hand."

A murmur of applause succeeded the specious sentiment, for the powerful rarely affect the noble attribute of justice, however limited may be its exercise, without their words finding an echo in the tongues of the selfish.

"Thou hearest—His Highness, who is the voice of the mighty state, says thou mayest remain;—though thou art still advised to withdraw."

"I will then see what virtue is left in this naked arm," returned Antonio, casting a mournful glance, and one that was not entirely free from the latent vanity of man, at his meagre and threadbare attire. "The limb hath its scars, but the infidels may have spared enough, for the little I ask."

"In whom is thy faith?"

"Blessed St. Anthony of the Miraculous Draught."

"Take thy place.—Ha! here cometh one unwilling to be known! How now! who appears with so false a face?"

"Call me Mask."

"So neat and just a leg and arm need not have hid their fellow, the countenance. Is it Your Highness's pleasure that one disguised should be entered for the sports?"

"Doubt it not. A mask is sacred in Venice. It is the glory of our excellent and wise laws, that he who seeketh to dwell within the privacy of his own thoughts, and to keep aloof from curiosity by shadowing his features, rangeth our streets and canals, as if he dwelt in the security of his own abode. Such are the high privileges of liberty, and such it is to be a citizen of a generous, a magnanimous, and a free state!"

A thousand bowed in approbation of the sentiment, and a rumor passed, from mouth to mouth, that a young noble was about to try his strength in the regatta in compliment to some wayward beauty.

"Such is justice!" exclaimed the herald, in a loud voice, admiration apparently overcoming respect, in the ardor of the moment. "Happy is he that is born in Venice, and envied are the people in whose councils, wisdom and mercy preside, like lovely and benignant sisters! On whom dost thou rely?"

"Mine own arm."

"Ha! This is impious! None so presuming may enter into these privileged sports."

The hurried exclamation of the herald was accompanied by a general stir, such as denotes sudden and strong emotion in a multitude.

"The children of the republic are protected by an even hand," observed the venerable prince. "It formeth our just pride, and blessed St. Mark forbid that aught resembling vainglory should be uttered! but it is truly our boast that we know no difference between our subjects of the islands, or those of the Dalmatian coast; between Padua, or Candia; Corfu, or St. Giorgio. Still it is not permitted for any to refuse the intervention of the saints."

"Name thy patron, or quit the place," continued the observant herald, anew.

The stranger paused, as if he looked into his mind, and then he answered—

"San Giovanni of the Wilderness."

"Thou namest one of blessed memory!"

"I name him who may have pity on me, in this living desert."

"The temper of thy soul is best known to thyself, but this reverend rank of patricians, yonder brilliant show of beauty, and that goodly multitude, may claim another name.—Take thy place."

While the herald proceeded to take the names of three or four more applicants, all gondoliers in private service, a murmur ran through the spectators, which proved how much their interest and curiosity had been awakened by the replies and appearance of the two last competitors. In the meantime, the young nobles who entertained those who came last began to move among the throng of boats, with the intention of making such manifestations of their gallant desires, and personal devotion, as suited the customs and opinions of the age. The list was now proclaimed to be full, and the gondolas were towed off, as before, towards the starting point, leaving the place beneath

114

the stern of the Bucentaur vacant. The scene that followed consequently passed directly before the eyes of those grave men who charged themselves with most of the private interests, as well as with the public concerns of Venice.

There were many unmasked and highborn dames, whirling about in their boats, attended by cavaliers in rich attire, and, here and there, appeared a pair of dark, lustrous eyes, peeping through the silk of a visor that concealed some countenance too youthful for exposure in so gay a scene. One gondola, in particular, was remarked for the singular grace and beauty of the form it held, qualities which made themselves apparent, even through the half-disguise of the simple habiliments she wore. The boat, the servants, and the ladies, for there were two, were alike distinguished for that air of severe but finished simplicity which oftener denotes the presence of high quality and true taste, than a more lavish expenditure of vulgar ornament. A Carmelite, whose features were concealed by his cowl, testified that their condition was high, and lent a dignity to their presence by his reverend and grave protection. A hundred gondolas approached this party, and after as many fruitless efforts to penetrate the disguises, glided away, while whispers and interrogatories passed from one to the other, to learn the name and station of the youthful beauty. At length, a gay bark, with watermen in gorgeous liveries, and in whose equipment there was a studied display of magnificence, came into the little circle that curiosity had drawn together. The single cavalier, who occupied the seat, arose, for few gondolas appeared that day with their gloomy-looking and mysterious pavillions, and saluted the masked females with the ease of one accustomed to all presences, but with the reserve of deep respect.

"I have a favorite follower in this race," he said gallantly, "and one in whose skill and force I put great trust. Until now, I have uselessly sought a lady of a beauty and merit so rare, as to warrant that I should place his fortune on her smiles. But I seek no farther."

"You are gifted with a keen sight, Signore, that you discover all you seek beneath these masks," returned one of the two females, while their companion, the Carmelite, bowed graciously to the compliment, which seemed little more than was warranted by the usage of such scenes.

"There are other means of recognition than the eyes, and

other sources of admiration than the senses, lady. Conceal your-selves as you will, here do I know that I am near the fairest face, the warmest heart, and the purest mind of Venice!"

"This is bold augury, Signore," returned she who was evidently the oldest of the two, glancing a look at her companion, as if to note the effect of this gallant speech. "Venice has a name for the beauty of its dames, and the sun of Italy warms many a generous heart."

"Better that such noble gifts should be directed to the worship of the Creator than of the creature," murmured the monk.

"Some there are, holy father, who have admiration for both. Such I would fain hope is the happy lot of her who is favored with the spiritual counsel of one so virtuous and wise as yourself. Here I place my fortune, let what may follow; and here would I gladly place a heavier stake, were it permitted."

As the cavalier spoke, he tendered to the silent fair a bouquet of the sweetest and most fragrant flowers; and among them were those to which poets and custom have ascribed the emblematic qualities of constancy and love. She to whom this offering of gallantry was made hesitated to accept it. It much exceeded the reserve imposed on one of her station and years, to allow of such homage from the other sex, though the occasion was generally deemed one that admitted of more than usual gallantry; and she evidently shrunk, with the sensitiveness of one whose feelings were unpractised, from an homage so public.

"Receive the flowers, my love," mildly whispered her companion; "the cavalier who offers them simply intends to show the quality of his breeding."

"That will be seen in the end," hastily returned Don Camillo—for it was he. "Signora, adieu; we have met on this water when there was less restraint between us."

He bowed, and signing to his gondolier, was quickly lost in the crowd of boats. Ere the barks, however, were separated, the mask of the silent fair was slightly moved, as if she sought relief from the air; and the Neapolitan was rewarded for his gallantry, by a momentary glance at the glowing countenance of Violetta.

"Thy guardian hath a displeased eye," hurriedly observed Donna Florinda. "I wonder that we should be known!"

"I should more wonder that we were not. I could recall the noble Neapolitan cavalier amid a million! Thou dost not remember all that I owe to him!"

Donna Florinda did not answer; but, in secret, she offered up a fervent prayer that the obligation might be blessed to the future happiness of her who had received it. There was a furtive and uneasy glance between her and the Carmelite; but, as neither spoke, a long and thoughtful silence succeeded the rencontre.

From this musing, the party, in common with all the gay and laughing multitude by which they were surrounded, were reminded of the business on which they were assembled by the signal-gun, the agitation on the Great Canal nearest the scene of strife, and a clear blast of the trumpets. But in order that the narrative may proceed regularly, it is fit that we should return, a little, in the order of time.

CHAPTER IX

"Here art thou in appointment fresh and fair,
Anticipating time with starting courage."
SHAKESPEARE

It has been seen that the gondolas, which were to contend in the race, had been towed towards the place of starting, in order that the men might enter on the struggle with undiminished vigor. In this precaution, even the humble and half-clad fisherman had not been neglected, but his boat, like the others, was attached to the larger barges to which this duty had been assigned. Still, as he passed along the canal, before the crowded balconies and groaning vessels which lined its sides, there arose that scornful and deriding laugh which seems ever to grow more strong and bold as misfortune weighs most heavily on its subject.

The old man was not unconscious of the remarks of which he was the subject; and, as it is rare indeed that our sensibilities do not survive our better fortunes, even he was so far conscious of a fall as not to be callous to contempt thus openly expressed. He looked wistfully on every side of him, and seemed to search, in every eye he encountered, some portion of the sympathy which his meek and humble feelings still craved. But even the men of his caste and profession threw jibes upon his ear; and, though of all the competitors perhaps the one whose motive most hallowed his ambition, he was held to be the only proper subject of mirth. For the solution of this revolting trait of human character, we are not to look to Venice and her institutions, since it is known that none are so arrogant, on occasions, as the ridden, and that the abject and insolent spirits are usually tenants of the same bosom.

The movement of the boats brought those of the masked waterman and the subject of these taunts side by side.

"Thou art not the favorite in this strife," observed the former, when a fresh burst of jibes were showered on the head of his unresisting associate. "Thou hast not been sufficiently heedful of thy attire; for this is a town of luxury, and he who would meet

118

applause must appear on the canals in the guise of one less borne upon by fortune."

"I know them! I know them!" returned the fisherman; "they are led away by their pride, and they think ill of one who cannot share in their vanities. But, friend unknown, I have brought with me a face which, old though it be, and wrinkled, and worn by the weather like the stones of the seashore, is uncovered to the eye, and without shame."

"There may be reasons which thou knowest not, why I wear a mask. But if my face be hid, the limbs are bare, and thou seest there is no lack of sinews to make good that which I have undertaken. Thou should'st have thought better of the matter, ere thou puttest thyself in the way of so much mortification. Defeat will not cause the people to treat thee more tenderly."

"If my sinews are old and stiffened, Signor Mask, they are long used to toil. As to shame, if it is a shame to be below the rest of mankind in fortune, it will not now come for the first time. A heavy sorrow hath befallen me, and this race may lighten the burthen of grief. I shall not pretend that I hear this laughter, and all these scornful speeches, as one listens to the evening breeze on the Lagunes—for a man is still a man, though he lives with the humblest, and eats of the coarsest. But let it pass; Sant' Antonio will give me heart to bear it."

"Thou hast a stout mind, fisherman; and I would gladly pray my patron to grant thee a stronger arm, but that I have much need of this victory myself. Wilt thou be content with the second prize, if, by any manner of skill, I might aid thee in thy efforts?—for, I suppose, the metal of the third is as little to thy taste as it is to my own."

"Nay, I count not on gold, or silver."

"Can the honor of such a struggle awaken the pride of one like thee?"

The old man looked earnestly at his companion; but he shook his head, without answer. Fresh merriment, at his expense, caused him to bend his face towards the scoffers; and he perceived they were, just then, passing a numerous group of his fellows of the Lagunes, who seemed to feel that his unjustifiable ambition reflected, in some degree, on the honor of their whole body.

"How now, old Antonio!" shouted the boldest of the band—"is it not enough that thou hast won the honors of the net, but thou would'st have a golden oar at thy neck?"

119

"We shall yet see him of the senate!" cried a second.

"He standeth in need of the horned bonnet for his naked head," continued a third. "We shall see the brave Admiral Antonio, sailing in the Bucentaur, with the nobles of the land!"

Their sallies were succeeded by coarse laughter. Even the fair, in the balconies, were not uninfluenced by these constant jibes, and the apparent discrepancy between the condition and the means of so unusual a pretender to the honors of the regatta. The purpose of the old man wavered; but he seemed goaded by some inward incentive that still enabled him to maintain his ground. His companion closely watched the varying expression of a countenance that was far too little trained in deception to conceal the feelings within; and, as they approached the place of starting, he again spoke.

"Thou mayest yet withdraw," he said;—"why should one of thy years make the little time he has to stay bitter, by bearing the ridicule of his associates for the rest of his life?"

"St. Anthony did a greater wonder, when he caused the fishes to come upon the waters to hear his preaching, and I will not show a cowardly heart, at a moment when there is most need of resolution."

The masked waterman crossed himself devoutly; and, relinquishing all further design to persuade the other to abandon the fruitless contest, he gave all his thoughts to his own interest in the coming struggle.

The narrowness of most of the canals of Venice, with the innumerable angles and the constant passing, have given rise to a fashion of construction and of rowing that are so peculiar to that city and its immediate dependencies as to require some explanation. The reader has doubtless already understood that a gondola is a long, narrow, and light boat, adapted to the uses of the place, and distinct from the wherries of all other towns. The distance between the dwellings, on most of the canals, is so small, that the width of the latter does not admit of the use of oars on both sides at the same time. The necessity of constantly turning aside to give room for others, and the frequency of the bridges and the corners, have suggested the expediency of placing the face of the waterman in the direction in which the boat is steering, and, of course, of keeping him on his feet. As every gondola, when fully equipped, has its pavilion in the centre, the height of the latter renders it necessary to place him who steers on such an elevation, as will enable him to overlook it. From these several causes, a one-oared boat, in Venice, is propelled by a gondolier who stands on a little angular deck in its stern, formed like the low roof of a house; and the stroke of the oar is given by a push, instead of a pull, as is common elsewhere. This habit of rowing erect, however, which is usually done by a foward, instead of a backward, movement of the body, is not unfrequent in all the ports of the Mediterranean, though in no other is there a boat which resembles the gondola in all its properties, or uses. The upright position of the gondolier requires that the pivot on which the oar rests should have a corresponding elevation; and there is, consequently, a species of bumkin, raised from the side of the boat, to the desired height, and which, being formed of a crooked and very irregular knee of wood, has two or three rowlocks, one above the other, to suit the stature of different individuals, or to give a broader or a narrower sweep of the blade as the movement shall require. As there is frequent occasion to cast the oar from one of these rowlocks to the other, and not unfrequently to change its side, it rests in a very open bed; and the instrument is kept in its place by great dexterity alone, and by a perfect knowledge of the means of accommodating the force and the rapidity of the effort to the forward movement of the boat and the resistance of the water. All these difficulties united render skill in a gondolier one of the most delicate branches of a waterman's art, as it is clear that muscular strength alone, though of great aid, can avail but little in such a practice.

The Great Canal of Venice, following its windings, being more than a league in length, the distance in the present race was reduced nearly half, by causing the boats to start from the Rialto. At this point, then, the gondolas were all assembled, attended by those who were to place them. As the whole of the population which, before, had been extended along the entire course of the water was now crowded between the bridge and the Bucentaur, the long and graceful avenue resembled a vista of human heads. It was an imposing sight to look along that bright and living lane, and the hearts of each competitor beat high, as hope, or pride, or apprehension became the feeling of the moment.

"Gino of Calabria," cried the marshal who placed the gondolas, "thy station is on the right. Take it, and St. Januarius speed thee!"

The servitor of Don Camillo assumed his oar, and the boat glided gracefully into its berth.

"Thou comest next, Enrico of Fusina. Call stoutly on thy Paduan patron, and husband thy strength; for none of the main have ever yet borne away a prize in Venice."

He then summoned, in succession, those whose names have not been mentioned, and placed them, side by side, in the centre of the canal.

"Here is place for thee, Signore," continued the officer, inclining his head to the unknown gondolier; for he had imbibed the general impression that the face of some young patrician was concealed beneath the mask, to humor the fancy of some capricious fair.—"Chance hath given thee the extreme left."

"Thou hast forgotten to call the fisherman," observed the masker, as he drove his own gondola into its station.

"Does the hoary fool persist in exposing his vanity and his rags to the best of Venice?"

"I can take place in the rear," meekly observed Antonio. "There may be those in the line it doth not become one like me to crowd; and a few strokes of the oar, more or less, can differ but little, in so long a strife."

"Thou hadst better push modesty to discretion, and remain."

"If it be your pleasure, Signore, I would rather see what St. Anthony may do for an old fisherman who has prayed to him, night and morning, these sixty years!"

"It is thy right; and, as thou seemest content with it, keep the place thou hast in the rear. It is only occupying it a little earlier than thou would'st otherwise. Now, recall the rules of the games, hardy gondoliers, and make thy last appeal to thy patrons. There is to be no crossing, or other foul expedients; naught except ready oars, and nimble wrists. He who varies, needlessly, from his line until he leadeth, shall be recalled by name; and whoever is guilty of any act to spoil the sports, or otherwise to offend the patricians, shall be both checked and punished. Be ready for the signal."

The assistant, who was in a strongly manned boat, fell back a little, while runners, similarly equipped, went ahead to order the curious from the water. These preparations were scarcely made, when a signal floated on the nearest dome. It was repeated on the campanile, and a gun was fired at the arsenal. A deep but suppressed murmur arose in the throng, which was as quickly succeeded by suspense.

Each gondolier had suffered the bows of his boat to incline slightly toward the left shore of the canal, as the jockey is seen, at the starting-post, to turn his courser aside, in order to repress its ardor, or divert its attention. But the first long and broad sweep of the oar brought them all in a line again, and away they glided in a body.

For the first few minutes there was no difference in speed, nor any sign by which the instructed might detect the probable evidence of defeat or success. The whole ten which formed the front line skimmed the water with an equal velocity, beak to beak, as if some secret attraction held each in its place, while the humble, though equally light bark of the fisherman steadily kept its position in the rear.

The boats were soon held in command. The oars got their justest poise and widest sweep, and the wrists of the men accustomed to their play. The line began to waver. It undulated, the glittering prow of one protruding beyond the others; and then it changed its form. Enrico of Fusina shot ahead, and, privileged by success, he insensibly sheered more into the centre of the canal, avoiding, by the change, the eddies, and the other obstructions of the shore. This manœuvre, which, in the language of the course, would have been called "taking the track," had the additional advantage of throwing upon those who followed some trifling impediment from the back-water. The sturdy and practised Bartolomeo of the Lido, as his companions usually called him, came next, occupying the space on his leader's quarter, where he suffered least from the reaction caused by the stroke of his oar. The gondolier of Don Camillo, also, soon shot out of the crowd, and was seen plying his arms vigorously still farther to the right, and a little in the rear of Bartolomeo. Then came, in the centre of the canal, and near as might be in the rear of the triumphant waterman of the main, a dense body, with little order and varying positions, compelling each other to give way, and otherwise increasing the difficulties of their struggle. More to the left, and so near to the palaces as barely to allow room for the sweep of his oar, was the masked competitor, whose progress seemed retarded by some unseen cause, for he gradually fell behind all the others, until several boats' lengths of open water lay between him and even the group of his nameless opponents. Still he plied his arms steadily, and with sufficient skill. As the interest of mystery had been excited in his favor, a rumor passed up the canal, that the young cavalier had been little favored by fortune in the choice of a boat. Others, who reflected more deeply on causes, whispered of the folly of one of his habits taking the risk of mortification by a competition with men whose daily labor had hardened their sinews, and whose practice enabled them to judge closely of every chance of the race. But when the eyes of the multitude turned from the cluster of passing boats to the solitary barge of the fisherman, who came singly on in the rear, admiration was again turned to derision.

Antonio had cast aside the cap he wore of wont, and the few straggling hairs that were left streamed about his hollow temples, leaving the whole of his swarthy features exposed to view. More than once, as the gondola came on, his eyes turned aside reproachfully, as if he keenly felt the stings of so many unlicensed tongues applied to feelings which, though blunted by his habits and condition, were far from extinguished. Laugh rose above laugh, however, and taunt succeeded taunt more bitterly, as the boats came among the gorgeous palaces, which lined the canal nearer to the goal. It was not that the owners of these lordly piles indulged in the unfeeling triumph, but their dependants, constantly subject themselves to the degrading influence of a superior presence, let loose the long-pent torrents of their arrogance, on the head of the first unresisting subject which offered.

Antonio bore all these jibes manfully, if not in tranquillity, and always without retort, until he again approached the spot occupied by his companions of the Lagunes. Here his eye sunk under the reproaches, and his oar faltered. The taunts and denunciations increased as he lost ground, and there was a moment when the rebuked and humbled spirit of the old man seemed about to relinquish the contest. But dashing a hand across his brow, as if to clear a sight which had become dimmed and confused, he continued to ply the oar, and, happily, he was soon past the point most trying to his resolution. From this moment the cries against the fisherman diminished, and as the Bucentaur, though still distant, was now in sight, interest in the issue of the race absorbed all other feelings.

Enrico still kept the lead; but the judges of the gondolier's skill began to detect signs of exhaustion in his faltering stroke. The waterman of the Lido pressed him hard, and the Calabrian was drawing more into a line with them both. At this moment, too, the masked competitor exhibited a force and skill that none had expected to see in one of his supposed rank. His body was thrown more upon the effort of the oar, and as his leg was stretched behind to aid the stroke, it discovered a volume of muscle, and an excellence of proportion, that excited murmurs of applause. The consequence was soon apparent. His gondola glided past the crowd, in the centre of the canal, and by a change that was nearly insensible, he became the fourth in the race. The shouts which rewarded his success had scarcely parted from the multitude, ere their admiration was called to a new and an entirely unexpected aspect in the struggle.

Left to his own exertions, and less annoyed by that derision and contempt which often defeat even more generous exertions, Antonio had drawn nearer to the crowd of nameless competitors. Though undistinguished in this narrative, there were seen, in that group of gondoliers, faces well known on the canals of Venice, as belonging to watermen in whose dexterity and force the city took pride. Either favored by his isolated position, or availing himself of the embarrassment these men gave to each other, the despised fisherman was seen a little on their left, coming up abreast, with a stroke and velocity that promised farther success. The expectation was quickly realized. He passed them all, amid a dead and wondering silence, and took his station, as fifth in the struggle.

From this moment all interest in those who formed the vulgar mass was lost. Every eye was turned towards the front, where the strife increased at each stroke of the oar, and where the issue began to assume a new and doubtful character. The exertions of the waterman of Fusina were seemingly redoubled, though his boat went no faster. The gondola of Bartolomeo shot past him; it was followed by those of Gino and the masked gondolier, while not a cry betrayed the breathless interest of the multitude. But when the boat of Antonio also swept ahead, there arose such a hum of voices as escapes a throng, when a sudden and violent change of feeling is produced in their wayward sentiments. Enrico was frantic with the disgrace. He urged every power of his frame to avert the dishonor, with the desperate energy of an Italian, and then he cast himself into the bottom of the gondola, tearing his hair and weeping in agony. His example was followed by those in the rear, though with more governed feelings, for they shot aside among the boats which lined the canal, and were lost to view.

From this open and unexpected abandonment of the struggle, the spectators got the surest evidence of its desperate character. But as a man has little sympathy for the unfortunate, when his feelings are excited by competition, the defeated were quickly forgotten. The name of Bartolomeo was borne high upon the winds, by a thousand voices, and his fellows of the piazzetta and the Lido called upon him, aloud, to die for the honor of their craft. Well did the sturdy gondolier answer to their wishes, for palace after palace was left behind, and no further change was made in the relative positions of the boats. But, like his predecessor, the leader redoubled his efforts, with a diminished effect, and Venice had the mortification of seeing a stranger leading one of the most brilliant of her regattas. Bartolomeo no sooner lost place, than Gino, the masker, and the despised Antonio, in turn, shot by, leaving him who had so lately been first in the race, the last. He did not, however, relinquish the strife, but continued to struggle with the energy of one who merited a better fortune.

When this unexpected and entirely new character was given to the contest, there still remained a broad sheet of water, between the advancing gondolas and the goal. Gino led, and with many favorable symptoms of his being able to maintain his advantage. He was encouraged by the shouts of the multitude, who now forgot his Calabrian origin, in his success, while many of the serving-men of his master, cheered him on, by name. All would not do. The masked waterman, for the first time, threw the grandeur of his skill and force into the oar. The ashen instrument bent to the power of an arm whose strength appeared to increase at will, and the movements of his body became rapid as the leaps of the grayhound. The pliant gondola obeyed, and amid a shout which passed from the piazzetta to the Rialto, it glided ahead.

If success gives force and increases the physical and moral energies, there is a fearful and certain reaction in defeat. The follower of Don Camillo was no exception to the general law, and when the masked competitor passed him, the boat of Antonio followed as if it were impelled by the same strokes. The distance between the two leading gondolas even now seemed to lessen, and there was a moment of breathless interest, when all there expected to see the fisherman, in despite of his years and boat, shooting past his rival.

But expectation was deceived. He of the mask, notwithstand-

126

ing his previous efforts, seemed to sport with the toil, so ready was the sweep of his oar, so sure its stroke, and so vigorous the arm by which it was impelled. Nor was Antonio an antagonist to despise. If there was less of the grace of a practised gondolier of the canals in his attitudes, than in those of his companion, there was no relaxation in the force of his sinews. They sustained him to the last, with that enduring power which had been begotten by threescore years of unremitting labor, and while his still athletic form was exerted to the utmost, there appeared no failing of its energies.

A few moments sent the leading gondolas several lengths ahead of their nearest followers. The dark beak of the fisherman's boat hung upon the quarter of the more showy bark of his antagonist, but it could do no more. The port was open before them, and they glanced by church, palace, barge, mistic,* and felucca, without the slightest inequality in their relative speed. The masked waterman glanced a look behind, as if to calculate his advantage, and then bending again to his pliant oar, he spoke, loud enough to be heard only by him who pressed so hard upon his track.

"Thou hast deceived me, fisherman!" he said; "there is more of manhood in thee, yet, than I had thought."

"If there is manhood in my arms, there is childishness and sorrow at the heart," was the reply.

"Dost thou so prize a golden bauble? Thou art second; be content with thy lot."

"It will not do; I must be foremost, or I have wearied my old limbs in vain!"

This brief dialogue was uttered, with an ease that showed how far use had accustomed both to powerful bodily efforts, and with a firmness of tones that few could have equalled in a moment of so great physical effort. The masker was silent, but his purpose seemed to waver. Twenty strokes of his powerful oar-blade, and the goal was attained: but his sinews were not so much extended, and that limb which had shown so fine a development of muscle was less swollen and rigid. The gondola of old Antonio glided abeam.

"Push thy soul into the blade," muttered he of the mask, "or thou wilt yet be beaten!"

---

* A small Mediterranean vessel, lateen rigged.—Editor.

The fisherman threw every effort of his body on the coming effort, and he gained a fathom. Another stroke caused the boat to quiver to its centre, and the water curled from its bows, like the ripple of a rapid. Then the gondola darted between the two goal-barges, and the little flags that marked the point of victory fell into the water. The action was scarce noted, ere the glittering beak of the masker shot past the eyes of the judges, who doubted, for an instant, on whom success had fallen. Gino was not long behind, and after him came Bartolomeo, fourth and last, in the best-contested race which had ever been seen on the waters of Venice.

When the flags fell, men held their breaths in suspense. Few knew the victor, so close had been the struggle. But a flourish of the trumpets soon commanded attention, and then a herald proclaimed, that—

"Antonio, a fisherman of the Lagunes, favored by his holy patron of the Miraculous Draught, had borne away the prize of gold—while a waterman who wore his face concealed, but who hath trusted to the care of the blessed San Giovanni of the Wilderness, is worthy of the silver prize, and that the third had fallen to the fortunes of Gino of Calabria, a servitor of the illustrious Don Camillo Monforte, Duca di Sant' Agata, and lord of many Neapolitan seigniories."

When this formal announcement was made, there succeeded a silence like that of the tomb. Then there arose a general shout among the living mass, which bore on high the name of Antonio, as if they celebrated the success of some conqueror. All feeling of contempt was lost in the influence of his triumph. The fishermen of the Lagunes, who so lately had loaded their aged companion with contumely, shouted for his glory with a zeal that manifested the violence of the transition from mortification to pride, and, as has ever been and ever will be the meed of success, he who was thought least likely to obtain it was most greeted with praise and adulation, when it was found that the end had disappointed expectation. Ten thousand voices were lifted, in proclaiming his skill and victory, and young and old, the fair, the gay, the noble, the winner of sequins and he who lost, struggled alike, to catch a glimpse of the humble old man who had so unexpectedly wrought this change of sentiment in the feelings of a multitude.

Antonio bore his triumph meekly. When his gondola had

reached the goal, he checked its course, and, without discovering any of the usual signs of exhaustion, he remained standing, though the deep heaving of his broad and tawny chest proved that his powers had been taxed to their utmost. He smiled as the shouts arose on his ear, for praise is grateful, even to the meek; still he seemed oppressed, with an emotion of a character deeper than pride. Age had somewhat dimmed his eye, but it was now full of hope. His features worked, and a single burning drop fell on each rugged cheek. The fisherman then breathed more freely.

Like his successful antagonist, the waterman of the mask betrayed none of the debility which usually succeeds great bodily exertion. His knees were motionless, his hands still grasped the oar firmly, and he too kept his feet with a steadiness that showed the physical perfection of his frame. On the other hand, both Gino and Bartolomeo sunk in their respective boats, as they gained the goal, in succession; and so exhausted was each of these renowned gondoliers, that several moments elapsed before either had breath for speech. It was during this momentary pause that the multitude proclaimed its sympathy with the victor, by their longest and loudest shouts. The noise had scarcely died away, however, before a herald summoned Antonio of the Lagunes, the masked waterman of the Blessed St. John of the Wilderness, and Gino the Calabrian, to the presence of the doge, whose princely hand was to bestow the promised prizes of the regatta.

CHAPTER X

"We shall not spend a large expense of time,
Before we reckon with your several loves,
And make us even with you."

Macbeth

WHEN the three gondolas reached the side of the Bucentaur, the fisherman hung back, as if he distrusted his right to intrude himself into the presence of the senate. He was, however, commanded to ascend, and signs were made for his two companions to follow.

The nobles, clad in their attire of office, formed a long and imposing lane from the gangway to the stern, where the titular sovereign of that still more titular republic was placed, in the centre of the high officers of the state, gorgeous and grave in borrowed guise and natural qualities.

"Approach," said the prince, mildly, observing that the old and half-naked man that led the victors hesitated to advance. "Thou art the conqueror, fisherman, and to thy hands must I consign the prize."

Antonio bent his knee to the deck, and bowed his head lowly ere he obeyed. Then taking courage, he drew nearer to the person of the doge, where he stood with a bewildered eye and rebuked mien, waiting the further pleasure of his superiors. The aged prince paused for stillness to succeed the slight movements created by curiosity. When he spoke, it was amid a perfect calm.

"It is the boast of our glorious republic," he said, "that the rights of none are disregarded; that the lowly receive their merited rewards as surely as the great; that St. Mark holds the balance with an even hand, and that this obscure fisherman, having deserved the honors of this regatta, will receive them with the same readiness on the part of him who bestows, as if he were the most favored follower of our own house. Nobles and burghers of Venice, learn to prize your excellent and equable laws in this occasion, for it is most in acts of familiar and

130

common usage that the parental character of a government is seen, since in matters of higher moment, the eyes of a world impel a compliance with its own opinions."

The doge delivered these preliminary remarks in a firm tone, like one confident of his auditors' applause. He was not deceived. No sooner had he done, than a murmur of approbation passed through the assembly, and extended itself to thousands who were beyond the sound of his voice, and to more who were beyond the reach of his meaning. The senators bent their heads in acknowledgment of the justice of what their chief had uttered, and the latter, having waited to gather these signs of an approving loyalty, proceeded.

"It is my duty, Antonio, and, being a duty, it hath become a pleasure, to place around thy neck this golden chain. The oar which it bears is an emblem of thy skill; and among thy associates it will be a mark of the republic's favor and impartiality, and of thy merit. Take it, then, vigorous old man, for though age hath thinned thy temples and furrowed thy cheek, it hath scarce affected thy wonderful sinews and hardy courage!"

"Highness!" observed Antonio, recoiling apace, when he found that he was expected to stoop, in order that the bauble might be bestowed, "I am not fit to bear about me such a sign of greatness and good fortune. The glitter of the gold would mock my poverty, and a jewel, which comes from so princely a hand, would be ill placed on a naked bosom."

This unexpected refusal caused a general surprise, and a momentary pause.

"Thou hast not entered on the struggle, fisherman, without a view to its prize? But thou sayest truly, the golden ornament would, indeed, but ill befit thy condition and daily wants. Wear it for the moment, since it is meet that all should know the justice and impartiality of our decisions, and bring it to my treasurer when the sports are done; he will make such an exchange as better suits thy wishes. There is precedent for this practice, and it shall be followed."

"Illustrious Highness! I did not trust my old limbs in so hard a strife without hopes of reward. But it was not gold, nor any vanity to be seen among my equals with that glittering jewel, that led me to meet the scorn of the gondoliers, and the displeasure of the great."

"Thou art deceived, honest fisherman, if thou supposest that

131

we regard thy just ambition with displeasure. We love to see a generous emulation among our people, and take all proper means to encourage those aspiring spirits who bring honor to a state, and fortune to our shores."

"I pretend not to place my poor thoughts against those of my prince," answered the fisherman; "my fears and shame have led me to believe, that it would give more pleasure to the noble and gay had a younger and happier borne away this honor."

"Thou must not think this. Bend, then, thy knee, that I may bestow the prize. When the sun sets, thou wilt find those in my palace who will relieve thee of the ornament at a just remuneration."

"Highness!" said Antonio, looking earnestly at the doge, who again arrested his movement, in surprise, "I am old, and little wont to be spoilt by fortune. For my wants, the Lagunes, with the favor of the Holy St. Anthony, are sufficient; but it is in thy power to make the last days of an old man happy, and to have thy name remembered in many an honest and well-meant prayer. Grant me back my child, forget the boldness of a heart-broken father!"

"Is not this he who urged us with importunity, concerning a youth that is gone into the service of the state?" exclaimed the prince, across whose countenance passed that expression of habitual reserve which so often concealed the feelings of the man.

"The same," returned a cold voice which the ear of Antonio well knew came from the Signor Gradenigo.

"Pity for thy ignorance, fisherman, represses our anger. Receive thy chain, and depart."

Antonio's eye did not waver. He kneeled with an air of profound respect, and folding his hands on his bosom, he said—

"Misery has made me bold, dread Prince! What I say comes from a heavy heart, rather than from a licentious tongue, and I pray your royal ear to listen with indulgence."

"Speak briefly, for the sports are delayed."

"Mighty Doge! riches and poverty have caused a difference in our fortunes, which knowledge and ignorance have made wider. I am rude in my discourse, and little suited to this illustrious company. But, Signore, God hath given to the fisherman the same feelings, and the same love for his offspring, as he has given to a prince. Did I place dependence only on the aid of my poor learning, I should now be dumb, but there is a strength within

132

that gives me courage to speak to the first and noblest in Venice in behalf of my child."

"Thou canst not impeach the senate's justice, old man, nor utter aught, in truth, against the known impartiality of the laws!"

"Sovrano mio! deign to listen, and you shall hear. I am what your eyes behold—a man, poor, laborious, and drawing near to the hour when he shall be called to the side of the Blessed St. Anthony of Rimini, and stand in a presence even greater than this. I am not vain enough to think that my humble name is to be found among those of the patricians who have served the republic in her wars—that is an honor which none but the great, and the noble, and the happy, can claim; but if the little I have done for my country is not in the Golden Book, it is written here," as Antonio spoke, he pointed to the scars on his half-naked form; "these are signs of the enmity of the Turk, and I now offer them as so many petitions to the bounty of the senate."

"Thou speakest vaguely. What is thy will?"

"Justice, mighty Prince. They have forced the only vigorous branch from the dying trunk—they have lopped the withering stem of its most promising shoot—they have exposed the sole companion of my labors and pleasures, the child to whom I have looked to close my eyes, when it shall please God to call me away, untaught, and young in lessons of honesty and virtue, a boy in principle as in years, to all the temptation, and sin, and dangerous companionship of the galleys!"

"Is this all? I had thought thy gondola in the decay, or thy right to use the Lagunes in question!"

"Is this all?" repeated Antonio, looking around him in bitter melancholy. "Doge of Venice, it is more than one old, heart-stricken, and bereaved, can bear!"

"Go to; take thy golden chain and oar, and depart among thy fellows in triumph. Gladden thy heart at a victory on which thou could'st not, in reason, have counted, and leave the interests of the state to those that are wiser than thee, and more fitted to sustain its cares."

The fisherman arose with an air of rebuked submission, the result of long life passed in the habit of political deference; but he did not approach to receive the proffered reward.

"Bend thy head, fisherman, that his Highness may bestow the prize," commanded an officer.

"I ask not for gold, nor any oar, but that which carries me

to the Lagunes in the morning, and brings me back into the canals at night. Give me my child, or give me nothing."

"Away with him!" muttered a dozen voices; "he utters sedition! let him quit the galley."

Antonio was hurried from the presence, and forced into his gondola with very unequivocal signs of disgrace. This unwonted interruption of the ceremonies clouded many a brow, for the sensibilities of a Venetian noble were quick, indeed, to reprehend the immorality of political discontent, though the conventional dignity of the class suppressed all other ill-timed exhibition of dissatisfaction.

"Let the next competitor draw near," continuued the sovereign, with a composure that constant practice in dissimulation rendered easy.

The unknown waterman, to whose secret favor Antonio owed his success, approached, still concealed by the licensed mask.

"Thou art the gainer of the second prize," said the prince, "and were rigid justice done, thou should'st receive the first also, since our favor is not to be rejected with impunity.—Kneel, that I may bestow the favor."

"Highness, pardon!" observed the masker, bowing with great respect, but withdrawing a single step from the offered reward; "if it be your gracious will to grant a boon, for the success of the regatta, I, too, have to pray that it may be given in another form."

"This is unusual! It is not wont that prizes offered by the hand of a Venetian doge should go abegging."

"I would not seem to press more than is respectful, in this great presence. I ask but little, and, in the end, it may cost the republic less, than that which is now offered."

"Name it."

"I, too, and on my knee, in dutiful homage to the chief of the state, beg that the prayer of the old fisherman be heard, and that the father and son may be restored to each other, for the service will corrupt the tender years of the boy, and make the age of his parent miserable."

"This touches on importunity! Who art thou, that comest in this hidden manner, to support a petition, once refused?"

"Highness—the second victor in the ducal regatta."

"Dost trifle in thy answers? The protection of a mask, in all that does not tend to unsettle the peace of the city, is sacred.

But here seemeth matter to be looked into.—Remove thy disguise, that we see thee, eye to eye."

"I have heard that he who kept civil speech, and in naught offended against the laws, might be seen at will, disguised in Venice, without question of his affairs, or name."

"Most true, in all that does not offend St. Mark. But here is a concert worthy of inquiry: I command thee, unmask."

The waterman, reading in every face around him the necessity of obedience, slowly withdrew the means of concealment, and discovered the pallid countenance and glittering eyes of Jacopo. An involuntary movement of all near left this dreaded person standing, singly, confronted with the prince of Venice, in a wide circle of wondering and curious listeners.

"I know thee not!" exclaimed the doge, with an open amazement that proved his sincerity, after regarding the other earnestly for a moment. "Thy reasons for the disguise should be better than thy reasons for refusing the prize."

The Signor Gradenigo drew near to the sovereign, and whispered in his ear. When he had done, the latter cast one look, in which curiosity and aversion were in singular union, at the marked countenance of the Bravo, and then he silently motioned to him to depart. The throng drew about the royal person, with instinctive readiness, closing the space in his front.

"We shall look into this, at our leisure," said the doge. "Let the festivities proceed."

Jacopo bowed low, and withdrew. As he moved along the deck of the Bucentaur, the senators made way, as if pestilence was in his path, though it was quite apparent, by the expression of their faces, that it was in obedience to a feeling of a mixed character. The avoided, but still tolerated Bravo descended to his gondola, and the usual signals were given to the multitude beneath, who believed the customary ceremonies were ended.

"Let the gondolier of Don Camillo Monforte stand forth," cried a herald, obedient to the beck of a superior.

"Highness, here," answered Gino, troubled and hurried.

"Thou art of Calabria?"

"Highness, yes."

"But of long practice on our Venetian canals, or thy gondola could never have outstripped those of the readiest oarsmen.—Thou servest a noble master?"

"Highness, yes."

"And it would seem that the Duke of St. Agata is happy in the possession of an honest and faithful follower?"

"Highness, too happy."

"Kneel, and receive the reward of thy resolution and skill."

Gino, unlike those who had preceded him, bent a willing knee to the deck, and took the prize with a low and humble inclination of the body. At this moment the attention of the spectators was drawn from the short and simple ceremony by a loud shout which arose from the water, at no great distance from the privileged bark of the senate. A common movement drew all to the side of the galley, and the successful gondolier was quickly forgotten.

A hundred boats were moving, in a body, towards the Lido, while the space they covered on the water presented one compact mass of the red caps of fishermen. In the midst of this marine picture was seen the bare head of Antonio, borne along in the floating multitude, without any effort of his own. The general impulsion was received from the vigorous arms of some thirty or forty of their number, who towed those in the rear by applying their force to three or four large gondolas in advance.

There was no mistaking the object of this singular and characteristic procession. The tenants of the Lagunes, with the fickleness with which extreme ignorance acts on human passions, had suddenly experienced a violent revolution in their feelings towards their ancient comrade. He who, an hour before, had been derided as a vain and ridiculous pretender, and on whose head bitter imprecations had been so lavishly poured, was now lauded with cries of triumph.

The gondoliers of the canals were laughed to scorn, and the ears of even the haughty nobles were not respected, as the exulting band taunted their pampered menials.

In short, by a process which is common enough with man in all the divisions and subdivisions of society, the merit of one was at once intimately and inseparably connected with the glory and exultation of all.

Had the triumph of the fisherman confined itself to this natural and commonplace exhibition, it would not have given grave offence to the vigilant and jealous power that watched over the peace of Venice. But, amid the shouts of approbation were mingled cries of censure. Words of grave import were

136

even heard, denouncing those who refused to restore to Antonio his child; and it was whispered on the deck of the Bucentaur, that, filled with the imaginary importance of their passing victory, the hardy band of rioters had dared to menace a forcible appeal, to obtain what they audaciously termed the justice of the case.

This ebullition of popular feeling was witnessed by the assembled senate in ominous and brooding silence. One unaccustomed to reflection on such a subject, or unpractised in the world, might have fancied alarm and uneasiness were painted on the grave countenances of the patricians, and that the signs of the times were little favorable to the continuance of an ascendency that was dependent more on the force of convention, than on the possession of any physical superiority. But, on the other hand, one who was capable of judging between the power of political ascendency, strengthened by its combinations and order, and the mere ebullitions of passion, however loud and clamorous, might readily have seen that the latter was not yet displayed in sufficient energy to break down the barriers which the first had erected.

The fishermen were permitted to go their way unmolested, though here and there a gondola was seen stealing towards the Lido, bearing certain of those secret agents of the police whose duty it was to forewarn the existing powers of the presence of danger. Among the latter was the boat of the wine seller, which departed from the piazzetta, containing a stock of his merchandise, with Annina, under the pretence of making his profit out of the present turbulent temper of their ordinary customers. In the meantime, the sports proceeded, and the momentary interruption was forgotten; or, if remembered, it was in a manner suited to the secret and fearful power which directed the destinies of that remarkable republic.

There was another regatta, in which men of inferior powers contended; but we deem it unworthy to detain the narrative by a description.

Though the grave tenants of the Bucentaur seemed to take an interest in what was passing immediately before their eyes, they had ears for every shout that was borne on the evening breeze from the distant Lido; and more than once the doge himself was seen to bend his looks in that direction, in a manner

137

which betrayed the concern that was uppermost in his mind.

Still the day passed on as usual. The conquerors triumphed, the crowd applauded, and the collected senate appeared to sympathize with the pleasures of a people over whom they ruled with a certainty of power that resembled the fearful and mysterious march of destiny.

CHAPTER XI

"Which is the merchant here, and which the Jew?"
SHAKESPEARE

THE evening of such a day, in a city with the habits of Venice, was not likely to be spent in the dullness of retirement. The great square of St. Mark was again filled with its active and motley crowd, and the scenes already described in the opening chapters of this work were resumed, if possible, with more apparent devotion to the levities of the hour, than on the occasion mentioned. The tumblers and jugglers renewed their antics, the cries of the fruit sellers and other venders of light luxuries were again mingled with the tones of the flute and the notes of the guitar and harp, while the idle and the busy, the thoughtless and the designing, the conspirator and the agent of the police, once more met in privileged security.

The night had advanced beyond its turn, when a gondola came gliding through the shipping of the port, with that easy and swan-like motion which is peculiar to its slow movement, and touched the quay with its beak, at the point where the canal of St. Mark forms its junction with the bay.

"Thou art welcome, Antonio," said one who approached the solitary individual that had directed the gondola, when the latter had thrust the iron spike of his painter between the crevices of the stones, as gondoliers are accustomed to secure their barges; "thou art welcome, Antonio, though late."

"I begin to know the sounds of that voice, though they come from a masked face," said the fisherman. "Friend, I owe my success today to thy kindness, and though it has not had the end for which I had both hoped and prayed, I ought not to thank thee less. Thou hast thyself been borne hard upon by the world, or thou would'st not have bethought thee of an old and despised man, when the shouts of triumph were ringing in thy ear, and when thy own young blood was stirred with the feelings of pride and victory."

139

"Nature gives thee strong language, fisherman. I have not passed the hours, truly, in the games and levities of my years. Life has been no festa to me—but no matter. The senate was not pleased to hear of lessening the number of the galleys' crew, and thou wilt bethink thee of some other reward. I have, here, the chain and golden oar in the hope that it will still be welcome."

Antonio looked amazed, but, yielding to a natural curiosity, he gazed a moment with a longing at the prize. Then, recoiling with a shudder, he uttered moodily, and with the tones of one whose determination was made: "I should think the bauble coined of my grandchild's blood! Keep it: they have trusted it to thee, for it is thine of right, and now that they refuse to hear my prayer, it will be useless to all but to him who fairly earned it."

"Thou makest no allowance, fisherman, for difference of years and for sinews that are in their vigor. Methinks that in adjudging such a prize, thought should be had to these matters, and then wouldest thou be found outstripping us all. Holy St. Theodore! I passed my childhood with the oar in hand, and never before have I met one in Venice who has driven my gondola so hard! Thou touchest the water with the delicacy of a lady fingering her harp, and yet with the force of the wave rolling on the Lido!"

"I have seen the hour, Jacopo, when even thy young arm would have tired, in such a strife between us. That was before the birth of my eldest son, who died in battle with the Ottoman, when the dear boy he left me was but an infant in arms. Thou never sawest the comely lad, good Jacopo?"

"I was not so happy, old man; but if he resembled thee, well mayest thou mourn his loss. Body of Diana! I have little cause to boast of the small advantage youth and strength gave me."

"There was a force within that bore me and the boat on—but of what use hath it been? Thy kindness, and the pain given to an old frame that hath been long racked by hardship and poverty, are both thrown away on the rocky hearts of the nobles."

"We know not yet, Antonio. The good saints will hear our prayers, when we least think they are listening. Come with me, for I am sent to seek thee."

The fisherman regarded his new acquaintance with surprise, and then turning to bestow an instant of habitual care on his boat, he cheerfully professed himself ready to proceed. The

place where they stood was a little apart from the thorough-
fare of the quays, and though there was a brilliant moon, the
circumstance of two men, in their garbs, being there was not
likely to attract observation; but Jacopo did not appear to be
satisfied with this security from remark. He waited until Antonio
had left the gondola, and, then, unfolding a cloak which had
lain on his arm, he threw it, without asking permission, over
the shoulders of the other. A cap, like that he wore himself, was
next produced, and being placed on the gray hairs of the fisherman, effectually completed his metamorphosis.

"There is no need of a mask," he said, examining his companion attentively, when his task was accomplished. "None
would know thee, Antonio, in this garb."

"And is there need of what thou hast done, Jacopo? I owe
thee thanks for a well-meant, and, but for the hardness of heart
of the rich and powerful, for what would have proved, a great
kindness. Still I must tell thee that a mask was never yet put
before my face; for what reason can there be, why one who
rises with the sun to go to his toil, and who trusteth to the
favor of the blessed St. Anthony for the little he hath, should
go abroad like a gallant ready to steal the good name of a virgin,
or a robber at night?"

"Thou knowest our Venetian custom, and it may be well
to use some caution, in the business we are on."

"Thou forgettest that thy intention is yet a secret to me. I
say it again, and I say it with truth and gratitude, that I owe
thee many thanks, though the end is defeated, and the boy is
still a prisoner in the floating-school of wickedness—but thou
hast a name, Jacopo, that I could wish did not belong to thee. I
find it hard to believe all that they have this day said, on the
Lido, of one who has so much feeling for the weak and
wronged."

The Bravo ceased to adjust the disguise of his companion,
and the profound stillness which succeeded his remark proved
so painful to Antonio, that he felt like one reprieved from suffo-
cation, when he heard the deep respiration that announced the
relief of his companion.

"I would not willingly say—"

"No matter," interrupted Jacopo, in a hollow voice. "No
matter, fisherman; we will speak of these things on some other
occasion. At present, follow, and be silent."

141

As he ceased, the self-appointed guide of Antonio beckoned for the latter to come on, when he led the way from the water-side. The fisherman obeyed, for little did it matter to one poor and heart-stricken as he, whither he was conducted. Jacopo took first entrance into the court of the doge's palace. His footstep was leisurely, and to the passing multitude they appeared like any others of the thousands who were abroad to breathe the soft air of the night or to enter into the pleasures of the piazza.

When within the dimmer and broken light of the court, Jacopo paused, evidently to scan the persons of those it contained. It is to be presumed he saw no reason to delay, for with a secret sign to his companion to follow, he crossed the area, and mounted the well-known steps, down which the head of the Faliero* had rolled, and which, from the statues on the summit, is called the Giant's Stairs. The celebrated mouths of the lions were passed, and they were walking swiftly along the open gallery when they encountered a halberdier of the ducal guard.

"Who comes?" demanded the mercenary, throwing forward his long and dangerous weapon.

"Friends to the state and to St. Mark."

"None pass at this hour without the word."

Jacopo motioned to Antonio to stand fast, while he drew nearer to the halberdier and whispered. The weapon was instantly thrown up, and the sentinel again paced the long gallery with practised indifference. The way was no sooner cleared than they proceeded. Antonio, not a little amazed at what he had already seen, eagerly followed his guide, for his heart began to beat high with an exciting, but undefined hope. He was not so ignorant of human affairs as to require to be told that those who ruled would sometime concede that in secret which policy forbade them to yield openly. Full, therefore, of the expectation of being ushered into the presence of the doge himself, and of having his child restored to his arms, the old man stepped lightly along the gloomy gallery, and darting through an entrance, at the heels of Jacopo, he found himself at the foot of another flight of massive steps. The route now became confused to the fisherman, for, quitting the more public vomitories of the palace,

---

* Marino Falieri (or Faliero), 1279–1355. A doge of Venice who plotted to overthrow the republic and was beheaded April 17, 1355.— Editor.

his companion held his way by a secret door, through many dimly lighted and obscure passages. They ascended and descended frequently, as often quitting or entering rooms of but ordinary dimensions and decorations, until the head of Antonio was completely turned, and he no longer knew the general direction of their course. At length they stopped, in an apartment of inferior ornaments, and of a dusky color, which the feeble light rendered still more gloomy.

"Thou art well acquainted with the dwelling of our prince," said the fisherman, when his companion enabled him to speak, by checking his swift movements. "The oldest gondolier of Venice is not more ready on the canals, than thou appearest to be among these galleries and corridors."

" 'Tis my business to bring thee hither, and what I am to do, I endeavor to do well. Antonio, thou art a man that feareth not to stand in the presence of the great, as this day hath shown. Summon thy courage, for a moment of trial is before thee."

"I have spoken boldly to the doge. Except the Holy Father, himself, what power is there on earth beside to fear?"

"Thou mayest have spoken, fisherman, too boldly. Temper thy language, for the great love not words of disrespect."

"Is truth unpleasant to them?"

"That is as may be. They love to hear their own acts praised, when their acts have merited praise, but they do not like to hear them condemned, even though they know what is said to be just."

"I fear me," said the old man, looking with simplicity at the other, "there is little difference between the powerful and the weak, when the garments are stripped from both, and the man stands naked to the eye."

"That truth may not be spoken here."

"How! Do they deny that they are Christians, and mortals, and sinners?"

"They make a merit of the first, Antonio—they forget the second, and they never like to be called the last, by any but themselves."

"I doubt, Jacopo, after all, if I get from them the freedom of the boy."

"Speak them fair, and say naught to wound their self-esteem, or to menace their authority—they will pardon much, if the last, in particular, be respected."

143

"But it is that authority which has taken away my child! Can I speak in favor of the power which I know to be unjust?"

"Thou must feign it, or thy suit will fail."

"I will go back to the Lagunes, good Jacopo, for this tongue of mine hath ever moved at the bidding of the heart. I fear I am too old to say that a son may righteously be torn from the father by violence. Tell them, thou, from me, that I came thus far, in order to do them respect, but that, seeing the hopelessness of beseeching further, I have gone to my nets, and to my prayers to blessed St. Anthony."

As he ceased speaking, Antonio wrung the hand of his motionless companion, and turned away, as if to retire. Two halberds fell to the level of his breast, ere his foot had quitted the marble floor, and he now saw, for the first time, that armed men crossed his passage, and that, in truth, he was a prisoner. Nature had endowed the fisherman with a quick and just perception, and long habit had given great steadiness to his nerves. When he perceived his real situation, instead of entering into useless remonstrance, or in any manner betraying alarm, he again turned to Jacopo with an air of patience and resignation.

"It must be that the illustrious Signore wish to do me justice," he said, smoothing the remnant of his hair, as men of his class prepare themselves for the presence of their superiors, "and it would not be decent, in an humble fisherman, to refuse them the opportunity. It would be better, however, if there were less force used here in Venice, in a matter of simple right and wrong. But the great love to show their power, and the weak must submit."

"We shall see!" answered Jacopo, who had manifested no emotion during the abortive attempt of the other to retire.

A profound stillness succeeded. The halberdiers maintained their rigid attitudes, within the shadow of the wall, looking like two insensible statues, in the attire and armor of the age, while Jacopo and his companion occupied the centre of the room, with scarcely more of the appearance of consciousness and animation. It may be well to explain, here, to the reader, some of the peculiar machinery of the state, in the country of which we write, and which is connected with the scene that is about to follow: for the name of a republic, a word which, if it mean anything, strictly implies the representation and supremacy of the general interests, but which has so frequently been prostituted to the protection and monopolies of privileged classes, may have induced him to believe that there was, at least, a resemblance between the outlines of that government, and the more just, because more popular, institutions of his own country.

In an age when rulers were profane enough to assert, and the ruled weak enough to allow, that the right of a man to govern his fellows was a direct gift from God, a departure from the bold and selfish principle, though it were only in profession, was thought sufficient to give a character of freedom and common sense to the polity of a nation. This belief is not without some justification, since it establishes in theory, at least, the foundations of government on a base sufficiently different from that which supposes all power to be the property of one, and that one to be the representative of the faultless and omnipotent Ruler of the Universe. With the first of these principles we have nothing to do, except it be to add that there are propositions so inherently false that they only require to be fairly stated to produce their own refutation; but our subject necessarily draws us into a short digression on the errors of the second, as they existed in Venice.

It is probable that when the patricians of St. Mark created a community of political rights in their own body, they believed their state had done all that was necessary to merit the high and generous title it assumed. They had innovated on a generally received principle, and they cannot claim the distinction of being either the first, or the last, who have imagined that to take the incipient steps in political improvement is at once to reach the goal of perfection. Venice had no doctrine of divine right, and as her prince was little more than a pageant, she boldly laid claim to be called a republic. She believed that a representation of the most prominent and brilliant interests in society was the paramount object of government, and, faithful to the seductive, but dangerous error, she mistook to the last, collective power for social happiness.

It may be taken as a governing principle, in all civil relations, that the strong will grow stronger, and the feeble more weak, until the first become unfit to rule, or the last unable to endure. In this important truth is contained the secret of the downfall of all those states which have crumbled beneath the weight of their own abuses. It teaches the necessity of widening the foundations of society, until the base shall have a breadth capable of

145

securing the just representation of every interest, without which the social machine is liable to interruption from its own movement, and eventually to destruction from its own excesses.

Venice, though ambitious and tenacious of the name of a republic, was, in truth, a narrow, a vulgar, and an exceedingly heartless oligarchy. To the former title she had no other claim than her denial of the naked principle already mentioned, while her practice is liable to the reproach of the two latter, in the unmanly and narrow character of its exclusion, in every act of her foreign policy, and in every measure of her internal police. An aristocracy must ever want the high personal feeling which often tempers despotism by the qualities of the chief, or the generous and human impulses of a popular rule. It has the merit of substituting things for men, it is true, but unhappily it substitutes the things of a few men for those of the whole. It partakes, and it always has partaken, though necessarily tempered by circumstances and the opinions of different ages, of the selfishness of all corporations, in which the responsibility of the individual, while his acts are professedly submitted to the temporizing expedients of a collective interest, is lost in the subdivision of numbers. At the period of which we write, Italy had several of these self-styled commonwealths, in not one of which, however, was there ever a fair and just confiding of power to the body of the people, though perhaps there is not one that has not been cited, sooner or later, in proof of the inability of man to govern himself! In order to demonstrate the fallacy of a reasoning which is so fond of predicting the downfall of our own liberal system, supported by examples drawn from transAtlantic states of the Middle Ages, it is necessary only to recount here, a little in detail, the forms in which power was obtained and exercised, in the most important of them all.

Distinctions in rank, as separated entirely from the will of the nation, formed the basis of Venetian polity. Authority, though divided, was not less a birthright, than in those governments in which it was openly avowed to be a dispensation of Providence. The patrician order had its high and exclusive privileges, which were guarded and maintained with a most selfish and engrossing spirit. He who was not born to govern had little hope of ever entering into the possession of his natural rights; while he who was, by the intervention of chance, might wield a power of the most fearful and despotic character. At a certain age, all of senatorial rank (for, by a specious fallacy, nobility did not take its usual appellations) were admitted into the councils of the nation. The names of the leading families were inscribed in a register, which was well entitled the "Golden Book," and he who enjoyed the envied distinction of having an ancestor thus enrolled, could, with a few exceptions (such as that named in the case of Don Camillo), present himself in the senate, and lay claim to the honors of the "Horned Bonnet." Neither our limits nor our object will permit a digression of sufficient length to point out the whole of the leading features of a system so vicious, and which was, perhaps, only rendered tolerable to those it governed, by the extraneous contributions of captured and subsidiary provinces, on which, in truth, as in all cases of metropolitan rule, the oppression weighed most grievously. The reader will at once see that the very reason why the despotism of the self-styled republic was tolerable to its own citizens was but another cause of its eventual destruction.

As the senate became too numerous to conduct, with sufficient secrecy and dispatch, the affairs of a state that pursued a policy alike tortuous and complicated, the most general of its important interests were intrusted to a council composed of three hundred of its members. In order to avoid the publicity and delay of a body large even as this, a second selection was made, which was known as the Council of Ten, and to which much of the executive power that aristocratical jealousy withheld from the titular chief of the state was confided. To this point the political economy of the Venetian republic, however faulty, had at least some merit for simplicity and frankness. The ostensible agents of the administration were known, and though all real responsibility to the nation was lost, in the superior influence and narrow policy of the patricians, the rulers could not entirely escape from the odium that public opinion might attach to their unjust or illegal proceedings. But a state whose prosperity was chiefly founded on the contribution and support of dependants, and whose existence was equally menaced by its own false principles, and by the growth of other and neighboring powers, had need of a still more efficient body, in the absence of that executive which its own republican pretensions denied to Venice. A political inquisition, which came in time to be one of the most fearful engines of police ever known, was the consequence. An authority, as irresponsible as it was absolute, was

147

periodically confided to another and still smaller body, which met and exercised its despotic and secret functions, under the name of the Council of Three. The choice of these temporary rulers was decided by lot, and in a manner that prevented the result from being known to any but to their own number, and to a few of the most confidential of the more permanent officers of the government. Thus there existed, at all times, in the heart of Venice, a mysterious and despotic power that was wielded by men who moved in society unknown, and apparently surrounded by all the ordinary charities of life; but which, in truth, was influenced by a set of political maxims that were perhaps as ruthless, as tyrannic, and as selfish as ever were invented by the evil ingenuity of man. It was, in short, a power that could only be intrusted, without abuse, to infallible virtue and infinite intelligence, using the terms in a sense limited by human means; and yet it was here confided to men whose title was founded on the double accident, of birth—and the colors of balls, and by whom it was wielded, without even the check of publicity.

The Council of Three met in secret, ordinarily issued its decrees without communicating with any other body, and had them enforced with a fearfulness of mystery and a suddenness of execution that resembled the blows of fate. The doge himself was not superior to its authority, nor protected from its decisions, while it has been known that one of the privileged three has been denounced by his companions. There is still in existence a long list of the state maxims which this secret tribunal recognized as its rule of conduct, and it is not saying too much to affirm that they set at defiance every other consideration but expediency,—all the recognized laws of God, and every principle of justice which is esteemed among men. The advances of the human intellect, supported by the means of publicity, may temper the exercise of a similar irresponsible power, in our own age, but in no country has this substitution of a soulless corporation for an elective representation been made in which a system of rule has not been established that sets at naught the laws of natural justice and the rights of the citizen. Any pretension to the contrary, by placing profession in opposition to practice, is only adding hypocrisy to usurpation.

It appears to be an unavoidable general consequence that abuses should follow, when power is exercised by a permanent and irresponsible body from whom there is no appeal. When this power is secretly exercised, the abuses become still more grave. It is also worthy of remark, that in the nations which submit, or have submitted to these undue and dangerous influences, the pretensions to justice and generosity are of the most exaggerated character; for while the fearless democrat vents his personal complaints aloud, and the voice of the subject of professed despotism is smothered entirely, necessity itself dictates to the oligarchist the policy of seemliness, as one of the conditions of his own safety. Thus Venice prided herself on the justice of St. Mark, and few states maintained a greater show, or put forth a more lofty claim to the possession of the sacred quality, than that whose real maxims of government were veiled in a mystery that even the loose morality of the age exacted.

CHAPTER XII

"A power that if but named
In casual converse, be it where it might,
The speaker lower'd, at once, his voice, his eyes,
And pointed upward as at God in heaven."
                                    ROGERS

THE reader has probably anticipated that Antonio was now standing in an antechamber of the secret and stern tribunal described in the preceding chapter. In common with all of his class, the fisherman had a vague idea of the existence, and of the attributes, of the council before which he was to appear; but his simple apprehension was far from comprehending the extent, or the nature, of functions that equally took cognizance of the most important interests of the republic, and of the more trifling concerns of a patrician family. While conjectures on the probable result of the expected interview were passing through his mind, an inner door opened, and an attendant signed for Jacopo to advance.

The deep and imposing silence which instantly succeeded the entrance of the summoned into the presence of the Council of Three gave time for a slight examination of the apartment and of those it contained. The room was not large for that country and climate, but rather of a size suited to the closeness of the councils that had place within its walls. The floor was tessellated with alternate pieces of black and white marble; the walls were draped in one common and sombre dress of black cloth; a single lamp of dark bronze was suspended over a solitary table in its centre, which, like every other article of the scanty furniture, had the same melancholy covering as the walls. In the angles of the room there were projecting closets, which might have been what they seemed, or merely passages into the other apartments of the palace. All the doors were concealed from casual observation by the hangings, which gave one general and chilling aspect of gloom to the whole scene. On the side of the room opposite to that on which Antonio stood, three men were seated in curule

150

chairs; but their masks, and the drapery which concealed their forms, prevented all recognition of their persons. One of this powerful body wore a robe of crimson, as the representative that fortune had given to the select council of the doge, and the others robes of black, being those which had drawn the lucky, or rather the unlucky balls, in the Council of Ten, itself a temporary and chance-created body of the senate. There were one or two subordinates near the table, but these, as well as the still more humble officials of the place, were hid from all ordinary knowledge, by disguises similar to those of the chiefs. Jacopo regarded the scene like one accustomed to its effect, though with evident reverence and awe; but the impression on Antonio was too manifest to be lost. It is probable that the long pause which followed his introduction was intended to produce and to note this effect, for keen eyes were intently watching his countenance during its continuance.

"Thou art called Antonio of the Lagunes?" demanded one of the secretaries near the table, when a sign had been secretly made from the crimson member of that fearful tribunal to proceed.

"A poor fisherman, eccellenza, who owes much to blessed Saint Antonio of the Miraculous Draught."

"And thou hast a son who bears thine own name, and who follows the same pursuit?"

"It is the duty of a Christian to submit to the will of God! My boy has been dead twelve years, come the day when the republic's galleys chased the infidel from Corfu to Candia. He was slain, noble Signore, with many others of his calling, in that bloody fight."

There was a movement of surprise among the clerks, who whispered together, and appeared to examine the papers in their hands, with some haste and confusion. Glances were sent back at the judges, who sat motionless, wrapped in the impenetrable mystery of their functions. A secret sign, however, soon caused the armed attendants of the place to lead Antonio and his companion from the room.

"Here is some inadvertency!" said a stern voice, from one of the masked Three, so soon as the fall of the footsteps of those who retired was no longer audible. "It is not seemly that the inquisition of St. Mark should show this ignorance."

"It touches merely the family of an obscure fisherman, illustrious Signore," returned the trembling dependant; "and it may be that his art would wish to deceive us in the opening interrogatories."

"Thou art in error," interrupted another of the Three. "The man is named Antonio Vecchio, and, as he sayeth, his only child died in the hot affair with the Ottoman. He of whom there is question is a grandson, and is still a boy."

"The noble Signore is right!" returned the clerk.—"In the hurry of affairs, we have misconceived a fact, which the wisdom of the council has been quick to rectify. St. Mark is happy in having among his proudest and oldest names, senators who enter thus familiarly into the interests of his meanest children!"

"Let the man be again introduced," resumed the judge, slightly bending his head to the compliment. "These accidents are unavoidable in the press of affairs."

The necessary order was given, and Antonio, with his companion constantly at his elbow, was brought once more into the presence.

"Thy son died in the service of the republic, Antonio?" demanded the secretary.

"Signore, he did. Holy Maria have pity on his early fate, and listen to my prayers! So good a child and so brave a man can have no great need of masses for his soul, or his death would have been doubly grievous to me, since I am too poor to buy them."

"Thou hast a grandson?"

"I had one, noble senator; I hope he still lives."

"He is not with thee in thy labors on the Lagunes?"

"San Teodoro grant that he were! He is taken, Signore, with many more of tender years, into the galleys, whence may our Lady give him a safe deliverance! If your eccellenza has an opportunity to speak with the general of the galleys, or with any other who may have authority in such a matter, on my knees, I pray you to speak in behalf of the child, who is a good and pious lad that seldom casts a line into the water, without an ave or a prayer to St. Anthony, and who has never given me uneasiness, until he fell into the grip of St. Mark."

"Rise—This is not the affair in which I have to question thee. Thou hast this day spoken of thy prayer to our most illustrious prince, the doge?"

"I have prayed his Highness to give the boy liberty."

"And this thou hast done openly, and with little deference to the high dignity and sacred character of the chief of the republic?"

"I did it like a father and a man. If but half what they say of the justice and kindness of the state were true, his Highness would have heard me as a father and a man."

A slight movement among the fearful Three caused the secretary to pause; when he saw, however, that his superiors chose to maintain their silence, he continued—

"This didst thou once in public and among the senators, but when repulsed, as urging a petition both out of place and out of reason, thou soughtest other [means]* to prefer thy request?"

"True, illustrious Signore."

"Thou camest among the gondoliers of the regatta in an unseemly garb, and placed thyself foremost with those who contended for the favor of the senate and its prince?"

"I came in the garb which I wear before the Virgin and St. Antonio, and if I was foremost in the race, it was more owing to the goodness and favor of the man at my side, than any virtue which is still left in these withered sinews and dried bones. San Marco remember him in his need, for the kind wish, and soften the hearts of the great to hear the prayer of a childless parent!"

There was another slight expression of surprise, or curiosity, among the inquisitors, and once more the secretary suspended his examination.

"Thou hearest, Jacopo," said one of the Three. "What answer dost thou make the fisherman?"

"Signore, he speaketh truth."

"And thou hast dared to trifle with the pleasures of the city, and to set at naught the wishes of the doge!"

"If it be a crime, illustrious senator, to have pitied an old man who mourned for his offspring, and to have given up my own solitary triumph to his love for the boy, I am guilty."

There was a long and silent pause after this reply. Jacopo had spoken with habitual reverence, but with the grave composure that appeared to enter deeply into the composition of his character. The paleness of the cheek was the same, and the glowing eye, which so singularly lighted and animated a countenance

---

* So in the first British edition, London, 1831.

that possessed a hue not unlike that of death, scarce varied its gaze, while he answered. A secret sign caused the secretary to proceed with his duty.

"And thou owest thy success in the regatta, Antonio, to the favor of thy competitor—he who is now with thee, in the presence of the council?"

"Under San Teodoro and St. Antonio, the city's patron and my own."

"And thy whole desire was to urge again thy rejected petition in behalf of the young sailor?"

"Signore, I had no other. What is the vanity of a triumph among the gondoliers, or the bauble of a mimic oar and chain, to one of my years and condition?"

"Thou forgettest that the oar and chain are gold?"

"Excellent gentlemen, gold cannot heal the wounds which misery has left on a heavy heart. Give me back the child, that my eyes may not be closed by strangers, and that I may speak good counsel into his young ears, while there is hope my words may be remembered, and I care not for all the metals of the Rialto! Thou mayest see that I utter no vain vaunt, by this jewel which I offer to the nobles, with the reverence due to their greatness and wisdom."

When the fisherman had done speaking, he advanced, with the timid step of a man unaccustomed to move in superior presences, and laid upon the dark cloth of the table a ring that sparkled with, what at least seemed to be, very precious stones. The astonished secretary raised the jewel, and held it in suspense before the eyes of the judges.

"How is this?" exclaimed he of the Three who had oftenest interfered in the examination; "that seemeth the pledge of our nuptials!"

"It is no other, illustrious senator: with this ring did the doge wed the Adriatic, in the presence of the ambassadors and the people."

"Hadst thou aught to do with this, also, Jacopo?" sternly demanded the judge.

The Bravo turned his eye on the jewel with a look of interest, but his voice maintained its usual depth and steadiness as he answered.

"Signore, no—until now, I knew not the fortune of the fisherman."

A sign to the secretary caused him to resume his questions.

"Thou must account, and clearly account, Antonio," he said, "for the manner in which this sacred ring came into thy possession; hadst thou anyone to aid thee in obtaining it?"

"Signore, I had."

"Name him, at once, that we take measures for his security."

" 'Twill be useless, Signore; he is far above the power of Venice."

"What meanest thou, fellow? None are superior to the right and the force of the republic that dwell within her limits. Answer without evasion, as thou valuest thy person."

"I should prize that which is of little value, Signore, and be guilty of a great folly, as well as of a great sin, were I to deceive you, to save a body old and worthless as mine from stripes. If your excellencies are willing to hear, you will find that I am no less willing to tell the manner in which I got the ring."

"Speak, then, and trifle not."

"I know not, Signori, whether you are used to hearing untruths, that you caution me so much not to deal with them; but we of the Lagunes are not afraid to say what we have seen and done, for most of our business is with the winds and waves, which take their orders from God himself. There is a tradition, Signori, among us fisherman, that in times past, one of our body brought up from the bay the ring with which the doge is accustomed to marry the Adriatic. A jewel of that value was of little use to one who casts his nets daily for bread and oil, and he brought it to the doge, as became a fisherman into whose hands the saints had thrown a prize to which he had no title, as it were to prove his honesty. This act of our companion is much spoken of on the Lagunes and at the Lido, and it is said there is a noble painting done by some of our Venetian masters, in the halls of the palace, which tells the story as it happened; showing the prince on his throne, and the lucky fisherman with his naked legs, rendering back to his Highness that which had been lost. I hope there is foundation for this belief, Signori, which greatly flatters our pride, and is not without use in keeping some among us truer to the right, and better favored in the eyes of St. Anthony, than might otherwise be."

"The fact was so."

"And the painting, excellent Signore? I hope our vanity has not deceived us concerning the picture neither?"

"The picture you mention is to be seen within the palace."

"Corpo di Bacco! I have had my misgivings on that point, for it is not common that the rich and the happy should take such note of what the humble and the poor have done. Is the work from the hands of the great Tiziano himself, eccellenza?"

"It is not; one of little name hath put his pencil to the canvas."

"They say that Tiziano had the art of giving to his works the look and richness of flesh, and one would think that a just man might find, in the honesty of the poor fisherman, a color bright enough to have satisfied even his eye. But it may be that the senate saw danger in thus flattering us of the Lagunes."

"Proceed with the account of thine own fortune with the ring."

"Illustrious nobles, I have often dreamed of the luck of my fellow of the old times; and more than once have I drawn the nets with an eager hand in my sleep, thinking to find that very jewel entangled in its meshes, or embowelled by some fish. What I have so often fancied has at last happened. I am an old man, Signori, and there are few pools or banks between Fusina and Giorgio, that my lines or my nets have not fathomed or covered. The spot to which the Bucentoro is wont to steer in these ceremonies is well known to me, and I had a care to cover the bottom round about with all my nets in the hope of drawing up the ring. When his Highness cast the jewel, I dropped a buoy to mark the spot—Signori, this is all—my accomplice was St. Anthony."

"For doing this you had a motive?"

"Holy Mother of God! Was it not sufficient to get back my boy from the grip of the galleys?" exclaimed Antonio, with an energy and a simplicity that are often found to be in the same character. "I thought that if the doge and the senate were willing to cause pictures to be painted, and honors to be given to one poor fisherman for the ring, they might be glad to reward another, by releasing a lad who can be of no great service to the republic, but who is all to his parent."

"Thy petition to his Highness, thy strife in the regatta, and thy search for the ring, had the same object?"

"To me, Signore, life has but one."

There was a slight but suppressed movement among the council.

"When thy request was refused by his Highness as ill-timed—"

"Ah! eccellenza, when one has a white head and a failing arm, he cannot stop to look for the proper moment in such a cause!" interrupted the fisherman, with a gleam of that impetuosity which forms the true base of Italian character.

"When thy request was denied, and thou hadst refused the reward of the victor, thou went among thy fellows and fed their ears with complaints of the injustice of St. Mark, and of the senate's tyranny?"

"Signore, no. I went away sad and heartbroken, for I had not thought the doge and nobles would have refused a successful gondolier so light a boon."

"And this thou didst not hesitate to proclaim among the fishermen and idlers of the Lido?"

"Eccellenza, it was not needed—my fellows knew my unhappiness, and tongues were not wanting to tell the worst."

"There was a tumult, with thee at its head, and sedition was uttered, with much vain boasting of what the fleet of the Lagunes could perform against the fleet of the republic."

"There is little difference, Signore, between the two, except that the men of the one go in gondolas with nets, and the men of the other are in the galleys of the state. Why should brothers seek each other's blood?"

The movement among the judges was more manifest than ever. They whispered together, and a paper containing a few lines written rapidly in pencil was put into the hands of the examining secretary.

"Thou didst address thy fellows, and spoke openly of thy fancied wrongs; thou didst comment on the laws which require the services of the citizens, when the republic is compelled to send forth a fleet against its enemies."

"It is not easy to be silent, Signore, when the heart is full."

"And there was consultation among thee of coming to the palace in a body, and of asking the discharge of thy grandson from the doge, in the name of the rabble of the Lido."

"Signore, there were some generous enough to make the offer, but others were of advice it would be well to reflect before they took so bold a measure."

"And thou—what was thine own counsel on that point?"

"Eccellenza, I am old, and though unused to be thus ques-

157

tioned by illustrious senators, I had seen enough of the manner in which St. Mark governs, to believe a few unarmed fishermen and gondoliers would not be listened to with—"

"Ha! Did the gondoliers become of thy party? I should have believed them jealous, and displeased with the triumph of one who was not of their body."

"A gondolier is a man, and though they had the feelings of human nature on being beaten, they had also the feelings of human nature when they heard that a father was robbed of his son.—Signore," continued Antonio, with great earnestness and a singular simplicity, "there will be great discontent on the canals, if the galleys sail with the boy aboard them!"

"Such is thy opinion;—were the gondoliers on the Lido numerous?"

"When the sports ended, eccellenza, they came over by hundreds, and I will do the generous fellows the justice to say that they had forgotten their want of luck in the love of justice. Diamine! these gondoliers are not so bad a class as some pretend, but they are men like ourselves, and can feel for a Christian as well as another!"

The secretary paused, for his task was done; and a deep silence pervaded the gloomy apartment. After a short pause one of the three resumed—

"Antonio Vecchio," he said, "thou hast served thyself in these said galleys, to which thou now seemest so averse—and served bravely, as I learn?"

"Signore, I have done my duty by St. Mark. I played my part against the infidel, but it was after my beard was grown, and at an age when I had learnt to know good from evil. There is no duty more cheerfully performed by us all, than to defend the islands and the Lagunes against the enemy."

"And all the republic's dominions.—Thou canst make no distinctions between any of the rights of the state."

"There is a wisdom granted to the great which God hath denied the poor and the weak, Signore. To me it does not seem clear that Venice, a city built on a few islands, hath any more right to carry her rule into Crete or Candia, than the Turk hath to come here."

"How! Dost thou dare, on the Lido, to question the claim of the republic to her conquests! or do the irreverent fishermen dare thus to speak lightly of her glory!"

"Eccellenza, I know little of rights that come by violence. God hath given us the Lagunes, but I know not that he has given us more. This glory of which you speak may sit lightly on the shoulders of a senator, but it weighs heavily on a fisherman's heart."

"Thou speakest, bold man, of that which thou dost not comprehend."

"It is unfortunate, Signore, that the power to understand hath not been given to those who have so much power to suffer."

An anxious pause succeeded this reply.

"Thou mayest withdraw, Antonio," said he who apparently presided in the dread councils of the Three. "Thou wilt not speak of what has happened, and thou wilt await the inevitable justice of St. Mark, in full confidence of its execution."

"Thanks, illustrious senator; I will obey your excellency; but my heart is full, and I would fain say a few words concerning the child, before I quit this noble company."

"Thou mayest speak—and here thou mayest give free vent to all thy wishes, or to all thy griefs, if any thou hast. St. Mark has no greater pleasure than to listen to the wishes of his children."

"I believe they have reviled the republic in calling its chiefs heartless, and sold to ambition!" said the old man, with generous warmth, disregarding the stern rebuke which gleamed in the eye of Jacopo. "A senator is but a man, and there are fathers and children among them, as among us of the Lagunes."

"Speak, but refrain from seditious or discreditable discourse," uttered a secretary, in a half-whisper. "Proceed."

"I have little now to offer, Signori; I am not used to boast of my services to the state, excellent gentlemen, but there is a time when human modesty must give way to human nature. These scars were got in one of the proudest days of St. Mark, and in the foremost of all the galleys that fought among the Greek islands. The father of my boy wept over me then, as I have since wept over his own son—yes—I might be ashamed to own it among men; but if the truth must be spoken, the loss of the boy has drawn bitter tears from me in the darkness of night, and in the solitude of the Lagunes. I lay many weeks, Signori, less a man than a corpse, and when I got back again to my nets and my toil, I did not withhold my son from the call of the republic. He went in my place to meet the infidel—a service from which he never came back. This was the duty of men who had grown in experience, and who were not to be deluded into wickedness by the evil company of the galleys. But this calling of children into the snares of the devil grieves a father, and—I will own the weakness, if such it be—I am not of a courage and pride to send forth my own flesh and blood into the danger and corruption of war and evil society, as in days when the stoutness of the heart was like the stoutness of the limbs. Give me back, then, my boy, till he has seen my old head laid beneath the sands, and until, by the aid of blessed St. Anthony, and such councils as a poor man can offer, I may give him more steadiness in his love of the right, and until I may have so shaped his life, that he will not be driven about by every pleasant or treacherous wind that may happen to blow upon his bark. Signori, you are rich, and powerful, and honored, and though you may be placed in the way of temptations to do wrongs that are suited to your high names and illustrious fortunes, ye know little of the trials of the poor. What are the temptations of the blessed St. Anthony himself, to those of the evil company of the galleys! And now, Signori, though you may be angry to hear it, I will say, that when an aged man has no other kin on earth, or none so near as to feel the glow of the thin blood of the poor, than one poor boy, St. Mark would do well to remember that even a fisherman of the Lagunes can feel as well as the doge on his throne. This much I say, illustrious senators, in sorrow, and not in anger; for I would get back the child, and die in peace with my superiors, as with my equals."

"Thou mayest depart," said one of the Three.

"Not yet, Signore, I have still more to say of the men of the Lagunes, who speak with loud voices concerning this dragging of boys into the service of the galleys."

"We will hear their opinions."

"Noble gentlemen, if I were to utter all they have said, word for word, I might do some disfavor to your ears! Man is man, though the Virgin and the saints listen to his aves and prayers from beneath a jacket of serge and a fisherman's cap. But I know too well my duty to the senate to speak so plainly. But, Signori, they say, saving the bluntness of their language, that St. Mark should have ears for the meanest of his people as well as for the richest noble; and that not a hair should fall from the head of a fisherman, without its being counted as if it were a lock from beneath the horned bonnet; and that where God hath not made marks of his displeasure, man should not."

"Do they dare to reason thus?"

"I know not if it be reason, illustrious Signore, but it is what they say, and, eccellenza, it is holy truth. We are poor workmen of the Lagunes, who rise with the day to cast our nets, and return at night to hard beds and harder fare; but with this we might be content, did the senate count us as Christians and men. That God hath not given to all the same chances in life, I well know, for it often happens that I draw an empty net, when my comrades are groaning with the weight of their draughts; but this is done to punish my sins, or to humble my heart, whereas it exceeds the power of man to look into the secrets of the soul, or to foretell the evil of the still innocent child. Blessed St. Anthony knows how many years of suffering this visit to the galleys may cause to the child in the end. Think of these things, I pray you, Signori, and send men of tried principles to the wars."

"Thou mayest retire," rejoined the judge.

"I should be sorry that any who cometh of my blood," continued the inattentive Antonio, "should be the cause of ill will between them that rule and them that are born to obey. But nature is stronger even than the law, and I should discredit her feelings were I to go without speaking as becomes a father. Ye have taken my ch:ld and sent him to serve the state at the hazard of body and soul, without giving opportunity for a parting kiss, or a parting blessing—ye have used my flesh and blood as ye would use the wood of the arsenal, and sent it forth upon the sea as if it were the insensible metal of the balls ye throw against the infidel. Ye have shut your ears to my prayers, as if they were words uttered by the wicked, and when I have exhorted you on my knees, wearied my stiffened limbs to do ye pleasure, rendered ye the jewel which St. Anthony gave to my net, that it might soften your hearts, and reasoned with you calmly on the nature of your acts, you turn from me coldly, as if I were unfit to stand forth in defence of the offspring that God hath left my age! This is not the boasted justice of St. Mark, Venetian senators, but hardness of heart and a wasting of the means of the poor that would ill become the most grasping Hebrew of the Rialto!"

"Hast thou aught more to urge, Antonio?" asked the judge, with the wily design of unmasking the fisherman's entire soul.

"Is it not enough, Signore, that I urge my years, my poverty, my scars, and my love for the boy? I know ye not, but though ye are hid behind the folds of your robes and masks, still must ye be men. There may be among ye a father, or perhaps some one who hath a still more sacred charge, the child of a dead son. To him I speak. In vain ye talk of justice when the weight of your power falls on them least able to bear it; and though ye may delude yourselves, the meanest gondolier of the canal knows—"

He was stopped from uttering more by his companion, who rudely placed a hand on his mouth.

"Why hast thou presumed to stop the complaints of Antonio?" sternly demanded the judge.

"It was not decent, illustrious senators, to listen to such disrespect in so noble a presence," Jacopo answered, bending reverently as he spoke. "This old fisherman, dread Signori, is warmed by love for his offspring, and he will utter that which, in his cooler moments, he will repent."

"St. Mark fears not the truth! If he has more to say, let him declare it."

But the excited Antonio began to reflect. The flush which had ascended to his weather beaten cheek disappeared, and his naked breast ceased to heave. He stood like one rebuked, more by his discretion than his conscience, with a calmer eye, and a face that exhibited the composure of his years, and the respect of his condition—

"If I have offended, great patricians," he said, more mildly, "I pray you to forget the zeal of an ignorant old man, whose feelings are master of his breeding, and who knows less how to render the truth agreeable to noble ears, than to utter it."

"Thou mayest depart."

The armed attendants advanced, and, obedient to a sign from the secretary, they led Antonio and his companion through the door by which they had entered. The other officials of the place followed, and the secret judges were left by themselves in the chamber of doom.

CHAPTER XIII

"O! the days that we have seen."
SHELTON

A PAUSE like that which accompanies self-contemplation, and perhaps conscious distrust of purpose, succeeded. Then the Three arose, together, and began to lay aside the instruments of their disguise. When the masks were removed, they exposed the grave visages of men in the decline of life, athwart which worldly cares and worldly passions had drawn those deep lines which no subsequent ease or resignation can erase. During the process of unrobing neither spoke, for the affair on which they had just been employed caused novel and disagreeable sensations to them all. When they were delivered from their superfluous garments and their masks, however, they drew near the table, and each sought that relief for his limbs and person which was natural to the long restraint he had undergone.

"There are letters from the French king intercepted," said one, after time had permitted them to rally their thoughts;—"it would appear they treat of the new intentions of the emperor."

"Have they been restored to the ambassador? or are the originals to go before the senate?" demanded another.

"On that we must take counsel, at our leisure. I have naught else to communicate, except that the order given to intercept the messenger of the Holy See hath failed of its object."

"Of this the secretaries advertised me. We must look into the negligence of the agents, for there is good reason to believe much useful knowledge would have come from that seizure."

"As the attempt is already known and much spoken of, care must be had to issue orders for the arrest of the robbers, else may the republic fall into disrepute with its friends. There are names on our list which might be readily marked for punishment, for that quarter of our patrimony is never in want of proscribed, to conceal an accident of this nature."

"Good heed will be had to this, since, as you say, the affair is weighty. The government or the individual that is negligent of

163

reputation cannot expect long to retain the respect of its equals."

"The ambition of the House of Hapsburgh robs me of my sleep!" exclaimed the other, throwing aside some papers, over which his eye had glanced, in disgust. "Holy St. Theodore! what a scourge to the race is the desire to augment territories and to extend an unjust rule, beyond the boundaries of reason and nature! Here have we, in Venice, been in undisputed possession of provinces that are adapted to our institutions, convenient to our wants, and agreeable to our desires, for ages;—provinces that were gallantly won by our ancestors, and which cling to us as habits linger in our age: and yet are they become objects of a covetous ambition to our neighbor, under a vain pretext of a policy that I fear is strengthened by our increasing weakness. I sicken, Signori, of my esteem for men, as I dive deeper into their tempers and desires, and often wish myself a dog, as I study their propensities. In his appetite for power, is not the Austrian the most rapacious of all the princes of the earth?"

"More so, think you, worthy Signore, than the Castilian? You overlook the unsatiated desire of the Spanish king to extend his sway in Italy."

"Hapsburgh or Bourbon; Turk or Englishman; they all seem actuated by the same fell appetite for dominion; and now that Venice hath no more to hope, than to preserve her present advantages, the least of all our enjoyments becomes a subject of covetous envy to our enemies. There are passions to weary one of an interference with governments, and to send him to his cord of penitence and the cloisters!"

"I never listen to your observations, Signore, without quitting the chamber an edified man! Truly this desire in the strangers to trespass on our privileges, and it may be well said, privileges which have been gained by our treasures and our blood, becomes more manifest, daily. Should it not be checked, St. Mark will be stripped, in the end, of even a landing place for a gondola on the main."

"The leap of the winged lion is much curtailed, excellent Sir, or these things might not be! It is no longer in our power to persuade, or to command, as of old, and our canals begin to be encumbered with slimy weeds, instead of well-freighted argosies, and swift-sailing feluccas."

"The Portuguese hath done us irretrievable harm, for without his African discoveries, we might yet have retained the traffic in Indian commodities. I cordially dislike the mongrel race, being, as it is, half Gothic and half Moorish!"

"I trust not myself to think of their origin or of their deeds, my friends, lest prejudice should kindle feelings unbecoming a man and a Christian.—How now, Signor Gradenigo; thou art thoughtful?"

The third member of the secret council, who had not spoken since the disappearance of the accused, and who was no other than the reader's old acquaintance of the name just mentioned, slowly lifted his head, from a meditative position, at this address.

"The examination of the fisherman hath recalled scenes of my boyhood," he answered, with a touch of nature that seldom found place in that chamber.

"I heard thee say he was thy foster brother," returned the other, struggling to conceal a gape.

"We drank of the same milk, and, for the first years of life, we sported at the same games."

"These imaginary kindred often give great uneasiness. I am glad your trouble hath no other source, for I had heard that the young heir of your house hath shown a prodigal disposition of late, and I feared that matter might have come to your knowledge, as one of the council, that a father might not wish to learn."

The selfish features of the Signor Gradenigo instantly underwent a change. He glanced curiously, and with a strong distrust, but in a covert manner, at the fallen eyes of his two companions, anxious to penetrate their secret thoughts ere he ventured to expose his own.

"Is there aught of complaint against the youth?" he demanded, in a voice of hesitation. "You understand a father's interest, and will not conceal the truth."

"Signore, you know that the agents of the police are active, and little that comes to their knowledge fails to reach the ears of the council. But, at the worst, the matter is not of life or death. It can only cost the inconsiderate young man a visit to Dalmatia, or an order to waste the summer at the foot of the Alps."

"Youth is the season of indiscretion, as ye know, Signori," returned the father, breathing more freely, "and as none become old that have not been young, I have little need to awaken your recollection of its weaknesses. I trust my son is incapable of designing aught against the republic?"

"Of that he is not suspected." A slight expression of irony crossed the features of the old senator, as he spoke. "But he is represented as aiming too freely at the person and wealth of your ward; and that she, who is the especial care of St. Mark, is not to be solicited without the consent of the senate, is an usage well known to one of its most ancient and most honorable members."

"Such is the law, and none coming of me shall show it disrespect. I have preferred my claims to that connexion, openly, but with diffidence; and I await the decision of the state, in respectful confidence."

His associates bowed in courteous acknowledgment of the justice of what he said, and of the loyalty of his conduct, but it was in the manner of men too long accustomed to duplicity, to be easily duped.

"None doubt it, worthy Signor Gradenigo, for thy faith to the state is ever quoted as a model for the young, and as a subject for the approbation of the more experienced. Hast thou any communications to make on the interest of the young heiress, thyself?"

"I am pained to say that the deep obligation conferred by Don Camillo Monforte seems to have wrought upon her youthful imagination, and I apprehend that, in disposing of my ward, the state will have to contend with the caprice of a female mind. The waywardness of that age will give more trouble, than the conduct of far graver matters."

"Is the lady attended by suitable companions, in her daily life?"

"Her companions are known to the senate. In so grave an interest, I would not act without their authority and sanction. But the affair hath great need of delicacy in its government. The circumstance that so much of my ward's fortune lies in the States of the Church renders it necessary to await the proper moment for disposing of her rights, and of transferring their substance within the limits of the republic, before we proceed to any act of decision. Once assured of her wealth, she may be disposed of, as seemeth best to the welfare of the state, without further delay."

166

"The lady hath a lineage and riches, and an excellence of person, that might render her of great account in some of these knotty negotiations which so much fetter our movements of late. The time hath been, when a daughter of Venice, not more fair, was wooed to the bed of a sovereign."

"Signore, those days of glory and greatness exist no longer. Should it be thought expedient to overlook the natural claims of my son, and to bestow my ward to the advantage of the republic, the most that can be expected through her means is a favorable concession in some future treaty, or a new prop to some of the many decaying interests of the city. In this particular, she may be rendered of as much, or even of more use, than the oldest and wisest of our body. But that her will may be free, and the child may have no obstacles to her happiness, it will be necessary to make a speedy determination of the claim preferred by Don Camillo. Can we do better than to recommend a compromise, that he may return without delay to his own Calabria?"

"The concern is weighty, and it demands deliberation."

"He complains of our tardiness already, and not without show of reason. It is five years since the claim was first preferred."

"Signor Gradenigo, it is for the vigorous and healthful to display their activity, the aged and the tottering must move with caution. Were we, in Venice, to betray precipitation in so weighty a concern, without seeing an immediate interest in the judgment, we should trifle with a gale of fortune that every sirocco will not blow into the canals. We must have terms with the lord of Sant' Agata, or we greatly slight our own advantage."

"I hinted of the matter to your excellencies, as a consideration for your wisdom; methinks it will be something gained to remove one so dangerous from the recollection, and from before the eyes, of a lovesick maiden."

"Is the damsel so amorous?"

"She is of Italy, Signore, and our sun bestows warm fancies and fervent minds."

"Let her to the confessional and her prayers! The godly priore of St. Mark will discipline her imagination, till she shall conceit the Neapolitan a Moor, and an infidel. Just San Teodoro, forgive me! But thou canst remember the time, my friends, when the penance of the church was not without service on thine own fickle tastes and truant practices."

167

"The Signor Gradenigo was a gallant in his time," observed the third, "as all well know who travelled in his company. Thou wert much spoken of at Versailles and at Vienna,—nay, thou canst not deny thy vogue to one who, if he hath no other merit, hath a memory."

"I protest against these false recollections," rejoined the accused, a withered smile lighting his faded countenance; "we have been young, Signori; but among us all, I never knew a Venetian of more general fashion and of better report, especially with the dames of France, than he who has just spoken."

"Account it not—account it not—'twas the weakness of youth and the use of the times!—I remember to have seen thee, Enrico, at Madrid, and a gayer or more accomplished gentleman was not known at the Spanish court."

"Thy friendship blinded thee—I was a boy and full of spirits; no more, I may assure thee. Didst hear of my affair with the mosquetaire, when at Paris?"

"Did I hear of the general war?—Thou art too modest, to raise this doubt of a meeting that occupied the coteries for a month, as it had been a victory of the powers! Signor Gradenigo, it was a pleasure to call him countryman at that time, for I do assure thee, a sprightlier or a more gallant gentleman did not walk the terrace."

"Thou tellest me of what my own eyes have been a witness. Did I not arrive when men's voices spoke of nothing else?—A beautiful court and a pleasant capital were those of France in our day, Signori."

"None pleasanter, or of greater freedom of intercourse—St. Mark aid me with his prayers! The many pleasant hours that I have passed between the Marais and the Chateau! Didst ever meet La Comtesse de Mignon in the gardens?"

"Zitto—thou growest loquacious, caro; nay, she wanted not for grace and affability, that I will say. In what a manner they played in the houses of resort, at that time!"

"I know it to my cost. Will you lend me your belief, dear friends? I arose from the table of La Belle Duchesse de—, the loser of a thousand sequins, and to this hour it seemeth but a moment that I was occupied."

"I remember the evening.—Thou wert seated between the wife of the Spanish ambassador, and a miladi of England. Thou

168

wert playing at rouge-et-noir, in more ways than one, for thy eyes were on thy neighbors instead of thy cards—Giulio, I would have paid half the loss, to have read the next epistle of the worthy senator thy father!"

"He never knew it—he never knew it—we had our friends on the Rialto, and the account was settled a few years later. Thou wast well with Ninon, Enrico?"

"A companion of her leisure, and one who basked in the sunshine of her wit."

"Nay, they said thou wert of more favor—"

"Mere gossip of the salons. I do protest, gentlemen,—not that others were better received—but idle tongues will have their discourse!"

"Wert thou of the party, Alessandro, that went in a fit of gaiety from country to country, till it numbered ten courts at which it appeared in as many weeks?"

"Was I not its mover? What a memory art thou getting! 'Twas for a hundred golden louis, and it was bravely won by an hour. A postponement of the reception by the elector of Bavaria went near to defeat us, but we bribed the groom of the chambers, as thou mayest remember, and got into the presence as it were by accident."

"Was that held to be sufficient?"

"That was it, for our terms mentioned the condition of holding discourse with ten sovereigns, in as many weeks, in their own palaces. Oh! it was fairly won; and I believe I may say that it was as gaily expended!"

"For the latter will I vouch, since I never quitted thee while a piece of it all remained. There are divers means of dispensing gold in those northern capitals, and the task was quickly accomplished. They are pleasant countries for a few years of youth and idleness!"

"It is a pity that their climates are so rude."

A slight and general shudder expressed their Italian sympathy, but the discourse did not the less proceed.

"They might have a better sun, and a clearer sky, but there is excellent cheer, and no want of hospitality," observed the Signor Gradenigo, who maintained his full share of the dialogue, though we have not found it necessary to separate sentiments that were so common among the different speakers. "I have seen pleasant hours even with the Genoese, though their town hath a cast of reflection and sobriety that is not always suited to the dispositions of youth."

"Nay, Stockholm and Copenhagen have their pleasures too, I do assure thee. I passed a season between them. Your Dane is a good joker and a hearty bottle companion."

"In that the Englishman surpasseth all! If I were to relate their powers of living in this manner, dear friends, ye would discredit me. That which I have seen often seemeth impossible even to myself. 'Tis a gloomy abode, and one that we of Italy little like, in common."

"Name it not in comparison with Holland—wert ever in Holland, friends?—didst ever enjoy the fashion of Amsterdam and the Hague? I remember to have heard a young Roman urge a friend to pass a winter there; for the witty rogue termed it the beau ideal of the land of petticoats!"

The three old Italians, in whom this sally excited a multitude of absurd recollections and pleasant fancies, broke out into a general and hearty fit of laughter. The sound of their cracked merriment, echoing in that gloomy and solemn room, suddenly recalled them to the recollection of their duties. Each listened an instant, as if in expectation that some extraordinary consequence was to follow so extraordinary an interruption of the usual silence of the place, like a child whose truant propensities were about to draw detection on his offence,—and then the principal of the council furtively wiped the tears from his eyes, and resumed his gravity.

"Signori," he said, fumbling in a bundle of papers, "we must take up the matter of the fisherman—but we will first inquire into the circumstance of the signet left, the past night, in the Lion's Mouth. Signor Gradenigo, you were charged with the examination."

"The duty hath been executed, noble Sirs, and with a success I had not hoped to meet with. Haste, at our last meeting, prevented a perusal of the paper to which it was attached, but it will now be seen that the two have a connexion. Here is an accusation which charges Don Camillo Monforte with a design to bear away, beyond the power of the senate, the Donna Violetta, my ward, in order to possess her person and riches. It speaketh of proofs in possession of the accuser, as if he were an agent in-

170

trusted by the Neapolitan. As a pledge of his truth, I suppose, for there is no mention made of any other use, he sends the signet of Don Camillo himself, which cannot have been obtained without that noble's confidence."

"Is it certain that he owns the ring?"

"Of that am I well assured. You know I am especially charged with conducting his personal demand with the senate, and frequent interviews have given me opportunity to note that he was wont to wear a signet, which is now wanting. My jeweller of the Rialto hath sufficiently identified this as the missing ring."

"Thus far it is clear, though there is an obscurity in the circumstance that the signet of the accused should be found with the accusation, which, being unexplained, renders the charge vague and uncertain. Have you any clue to the writing, or any means of knowing whence it comes?"

There was a small but nearly imperceptible red spot on the cheek of the Signor Gradenigo that did not escape the keen distrust of his companions; but he concealed his alarm, answering distinctly that he had none.

"We must then defer a decision for further proof. The justice of St. Mark hath been too much vaunted to endanger its reputation by a hasty decree, in a question which so closely touches the interest of a powerful noble of Italy. Don Camillo Monforte hath a name of distinction, and counteth too many of note among his kindred, to be dealt with as we might dispose of a gondolier, or the messenger of some foreign state."

"As respects him, Signore, you are undoubtedly right. But may we not endanger our heiress by too much tenderness?"

"There are many convents in Venice, Signore."

"The monastic life is ill suited to the temper of my ward," the Signor Gradenigo drily observed, "and I fear to hazard the experiment; gold is a key to unlock the strongest cell; besides, we cannot with due observance of propriety place a child of the state in durance."

"Signor Gradenigo, we have had this matter under long and grave consideration, and agreeably to our laws, when one of our number hath a palpable interest in the affair, we have taken counsel of his Highness, who is of accord with us in sentiment. Your personal interest in the lady might have warped your usually excellent judgment; else, be assured, we should have summoned you to the conference."

The old senator, who thus unexpectedly found himself excluded from consultation, on the very matter that, of all others, made him most value his temporary authority, stood abashed and silent—reading in his countenance, however, a desire to know more, his associates proceeded to communicate all it was their intention he should hear.

"It hath been determined to remove the lady to a suitable retirement, and for this purpose care hath been already had to provide the means. Thou wilt be temporarily relieved of a most grievous charge, which cannot but have worked heavily on thy spirits, and, in other particulars, have lessened thy much-valued usefulness to the republic."

This unexpected communication was made with marked courtesy of manner; but with an emphasis and tone that sufficiently acquainted the Signor Gradenigo with the nature of the suspicions that beset him. He had too long been familiar with the sinuous policy of the council, in which, at intervals, he had so often sat, not to understand that he would run the risk of a more serious accusation were he to hesitate in acknowledging its justice. Teaching his features, therefore, to wear a smile as treacherous as that of his wily companion, he answered with seeming gratitude.

"His Highness and you, my excellent colleagues, have taken counsel of your good wishes and kindness of heart, rather than of the duty of a poor subject of St. Mark, to toil on in his service while he hath strength and reason for the task," he said. "The management of a capricious female mind is a concern of no light moment, and while I thank you for this consideration of my case, you will permit me to express my readiness to resume the charge whenever it shall please the state again to confer it."

"Of this none are more persuaded than we, nor are any better satisfied of your ability to discharge the trust faithfully. But you enter, Signore, into all our motives, and will join us in the opinion, that it is equally unbecoming the republic, and one of its most illustrious citizens, to leave a ward of the former in a position that shall subject the latter to unmerited censure. Believe me, we have thought less of Venice in this matter, than of the honor and the interests of the house of Gradenigo; for, should

172

this Neapolitan thwart our views, you of us all would be most liable to be disapproved of."

"A thousand thanks, excellent Sir," returned the deposed guardian. "You have taken a load from my mind, and restored some of the freshness and elasticity of youth! The claim of Don Camillo now is no longer urgent, since it is your pleasure to remove the lady, for a season, from the city."

" 'Twere better to hold it in deeper suspense, if it were only to occupy his mind. Keep up thy communications, as of wont, and withhold not hope, which is a powerful exciter in minds that are not deadened by experience. We shall not conceal from one of our number, that a negotiation is already near a termination which will relieve the state from the care of the damsel, and at some benefit to the republic. Her estates lying without our limits greatly facilitate the treaty, which hath only been withheld from your knowledge, by the consideration, that of late, we have rather too much overloaded thee with affairs."

Again the Signor Gradenigo bowed submissively, and with apparent joy. He saw that his secret design had been penetrated, notwithstanding all his practised duplicity and specious candor; and he submitted with that species of desperate resignation which becomes a habit, if not a virtue, in men long accustomed to be governed despotically. When this delicate subject, which required the utmost finesse of Venetian policy, since it involved the interests of one who happened, at the moment, to be in the dreaded council itself, was disposed of, the three turned their attention to other matters, with that semblance of indifference to personal feeling which practice in tortuous paths of state intrigue enabled men to assume.

"Since we are so happily of opinion, concerning the disposition of the Donna Violetta," coolly observed the oldest senator, a rare specimen of hackneyed and worldly morality, "we may look into our list of daily duties—what say the Lions' Mouths tonight?"

"A few of the ordinary and unmeaning accusations that spring from personal hatred," returned another. "One chargeth his neighbor with oversight in religious duties, and with some carelessness of the fasts of Holy Church—a foolish scandal, fitted for the ears of a curate."

"Is there naught else?"

173

"Another complaineth of neglect in a husband. The scrawl is in a woman's hand, and beareth, on its face, the evidence of a woman's resentment."

"Sudden to rise and easy to be appeased. Let the neighborhood quiet the household by its sneers—What next?"

"A suitor in the courts maketh complaint of the tardiness of the judges."

"This toucheth the reputation of St. Mark; it must be looked to!"

"Hold!" interrupted the Signor Gradenigo. "The tribunal acteth advisedly—'tis in the matter of a Hebrew who is thought to have secrets of importance. The affair hath need of deliberation, I do assure you."

"Destroy the charge—Have we more?"

"Nothing of note. The usual number of pleasantries and hobbling verses which tend to nothing. If we get some useful gleanings, by these secret accusations, we gain much nonsense. I would whip a youngster of ten who could not mould our soft Italian into better rhyme than this."

" 'Tis the wantonness of security. Let it pass, for all that serveth to amuse suppresseth turbulent thoughts. Shall we now see his Highness, Signori?"

"You forget the fisherman," gravely observed the Signor Gradenigo.

"Your honor sayeth true. What a head for business hath he! Nothing that is useful escapeth his ready mind."

The old senator, while he was too experienced to be cajoled by such language, saw the necessity of appearing flattered. Again he bowed, and protested aloud and frequently against the justice of compliments that he so little merited. When this little byplay was over, they proceeded gravely to consider the matter before them.

As the decision of the Council of Three will be made apparent in the course of the narrative, we shall not continue to detail the conversation that accompanied their deliberations. The sitting was long, so long indeed that when they arose, having completed their business, the heavy clock of the square tolled the hour of midnight.

"The doge will be impatient," said one of the two nameless members, as they threw on their cloaks, before leaving the chamber. "I thought his Highness wore a more fatigued and

174

feeble air today, than he is wont to exhibit, at the festivities of the city."

"His Highness is no longer young, Signore. If I remember right, he greatly outnumbers either of us in years. Our Lady of Loretto lend him strength long to wear the ducal bonnet, and wisdom to wear it well!"

"He hath lately sent offerings to her shrine."

"Signore, he hath. His confessor hath gone in person with the offering, as I know of certainty. 'Tis not a serious gift, but a mere remembrance to keep himself in the odor of sanctity. I doubt that his reign will not be long!"

"There are, truly, signs of decay in his system. He is a worthy prince, and we shall lose a father when called to weep for his loss!"

"Most true, Signore: but the horned bonnet is not an invulnerable shield against the arrows of death. Age and infirmities are more potent than our wishes."

"Thou art moody tonight, Signor Gradenigo. Thou art not used to be so silent with thy friends."

"I am not the less grateful, Signore, for their favors. If I have a loaded countenance, I bear a lightened heart. One who hath a daughter of his own so happily bestowed in wedlock as thine may judge of the relief I feel by this disposition of my ward. Joy affects the exterior, frequently, like sorrow; ay, even to tears."

His two companions looked at the speaker with much obvious sympathy in their manners. They then left the chamber of doom together. The menials entered and extinguished the lights, leaving all behind them in an obscurity that was no bad type of the gloomy mysteries of the place.

CHAPTER XIV

"Then methought,
A serenade broke silence, breathing hope
Through walls of stone."
Italy

NOTWITHSTANDING the lateness of the hour, the melody of music
was rife on the water. Gondolas continued to glide along the
shadowed canals, while the laugh or the song was echoed among
the arches of the palaces. The piazza and piazzetta were yet brilliant with lights, and gay with their multitudes of unwearied
revellers.

The habitation of Donna Violetta was far from the scene of
general amusement. Though so remote, the hum of the moving
throng, and the higher strains of the wind instruments, came,
from time to time, to the ears of its inmates, mellowed and thrilling by distance.

The position of the moon cast the whole of the narrow passage which flowed beneath the windows of her private apartments into shadow. In a balcony which overhung the water,
stood the youthful and ardent girl, listening with a charmed ear
and a tearful eye to one of those soft strains, in which Venetian
voices answered to each other from different points on the canals,
in the songs of the gondoliers. Her constant companion and
mentor was near, while the ghostly father of them both stood
deeper in the room.

"There may be pleasanter towns on the main, and capitals of
more revelry," said the charmed Violetta, withdrawing her person from its leaning attitude, as the voices ceased; "but in such
a night and at this witching hour, what city may compare with
Venice?"

"Providence has been less partial in the distribution of its
earthly favors than is apparent to a vulgar eye," returned the
attentive Carmelite. "If we have our peculiar enjoyments and our
moments of divine contemplation, other towns have advantages
of their own; Genoa and Pisa, Firenze, Ancona, Roma, Palermo,
and, chiefest of all, Napoli—"

176

"Napoli, father!"

"Daughter, Napoli. Of all the towns of sunny Italy, 'tis the fairest and the most blessed in natural gifts. Of every region I have visited, during a life of wandering and penitence, that is the country on which the touch of the Creator hath been the most God-like!"

"Thou art imaginative tonight, good Father Anselmo. The land must be fair indeed, that can thus warm the fancy of a Carmelite."

"The rebuke is just. I have spoken more under the influence of recollections that came from days of idleness and levity, than with the chastened spirit of one who should see the hand of the Maker, in the most simple and least lovely of all His wondrous works."

"You reproach yourself causelessly, holy father," observed the mild Donna Florinda, raising her eyes towards the pale countenance of the monk; "to admire the beauties of nature is to worship Him who gave them being."

At that moment a burst of music rose on the air, proceeding from the water beneath the balcony. Donna Violetta started back, abashed, and as she held her breath in wonder, and haply with that delight which open admiration is apt to excite in a youthful female bosom, the color mounted to her temples.

"There passeth a band," calmly observed the Donna Florinda.

"No, it is a cavalier! There are gondoliers, servitors in his colors."

"This is as hardy as it may be gallant," returned the monk, who listened to the air with an evident and grave displeasure.

There was no longer any doubt but that a serenade was meant. Though the custom was of much use, it was the first time that a similar honor had been paid beneath the window of Donna Violetta. The studied privacy of her life, her known destiny, and the jealousy of the despotic state, and perhaps the deep respect which encircled a maiden of her tender years and high condition, had, until that moment, kept the aspiring, the vain, and the interested, equally in awe.

"It is for me!" whispered the trembling, the distressed, the delighted Violetta.

"It is for one of us, indeed," answered the cautious friend.

"Be it for whom it may, it is bold," rejoined the monk.

Donna Violetta shrunk from observation, behind the drapery

of the window, but she raised a hand in pleasure, as the rich strains rolled through the wide apartments.

"What a taste rules the band!" she half-whispered, afraid to trust her voice, lest a sound should escape her ears. "They touch an air of Petrarch's sonnatas! How indiscreet, and yet how noble!"

"More noble than wise," said the Donna Florinda, who entered the balcony, and looked intently on the water beneath.

"Here are musicians in the color of a noble in one gondola," she continued, "and a single cavalier in another."

"Hath he no servitor?—Doth he ply the oar himself?"

"Truly that decency hath not been overlooked; one in a flowered jacket guides the boat."

"Speak, then, dearest Florinda, I pray thee."

"Would it be seemly?"

"Indeed I think it. Speak them fair. Say that I am the senate's.—That it is not discreet to urge a daughter of the state thus—say what thou wilt—but speak them fair."

"Ha! It is Don Camillo Monforte! I know him by his noble stature and the gallant wave of his hand."

"This temerity will undo him! His claim will be refused— himself banished. Is it not near the hour when the gondola of the police passes? Admonish him to depart, good Florinda—and yet —can we use this rudeness to a Signor of his rank!"

"Father, counsel us; you know the hazards of this rash gallantry in the Neapolitan—aid us with thy wisdom, for there is not a moment to lose."

The Carmelite had been an attentive and an indulgent observer of the emotion, which sensations so novel had awakened in the ardent but unpractised breast of the fair Venetian. Pity, sorrow, and sympathy were painted on his mortified face, as he witnessed the mastery of feeling over a mind so guileless, and a heart so warm; but the look was rather that of one who knew the dangers of the passions, than of one who condemned them, without thought of their origin or power. At the appeal of the governess he turned away and silently quitted the room. Donna Florinda left the balcony and drew near her charge. There was no explanation, nor any audible or visible means of making their sentiments known to each other. Violetta threw herself into the arms of her more experienced friend, and struggled to conceal her face in her bosom. At this moment the music suddenly ceased, and the plash of oars, falling into the water, succeeded.

178

"He is gone!" exclaimed the young creature, who had been the object of the serenade, and whose faculties, spite of her confusion, had lost none of their acuteness. "The gondolas are moving away, and we have not made even the customary acknowledgments for their civility!"

"It is not needed—or rather it might increase a hazard that is already too weighty. Remember thy high destiny, my child, and let them depart."

"And yet, methinks one of my station should not fail in courtesy. The compliment may mean no more than any other idle usage, and they should not quit us unthanked."

"Rest you, within. I will watch the movement of the boats, for it surpasseth female endurance not to note their aspect."

"Thanks, dearest Florinda! hasten, lest they enter the other canal ere thou seest them."

The governess was quickly in the balcony. Active as was her movement, her eyes were scarcely cast upon the shadow beneath, before a hurried question demanded what she beheld.

"Both gondolas are gone," was the answer. "That with the musicians is already entering the Great Canal, but that of the cavalier hath unaccountably disappeared!"

"Nay, look again; he cannot be in such haste to quit us."

"I had not sought him in the right direction. Here is his gondola, by the bridge of our own canal."

"And the cavalier? He waits for some sign of courtesy; it is meet that we should not withhold it."

"I see him not. His servitor is seated on the steps of the landing, while the gondola appeareth to be empty. The man hath an air of waiting, but I nowhere see the master!"

"Blessed Maria! can aught have befallen the gallant Duca di Sant' Agata?"

"Naught but the happiness of casting himself here!" exclaimed a voice near the person of the heiress. The Donna Violetta turned her gaze from the balcony, and beheld him who filled all her thoughts, at her feet.

The cry of the girl, the exclamation of her friend, and a rapid and eager movement of the monk, brought the whole party into a group.

"This may not be," said the latter in a reproving voice. "Arise, Don Camillo, lest I repent listening to your prayer; you exceed our conditions."

"As much as this emotion exceedeth my hopes," answered the

noble. "Holy father, it is vain to oppose Providence! Providence brought me to the rescue of this lovely being, when accident threw her into the Giudecca, and, once more, Providence is my friend, by permitting me to be a witness of this feeling. Speak, fair Violetta, thou wilt not be an instrument of the senate's selfishness—thou wilt not hearken to their wish of disposing of thy hand on the mercenary, who would trifle with the most sacred of all vows, to possess thy wealth?"

"For whom am I destined?" demanded Violetta.

"No matter, since it be not for me. Some trafficker in happiness, some worthless abuser of the gifts of fortune."

"Thou knowest, Camillo, our Venetian custom, and must see that I am hopelessly in their hands."

"Arise, Duke of St. Agata," said the monk, with authority; "when I suffered you to enter this palace, it was to remove a scandal from its gates, and to save you from your own rash disregard of the state's displeasure. It is idle to encourage hopes that the policy of the republic opposes. Arise then, and respect your pledges."

"That shall be as this lady may decide. Encourage me with but an approving look, fairest Violetta, and not Venice, with its doge and inquisition, shall stir me an inch from thy feet!"

"Camillo!" answered the trembling girl, "thou, the preserver of my life, hast little need to kneel to me!"

"Duke of St. Agata—daughter!"

"Nay, heed him not, generous Violetta. He utters words of convention—he speaks as all speak in age, when men's tongues deny the feelings of their youth. He is a Carmelite, and must feign this prudence. He never knew the tyranny of the passions. The dampness of his cell has chilled the ardor of the heart. Had he been human, he would have loved; had he loved, he would never have worn a cowl."

Father Anselmo receded a pace, like one pricked in conscience, and the paleness of his ascetic features took a deadly hue. His lips moved as if he would have spoken, but the sounds were smothered by an oppression that denied him utterance. The gentle Florinda saw his distress, and she endeavored to interpose between the impetuous youth and her charge.

"It may be as you say, Signor Monforte," she said, "and that the senate, in its fatherly care, searches a partner worthy of an heiress of a house so illustrious and so endowed as that of Tiepolo. But in this, what is there more than of wont? Do not the nobles of all Italy seek their equals in condition and in the gifts of fortune, in order that their union may be fittingly assorted. How know we that the estates of my young friend have not a value in the eye of the Duke of St. Agata, as well as in those of him that the senate may elect for thy husband?"

"Can this be true!" exclaimed Violetta.

"Believe it not; my errand in Venice is no secret. I seek the restitution of lands and houses long withheld from my family, with the honors of the senate that are justly mine. All these do I joyfully abandon for the hope of thy favor."

"Thou hearest, Florinda: Don Camillo is not to be distrusted!"

"What are the senate and the power of St. Mark, that they should cross our lives with misery? Be mine, lovely Violetta, and in the fastnesses of my own good Calabrian castle we will defy their vengeance and policy. Their disappointment shall furnish merriment for my vassals, and our felicity shall make the happiness of thousands. I affect no disrespect for the dignity of the councils, nor any indifference to that I lose, but to me art thou far more precious than the horned bonnet itself, with all its fancied influence and glory."

"Generous Camillo!"

"Be mine, and spare the cold calculators of the senate another crime. They think to dispose of thee, as if thou wert worthless merchandise, to their own advantage. But thou wilt defeat their design. I read the generous resolution in thine eye, Violetta; thou wilt manifest a will superior to their arts and egotism."

"I would not be trafficked for, Don Camillo Monforte, but wooed and won as befitteth a maiden of my condition. They may still leave me liberty of choice. The Signor Gradenigo hath much encouraged me of late with this hope, when speaking of the establishment suited to my years."

"Believe him not; a colder heart, a spirit more removed from charity, exists not in Venice. He courts thy favor for his own prodigal son; a cavalier without honor, the companion of profligates, and the victim of the Hebrews. Believe him not, for he is stricken in deceit."

"He is the victim of his own designs, if this be true. Of all the youths of Venice I esteem Giacomo Gradenigo least."

"This interview must have an end," said the monk, interposing effectually, and compelling the lover to rise. "It would be easier to escape the toils of sin than to elude the agents of the police. I tremble lest this visit should be known, for we are encircled with the ministers of the state, and not a palace in Venice is more narrowly watched than this. Were thy presence here detected, indiscreet young man, thy youth might pine in a prison, while thou would'st be the cause of persecution and unmerited sorrow to this innocent and inexperienced maiden."

"A prison, sayest thou, father!"

"No less, daughter. Lighter offences are often expiated by heavier judgments, when the pleasure of the senate is thwarted."

"Thou must not be condemned to a prison, Camillo!"

"Fear it not. The years and peaceful calling of the father make him timid. I have long been prepared for this happy moment, and I ask but a single hour to put Venice and all her toils at defiance. Give me the blessed assurance of thy truth, and confide in my means for the rest."

"Thou hearest, Florinda!"

"This bearing is suited to the sex of Don Camillo, dearest, but it ill becometh thee. A maiden of high quality must await the decision of her natural guardians."

"But should that choice be Giacomo Gradenigo?"

"The senate will not hear of it. The arts of his father have long been known to thee; and thou must have seen, by the secrecy of his own advances, that he distrusts their decision. The state will have a care to dispose of thee as befitteth thy hopes. Thou art sought of many, and those who guard thy fortune only await the proposals which best become thy birth."

"Proposals that become my birth!"

"Suitable in years, condition, expectations, and character."

"Am I to regard Don Camillo Monforte as one beneath me?"
The Monk again interposed.

"This interview must end," he said. "The eyes drawn upon us, by your indiscreet music, are now turned on other objects, Signore, and you must break your faith, or depart."

"Alone, father?"

"Is the Donna Violetta to quit the roof of her father with as little warning as an unfavored dependant?"

"Nay, Signor Monforte, you could not, in reason, have expected more, in this interview, than the hope of some future termination to your suit—some pledge—"

182

"And that pledge?"

The eye of Violetta turned from her governess to her lover, from her lover to the monk, and from the latter to the floor.

"Is thine, Camillo."

A common cry escaped the Carmelite and the governess.

"Thy mercy, excellent friends," continued the blushing but decided Violetta. "If I have encouraged Don Camillo, in a manner that thy counsels and maiden modesty would reprove, reflect that had he hesitated to cast himself into the Giudecca, I should have wanted the power to confer this trifling grace. Why should I be less generous than my preserver? No, Camillo, when the senate condemns me to wed another than thee, it pronounces the doom of celibacy; I will hide my griefs in a convent till I die!"

There was a solemn and fearful interruption to a discourse which was so rapidly becoming explicit, by the sound of the bell that the groom of the chambers, a long-tried and confidential domestic, had been commanded to ring before he entered. As this injunction had been accompanied by another not to appear unless summoned, or urged by some grave motive, the signal caused a sudden pause, even at that interesting moment.

"How now!" exclaimed the Carmelite to the servant, who abruptly entered. "What means this disregard of my injunctions?"

"Father, the republic!"

"Is St. Mark in jeopardy, that females and priests are summoned to aid him?"

"There are officials of the state below who demand admission in the name of the republic."

"This grows serious," said Don Camillo, who alone retained his self-possession. "My visit is known, and the active jealousy of the state anticipates its object. Summon your resolution, Donna Violetta, and you, father, be of heart! I will assume the responsibility of the offence, if offence it be, and exonerate all others from censure."

"Forbid it, Father Anselmo. Dearest Florinda, we will share his punishment!" exclaimed the terrified Violetta, losing all self-command in the fear of such a moment. "He has not been guilty of this indiscretion without participation of mine; he has not presumed beyond his encouragement."

The monk and Donna Florinda regarded each other in mute

183

amazement, and haply there was some admixture of feeling in the look that denoted the uselessness of caution when the passions were intent to elude the vigilance of those who were merely prompted by prudence. The former simply motioned for silence, while he turned to the domestic.

"Of what character are these ministers of the state?" he demanded.

"Father, they are its known officers, and wear the badges of their condition."

"And their request?"

"Is to be admitted to the presence of the Donna Violetta."

"There is still hope!" rejoined the monk, breathing more freely. Moving across the room, he opened a door which communicated with the private oratory of the palace. "Retire within this sacred chapel, Don Camillo, while we await the explanation of so extraordinary a visit."

As the time pressed, the suggestion was obeyed on the instant. The lover entered the oratory, and when the door was closed upon his person, the domestic, one known to be worthy of all confidence, was directed to usher in those who waited without.

But a single individual appeared. He was known, at a glance, for a public and responsible agent of the government who was often charged with the execution of secret and delicate duties. Donna Violetta advanced to meet him, in respect to his employers, and with the return of that self-possession which long practice interweaves with the habits of the great.

"I am honored by this care of my dreaded and illustrious guardians," she said, making an acknowledgment for the low reverence with which the official saluted the richest ward of Venice. "To what circumstance do I owe this visit?"

The officer gazed an instant about him, with an habitual and suspicious caution, and then repeating his salutations, he answered.

"Lady," he said, "I am commanded to seek an interview with the daughter of the state, the heiress of the illustrious house of Tiepolo, with the Donna Florinda Mercato, her female companion, with the Father Anselmo, her commissioned confessor, and with any other who enjoy the pleasure of her society and the honor of her confidence."

"Those you seek are here; I am Violetta Tiepolo; to this lady am I indebted for a mother's care; and this reverend Carmelite is my spiritual counsellor. Shall I summon my household?"

"It is unnecessary. My errand is rather of private than of public concern. At the decease of your late most honored and much-lamented parent, the illustrious Senator Tiepolo, the care of your person, lady, was committed by the republic, your natural and careful protector, to the especial guardianship and wisdom of Signor Alessandro Gradenigo, of illustrious birth and estimable qualities."

"Signore, you say true."

"Though the parental love of the councils may have seemed to be dormant, it has ever been wakeful and vigilant. Now that the years, instruction, beauty, and other excellencies of their daughter, have come to so rare perfection, they wish to draw the ties that unite them nearer, by assuming their own immediate duties about her person."

"By this I am to understand that I am no longer a ward of the Signor Gradenigo?"

"Lady, a ready wit has helped you to the explanation. That illustrious patrician is released from his cherished and well-acquitted duties. Tomorrow new guardians will be charged with the care of your prized person, and will continue their honorable trust, until the wisdom of the senate shall have formed for you such an alliance, as shall not disparage a noble name and qualities that might adorn a throne."

"Am I to be separated from those I love?" demanded Violetta, impetuously.

"Trust to the senate's wisdom. I know not its determination concerning those who have long dwelt with you, but there can be no reason to doubt its tenderness or discretion. I have now only to add, that until those charged anew with the honorable office of your protectors shall arrive, it will be well to maintain the same modest reserve in the reception of visitors as of wont, and that your door, lady, must in propriety be closed against the Signor Gradenigo as against all others of his sex."

"Shall I not even thank him for his care?"

"He is tenfold rewarded in the senate's gratitude."

"It would have been gracious to have expressed my feelings towards the Signor Gradenigo in words; but that which is refused to the tongue will be permitted to the pen."

185

"The reserve that becomes the state of one so favored is absolute. St. Mark is jealous where he loves. And, now my commission is discharged, I humbly take my leave, flattered in having been selected to stand in such a presence, and to have been thought worthy of so honorable a duty."

As the officer ceased speaking and Violetta returned his bows, she turned her eyes, filled with apprehension, on the sorrowful features of her companions. The ambiguous language of those employed in such missions was too well known to leave much hope for the future. They all anticipated their separation on the morrow, though neither could penetrate the reason of this sudden change in the policy of the state. Interrogation was useless, for the blow evidently came from the secret council, whose motives could no more be fathomed than its decrees foreseen. The monk raised his hands in silent benediction towards his spiritual charge, and, unable, even in the presence of the stranger, to repress their grief, Donna Florinda and Violetta sunk into each other's arms, and wept.

In the meantime the minister of this cruel blow had delayed his departure, like one who had a half-formed resolution. He regarded the countenance of the unconscious Carmelite intently, and in a manner that denoted the habit of thinking much before he decided.

"Reverend Father," he said, "may I crave a moment of your time, for an affair that concerns the soul of a sinner?"

Though amazed, the monk could not hesitate about answering such an appeal. Obedient to a gesture of the officer, he followed him from the apartment, and continued at his side while the other threaded the magnificent rooms and descended to his gondola.

"You must be much honored of the senate, holy monk," observed the latter while they proceeded, "to hold so near a trust about the person of one in whom the state takes so great an interest?"

"I feel it as such, my son. A life of peace and prayer should have made me friends."

"Men like you, father, merit the esteem they crave. Are you long of Venice?"

"Since the last conclave. I came into the republic as confessor to the late minister from Florence."

"An honorable trust. You have been with us then long

186

enough to know that the republic never forgets a servitor, nor forgives an affront."

" 'Tis an ancient state, and one whose influence still reaches far and near."

"Have a care of the step. These marbles are treacherous to an uncertain foot."

"Mine is too practised in the descent to be unsteady. I hope I do not now descend these stairs for the last time?"

The minister of the council affected not to understand the question, but he answered as if replying only to the previous observation.

" 'Tis truly a venerable state," he said, "but a little tottering with its years. All who love liberty, father, must mourn to see so glorious a sway on the decline. *Sic transit gloria mundi!* You barefooted Carmelites do well to mortify the flesh in youth, by which you escape the pains of a decreasing power. One like you can have few wrongs of his younger days to repair."

"We are none of us without sin," returned the monk, crossing himself. "He who would flatter his soul with being perfect lays the additional weight of vanity on his life."

"Men of my occupation, holy Carmelite, have few opportunities of looking into themselves, and I bless the hour that hath brought me into company so godly. My gondola waits—will you enter?"

The monk regarded his companion in distrust, but knowing the uselessness of resistance, he murmured a short prayer and complied. A strong dash of the oars announced their departure from the steps of the palace.

CHAPTER XV

"O pescator! dell' onda,
        Fi da lin;
O pescator! dell' onda,
        Fi da lin:
Vien pescar in qua,
Colla bella tua barca,
Colla bella se ne va,
Fi da lin, lin, la—"
Venetian Boat Song

THE moon was at the height. Its rays fell in a flood on the swelling domes and massive roofs of Venice, while the margin of the town was brilliantly defined by the glittering bay. The natural and gorgeous setting was more than worthy of that picture of human magnificence; for at that moment, rich as was the queen of the Adriatic in her works of art, the grandeur of her public monuments, the number and splendor of her palaces, and most else that the ingenuity and ambition of man could attempt, she was but secondary in the glories of the hour.

Above was the firmament, gemmed with worlds, and sublime in immensity. Beneath lay the broad expanse of the Adriatic, endless to the eye, tranquil as the vault it reflected, and luminous with its borrowed light. Here and there a low island, reclaimed from the sea by the patient toil of a thousand years, dotted the Lagunes, burthened with the group of some conventual dwellings, or picturesque with the modest roofs of a hamlet of the fishermen. Neither oar, nor song, nor laugh, nor flap of sail, nor jest of mariner, disturbed the stillness. All in the near view was clothed in midnight loveliness, and all in the distance bespoke the solemnity of nature at peace. The city and the Lagunes, the gulf and the dreamy Alps, the interminable plain of Lombardy, and the blue void of heaven, lay alike, in a common and grand repose.

There suddenly appeared a gondola. It issued from among the watery channels of the town, and glided upon the vast bosom of the bay, noiseless as the fancied progress of a spirit. A practised and nervous arm guided its movement, which was unceasing and rapid. So swift indeed was the passage of the boat, as to denote pressing haste on the part of the solitary individual it contained. It held the direction of the Adriatic, steering between one of the more southern outlets of the bay and the well-known island of St. Giorgio. For half an hour the exertions of the gondolier were unrelaxed, though his eye was often cast behind him, as if he distrusted pursuit; and as often did he gaze ahead, betraying an anxious desire to reach some object that was yet invisible. When a wide reach of water lay between him and the town, however, he permitted his oar to rest, and he lent all his faculties to a keen and anxious search.

A small dark spot was discovered on the water still nearer to the sea. The oar of the gondolier dashed the element behind him, and his boat again glided away, so far altering its course as to show that all indecision was now ended. The darker spot was shortly beheld quivering in the rays of the moon, and it soon assumed the form and dimensions of a boat at anchor. Again the gondolier ceased his efforts, and he leaned forward, gazing intently at this undefined object, as if he would aid his powers of sight by the sympathy of his other faculties. Just then the notes of music came softly across the Lagunes. The voice was feeble even to trembling, but it had the sweetness of tone and the accuracy of execution which belong so peculiarly to Venice. It was the solitary man, in the distant boat, indulging in the song of a fisherman. The strains were sweet, and the intonations plaintive to melancholy. The air was common to all who plied the oar in the canals, and familiar to the ear of the listener. He waited until the close of a verse had died away, and then he answered with a strain of his own. The alternate parts were thus maintained until the music ceased, by the two singing a final verse in chorus.

When the song was ended, the oar of the gondolier stirred the water again, and he was quickly by the other's side.

"Thou art busy with thy hook betimes, Antonio," said he who had just arrived, as he stepped into the boat of the old fisherman already so well known to the reader. "There are men that an interview with the Council of Three would have sent to their prayers and a sleepless bed."

"There is not a chapel in Venice, Jacopo, in which a sinner may so well lay bare his soul as in this. I have been here on the empty Lagunes, alone with God, having the gates of Paradise open before my eyes."

"One like thee hath no need of images to quicken his devotion."

"I see the image of my Savior, Jacopo, in those bright stars, that moon, the blue heavens, the misty bank of mountain, the waters on which we float, ay, even in my own sinking form, as in all which has come from His wisdom and power. I have prayed much since the moon has risen."

"And is habit so strong in thee, that thou thinkest of God and thy sins, while thou anglest?"

"The poor must toil and the sinful must pray. My thoughts have dwelt so much of late on the boy, that I have forgotten to provide myself with food. If I fish later or earlier than common, 'tis because a man cannot live on grief."

"I have bethought me of thy situation, honest Antonio; here is that which will support life and raise thy courage. See," added the Bravo, stretching forth an arm into his own gondola, from which he drew a basket, "here is bread from Dalmatia, wine of Lower Italy, and figs from the Levant—eat, then, and be of cheer."

The fisherman threw a wistful glance at the viands, for hunger was making powerful appeals to the weakness of nature, but his hand did not relinquish its hold of the line, with which he still continued to angle.

"And these are thy gifts, Jacopo?" he asked in a voice that, spite of his resignation, betrayed the longings of appetite.

"Antonio, they are the offerings of one who respects thy courage and honors thy nature."

"Bought with his earnings?"

"Can it be otherwise?—I am no beggar, for the love of the saints, and few in Venice give unasked. Eat then, without fear; seldom wilt thou be more welcome."

"Take them away, Jacopo, if thou lovest me. Do not tempt me beyond what I can bear."

"How! art thou commanded to a penance?" hastily exclaimed the other.

"Not so—not so. It is long since I have found leisure or heart for the confessional."

"Then why refuse the gift of a friend? Remember thy years and necessities."

"I cannot feed on the price of blood!"

The hand of the Bravo was withdrawn, as if repelled by an electric touch. The action caused the rays of the moon to fall athwart his kindling eye, and firm as Antonio was in honesty and principle, he felt the blood creep to his heart, as he encountered the fierce and sudden glance of his companion. A long pause succeeded, during which the fisherman diligently plied his line, though utterly regardless of the object for which it had been cast.

"I have said it, Jacopo," he added, at length, "and tongue of mine shall not belie the thought of my heart. Take away thy food then, and forget all that is past; for what I have said hath not been said in scorn, but out of regard to my own soul. Thou knowest how I have sorrowed for the boy, but next to his loss I could mourn over thee—ay, more bitterly than over any other of the fallen!"

The hard breathing of the Bravo was audible, but still he spoke not.

"Jacopo," continued the anxious fisherman, "do not mistake me. The pity of the suffering and poor is not like the scorn of the rich and worldly. If I touch a sore, I do not bruise it with my heel. Thy present pain is better than the greatest of all thy former joys."

"Enough, old man," said the other in a smothered voice; "thy words are forgotten. Eat without fear, for the offering is bought with earnings as pure as the gleanings of a mendicant friar."

"I will trust to the kindness of St. Anthony and the fortune of my hook," simply returned Antonio. " 'Tis common for us of the Lagunes to go to a supperless bed: take away the basket, good Jacopo, and let us speak of other things."

The Bravo ceased to press his food upon the fisherman. Laying aside his basket, he sat brooding over what had occurred.

"Hast thou come thus far for naught else, good Jacopo?" demanded the old man, willing to weaken the shock of his refusal.

The question appeared to restore Jacopo to a recollection of his errand. He stood erect, and looked about him, for more than a minute, with a keen eye and an entire intentness of purpose. The look in the direction of the city was longer and more earnest than those thrown toward the sea and the main, nor was it withdrawn, until an involuntary start betrayed equally surprise and alarm.

"Is there not a boat, here, in a line with the tower of the campanile?" he asked quickly, pointing towards the city.

"It so seems. It is early for my comrades to be abroad, but the draughts have not been heavy of late, and the revelry of yesterday drew many of our people from their toil. The patricians must eat, and the poor must labor, or both would die."

The Bravo slowly seated himself, and he looked with concern into the countenance of his companion.

"Art thou long here, Antonio?"

"But an hour. When they turned us away from the palace, thou knowest that I told thee of my necessities. There is not, in common, a more certain spot on the Lagunes than this, and yet have I long played the line in vain. The trial of hunger is hard, but, like all other trials, it must be borne. I have prayed to my patron thrice, and sooner or later he will listen to my wants. Thou art used to the manners of these masked nobles, Jacopo; dost thou think them likely to hearken to reason? I hope I did the cause no wrong for want of breeding, but I spoke them fair and plainly as fathers and men with hearts."

"As senators they have none. Thou little understandest, Antonio, the distinctions of these patricians. In the gaiety of their palaces, and among the companions of their pleasures, none will speak you fairer of humanity and justice—ay—even of God! But when met to discuss what they call the interests of St. Mark, there is not a rock on the coldest peak of yonder Alp, with less humanity, or a wolf among their valleys more heartless!"

"Thy words are strong, Jacopo—I would not do injustice even to those who have done me this wrong. The senators are men, and God has given all feelings and nature alike."

"The gift is then abused. Thou hast felt the want of thy daily assistant, fisherman, and thou hast sorrowed for thy child; for thee it is easy to enter into another's grief; but the senators know nothing of suffering. Their children are not dragged to the galleys, their hopes are never destroyed by laws coming from hard taskmasters, nor are their tears shed for sons ruined by being made companions of the dregs of the republic. They will talk of public virtue and services to the state, but in their own cases they mean the virtue of renown, and services that bring with them honors and rewards. The wants of the state is their conscience, though they take heed those wants shall do themselves no harm."

"Jacopo, Providence itself hath made a difference in men. One is large, another small; one weak, another strong; one wise, another foolish. At what Providence hath done, we should not murmur."

"Providence did not make the senate; 'tis an invention of man. Mark me, Antonio, thy language hath given offence, and thou art not safe in Venice. They will pardon all but complaints against their justice. That is too true to be forgiven."

"Can they wish to harm one who seeks his own child?"

"If thou wert great and respected, they would undermine thy fortune and character, ere thou should'st put their system in danger—as thou art weak and poor, they will do thee some direct injury, unless thou art moderate. Before all, I warn thee that their system must stand!"

"Will God suffer this?"

"We may not enter into His secrets," returned the Bravo, devoutly crossing himself. "Did His reign end with this world, there might be injustice in suffering the wicked to triumph, but, as it is, we—Yon boat approaches fast! I little like its air and movements."

"They are not fishermen, truly, for there are many oars and a canopy!"

"It is a gondola of the state!" exclaimed Jacopo, rising and stepping into his own boat, which he cast loose from that of his companion, when he stood in evident doubt as to his future proceedings. "Antonio, we should do well to row away."

"Thy fears are natural," said the unmoved fisherman, "and 'tis a thousand pities that there is cause for them. There is yet time for one skilful as thou to outstrip the fleetest gondola on the canals."

"Quick, lift thy anchor, old man, and depart,—my eye is sure. I know the boat."

"Poor Jacopo! what a curse is a tender conscience! Thou hast been kind to me in my need, and if prayers, from a sincere heart, can do thee service, thou shalt not want them."

"Antonio!" cried the other, causing his boat to whirl away, and then pausing an instant like a man undecided—"I can stay no longer—trust them not—they are false as fiends—there is no time to lose—I must away."

The fisherman murmured an ejaculation of pity, as he waved a hand, in adieu!

"Holy St. Anthony, watch over my own child, lest he come to some such miserable life!" he added, in an audible prayer—"There hath been good seed cast on a rock, in that youth, for a warmer or kinder heart is not in man. That one like Jacopo should live by striking the assassin's blow!"

The near approach of the strange gondola now attracted the whole attention of the old man. It came swiftly towards him, impelled by six strong oars, and his eye turned feverishly in the direction of the fugitive. Jacopo, with a readiness that necessity and long practice rendered nearly instinctive, had taken a direction which blended his wake in a line with one of those bright streaks that the moon drew on the water, and which, by dazzling the eye, effectually concealed the objects within its width. When the fisherman saw that the Bravo had disappeared, he smiled and seemed at ease.

"Ay, let them come here," he said; "it will give Jacopo more time. I doubt not the poor fellow hath struck a blow, since quitting the palace, that the council will not forgive! The sight of gold hath been too strong, and he hath offended those who have so long borne with him. God forgive me, that I have had communion with such a man! But when the heart is heavy, the pity of even a dog will warm our feelings. Few care for me, now, or the friendship of such as he could never have been welcome."

Antonio ceased, for the gondola of the state came with a rushing noise to the side of his own boat, where it was suddenly stopped by a backward sweep of the oars. The water was still in ebullition, when a form passing into the gondola of the fisherman, the larger boat shot away again, to the distance of a few hundred feet, and remained at rest.

Antonio witnessed this movement in silent curiosity; but when he saw the gondoliers of the state lying on their oars, he glanced his eye again furtively in the direction of Jacopo, saw that all was safe, and faced his companion with confidence. The brightness of the moon enabled him to distinguish the dress and aspect of a barefooted Carmelite. The latter seemed more confounded than his companion, by the rapidity of the movement, and the novelty of his situation. Notwithstanding his confusion, however, an evident look of wonder crossed his mortified features when he first beheld the humble condition, the thin and whitened locks, and the general air and bearing of the old man with whom he now found himself.

"Who art thou?" escaped him, in the impulse of surprise.

"Antonio of the Lagunes! A fisherman that owes much to St. Anthony, for favors little deserved."

"And why hath one like thee fallen beneath the senate's displeasure!"

"I am honest and ready to do justice to others. If that offend the great, they are men more to be pitied than envied."

"The convicted are always more disposed to believe themselves unfortunate than guilty. The error is fatal, and it should be eradicated from the mind, lest it lead to death."

"Go tell this to the patricians. They have need of plain counsel, and a warning from the church."

"My son, there is pride and anger, and a perverse heart in thy replies. The sins of the senators—and as they are men, they are not without spot—can in no manner whiten thine own. Though an unjust sentence should condemn one to punishment, it leaves the offences against God in their native deformity. Men may pity him who hath wrongfully undergone the anger of the world, but the church will only pronounce pardon on him who confesseth his errors, with a sincere admission of their magnitude."

"Have you come, father, to shrive a penitent?"

"Such is my errand. I lament the occasion, and if what I fear be true, still more must I regret that one so aged should have brought his devoted head beneath the arm of justice."

Antonio smiled, and again he bent his eyes along that dazzling streak of light which had swallowed up the gondola and the person of the Bravo.

"Father," he said, when a long and earnest look was ended, "there can be little harm in speaking truth to one of thy holy office. They have told thee there was a criminal here in the Lagunes who hath provoked the anger of St. Mark?"

"Thou art right."

"It is not easy to know when St. Mark is pleased, or when he is not," continued Antonio, plying his line with indifference, "for the very man he now seeks has he long tolerated; ay, even in presence of the doge. The senate hath its reasons which lie beyond the reach of the ignorant, but it would have been better

195

for the soul of the poor youth, and more seemly for the republic, had it turned a discouraging countenance on his deeds from the first."

"Thou speakest of another!—thou art not then the criminal they seek?"

"I am a sinner, like all born of woman, reverend Carmelite, but my hand hath never held any other weapon than the good sword with which I struck the infidel. There was one lately here that, I grieve to add, cannot say this!"

"And he is gone?"

"Father, you have your eyes, and you can answer that question for yourself. He is gone; though he is not far, still is he beyond the reach of the swiftest gondola in Venice, praised be St. Mark!"

The Carmelite bowed his head, where he was seated, and his lips moved, either in prayer or in thanksgiving.

"Are you sorry, monk, that a sinner has escaped?"

"Son, I rejoice that this bitter office hath passed from me, while I mourn that there should be a spirit so depraved as to require it. Let us summon the servants of the republic, and inform them that their errand is useless."

"Be not of haste, good father. The night is gentle, and these hirelings sleep on their oars, like gulls in the Lagunes. The youth will have more time for repentance, should he be undisturbed."

The Carmelite, who had arisen, instantly reseated himself, like one actuated by a strong impulse.

"I thought he had already been far beyond pursuit," he muttered, unconsciously apologizing for his apparent haste.

"He is over bold, and I fear he will row back to the canals, in which case you might meet nearer to the city—or, there may be more gondolas of the state out—in short, father, thou wilt be more certain to escape hearing the confession of a Bravo, by listening to that of a fisherman, who has long wanted an occasion to acknowledge his sins."

Men who ardently wish the same result require few words to understand each other. The Carmelite took, intuitively, the meaning of his companion, and throwing back his cowl, a movement that exposed the countenance of Father Anselmo, he prepared to listen to the confession of the old man.

"Thou art a Christian, and one of thy years hath not to learn the state of mind that becometh a penitent," said the monk, when each was ready.

"I am a sinner, father; give me counsel and absolution, that I may have hope."

"Thy will be done—thy prayer's heard—approach and kneel."

Antonio, who had fastened his line to his seat, and disposed of his net with habitual care, now crossed himself devoutly, and took his station before the Carmelite. His acknowledgments of error then began. Much mental misery clothed the language and ideas of the fisherman with a dignity that his auditor had not been accustomed to find in men of his class. A spirit so long chastened by suffering had become elevated and noble. He related his hopes for the boy, the manner in which they had been blasted by the unjust and selfish policy of the state, of his different efforts to procure the release of his grandson, and his bold expedients at the regatta and the fancied nuptials with the Adriatic. When he had thus prepared the Carmelite to understand the origin of his sinful passions, which it was now his duty to expose, he spoke of those passions themselves, and of their influence on a mind that was ordinarily at peace with mankind. The tale was told simply and without reserve, but in a manner to inspire respect, and to awaken powerful sympathy in him who heard it.

"And these feelings thou didst indulge against the honored and powerful of Venice!" demanded the monk, affecting a severity he could not feel.

"Before my God do I confess the sin! In bitterness of heart I cursed them; for to me they seemed men without feeling for the poor, and heartless as the marbles of their own palaces."

"Thou knowest that to be forgiven, thou must forgive. Dost thou, at peace with all of earth, forget this wrong, and canst thou in charity with thy fellows, pray to Him who died for the race, in behalf of those who have injured thee?"

Antonio bowed his head on his naked breast, and he seemed to commune with his soul.

"Father," he said, in a rebuked tone, "I hope I do."

"Thou must not trifle with thyself to thine own perdition. There is an eye in yon vault above us which pervades space, and which looks into the inmost secrets of the heart. Canst thou pardon the error of the patricians, in a contrite spirit for thine own sins?"

"Holy Maria, pray for them, as I now ask mercy in their behalf!—Father, they are forgiven."

"Amen!"

The Carmelite arose and stood over the kneeling Antonio, with the whole of his benevolent countenance illuminated by the moon. Stretching his arms towards the stars, he pronounced the absolution in a voice that was touched with pious fervor. The upward expectant eye, with the withered lineaments of the fisherman, and the holy calm of the monk, formed a picture of resignation and hope that angels would have loved to witness.

"Amen! amen!" exclaimed Antonio, as he arose, crossing himself; "St. Anthony and the Virgin aid me to keep these resolutions!"

"I will not forget thee, my son, in the offices of Holy Church. Receive my benediction, that I may depart."

Antonio again bowed his knee, while the Carmelite firmly pronounced the words of peace. When this last office was performed, and a decent interval of mutual but silent prayer had passed, a signal was given to summon the gondola of the state. It came rowing down with great force, and was instantly at their side. Two men passed into the boat of Antonio, and with officious zeal assisted the monk to resume his place in that of the republic.

"Is the penitent shrived?" half whispered one, seemingly the superior of the two.

"Here is an error. He thou seekst has escaped. This aged man is a fisherman named Antonio, and one who cannot have gravely offended St. Mark. The Bravo hath passed toward the island of San Giorgio, and must be sought elsewhere."

The officer released the person of the monk, who passed quickly beneath the canopy, and he turned to cast a hasty glance at the features of the fisherman. The rubbing of a rope was audible, and the anchor of Antonio was lifted by a sudden jerk. A heavy plashing of the water followed, and the two boats shot away together, obedient to a violent effort of the crew. The gondola of the state exhibited its usual number of gondoliers bending to their toil, with its dark and hearse-like canopy, but that of the fisherman was empty!

The sweep of the oars and the plunge of the body of Antonio had been blended in a common wash of the surge. When the fisherman came to the surface, after his fall, he was alone in the centre of the vast but tranquil sheet of water. There might have been a glimmering of hope, as he arose from the darkness of the sea to the bright beauty of that moonlit night. But the sleeping domes were too far for human strength, and the gondolas were sweeping madly towards the town. He turned, and swimming feebly, for hunger and previous exertion had undermined his strength, he bent his eye on the dark spot which he had constantly recognized as the boat of the Bravo.

Jacopo had not ceased to watch the interview, with the utmost intentness of his faculties. Favored by position, he could see without being distinctly visible. He saw the Carmelite pronouncing the absolution, and he witnessed the approach of the larger boat. He heard a plunge heavier than that of falling oars, and he saw the gondola of Antonio towing away empty. The crew of the republic had scarcely swept the Lagunes with their oar-blades, before his own stirred the water.

"Jacopo!—Jacopo!" came fearfully and faintly to his ears.

The voice was known and the occasion thoroughly understood. The cry of distress was succeeded by the rush of the water, as it piled before the beak of the Bravo's gondola. The sound of the parted element was like the sighing of a breeze. Ripples and bubbles were left behind, as the driven scud floats past the stars, and all those muscles which had once before that day been so finely developed in the race of the gondoliers were now expanded, seemingly in twofold volumes. Energy and skill were in every stroke, and the dark spot came down the streak of light, like the swallow touching the water with its wing.

"Hither, Jacopo—thou steerest wide!"

The beak of the gondola turned, and the glaring eye of the Bravo caught a glimpse of the fisherman's head.

"Quickly, good Jacopo,—I fail!"

The murmuring of the water again drowned the stifled words. The efforts of the oar were frenzied, and at each stroke the light gondola appeared to rise from its element.

"Jacopo—hither—dear Jacopo!"

"The mother of God aid thee, fisherman!—I come."

"Jacopo—the boy!—the boy!"

The water gurgled; an arm was visible in the air, and it disappeared. The gondola drove upon the spot where the limb had just been visible, and a backward stroke that caused the ashen blade to bend like a reed laid the trembling boat motionless. The furious action threw the Lagune into ebullition, but, when the foam subsided, it lay calm as the blue and peaceful vault it reflected.

"Antonio!"—burst from the lips of the Bravo.

A frightful silence succeeded the call. There was neither answer nor human form. Jacopo compressed the handle of his oar with fingers of iron, and his own breathing caused him to start. On every side he bent a frenzied eye, and on every side he beheld the profound repose of that treacherous element which is so terrible in its wrath. Like the human heart, it seemed to sympathize with the tranquil beauty of the midnight view; but, like the human heart, it kept its own fearful secrets.

END VOLUME 1

CHAPTER XVI

"Yet a few days and dream-perturbed nights,
And I shall slumber well—but where?—no matter.
Adieu, my Angiolina."

Marino Faliero

WHEN the Carmelite re-entered the apartment of Donna Violetta, his face was covered with the hue of death, and his limbs with difficulty supported him to a chair. He scarcely observed that Don Camillo Monforte was still present, nor did he note the brightness and joy which glowed in the eyes of the ardent Violetta. Indeed his appearance was at first unseen by the happy lovers, for the Lord of St. Agata had succeeded in wresting the secret from the breast of his mistress, if that may be called a secret which Italian character had scarcely struggled to retain, and he had crossed the room before even the more tranquil look of the Donna Florinda rested on his person.

"Thou art ill!" exclaimed the governess. "Father Anselmo hath not been absent without grave cause!"

The monk threw back his cowl for air, and the act discovered the deadly paleness of his features. But his eye, charged with a meaning of horror, rolled over the faces of those who drew around him, as if he struggled with memory to recall their persons.

"Ferdinando! Father Anselmo!" cried the Donna Florinda, correcting the unbidden familiarity, though she could not command the anxiety of her rebel features; "speak to us—thou art suffering!"

"Ill at heart, Florinda."

"Deceive us not—haply thou hast more evil tidings—Venice—"

"Is a fearful state!"

"Why hast thou quitted us?—why, in a moment of so much importance to our pupil—a moment that may prove of the last influence on her happiness—hast thou been absent for a long hour?"

Violetta turned a surprised and unconscious glance towards the clock, but she spoke not.

"The servants of the state had need of me," returned the monk, easing the pain of his spirit by a groan.

"I understand thee, father;—thou hast shrived a penitent?"

"Daughter, I have: and fewer depart more at peace with God and their fellows!"

Donna Florinda murmured a short prayer for the soul of the dead, piously crossing herself as she concluded. Her example was imitated by her pupil, and even the lips of Don Camillo moved, while his head was bowed by the side of his fair companion, in seeming reverence.

" 'Twas a just end, father?" demanded Donna Florinda.

"It was an unmerited one!" cried the monk, with fervor, "or there is no faith in man. I have witnessed the death of one who was better fitted to live, as happily he was better fitted to die, than those who pronounced his doom. What a fearful state is Venice!"

"And such are they who are masters of thy person, Violetta," said Don Camillo; "to these midnight murderers will thy happiness be consigned! Tell us, father, does thy sad tragedy touch in any manner on the interests of this fair being? for we are encircled here by mysteries that are as incomprehensible, while they are nearly as fearful, as fate itself."

The monk looked from one to the other, and a more human expression began to appear in his countenance.

"Thou art right," he said; "such are the men who mean to dispose of the person of our pupil. Holy St. Mark, pardon the prostitution of his revered name, and shield her with the virtue of his prayers!"

"Father, are we worthy to know more of that thou hast witnessed?"

"The secrets of the confessional are sacred, my son; but this hath been a disclosure to cover the living, and not the dead, with shame."

"I see the hand of those up above in this!" for so most spoke of the Council of Three. "They have tampered with my right, for years, to suit their selfish purposes, and, to my shame must I own it, they have driven me to a submission, in order to obtain justice, that as ill accords with my feelings as with my character."

202

"Nay, Camillo, thou art incapable of this injustice to thyself!"

" 'Tis a fearful government, dearest, and its fruits are equally pernicious to the ruler and the subject. It hath, of all other dangers the greatest, the curse of secrecy on its intentions, its acts, and its responsibilities!"

"Thou sayest true, my son; there is no security against oppression and wrong in a state, but the fear of God, or the fear of man. Of the first, Venice hath none, for too many souls share the odium of her sins; and as for the last, her deeds are hid from their knowledge."

"We speak boldly, for those who live beneath her laws," observed Donna Florinda, glancing a look timidly around her. "As we can neither change nor amend the practices of the state, better that we should be silent."

"If we cannot alter the power of the council, we may elude it," hastily answered Don Camillo, though he too dropped his voice, and assured himself of their security, by closing the casement, and casting his eyes towards the different doors of the room. "Are you assured of the fidelity of the menials, Donna Florinda?"

"Far from it, Signore; we have those who are of ancient service and of tried character; but we have those who are named by the senator, Gradenigo, and who are doubtless no other than the agents of the state."

"In this manner do they pry into the privacy of all! I am compelled to entertain, in my palace, varlets that I know to be their hirelings; and yet do I find it better to seem unconscious of their views, lest they environ me in a manner that I cannot even suspect. Think you, father, that my presence here hath escaped the spies?"

"It would be to hazard much were we to rely on such security. None saw us enter, as I think, for we used the secret gate and the more private entrance; but who is certain of being unobserved when every fifth eye is that of a mercenary?"

The terrified Violetta laid her hand on the arm of her lover. "Even now, Camillo," she said, "thou mayest be observed, and secretly devoted to punishment!"

"If seen, doubt it not: St. Mark will never pardon so bold an interference with his pleasure. And yet, sweetest Violetta, to gain thy favor, this risk is nothing; nor will a far greater hazard turn me from my purpose."

"These inexperienced and confiding spirits have taken advantage of my absence to communicate more freely than was discreet," said the Carmelite, in the manner of one who foresaw the answer.

"Father, nature is too strong for the weak preventives of prudence."

The brow of the monk became clouded. His companions watched the workings of his mind, as they appeared in a countenance that in common was so benevolent, though always sad. For a few moments none broke the silence.

The Carmelite at length demanded, raising his troubled look to the countenance of Don Camillo—

"Hast thou duly reflected on the consequences of this rashness, son? What dost thou purpose, in thus braving the anger of the republic, and in setting at defiance her arts, her secret means of intelligence, and her terrors?"

"Father, I have reflected as all of my years reflect, when in heart and soul they love. I have brought myself to feel that any misery would be happiness compared to the loss of Violetta, and that no risk can exceed the reward of gaining her favor. Thus much for the first of thy questions—for the last I can only say that I am too much accustomed to the wiles of the senate to be a novice in the means of counteracting them."

"There is but one language for youth, when seduced by that pleasing delusion which paints the future with hues of gold. Age and experience may condemn it, but the weakness will continue to prevail in all, until life shall appear in its true colors. Duke of Sant' Agata, though a noble of high lineage and illustrious name, and though lord of many vassals, thou art not a power—thou canst not declare thy palace in Venice a fortress, nor send a herald to the doge with defiance."

"True, reverend monk; I cannot do this; nor would it be well for him who could, to trust his fortune on so reckless a risk. But the states of St. Mark do not cover the earth—we can fly."

"The senate hath a long arm; and it hath a thousand secret hands."

"None know it better than I; still it does no violence without motive; the faith of their ward irretrievably mine, the evil, as respects them, becomes irreparable."

"Think'st thou so! Means would quickly be found to separate

you. Believe not that Venice would be thwarted of its design so easily; the wealth of a house like this would purchase many an unworthy suitor, and thy right would be disregarded, or haply denied."

"But, father, the ceremony of the church may not be despised!" exclaimed Violetta; "it comes from heaven and is sacred."

"Daughter, I say it with sorrow, but the great and the powerful find means even to set aside that venerable and holy sacrament. Thine own gold would serve to seal thy misery."

"This might arrive, father, were we to continue within the grasp of St. Mark," interrupted the Neapolitan; "but once beyond his borders, 'twould be a bold interference with the right of a foreign state to lay hand on our persons. More than this, I have a castle, in St. Agata, that will defy their most secret means, until events might happen which should render it more prudent for them to desist than to persevere."

"This reason hath force wert thou within the walls of St. Agata, instead of being, as thou art, among the canals."

"Here is one of Calabria, a vassal born of mine, a certain Stefano Milano, the padrone of a Sorrentine felucca, now lying in the port; the man is in strict amity with my own gondolier— he who was third in this day's race. Art thou ill, father, that thou appearest troubled?"

"Proceed with thy expedient," answered the monk, motioning that he wished not to be observed.

"My faithful Gino reports that this Stefano is on the canals, on some errand of the republic, as he thinks, for though the mariner is less disposed to familiarity than is wont, he hath let drop hints that lead to such a conclusion—the felucca is ready, from hour to hour, to put upon the sea, and doubt not the padrone would rather serve his natural lord than these double-dealing miscreants of the senate. I can pay as well as they, if served to my pleasure, and I can punish too, when offended."

"There is reason in this, Signore, wert thou beyond the wiles of this mysterious city. But in what manner canst thou embark, without drawing the notice of those, who doubtless watch our movements, on thy person?"

"There are maskers on the canals at all hours, and if Venice be so impertinent in her system of watchfulness, thou knowest, father, that, without extraordinary motive, that disguise is sacred.

Without this narrow privilege, the town would not be habitable a day."

"I fear the result," observed the hesitating monk, while it was evident, from the thoughtfulness of his countenance, that he calculated the chances of the adventure. "If known and arrested, we are all lost!"

"Trust me, father, that thy fortune shall not be forgotten, even in that unhappy issue. I have an uncle, as you know, high in the favor of the pontiff, and who wears the scarlet hat. I pledge to you the honor of a cavalier, all my interest with this relative, to gain such intercession from the church as shall weaken the blow to her servant."

The features of the Carmelite flushed, and, for the first time, the ardent young noble observed around his ascetic mouth an expression of worldly pride.

"Thou hast unjustly rated my apprehensions, Lord of St. Agata," he said; "I fear not for myself, but for others. This tender and lovely child hath not been confided to my care, without creating a parental solicitude in her behalf, and"—he paused, and seemed to struggle with himself—"I have too long known the mild and womanly virtues of Donna Florinda, to witness, with indifference, her exposure to a near and fearful danger. Abandon our charge, we cannot; nor do I see in what manner, as prudent and watchful guardians, we may in any manner consent to this risk. Let us hope that they who govern will yet consult the honor and happiness of Donna Violetta."

"That were to hope the winged lion would become a lamb, or the dark and soulless senate a community of self-mortifying and godly Carthusians! No, reverend monk, we must seize the happy moment, and none is likely to be more fortunate than this, or trust our hopes to a cold and calculating policy that disregards all motives but its own object. An hour, nay, half the time, would suffice to apprize the mariner, and ere the morning light, we might see the domes of Venice sinking into their own hated Lagunes."

"These are the plans of confident youth, quickened by passion. Believe me, son, it is not easy as thou imaginest, to mislead the agents of the police. This palace could not be quitted, the felucca entered, or any one of the many necessary steps hazarded, without drawing upon us their eyes. Hark!—I hear the wash of oars—a gondola is even now at the water gate!"

Donna Florinda went hastily to the balcony, and as quickly

returned to report that she had seen an officer of the republic enter the palace. There was no time to lose, and Don Camillo was again urged to conceal himself in the little oratory. This necessary caution had hardly been observed before the door of the room opened, and the privileged messenger of the senate announced his own appearance. It was the very individual who had presided at the fearful execution of the fisherman, and who had already announced the cessation of the Signor Gradenigo's powers. His eye glanced suspiciously around the room, as he entered, and the Carmelite trembled in every limb, at the look which encountered his own. But all immediate apprehensions vanished, when the usual artful smile, with which he was wont to soften his disagreeable communications, took place of the momentary expression of a vague and an habitual suspicion.

"Noble lady," he said, bowing with deference to the rank of her he addressed, "you may learn by this assiduity, on the part of their servant, the interest which the senate takes in your welfare. Anxious to do you pleasure, and ever attentive to the wishes of one so young, it hath been decided to give you the amusement and variety of another scene, at a season when the canals of our city become disagreeable, from their warmth and the crowds which live in the air. I am sent to request you will make such preparations, as may befit your convenience during a few months' residence in a purer atmosphere, and that this may be done speedily; as your journey, always to prevent discomfort to yourself, will commence before the rising of the sun."

"This is short notice, Signore, for a female about to quit the dwelling of her ancestors!"

"St. Mark suffers his love and parental care to overlook the vain ceremonies of form. It is thus the parent dealeth with the child. There is little need of unusual notice, since it will be the business of the government to see all that is necessary dispatched to the residence which is to be honored with the presence of so illustrious a lady."

"For myself, Signore, little preparation is needed. But I fear the train of servitors that befit my condition will require more leisure for their arrangements."

"Lady, that embarrassment hath been foreseen, and to remove it, the council hath decided to supply you with the only attendant you will require, during an absence from the city which will be so short."

"How, Signore! am I to be separated from my people?"

"From the hired menials of your palace, lady, to be confided to those who will serve your person, from a nobler motive."

"And my maternal friend—my ghostly adviser?"

"They will be permitted to repose from their trusts, during your absence."

An exclamation from Donna Florinda, and an involuntary movement of the monk, betrayed their mutual concern. Donna Violetta suppressed the exhibition of her own resentment, and of her wounded affections, by a powerful effort, in which she was greatly sustained by her pride; but she could not entirely conceal the anguish of another sort that was seated in her eye.

"Do I understand that this prohibition extends to her who, in common, serves my person?"

"Signora, such are my instructions."

"Is it expected that Violetta Tiepolo will do these menial offices for herself?"

"Signora, no. A most excellent and agreeable attendant has been provided for that duty. Annina," he continued, approaching the door, "thy noble mistress is impatient to see thee."

As he spoke, the daughter of the wine seller appeared. She wore an air of assumed humility, but it was accompanied by a secret mien that betrayed independence of the pleasure of her new mistress.

"And this damsel is to be my nearest confidant!" exclaimed Donna Violetta, after studying the artful and demure countenance of the girl, a moment, with a dislike she did not care to conceal.

"Such hath been the solicitude of your illustrious guardians, lady. As the damsel is instructed in all that is necessary, I will intrude no longer, but take my leave, recommending that you improve the hours, which are now few, between this and the rising sun, that you may profit by the morning breeze in quitting the city."

The officer glanced another look around the room, more, however, through habitual caution than any other reason, bowed, and departed.

A profound and sorrowful silence succeeded. Then the apprehension that Don Camillo might mistake their situation and appear, flashed upon the mind of Violetta, and she hastened to apprize him of the danger, by speaking to the new attendant. wardrobe."

"Thou hast served before this, Annina?" she asked so loud as to permit the words to be heard in the oratory.

"Never a lady so beautiful and illustrious, Signora. But I hope to make myself agreeable to one that I hear is kind to all around her."

"Thou art not new to the flattery of thy class; go then, and acquaint my ancient attendants with this sudden resolution, that I may not disappoint the council by tardiness. I commit all to thy care, Annina, since thou knowest the pleasure of my guardians—those without will furnish the means."

The girl lingered, and her watchful observers noted suspicion and hesitation in her reluctant manner of compliance. She obeyed, however, leaving the room with the domestic Donna Violetta summoned from the antechamber. The instant the door was closed behind her, Don Camillo was in the group, and the whole four stood regarding each other in a common panic.

"Canst thou still hesitate, father?" demanded the lover.

"Not a moment, my son, did I see the means of accomplishing flight."

"How! Thou wilt not then desert me!" exclaimed Violetta, kissing his hands in joy. "Nor thou, my second mother!"

"Neither," answered the governess, who possessed intuitive means of comprehending the resolutions of the monk; "we will go with thee, love, to the Castle of St. Agata, or to the dungeon of St. Mark."

"Virtuous and sainted Florinda, receive my thanks!" cried the reprieved Violetta, clasping her hands on her bosom, with an emotion in which piety and gratitude were mingled.—"Camillo, we await thy guidance."

"Refrain," observed the monk,—"a footstep—thy concealment."

Don Camillo was scarce hid from view, when Annina reappeared. She had the same suspicious manner of glancing her eye around as the official, and it would seem, by the idle question she put, that her entrance had some other object than the mere pretence which she made of consulting her new mistress's humor in the color of a robe.

"Do as thou wilt, girl," said Violetta, with impatience; "thou knowest the place of my intended retirement, and canst judge of the fitness of my attire. Hasten thy preparations, that I be not the cause of delay. Enrico, attend my new maid to the

Annina reluctantly withdrew, for she was far too much prac-

209

tised in wiles not to distrust this unexpected compliance with the will of the council, or not to perceive that she was admitted with displeasure to the discharge of her new duties. As the faithful domestic of Donna Violetta kept at her side, she was fain, however, to submit, and suffered herself to be led a few steps from the door. Suddenly pretending to recollect a new question, she returned with so much rapidity, as to be again in the room, before Enrico could anticipate the intention.

"Daughter, complete thy errands, and forbear to interrupt our privacy," said the monk, sternly.—"I am about to confess this penitent, who may pine long for the consolations of the holy office, ere we meet again. If thou hast not aught urgent, withdraw, ere thou seriously givest offence to the church."

The severity of the Carmelite's tone, and the commanding, though subdued gleaming of his eye, had the effect to awe the girl. Quailing before his look, and in truth startled at the risk she ran in offending against opinions so deeply seated in the minds of all, and from which her own superstitious habits were far from free, she muttered a few words of apology, and finally withdrew. There was another uneasy and suspicious glance thrown around her, however, before the door was closed. When they were once more alone, the monk motioned for silence to the impetuous Don Camillo, who could scarce restrain his impatience until the intruder departed.

"Son, be prudent," he said; "we are in the midst of treachery; in this unhappy city none know in whom they can confide."

"I think we are sure of Enrico," said the Donna Florinda, though the very doubts she affected not to feel lingered in the tones of her voice.

"It matters not, daughter.—He is ignorant of the presence of Don Camillo, and in that we are safe. Duke of Sant' Agata, if you can deliver us from these toils, we will accompany you."

A cry of joy was near bursting from the lips of Violetta; but obedient to the eye of the monk, she turned to her lover, as if to learn his decision. The expression of Don Camillo's face was the pledge of his assent. Without speaking, he wrote hastily, with a pencil, a few words on the envelope of a letter, and inclosing a piece of coin in its folds, he moved with a cautious step to the balcony. A signal was given, and all awaited in breathless silence the answer. Presently they heard the wash of the water, caused by the movement of a gondola beneath the window. Stepping forward again, Don Camillo dropped the paper with such precision, that he distinctly heard the fall of the coin in the bottom of the boat. The gondolier scarce raised his eyes to the balcony, but commencing an air much used on the canals, he swept onward, like one whose duty called for no haste.

"That has succeeded!" said Don Camillo, when he heard the song of Gino. "In an hour my agent will have secured the felucca, and all now depends on our own means of quitting the palace unobserved. My people will await us, shortly, and perhaps 'twould be well to trust openly to our speed in gaining the Adriatic."

"There is a solemn and necessary duty to perform," observed the monk;—"daughters, withdraw to your rooms, and occupy yourselves with the preparation necessary for your flight, which may readily be made to appear as intended to meet the senate's pleasure. In a few minutes I shall summon you hither, again."

Wondering, but obedient, the females withdrew. The Carmelite then made a brief but clear explanation of his intention. Don Camillo listened eagerly, and when the other had done speaking they retired together into the oratory. Fifteen minutes had not passed, before the monk reappeared, alone, and touched the bell which communicated with the closet of Violetta. Donna Florinda and her pupil were quickly in the room.

"Prepare thy mind for the confessional," said the priest, placing himself, with grave dignity, in that chair which he habitually used, when listening to the self-accusations and failings of his spiritual child.

The brow of Violetta paled and flushed again, as if there lay a heavy sin on her conscience. She turned an imploring look on her maternal monitor, in whose mild features she met an encouraging smile, and then, with a beating heart, though ill-collected for the solemn duty, but with a decision that the occasion required, she knelt on the cushion at the feet of the monk.

The murmured language of Donna Violetta was audible to none but him for whose paternal ear it was intended, and that dread Being whose just anger it was hoped it might lessen. But Don Camillo gazed, through the half-opened door of the chapel, on the kneeling form, the clasped hands, and the uplifted countenance of the beautiful penitent. As she proceeded with the acknowledgment of her errors, the flush on her cheek deepened,

211

and a pious excitement kindled in those eyes, which he had so lately seen glowing with a very different passion. The ingenuous and disciplined soul of Violetta was not so quickly disburthened of its load of sin as that of the more practised mind of the Lord of Sant' Agata. The latter fancied that he could trace in the movement of her lips the sound of his own name, and a dozen times during the confession, he thought he could even comprehend sentences of which he himself was the subject. Twice the good father smiled, involuntarily, and at each indiscretion, he laid a hand in affection on the bared head of the suppliant. But Violetta ceased to speak, and the absolution was pronounced, with a fervor that the remarkable circumstances in which they all stood did not fail to heighten.

When this portion of his duty was ended, the Carmelite entered the oratory. With steady hands he lighted the candles of the altar, and made the other dispositions for the mass. During this interval Don Camillo was at the side of his mistress, whispering with the warmth of a triumphant and happy lover. The governess stood near the door, watching for the sound of footsteps in the antechamber. The monk then advanced to the entrance of the little chapel, and was about to speak, when a hurried step from Donna Florinda arrested his words. Don Camillo had just time to conceal his person within the drapery of a window, before the door opened and Annina entered.

When the preparations of the altar and the solemn countenance of the priest first met her eye, the girl recoiled, with the air of one rebuked. But rallying her thoughts, with that readiness which had gained her the employment she filled, she crossed herself, reverently, and took a place apart, like one who, while she knew her station, wished to participate in the mysteries of the holy office.

"Daughter, none who commence this mass with us, can quit the presence, ere it be completed," observed the monk.

"Father, it is my duty to be near the person of my mistress, and it is a happiness to be near it on the occasion of this early matin."

The monk was embarrassed. He looked from one to the other, in indecision, and was about to frame some pretence to get rid of the intruder, when Don Camillo appeared in the middle of the room.

"Reverend monk, proceed," he said; " 'tis but another witness of my happiness."

212

While speaking, the noble touched the handle of his sword, significantly, with a finger, and cast a look at the half-petrified Annina which effectually controlled the exclamation that was about to escape her. The monk appeared to understand the terms of this silent compact; for with a deep voice he commenced the offices of the mass. The singularity of their situation, the important results of the act in which they were engaged, the impressive dignity of the Carmelite, and the imminent hazard which they all ran of exposure, together with the certainty of punishment for their daring to thwart the will of Venice, if betrayed, caused a deeper feeling, than that which usually pervades a marriage ceremony, to preside at nuptials thus celebrated. The youthful Violetta trembled at every intonation of the solemn voice of the monk, and towards the close, she leaned in helplessness on the arm of the man to whom she had just plighted her vows. The eye of the Carmelite kindled, as he proceeded with the office, however; and, long ere he had done, he had obtained such a command over the feelings of even Annina, as to hold her mercenary spirit in awe. The final union was pronounced, and the benediction given.

"Maria, of pure memory, watch over thy happiness, daughter!" said the monk, for the first time in his life saluting the fair brow of the weeping bride.—"Duke of Sant' Agata, may thy patron hear thy prayers, as thou provest kind to this innocent and confiding child!"

"Amen!—Ha!—we are not too soon united, my Violetta; I hear the sound of oars."

A glance from the balcony assured him of the truth of his words, and rendered it apparent that it had now become necessary to take the most decided step of all. A six-oared gondola, of a size suited to endure the waves of the Adriatic at that mild season, and with a pavilion of fit dimensions, stopped at the water gate of the palace.

"I wonder at this boldness!" exclaimed Don Camillo. "There must be no delay, lest some spy of the republic apprize the police. Away, dearest Violetta—away, Donna Florinda—Father, away!"

The governess and her charge passed swiftly into the inner rooms. In a minute, they returned bearing the caskets of Donna Violetta, and a sufficient supply of necessaries, for a short voyage. The instant they reappeared, all was ready; for Don Camillo had long held himself prepared for this decisive moment, and the self-denying Carmelite had little need of superfluities. It was no moment for unnecessary explanation or trivial objections.

"Our hope is in celerity," said Don Camillo; "secrecy is impossible."

He was still speaking, when the monk led the way from the room. Donna Florinda and the half-breathless Violetta followed; Don Camillo drew the arm of Annina under his own, and in a low voice bid her, at her peril, refuse to obey.

The long suite of outer rooms was passed, without meeting a single observer of the extraordinary movement. But when the fugitives entered the great hall that communicated with the principal stairs, they found themselves in the centre of a dozen menials of both sexes.

"Place," cried the Duke of Sant' Agata, whose person and voice were alike unknown to them. "Your mistress will breathe the air of the canals."

Wonder and curiosity were alive in every countenance, but suspicion and eager attention were uppermost in the features of many. The foot of Donna Violetta had scarcely touched the pavement of the lower hall, when several menials glided down the flight, and quitted the palace by its different outlets. Each sought those who engaged him in the service. One flew along the narrow streets of the islands, to the residents of the Signor Gradenigo; another sought his son; and one, ignorant of the person of him he served, actually searched an agent of Don Camillo, to impart a circumstance in which that noble was himself so conspicuous an actor. To such a pass of corruption had a double-dealing and mystery reduced the household of the fairest and richest in Venice! The gondola lay at the marble steps of the water gate, held against the stones by two of its crew. Don Camillo saw, at a glance, that the masked gondoliers had neglected none of the precautions he had prescribed, and he inwardly commended their punctuality. Each wore a short rapier at his girdle, and he fancied he could trace beneath the folds of their garments, evidence of the presence of the clumsy firearms in use at that period. These observations were made, while the Carmelite and Violetta entered the boat. Donna Florinda followed, and Annina was about to imitate her example, when she was arrested by the arm of Don Camillo.

"Thy service ends here," whispered the bridegroom. "Seek another mistress; in fault of a better, thou mayest devote thyself to Venice."

The little interruption caused Don Camillo to look backward, and, for a single moment, he paused to scrutinize the group of eyes that crowded the hall of the palace, at a respectful distance.

"Adieu, my friends!" he added; "Those among ye who love your mistress shall be remembered."

He would have said more, but a rude seizure of his arms caused him to turn hastily away. He was firm in the grasp of the two gondoliers who had landed. While he was yet in too much astonishment to struggle, Annina, obedient to a signal, darted past him and leaped into the boat. The oars fell into the water; Don Camillo was repelled by a violent shove backward into the hall, the gondoliers stepped lightly into their places, and the gondola swept away from the steps, beyond the power of him they left to follow.

"Gino!—miscreant!—what means this treachery?"

The moving of the parting gondola was accompanied by no other sound than the usual washing of the water. In speechless agony, Don Camillo saw the boat glide, swifter and swifter at each stroke of the oars, along the canal, and then, whirling round the angle of a palace, disappear.

Venice admitted not of pursuit like another city, for there was no passage along the canal taken by the gondola, but by water. Several of the boats used by the family lay within the piles on the great canal at the principal entrance, and Don Camillo was about to rush into one, and to seize its oars, with his own hands, when the usual sounds announced the approach of a gondola from the direction of the bridge that had so long served as a place of concealment to his own domestic. It soon issued from the obscurity, cast by the shadows of the houses, and proved to be a large gondola pulled, like the one which had just disappeared, by six masked gondoliers. The resemblance between the equipments of the two was so exact, that at first not only the wondering Camillo, but all the others present fancied the latter, by some extraordinary speed, had already made the tour of the adjoining palaces, and was once more approaching the private entrance of that of Donna Violetta.

"Gino!" cried the bewildered bridegroom.

"Signore mio?" answered the faithful domestic.

"Draw nearer, varlet. What meaneth this idle trifling, at a moment like this?"

Don Camillo leaped a fearful distance, and happily he reached the gondola. To pass the men and rush into the canopy needed but a moment; to perceive that it was empty was the work of a glance.

"Villains, have you dared to be false!" cried the confounded noble.

At that instant the clock of the city began to tell the hour of two, and it was only as that appointed signal sounded heavy and melancholy on the night air, that the undeceived Camillo got a certain glimpse of the truth.

"Gino," he said, repressing his voice, like one summoning a desperate resolution—"Are thy fellows true?"

"As faithful as your own vassals, Signore."

"And thou didst not fail to deliver the note to my agent?"

"He had it before the ink was dry, eccellenza."

"The mercenary villain!—He told thee where to find the gondola, equipped as I see it?"

"Signore, he did; and I do the man the justice to say that nothing is wanting, either to speed or comfort."

"Ay, he even deals in duplicates, so tender is his care!" muttered .Don Camillo, between his teeth.—"Pull away, men; your own safety and my happiness now depend on your arms. A thousand ducats if you equal my hopes—my just anger if you disappoint them!"

Don Camillo threw himself on the cushions as he spoke, in bitterness of heart, though he seconded his words by a gesture which bid the men proceed. Gino, who occupied the stern and managed the directing oar, opened a small window in the canopy, which communicated with the interior, and bent to take his master's directions as the boat sprang ahead. Rising from his stooping posture, the practised gondolier gave a sweep with his blade, which caused the sluggish element of the narrow canal to whirl in eddies, and then the gondola glided into the Great Canal, as if it obeyed an instinct.

CHAPTER XVII

"Why liest thou so on the green earth?
'Tis not the hour of slumber:—why so pale?"
                                        Cain

NOTWITHSTANDING his apparent decision, the Duke of Sant' Agata was completely at a loss in what manner to direct his future movements. That he had been duped, by one or more of the agents to whom he had been compelled to confide his necessary preparations for the flight he had meditated several days, was too certain to admit of his deceiving himself with the hopes that some unaccountable mistake was the cause of his loss. He saw, at once, that the senate was master of the person of his bride, and he too well knew its power, and its utter disregard of human obligations, when any paramount interest of the state was to be consulted, to doubt for an instant its willingness to use its advantage in any manner that was most likely to contribute to its own views. By the premature death of her uncle, Donna Violetta had become the heiress of vast estates in the dominions of the church, and a compliance with that jealous and arbitrary law of Venice, which commanded all of its nobles to dispose of any foreign possessions they might acquire, was only suspended on account of her sex, and, as has already been seen, with the hope of disposing of her hand in a manner that would prove more profitable to the republic. With this object still before them, and with the means of accomplishing it in their own hands, the bridegroom well knew that his marriage would not only be denied, but he feared the witnesses of the ceremony would be so disposed of, as to give little reason ever to expect embarrassment from their testimony. For himself, personally, he felt less apprehension, though he foresaw that he had furnished his opponents with an argument that was likely to defer to an indefinite period, if it did not entirely defeat, his claims to the disputed succession. But he had already made up his mind to this result, though it is probable that his passion for Violetta had not entirely blinded him to the fact, that her Roman seigniories would be no unequal

217

offset for the loss. He believed that he might possibly return to his palace with impunity, so far as any personal injury was concerned; for the great consideration he enjoyed in his native land, and the high interest he possessed at the court of Rome, were sufficient pledges that no open violence would be done him. The chief reason why his claim had been kept in suspense was the wish to profit by his near connexion with the favorite cardinal, and though he had never been able entirely to satisfy the ever-increasing demands of the council, in this respect, he thought it probable that the power of the Vatican would not be spared to save him from any very imminent personal hazard. Still he had given the state of Venice plausible reasons for severity, and liberty, just at that moment, was of so much importance, that he dreaded falling into the hands of the officials, as one of the greatest misfortunes which could momentarily overtake him. He so well knew the crooked policy of those with whom he had to deal, that he believed he might be arrested solely that the government could make an especial merit of his future release, under circumstances of so seeming gravity. His order to Gino, therefore, had been to pull down the principal passage toward the port.

Before the gondola, which sprung at each united effort of its crew like some bounding animal, entered among the shipping, its master had time to recover his self-possession, and to form some hasty plans for the future. Making a signal for the crew to cease rowing, he came from beneath the canopy. Notwithstanding the lateness of the hour, boats were plying on the water within the town, and the song was still audible on the canals. But among the mariners a general stillness prevailed, such as befitted their toil during the day, and their ordinary habits.

"Call the first idle gondolier of thy acquaintance hither, Gino," said Don Camillo, with assumed calmness; "I would question him."

In less than a minute he was gratified.

"Hast seen any strongly manned gondola plying, of late, in this part of the canal?" demanded Don Camillo, of the man they had stopped.

"None, but this of your own, Signore; which is the fastest of all that passed beneath the Rialto, in this day's regatta."

"How knowest thou, friend, aught of the speed of my boat?"

"Signore, I have pulled an oar on the canals of Venice six-

and-twenty years, and I do not remember to have seen a gondola move more swiftly on them than did this very boat but a few minutes ago, when it dashed among the feluccas, further down in the port, as if it were again running for the oar. Corpo di Bacco! There are rich wines in the palaces of the nobles, that men can give such life to wood!"

"Whither did we steer?" eagerly asked Don Camillo.

"Blessed San Teodoro! I do not wonder, eccellenza, that you ask that question, for though it is but a moment since, here I see you lying as motionless on the water as a floating weed!"

"Friend, here is silver—addio."

The gondolier swept slowly onward, singing a strain in honor of his bark, while the boat of Don Camillo darted ahead. Mistic, felucca, xebec,* brigantine, and three-masted ship, were apparently floating past them, as they shot through the maze of shipping, when Gino bent forward and drew the attention of his master to a large gondola, which was pulling with a lazy oar toward them, from the direction of the Lido. Both boats were in a wide avenue in the midst of the vessels, the usual track of those who went to sea, and there was no object whatever between them. By changing the course of his own boat, Don Camillo soon found himself within an oar's length of the other. He saw, at a glance, it was the treacherous gondola by which he had been duped.

"Draw, men, and follow!" shouted the desperate Neapolitan, preparing to leap into the midst of his enemies.

"You draw against St. Mark!" cried a warning voice from beneath the canopy. "The chances are unequal Signore; for the smallest signal would bring twenty galleys to our succor."

Don Camillo might have disregarded this menace, had he not perceived that it caused the half-drawn rapiers of his followers to return to their scabbards.

"Robber!" he answered, "restore her whom you have spirited away."

"Signore, you young nobles are often pleased to play your extravagances with the servants of the republic. Here are none but the gondoliers and myself." A movement of the boat permitted Don Camillo to look into the covered part, and he saw

---

* A Mediterranean vessel, both lateen and square rigged, frequently used as corsairs.—Editor.

that the other uttered no more than the truth. Convinced of the uselessness of further parley, knowing the value of every moment, and believing he was on a track which might still lead to success, the young Neapolitan signed to his people to go on. The boats parted in silence, that of Don Camillo proceeding in the direction from which the other had just come.

In a short time the gondola of Don Camillo was in an open part of the Giudecca, and entirely beyond the tiers of the shipping. It was so late that the moon had begun to fall, and its light was cast obliquely on the bay, throwing the eastern sides of the buildings and the other objects into shadow. A dozen different vessels were seen, aided by the landbreeze, steering towards the entrance of the port. The rays of the moon fell upon the broad surface of those sides of their canvas which were nearest to the town, and they resembled so many spotless clouds, sweeping the water and floating seaward.

"They are sending my wife to Dalmatia!" cried Don Camillo, like a man on whom the truth began to dawn.

"Signore mio!" exclaimed the astonished Gino.

"I tell thee, sirrah, that this accursed senate hath plotted against my happiness, and having robbed me of thy mistress, hath employed one of the many feluccas that I see, to transport her to some of its strongholds, on the eastern coast of the Adriatic."

"Blessed Maria! Signor Duca, and my honored master; they say that the very images of stone in Venice have ears, and that the horses of bronze will kick if an evil word is spoken against those up above."

"Is it not enough, varlet, to draw curses from the meek Job, to rob him of a wife? Hast thou no feeling for thy mistress?"

"I did not dream, eccellenza, that you were so happy as to have the one, or that I was so honored as to have the other."

"Thou remindest me of my folly, good Gino. In aiding me on this occasion, thou wilt have thy own fortune in view, as thy efforts, like those of thy fellows, will be made in behalf of the lady to whom I have just plighted a husband's vows."

"San Teodoro help us all, and hint what is to be done! The lady is most happy, Signor Don Camillo, and if I only knew by what name to mention her, she should never be forgotten in any prayer that so humble a sinner might dare to offer."

"Thou hast not forgotten the beautiful lady I drew from the Giudecca?"

"Corpo di Bacco! Your eccellenza floated like a swan, and swam faster than a gull. Forgotten! Signore, no,—I think of it every time I hear a plash in the canals, and every time I think of it I curse the Ancona man in my heart. St. Theodore forgive me, if it be unlike a Christian to do so. But, though we all tell marvels of what our lord did in the Giudecca, the dip of its waters is not the marriage ceremony, nor can we speak with much certainty of beauty that was seen to so great disadvantage."

"Thou art right, Gino.—But that lady, the illustrious Donna Violetta Tiepolo, the daughter and heiress of a famed senator, is now thy mistress. It remains for us to establish her in the Castle of Sant' Agata, where I shall defy Venice and its agents."

Gino bowed his head in submission, though he cast a look behind, to make sure that none of those agents, whom his master set so openly at defiance, were within earshot.

In the meantime the gondola proceeded, for the dialogue in no manner interrupted the exertions of Gino, still holding the direction of the Lido. As the land breeze freshened, the different vessels in sight glided away, and by the time Don Camillo reached the barrier of sand which separates the Lagunes from the Adriatic, most of them had glided through the passages, and were now shaping their courses, according to their different destinations, across the open gulf. The young noble had permitted his people to pursue the direction originally taken, in pure indecision. He was certain that his bride was in one of the many barks in sight, but he possessed no clue to lead him towards the right one, nor any sufficient means of pursuit, were he even master of that important secret. When he landed, therefore, it was with the simple hope of being able to form some general conjecture as to the portion of the republic's dominions in which he might search for her he had lost, by observing to what part of the Adriatic the different feluccas held their way. He had determined on immediate pursuit, however, and before he quitted the gondola, he once more turned to his confidential gondolier to give the necessary instructions.

"Thou knowest, Gino," he said, "that there is one born a vassal on my estates, here in the port, with a felucca from the Sorrentine shore?"

"I know the man better than I know my own faults, Signore, or even my own virtues."

221

"Go to him, at once, and make sure of his presence. I have imagined a plan to decoy him into the service of his lord; but I would now know the condition of his vessel."

Gino said a few words in commendation of the zeal of his friend Stefano, and in praise of the *Bella Sorrentina*, as the gondola receded from the shore; and then he dashed his oar into the water, like a man in earnest to execute the commission.

There is a lonely spot on the Lido di Palestrina, where Catholic exclusion has decreed that the remains of all who die in Venice without the pale of the church of Rome shall moulder into their kindred dust. Though it is not distant from the ordinary landing and the few buildings which line the shore, it is a place that, in itself, is no bad emblem of a hopeless lot. Solitary, exposed equally to the hot airs of the south and the bleak blasts of the Alps, frequently covered with the spray of the Adriatic, and based on barren sands, the utmost that human art, aided by a soil which has been fattened by human remains, can do, has been to create around the modest graves a meager vegetation, that is in slight contrast to the sterility of most of the bank. This place of interment is without the relief of trees, at the present day it is uninclosed, and in the opinions of those who have set it apart for heretic and Jew, it is unblessed. And yet, though condemned alike to this, the last indignity which man can inflict on his fellow, the two proscribed classes furnish a melancholy proof of waywardness of human passions and prejudice, by refusing to share in common the scanty pittance of earth which bigotry has allowed for their everlasting repose! While the Protestant sleeps by the side of Protestant in exclusive obloquy, the children of Israel moulder apart on the same barren heath, sedulous to preserve, even in the grave, the outward distinctions of faith. We shall not endeavor to seek that deeply seated principle which renders man so callous to the most eloquent and striking appeals to liberality, but rest satisfied with being grateful that we have been born in a land in which the interests of religion are as little as possible sullied by the vicious contamination of those of life; in which Christian humility is not exhibited beneath the purple, nor Jewish adhesion by intolerance; in which man is left to care for the welfare of his own soul; and in which, so far as the human eye can penetrate, God is worshipped for himself.

Don Camillo Monforte landed near the retired graves of the

222

proscribed. As he wished to ascend the low sandhills, which have been thrown up by the waves and the winds of the gulf, on the outer edge of the Lido, it was necessary that he should pass directly across the contemned spot, or make such a circuit as would have been inconvenient. Crossing himself, with a superstition that was interwoven with all his habits and opinions, and loosening his rapier, in order that he might not miss the succor of that good weapon, at need, he moved across the heath tenanted by the despised dead, taking care to avoid the mouldering heaps of earth which lay above the bones of heretic or Jew. He had not threaded more than half the graves, however, when a human form arose from the grass, and seemed to walk like one who mused on the moral that the piles at his feet would be apt to excite. Again Don Camillo touched the handle of his rapier; then moving aside, in a manner to give himself an equal advantage from the light of the moon, he drew near the stranger. His footstep was heard, for the other paused, regarded the approaching cavalier, and folding his arms, as it might be in sign of neutrality, awaited his nearer approach.

"Thou hast chosen a melancholy hour for thy walk, Signore," said the young Neapolitan; "and a still more melancholy scene. I hope I do not intrude on an Israelite, or a Lutheran, who mourns for his friend?"

"Don Camillo Monforte, I am, like yourself, a Christian."

"Ha! Thou knowest me—'tis Battista, the gondolier that I once entertained in my household?"

"Signore, 'tis not Battista."

As he spoke, the stranger faced the moon, in a manner that threw all of its mild light upon his features.

"Jacopo!" exclaimed the duke, recoiling, as did all in Venice habitually, when that speaking eye was unexpectedly met.

"Signore—Jacopo."

In a moment the rapier of Don Camillo glittered in the rays of the moon.

"Keep thy distance, fellow, and explain the motive that hath brought thee thus across my solitude!"

The Bravo smiled, but his arms maintained their fold.

"I might, with equal justice, call upon the Duke of Sant' Agata to furnish reasons, why he wanders at this hour among the Hebrew graves."

"Nay, spare thy pleasantry; I trifle not with men of thy

reputation; if any in Venice have thought fit to employ thee against my person, thou wilt have need of all thy courage and skill, ere thou earnest thy fee."

"Put up thy rapier, Don Camillo; here is none to do you harm. Think you, if employed in the manner you name, I would be in this spot to seek you? Ask yourself whether your visit here was known, or whether it was more than the idle caprice of a young noble who finds his bed less easy than his gondola. We have met, Duke of Sant' Agata, when you distrusted my honor less."

"Thou speakest true, Jacopo," returned the noble, suffering the point of his rapier to fall from before the breast of the Bravo, though he still hesitated to withdraw the point. "Thou sayest the truth. My visit to this spot is indeed accidental, and thou could'st not have possibly foreseen it. Why art thou here?"

"Why are these here?" demanded Jacopo, pointing to the graves at his feet. "We are born, and we die—that much is known to us all; but the when and the where are mysteries, until time reveals them."

"Thou art not a man to act without good motive. Though these Israelites could not foresee their visit to the Lido, thine hath not been without intention."

"I am here, Don Camillo Monforte, because my spirit hath need of room. I want the air of the sea—the canals choke me—I can only breathe in freedom on this bank of sand!"

"Thou hast another reason, Jacopo?"

"Ay, Signore—I loathe yon city of crimes!"

As the Bravo spoke, he shook his hand in the direction of the domes of St. Mark, and the deep tones of his voice appeared to heave up from the depths of his chest.

"This is extraordinary language for a—"

"Bravo; speak the word boldly, Signore—it is no stranger to my ears. But even the stiletto of a Bravo is honorable, compared to that sword of pretended justice which St. Mark wields! The commonest hireling of Italy—he who will plant his dagger in the heart of his friend for two sequins, is a man of open dealing, compared to the merciless treachery of some in yonder town!"

"I understand thee, Jacopo; thou art, at length, proscribed. The public voice, faint as it is in the republic, has finally reached the ears of thy employers, and they withdraw their protection."

Jacopo regarded the noble, for an instant, with an expression so ambiguous, as to cause the latter insensibly to raise the point of his rapier, but when he answered, it was with his ordinary quiet.

"Signor Duca," he said, "I have been thought worthy to be retained by Don Camillo Monforte!"

"I deny it not—and now that thou recallest the occasion, new light breaks in upon me. Villain, to thy faithlessness I owe the loss of my bride!"

Though the rapier was at the very throat of Jacopo, he did not flinch. Gazing at his excited companion, he laughed in a smothered manner, but bitterly.

"It would seem that the Lord of Sant' Agata wishes to rob me of my trade," he said. "Arise, ye Israelites, and bear witness, lest men doubt the fact! A common Bravo of the canals is way-laid, among your despised graves, by the proudest Signor of Calabria! You have chosen your spot, in mercy, Don Camillo, for sooner or later this crumbling and sea-worn earth is to re-ceive me. Were I to die at the altar itself, with the most penitent prayer of Holy Church on my lips, the bigots would send my body to rest among those hungry Hebrews and accursed here-tics. Yes, I am a man proscribed, and unfit to sleep with the faithful!"

His companion spoke with so strange a mixture of irony and melancholy, that the purpose of Don Camillo wavered. But remembering his loss, he shook the rapier's point, and contin-ued:—

"Thy taunts and effrontery will not avail thee, knave," he cried. "Thou knowest that I would have engaged thee as the leader of a chosen band, to favor the flight of one dear from Venice."

"Nothing more true, Signore."

"And thou didst refuse the service?"

"Noble duke, I did."

"Not content with this, having learned the particulars of my project, thou sold the secret to the senate?"

"Don Camillo Monforte, I did not. My engagements with the council would not permit me to serve you; else, by the brightest star of yonder vault! it would have gladdened my heart to have witnessed the happiness of two young and faithful lovers. No—no—no; they know me not who think I cannot find pleasure in the joy of another. I told you that I was the senate's,—and there the matter ended."

"And I had the weakness to believe thee, Jacopo, for thou

225

hast a character so strangely compounded of good and evil, and bearest so fair a name for observance of thy faith, that the seeming frankness of the answer lulled me to security. Fellow, I have been betrayed, and that at the moment when I thought success most sure."

Jacopo manifested interest, but, as he moved slowly on, accompanied by the vigilant and zealous noble, he smiled coldly, like one who had pity for the other's credulity.

"In bitterness of soul, I have cursed the whole race for its treachery," continued the Neapolitan.

"This is rather for the priore of St. Mark, than for the ear of one who carries a public stiletto."

"My gondola has been imitated—the liveries of my people copied—my bride stolen.—Thou answerest not, Jacopo?"

"What answer would you have? You have been cozened, Signore, in a state whose very prince dare not trust his secrets to his wife. You would have robbed Venice of an heiress, and Venice has robbed you of a bride. You have played high, Don Camillo, and have lost a heavy stake. You have thought of your own wishes and rights, while you have pretended to serve Venice with the Spaniard."

Don Camillo started in surprise.

"Why this wonder, Signore?—You forget that I have lived much among those who weigh the chances of every political interest, and that your name is often in their mouths. This marriage is doubly disagreeable to Venice, who has nearly as much need of the bridegroom as of the bride. The council hath long ago forbidden the banns."

"Ay—but the means?—explain the means by which I have been duped, lest the treachery be ascribed to thee."

"Signore, the very marbles of the city give up their secrets to the state. I have seen much, and understood much, when my superiors have believed me merely a tool; but I have seen much that even those who employed me could not comprehend. I could have foretold this consummation of your nuptials, had I known of their celebration."

"This thou could'st not have done, without being an agent of their treachery."

"The schemes of the selfish may be foretold; it is only the generous and the honest that baffle calculation. He who can gain a knowledge of the present interest of Venice is master of her dearest secrets of state; for what she wishes she will do, unless the service cost too dear. As for the means—how can they be wanting in a household like yours, Signore?"

"I trusted none but those deepest in my confidence."

"Don Camillo, there is not a servitor in your palace, Gino alone excepted, who is not a hireling of the senate, or of its agents. The very gondoliers who row you to your daily pleasures have had their hands crossed with the republic's sequins. Nay, they are not only paid to watch you, but to watch each other."

"Can this be true!"

"Have you ever doubted it, Signore?" asked Jacopo, looking up like one who admired at another's simplicity.

"I knew them to be false—pretenders to a faith that in secret they mock; but I had not believed they dared to tamper with the very menials of my person. This undermining of the security of families is to destroy society at its core!"

"You talk like one who hath not been long a bridegroom, Signore," said the Bravo with a hollow laugh. "A year hence, you may know what it is to have your own wife turning your secret thoughts into gold."

"And thou servest them, Jacopo?"

"Who does not, in some manner suited to his habits? We are not masters of our fortune, Don Camillo, or the Duke of Sant' Agata would not be turning his influence with a relative, to the advantage of the republic. What I have done hath not been done without bitter penitence, and an agony of soul, that your own light servitude may have spared you, Signore."

"Poor Jacopo!"

"If I have lived through it all, 'tis because one mightier than the state hath not deserted me. But, Don Camillo Monforte, there are crimes which pass beyond the powers of man to endure."

The Bravo shuddered, and he moved among the despised graves, in silence.

"They have then proved too ruthless even for thee?" said Don Camillo, who watched the contracting eye and heaving form of his companion, in wonder.

"Signore, they have. I have witnessed, this night, a proof of their heartlessness and bad faith, that hath caused me to look forward to my own fate. The delusion is over; from this hour I serve them no longer."

The Bravo spoke with deep feeling, and his companion fancied, strange as it was coming from such a man, with an air of wounded integrity. Don Camillo knew that there was no condition of life, however degraded or lost to the world, which had not its own particular opinions of the faith due to its fellows; and he had seen enough of the sinuous course of the oligarchy of Venice, to understand that it was quite possible its shameless and irresponsible duplicity might offend the principles of even an assassin. Less odium was attached to men of that class, in Italy and at that day, than will be easily imagined in a country like this; for the radical defects and the vicious administration of the laws, caused an irritable and sensitive people too often to take into their own hands, the right of redressing their own wrongs. Custom had lessened the odium of the crime, and though society denounced the assassin himself, it is scarcely too much to say, that his employer was regarded with little more disgust than the religious of our time regard the survivor of a private combat. Still it was not usual for nobles like Don Camillo to hold intercourse, beyond that which the required service exacted, with men of Jacopo's cast; but the language and manner of the Bravo so strongly attracted the curiosity, and even the sympathy of his companion, that the latter unconsciously sheathed his rapier and drew nearer.

"Thy penitence and regrets, Jacopo, may lead thee yet nearer to virtue," he said, "than mere abandonment of the senate's service. Seek out some godly priest, and ease thy soul, by confession and prayer."

The Bravo trembled in every limb, and his eye turned wistfully to the countenance of the other.

"Speak, Jacopo; even I will hear thee, if thou would'st remove the mountain from thy breast."

"Thanks, noble Signore! a thousand thanks for this glimpse of sympathy, to which I have long been a stranger! None know how dear a word of kindness is, as he who has been condemned by all, as I have been. I have prayed—I have craved—I have wept for some ear to listen to my tale, and I thought I had found one who would have heard me without scorn, when the cold policy of the senate struck him. I came here to commune with the hated dead, when chance brought us together. Could I—" the Bravo paused and looked doubtfully, again, at his companion.

"Say on, Jacopo."

"I have not dared to trust my secrets even to the confessional, Signore, and can I be so bold as to offer them to you?"

"Truly, it is a strange behest!"

"Signore, it is. You are noble, I am of humble blood. Your ancestors were senators and doges of Venice, while mine have been, since the fishermen first built their huts in the Lagunes, laborers on the canals, and rowers of gondolas. You are powerful, and rich, and courted; while I am denounced, and, in secret, I fear, condemned. In short, you are Don Camillo Monforte, and I am Jacopo Frontoni!"

Don Camillo was touched, for the Bravo spoke without bitterness, and in deep sorrow.

"I would thou wert at the confessional, poor Jacopo!" he said; "I am little able to give ease to such a burthen."

"Signore, I have lived too long, shut out from the good wishes of my fellows, and I can bear with it no longer. The accursed senate may cut me off without warning, and then who will stop to look at my grave. Signore, I must speak, or die!"

"Thy case is piteous, Jacopo!—Thou hast need of ghostly counsel."

"Here is no priest, Signore, and I carry a weight past bearing. The only man who has shown interest in me, for three long and dreadful years, is gone!"

"But he will return, poor Jacopo."

"Signore, he will never return. He is with the fishes of the Lagunes."

"By thy hand, monster!"

"By the justice of the illustrious republic," said the Bravo, with a smothered but bitter smile.

"Ha! they are then awake to the acts of thy class? Thy repentance is the fruit of fear!"

Jacopo seemed choked. He had evidently counted on the awakened sympathy of his companion, notwithstanding the difference in their situations, and to be thus thrown off again, unmanned him. He shuddered, and every muscle and nerve appeared about to yield its power. Touched by so unequivocal signs of suffering, Don Camillo kept close at his side, reluctant to enter more deeply into the feelings of one of his known character, and yet unable to desert a fellow creature in so grievous agony.

"Signor Duca," said the Bravo, with a pathos in his voice that went to the heart of his auditor, "leave me. If they ask for a proscribed man, let them come here; in the morning they will find my body near the graves of the heretics."

"Speak, I will hear thee."

Jacopo looked up with doubt expressed on his features.

"Unburden thyself; I will listen, though thou recounted the assassination of my dearest friend."

The oppressed Bravo gazed at him, as if he still distrusted his sincerity. His face worked, and his look became still more wistful; but as Don Camillo faced the moon, and betrayed the extent of his sympathy, the other burst into tears.

"Jacopo, I will hear thee—I will hear thee, poor Jacopo!" cried Don Camillo, shocked at this exhibition of distress in one so stern by nature. A wave from the hand of the Bravo silenced him, and Jacopo, struggling with himself for a moment, spoke.

"You have saved a soul from perdition, Signore," he said, smothering his emotion. "If the happy knew how much power belongs to a single word of kindness—a glance of feeling, when given to the despised, they would not look so coldly on the miserable. This night must have been my last, had you cast me off without pity—but you will hear my tale, Signore—you will not scorn the confession of a Bravo?"

"I have promised. Be brief, for at this moment I have great care of my own."

"Signore, I know not the whole of your wrongs, but they will not be less likely to be redressed for this grace."

Jacopo made an effort to command himself, when he commenced his tale.

The course of the narrative does not require that we should accompany this extraordinary man, through the relation of the secrets he imparted to Don Camillo. It is enough, for our present purposes, to say, that, as he proceeded, the young Calabrian noble drew nearer to his side, and listened with growing interest. The Duke of Sant' Agata scarcely breathed, while his companion, with that energy of language and feeling which marks Italian character, recounted his secret sorrows, and the scenes in which he had been an actor. Long before he was done, Don Camillo had forgotten his own private causes of concern, and, by the time the tale was finished, every shade of disgust had given place to an ungovernable expression of pity. In short, so eloquent was the speaker, and so interesting the facts with which he dealt, that he seemed to play with the sympathies of the listener, as the improvisatore of that region is known to lead captive the passions of the admiring crowd.

During the time Jacopo was speaking, he and his wondering auditor had passed the limits of the despised cemetery; and as the voice of the former ceased, they stood on the outer beach of the Lido. When the low tones of the Bravo were no longer audible, they were succeeded by the sullen wash of the Adriatic.

"This surpasseth belief!" Don Camillo exclaimed, after a long pause, which had only been disturbed by the rush and retreat of the waters.

"Signore, as holy Maria is kind! it is true."

"I doubt you not, Jacopo—poor Jacopo! I cannot distrust a tale thus told! Thou hast, indeed, been a victim of their hellish duplicity, and well mayest thou say, the load was past bearing. What is thy intention?"

"I serve them no longer, Don Camillo—I wait only for the last solemn scene, which is now certain, and then I quit this city of deceit, to seek my fortune in another region. They have blasted my youth, and loaded my name with infamy.—God may yet lighten the load!"

"Reproach not thyself beyond reason, Jacopo, for the happiest and most fortunate of us all are not above the power of temptation. Thou knowest that even my name and rank have not, altogether, protected me from their arts."

"I know them capable, Signore, of deluding angels! Their arts are only surpassed by their means, and their pretence of virtue by their indifference to its practice."

"Thou sayest true, Jacopo: the truth is never in greater danger, than when whole communities lend themselves to the vicious deception of seemliness, and without truth there is no virtue. This it is to substitute profession for practice—to use the altar for a worldly purpose—and to bestow power without any other responsibility than that which is exacted by the selfishness of caste! Jacopo—poor Jacopo! thou shalt be my servitor—I am lord of my own seigniories, and once rid of this specious republic, I charge myself with the care of thy safety and fortunes. Be at peace as respects thy conscience: I have interest near the Holy See, and thou shalt not want absolution!"

The gratitude of the Bravo was more vivid in feeling than in expression. He kissed the hand of Don Camillo, but it was with a reservation of self-respect that belonged to the character of the man.

"A system like this of Venice," continued the musing noble,

231

"leaves none of us masters of our own acts. The wiles of such a combination are stronger than the will. It cloaks its offences against right in a thousand specious forms, and it enlists the support of every man, under the pretence of a sacrifice for the common good. We often fancy ourselves simple dealers in some justifiable state intrigue, when in truth we are deep in sin. Falsehood is the parent of all crimes, and in no case has it a progeny so numerous, as that in which its own birth is derived from the state. I fear I may have made sacrifices, to this treacherous influence, I could wish forgotten."

Though Don Camillo soliloquized, rather than addressed his companion, it was evident, by the train of his thoughts, that the narrative of Jacopo had awakened disagreeable reflections, on the manner in which he had pushed his own claims with the senate. Perhaps he felt the necessity of some apology to one who, though so much his inferior in rank, was so competent to appreciate his conduct, and who had just denounced in the strongest language, his own fatal subserviency to the arts of that irresponsible and meretricious body.

Jacopo uttered a few words of a general nature, but such as had a tendency to quiet the uneasiness of his companion; after which, with a readiness that proved him qualified for the many delicate missions with which he had been charged, he ingeniously turned the discourse to the recent abduction of Donna Violetta, with the offer of rendering his new employer all the services in his power to regain his bride.

"That thou mayest know all thou hast undertaken," rejoined Don Camillo, "listen, Jacopo, and I will conceal nothing from thy shrewdness."

The Duke of Sant' Agata now briefly, but explicitly, laid bare to his companion all his own views and measures, with respect to her he loved, and all those events with which the reader has already become acquainted.

The Bravo gave great attention to the minutest parts of the detail, and more than once, as the other proceeded, he smiled to himself, like a man who was able to trace the secret means by which this or that intrigue had been effected. The whole was just related, when the sound of a footstep announced the return of Gino.

CHAPTER XVIII

"Pale she look'd,
Yet cheerful; though methought, once, if not twice,
She wiped away a tear that would be coming."
ROGERS

THE hours passed as if naught had occurred, within the barriers of the city, to disturb their progress. On the following morning men proceeded to their several pursuits, of business or of pleasure, as had been done for ages, and none stopped to question his neighbor of the scene which might have taken place during the night. Some were gay, and others sorrowing; some idle, and others occupied; here one toiled, there another sported; and Venice presented, as of wont, its noiseless, suspicious, busy, mysterious, and yet stirring throngs, as it had before done at a thousand similar risings of the sun.

The menials lingered around the water gate of Donna Violetta's palace, with distrustful but cautious faces, scarce whispering among themselves their secret suspicions of the fate of their mistress. The residence of the Signor Gradenigo presented its usual gloomy magnificence, while the abode of Don Camillo Monforte betrayed no sign of the heavy disappointment which its master had sustained. The *Bella Sorrentina* still lay in the port, with a yard on deck, while the crew repaired its sail in the lazy manner of mariners, who work without excitement.

The Lagunes were dotted with the boats of fishermen, and travellers arrived and departed from the city, by the well-known channels of Fusina and Mestre. Here, some adventurer from the north quitted the canals, on his return towards the Alps, carrying with him a pleasing picture of the ceremonies he had witnessed, mingled with some crude conjectures of that power which predominated in the suspected state; and there, a countryman of the Main sought his little farm, satisfied with the pageants and regatta of the previous day. In short, all seemed as usual, and the events we have related remained a secret with the actors,

233

and that mysterious council which had so large a share in their existence.

As the day advanced, many a sail was spread for the pillars of Hercules, or the genial Levant, and feluccas, mistics and golettas,* went and came as the land or sea breeze prevailed. Still the mariner of Calabria lounged beneath the awning which sheltered his deck, or took his siesta on a pile of old sails, which were ragged with the force of many a hot sirocco. As the sun fell, the gondolas of the great and idle began to glide over the water; and when the two squares were cooled by the air of the Adriatic, the Broglio began to fill with those privileged to pace its vaulted passage. Among these came the Duke of Sant' Agata, who, though an alien to the laws of the republic, being of so illustrious descent, and of claims so equitable, was received among the senators, in their moments of ease, as a welcome sharer in this vain distinction. He entered the Broglio at the wonted hour, and with his usual composure, for he trusted to his secret influence at Rome, and something to the success of his rivals, for impunity. Reflection had shown Don Camillo that, as his plans were known to the council, they would long since have arrested him, had such been their intention; and it had also led him to believe that the most efficient manner of avoiding the personal consequences of his adventure was to show confidence in his own power to withstand them. When he appeared, therefore, leaning on the arm of a high officer of the papal embassy, and with an eye that spoke assurance in himself, he was greeted, as usual, by all who knew him, as was due to his rank and expectations. Still Don Camillo walked among the patricians of the republic with novel sensations. More than once he thought he detected, in the wandering glances of those with whom he conversed, signs of their knowledge of his frustrated attempt, and more than once, when he least suspected such scrutiny, his countenance was watched, as if the observer sought some evidence of his future intentions. Beyond this, none might have discovered that an heiress of so much importance had been so near being lost to the state, or, on the other hand, that a bridegroom had been robbed of his bride. Habitual art, on the part of the state, and resolute but wary intention, on the part of the young noble, concealed all else from observation.

_____
* Schooners.—Editor.

In this manner the day passed, not a tongue in Venice, beyond those which whispered in secret, making any allusion to the incidents of our tale.

Just as the sun was setting, a gondola swept slowly up to the water gate of the ducal palace. The gondolier landed, fastened his boat in the usual manner to the steppingstones, and entered the court. He wore a mask, for the hour of disguise had come, and his attire was so like the ordinary fashion of men of his class, as to defeat recognition by its simplicity. Glancing an eye about him, he entered the building by a private door.

The edifice in which the doges of Venice dwelt still stands a gloomy monument of the policy of the republic, furnishing evidence, in itself, of the specious character of the prince whom it held. It is built around a vast but gloomy court, as is usual with nearly all of the principal edifices of Europe. One of its fronts forms a side of the piazzetta, so often mentioned, and another lines the quay next the port. The architecture of these two exterior faces of the palace renders the structure remarkable. A low portico, which forms the Broglio, sustains a row of massive oriental windows, and above these again lies a pile of masonry, slightly relieved by apertures, which reverses the ordinary uses of the arts. A third front is nearly concealed by the cathedral of St. Mark, and the fourth is washed by its canal. The public prison of the city forms the other side of this canal, eloquently proclaiming the nature of the government by the close approximation of the powers of legislation and of punishment. The famous Bridge of Sighs is the material, and we might add the metaphorical, link between the two. The latter edifice stands on the quay, also, and though less lofty and spacious, in point of architectural beauty it is the superior structure, though the quaintness and unusual style of the palace is most apt to attract attention.

The masked gondolier soon reappeared beneath the arch of the water gate, and with a hurried step he sought his boat. It required but a minute to cross the canal, to land on the opposite quay, and to enter the public door of the prison. It would seem that he had some secret means of satisfying the vigilance of the different keepers, for bolts were drawn, and doors unlocked, with little question, wherever he presented himself. In this manner he quickly passed all the outer barriers of the palace, and reached a part of the building which had the appearance of being fitted for the accommodation of a family. Judging from the air of all around him, those who dwelt there took the luxury of their abode but little into the account, though neither the furniture nor the rooms were wanting in most of the necessaries suited to people of their class and the climate, and in that age.

The gondolier had ascended a private stairway, and he was now before a door which had none of those signs of a prison that so freely abounded in other parts of the building. He paused to listen, and then tapped, with singular caution.

"Who is without?" asked a gentle female voice, at the same instant that the latch moved and fell again, as if she within waited to be assured of the character of her visitor, before she opened the door.

"A friend to thee, Gelsomina," was the answer.

"Nay, here all are friends to the keepers, if words can be believed. You must name yourself, or go elsewhere for your answer."

The gondolier removed the mask a little, which had altered his voice as well as concealed his face.

"It is I, Gessina," he said, using the diminutive of her name.

The bolts grated, and the door was hurriedly opened.

"It is wonderful that I did not know thee, Carlo!" said the female, with eager simplicity; "but thou takest so many disguises of late, and so counterfeitest strange voices, that thine own mother might have distrusted her ear."

The gondolier paused to make certain they were alone; then, laying aside the mask altogether, he exposed the features of the Bravo.

"Thou knowest the need of caution," he added, "and wilt not judge me harshly."

"I said not that, Carlo—but thy voice is so familiar, that I thought it wonderful thou could'st speak as a stranger."

"Hast thou aught for me?"

The gentle girl, for she was both young and gentle, hesitated.

"Hast thou aught new, Gelsomina?" repeated the Bravo, reading her innocent face with his searching glance.

"Thou art fortunate in not being sooner in the prison. I have just had a visitor. Thou would'st not have liked to be seen, Carlo?"

"Thou knowest I have good reasons for coming masked. I might, or I might not have disliked thy acquaintance, as he should have proved."

"Nay, now thou judgest wrong," returned the female, hastily, "I had no other, here, but my cousin, Annina."

"Dost thou think me jealous?" said the Bravo, smiling in kindness, as he took her hand. "Had it been thy cousin Pietro, or Michele, or Roberto, or any other youth of Venice, I should have no other dread than that of being known."

"But it was only Annina—my cousin, Annina, whom thou hast never seen—and I have no cousins Pietro, and Michele, and Roberto. We are not many, Carlo. Annina has a brother, but he never comes hither. Indeed it is long since she has found it convenient to quit her trade to come to this dreary place. Few children of sisters see each other so seldom as Annina and I!"

"Thou art a good girl, Gessina, and art always to be found near thy mother. Hast thou naught in particular for my ear?"

Again the soft eyes of Gelsomina, or Gessina, as she was familiarly called, dropped to the floor—but raising them, ere he could note the circumstance, she hurriedly continued the discourse.

"I fear Annina will return, or I would go with thee at once."

"Is this cousin of thine still here, then?" asked the Bravo, with uneasiness.—"Thou knowest I would not be seen."

"Fear not. She cannot enter without touching that bell, for she is above with my poor bedridden mother. Thou canst go into the inner room, as usual, when she comes, and listen to her idle discourse, if thou wilt—or—but we have not time—for Annina comes seldom, and I know not why, but she seems to love a sick room little, as she never stays many minutes with her aunt."

"Thou would'st have said, or I might go on my errand, Gessina?"

"I would, Carlo—but I am certain we should be recalled by my impatient cousin."

"I can wait; I am patient when with thee, dearest Gessina."

"Hist!—'Tis my cousin's step.—Thou canst go in."

While she spoke, a small bell rang, and the Bravo withdrew into the inner room, like one accustomed to that place of retreat. He left the door ajar, for the darkness of the closet sufficiently concealed his person. In the meantime, Gelsomina opened the outer door for the admission of her visitor. At the first sound of the latter's voice, Jacopo, who had little suspected the fact from a name which was so common, recognized the artful daughter of the wine seller.

"Thou art at thy ease, here, Gelsomina," cried the latter,

entering and throwing herself into a seat, like one fatigued. "Thy mother is better, and thou art truly mistress of the house."

"I would I were not, Annina, for I am young to have this trust, with this affliction."

"It is not so insupportable, Gessina, to be mistress within doors at seventeen! Authority is sweet, and obedience is odious."

"I have found neither so, and I will give up the first with joy, whenever my poor mother shall be able to take command of her own family again."

"This is well, Gessina, and does credit to the good father confessor. But authority is dear to woman, and so is liberty. Thou wast not with the maskers yesterday, in the square?"

"I seldom wear a disguise, and I could not quit my mother."

"Which means that thou would'st have been glad to do it. Thou hast good reason for thy regrets, since a gayer marriage of the sea, or a braver regatta, has not been witnessed in Venice, since thou wast born. But the first was to be seen from thy window?"

"I saw the galley of state sweeping toward the Lido, and the train of patricians on its deck; but little else."

"No matter. Thou shalt have as good an idea of the pageant as if thou hadst played the part of the doge himself. First came the men of the guard, with their ancient dresses—"

"Nay, this I remember to have often seen; for the same show is kept from year to year."

"Thou art right; but Venice never witnessed such a brave regatta! Thou knowest that the first trial is always between gondolas of many oars, steered by the best esteemed of the canals. Luigi was there, and though he did not win, he more than merited success, by the manner in which he directed his boat. Thou knowest Luigi?"

"I scarce know any in Venice, Annina, for the long illness of my mother, and this unhappy office of my father, keep me within, when others are on the canals."

"True. Thou art not well placed to make acquaintances. But Luigi is second to no gondolier, in skill or reputation, and he is much the merriest rogue of them all that put foot on the Lido."

"He was foremost, then, in the grand race?"

"He should have been, but the awkwardness of his fellows, and some unfairness in the crossing, threw him back to be second. 'Twas a sight to behold, that of many noble watermen

238

struggling to maintain or to get a name on the canals. Santa Maria! I would thou could'st have seen it, girl!"

"I should not have been glad to see a friend defeated."

"We must take fortune as it offers. But the most wonderful sight of the day, after all, though Luigi and his fellows did so well, was to see a poor fisherman, named Antonio, in his bare head and naked legs, a man of seventy years, and with a boat no better than that I use to carry liquors to the Lido, entering on the second race, and carrying off the prize!"

"He could not have met with powerful rivals?"

"The best of Venice; though Luigi, having strived for the first, could not enter for the second trial. 'Tis said, too," continued Annina, looking about her with habitual caution, "that one who may scarce be named in Venice had the boldness to appear in that regatta masked; and yet the fisherman won! Thou hast heard of Jacopo?"

"The name is common."

"There is but one who bears it now, in Venice.—All mean the same when they say Jacopo."

"I have heard of a monster of that name. Surely he hath not dared to show himself among the nobles, on such a festa!"

"Gessina, we live in an unaccountable country! The man walks the piazza with a step as lordly as the doge, at his pleasure, and yet none say aught to him! I have seen him, at noonday, leaning against the triumphal mast, or the column of San Teodoro, with as proud an air as if he were put there to celebrate a victory of the republic!"

"Perhaps he is master of some terrible secret, which they fear he will reveal?"

"Thou knowest little of Venice, child! Holy Maria! a secret of that kind is a death warrant of itself. It is as dangerous to know too much, as it is to know too little, when one deals with St. Mark. But they say Jacopo was there, standing eye to eye with the doge, and scaring the senators as if he had been an uncalled spectre from the vaults of their fathers. Nor is this all; as I crossed the Lagunes this morning, I saw the body of a young cavalier drawn from the water, and those who were near it said it had the mark of his fatal hand!"

The timid Gelsomina shuddered.

"They who rule," she said, "will have to answer for this negligence to God, if they let the wretch longer go at large."

239

"Blessed St. Mark protect his children! They say there is much of this sort of sin to answer for—but see the body I did, with my own eyes, in entering the canals this morning."

"And didst thou sleep on the Lido, that thou wert abroad so early?"

"The Lido—yes—nay—I slept not, but thou knowest my father had a busy day during the revels, and I am not like thee, Gessina, mistress of the household, to do as I would. But I tarry here to chat with thee, when there is great need of industry at home. Hast thou the package, child, which I trusted to thy keeping, at my last visit?"

"It is here," answered Gelsomina, opening a drawer, and handing to her cousin a small but closely enveloped package, which, unknown to herself, contained some articles of forbidden commerce, and which the other, in her indefatigable activity, had been obliged to secrete for a time. "I had begun to think that thou hadst forgotten it, and was about to send it to thee."

"Gelsomina, if thou lovest me, never do so rash an act! My brother Giuseppe—thou scarce knowest Giuseppe?"

"We have little acquaintance, for cousins."

"Thou art fortunate in thy ignorance. I cannot say what I might of the child of the same parents, but had Giuseppe seen this package, by any accident, it might have brought thee into great trouble!"

"Nay, I fear not thy brother, nor any else," said the daughter of the prison keeper, with the firmness of innocence; "he could do me no harm for dealing kindly by a relative."

"Thou art right; but he might have caused me great vexation. Sainted Maria! if thou knewest the pain that unthinking and misguided boy gives his family! He is my brother, after all, and you will fancy the rest. Addio, good Gessina; I hope thy father will permit thee to come and visit, at last, those who so much love thee."

"Addio, Annina; thou knowest I would come gladly, but that I scarce quit the side of my poor mother."

The wily daughter of the wine seller gave her guileless and unsuspecting friend a kiss, and then she was let out and departed.

"Carlo," said the soft voice of Gessina; "thou canst come forth, for we have no further fear of visits."

The Bravo appeared, but with a paleness deeper than common on his cheek. He looked mournfully at the gentle and

240

affectionate being who awaited his return, and when he struggled to answer her ingenuous smile, the abortive effort gave his features an expression of ghastliness.

"Annina has wearied thee with her idle discourse of the regatta, and of murders on the canals. Thou wilt not judge her harshly, for the manner in which she spoke of Giuseppe, who may deserve this, and more. But, I know thy impatience, and I will not increase thy weariness."

"Hold, Gessina—this girl is thy cousin?"

"Have I not told thee so? Our mothers are sisters."

"And she is here often?"

"Not as often as she could wish, I am certain, for her aunt has not quitted her room for many, many months."

"Thou art an excellent daughter, kind Gessina, and would make all others as virtuous as thyself.—And thou hast been to return these visits?"

"Never. My father forbids it, for they are dealers in wines, and entertain the gondoliers in revelry. But Annina is blameless for the trade of her parents."

"No doubt—and that package? it hath been long in thy keeping?"

"A month; Annina left it at her last visit, for she was hurried to cross to the Lido. But why these questions? You do not like my cousin, who is giddy, and given to idle conversation, but who, I think, must have a good heart. Thou heard'st the manner in which she spoke of the wretched Bravo, Jacopo, and of this late murder?"

"I did."

"Thou could'st not have shown more horror at the monster's crime thyself, Carlo. Nay, Annina is thoughtless, and she might be less worldly; but she hath, like all of us, a holy aversion to sin. Shall I lead thee to the cell?"

"Go on."

"Thy honest nature revolts, Carlo, at the cold villainy of the assassin. I have heard much of his murders, and of the manner in which those up above bear with him. They say, in common, that his art surpasseth theirs, and that the officers wait for proof, that they may not do injustice."

"Is the senate so tender, think you?" asked the Bravo, huskily, but motioning for his companion to proceed.

The girl looked sad, like one who felt the force of this ques-

241

tion; and she turned away to open a private door, whence she brought forth a litle box.

"This is the key, Carlo," she said, showing him one of a massive bunch, "and I am now the sole warder. This much, at least, we have effected; the day may still come when we shall do more."

The Bravo endeavored to smile, as if he appreciated her kindness; but he only succeeded in making her understand his desire to go on. The eye of the gentle-hearted girl lost its gleam of hope in an expression of sorrow, and she obeyed.

CHAPTER XIX

"But let us to the roof,
And, when thou hast survey'd the sea, the land,
Visit the narrow cells that cluster there,
As in a place of tombs."

St. Mark's Place

WE shall not attempt to thread the vaulted galleries, the gloomy corridors, and all the apartments, through which the keeper's daughter led her companion. Those who have ever entered an extensive prison will require no description to revive the feeling of pain which it excited, by barred windows, creaking hinges, grating bolts, and all those other signs which are alike the means and evidence of incarceration. The building, unhappily like most other edifices intended to repress the vices of society, was vast, strong, and intricate within, although, as has been already intimated, of a chaste and simple beauty externally, that might seem to have been adopted in mockery of its destination.

Gelsomina entered a low, narrow, and glazed gallery, when she stopped.

"Thou soughtest me, as wont, beneath the water gate, Carlo," she asked, "at the usual hour?"

"I should not have entered the prison had I found thee there, for thou knowest I would be little seen. But I bethought me of thy mother, and crossed the canal."

"Thou wast wrong. My mother rests much as she has done, for many months—thou must have seen that we are not taking the usual route to the cell?"

"I have; but as we are not accustomed to meet in thy father's rooms, on this errand, I thought this the necessary direction."

"Hast thou much knowledge of the palace and the prison, Carlo?"

"More than I could wish, good Gelsomina;—but why am I thus questioned, at a moment when I would be otherwise employed?"

The timid and conscious girl did not answer. Her cheek was

243

never bright, for like a flower reared in the shade, it had the delicate hue of her secluded life; but at this question it became pale. Accustomed to the ingenuous habits of the sensitive being at his side, the Bravo studied her speaking features intently. He moved swiftly to a window, and looking out, his eye fell upon a narrow and gloomy canal. Crossing the gallery, he cast a glance beneath him, and saw the same dark watery passage, leading between the masonry of two massive piles to the quay and the port.

"Gelsomina!" he cried, recoiling from the sight, "this is the Bridge of Sighs!"

"It is, Carlo; hast thou ever crossed it before?"

"Never: nor do I understand why I cross it now. I have long thought that it might one day be my fortune to walk this fatal passage, but I could not dream of such a keeper!"

The eye of Gelsomina brightened, and her smile was cheerful.

"Thou wilt never cross it, to thy harm, with me."

"Of that I am certain, kind Gessina," he answered, taking her hand. "But this is a riddle that I cannot explain. Art thou in the habit of entering the palace by this gallery?"

"It is little used, except by the keepers and the condemned, as doubtless thou hast often heard; but yet they have given me the keys, and taught me the windings of the place, in order that I might serve, as usual, for thy guide."

"Gelsomina, I fear I have been too happy in thy company to note, as prudence would have told me, the rare kindness of the council in permitting me to enjoy it!"

"Dost thou repent, Carlo, that thou hast known me?"

The reproachful melancholy of her voice touched the Bravo, who kissed the hand he held, with Italian fervor.

"I should then repent me of the only hours of happiness I have known for years," he said. "Thou hast been to me, Gelsomina, like a flower in a desert—a pure spring to a feverish man—a gleam of hope to one suffering under malediction.—No, no; not for a moment have I repented knowing thee, my Gelsomina!"

" 'Twould not have made my life more happy, Carlo, to have thought I had added to thy sorrows. I am young, and ignorant of the world, but I know we should cause joy, and not pain, to those we esteem."

244

"Thy nature would teach thee this gentle lesson. But, is it not strange that one like me should be suffered to visit the prison unattended by any other keeper?"

"I had not thought it so, Carlo; but, surely it is not common!"

"We have found so much pleasure in each other, dear Gessina, that we have overlooked what ought to have caused alarm."

"Alarm, Carlo!"

"Or, at least, distrust; for these wily senators do no act of mercy without a motive. But it is now too late to recall the past, if we would; and in that which relates to thee I would not lose the memory of a moment. Let us proceed."

The slight cloud vanished from the face of the mild auditor of the Bravo; but still she did not move.

"Few pass this bridge, they say," she added tremulously, "and enter the world again; and yet thou dost not even ask why we are here, Carlo!"

There was a transient gleam of distrust in the hasty glance of the Bravo, as he shot a look at the undisturbed eye of the innocent being who put this question. But it scarcely remained long enough to change the expression of manly interest she was accustomed to meet in his look.

"Since thou wilt have me curious," he said, "why hast thou come hither, and more than all, being here, why dost thou linger?"

"The season is advanced, Carlo," she answered, speaking scarcely above her breath, "and we should look in vain among the cells."

"I understand thee," he said; "we will proceed."

Gelsomina lingered to gaze wistfully into the face of her companion, but finding no visible sign of the agony he endured, she went on. Jacopo spoke hoarsely, but he was too long accustomed to disguise, to permit the weakness to escape, when he knew how much it would pain the sensitive and faithful being who had yielded her affections to him with a singleness and devotion which arose nearly as much from her manner of life, as from natural ingenuousness.

In order that the reader may be enabled to understand the allusions which seem to be so plain to our lovers, it may be necessary to explain another odious feature in the policy of the republic of Venice.

245

Whatever may be the pretension of a state, in its acknowledged theories, an unerring clue to its true character is ever to be found in the machinery of its practice. In those governments which are created for the good of the people, force is applied with caution and reluctance, since the protection and not the injury of the weak is their object; whereas the more selfish and exclusive the system becomes, the more severe and ruthless are the coercive means employed by those in power. Thus, in Venice, whose whole political fabric reposed on the narrow foundation of an oligarchy, the jealousy of the senate brought the engines of despotism in absolute contact with even the pageantry of their titular prince, and the palace of the doge himself was polluted by the presence of the dungeons. The princely edifice had its summer and winter cells. The reader may be ready to believe that mercy had dictated some slight solace for the miserable, in this arrangement. But this would be ascribing pity to a body which, to its latest moment, had no tie to subject it to the weakness of humanity. So far from consulting the sufferings of the captive, his winter cell was below the level of the canals, while his summers were to be passed beneath the leads, exposed to the action of the burning sun of that climate. As the reader has probably anticipated already that Jacopo was in the prison on an errand connected with some captive, this short explanation will enable him to understand the secret allusion of his companion. He they sought had, in truth, been recently conveyed from the damp cells, where he had passed the winter and spring, to the heated chambers beneath the roof.

Gelsomina continued to lead the way, with a sadness of eye and feature that betrayed her strong sympathy with the sufferings of her companion, but without appearing to think further delay necessary. She had communicated a circumstance which weighed heavily on her own mind, and, like most of her mild temperament, who had dreaded such a duty, now that it was discharged, she experienced a sensible relief. They ascended many flights of steps, opened and shut numberless doors, and threaded several narrow corridors, in silence, before reaching the place of destination. While Gelsomina sought the key of the door before which they stopped, in the large bunch she carried, the Bravo breathed the hot air of the attic, like one who was suffocating.

"They promised me that this should not be done again!" he said.—"But they forget their pledges, fiends as they are!"

"Carlo!—thou forgettest that this is the palace of the doge!" whispered the girl, while she threw a timid glance behind her.

"I forget nothing that is connected with the republic!—It is all here," striking his flushed brow—"what is not there, is in my heart!"

"Poor Carlo! this cannot last forever—there will be an end."

"Thou art right," answered the Bravo, hoarsely.—"The end is nearer than thou thinkest.—No matter; turn the key, that we may go in."

The hand of Gelsomina lingered on the lock, but admonished by his impatient eye, she complied, and they entered the cell.

"Father!" exclaimed the Bravo, hastening to the side of a pallet, that lay on the floor.

The attenuated and feeble form of an old man rose at the word, and an eye which, while it spoke mental feebleness, was at that moment even brighter than that of his son, glared on the faces of Gelsomina and her companion.

"Thou hast not suffered, as I had feared, by this sudden change, father!" continued the latter, kneeling by the side of the straw.—"Thine eye, and cheek, and countenance are better, than in the damp caves below!"

"I am happy here," returned the prisoner;—"there is light, and though they have given me too much of it, thou canst never know, my boy, the joy of looking at the day, after so long a night."

"He is better, Gelsomina!—They have not yet destroyed him. See!—his eye is bright even, and his cheek has a glow!"

"They are ever so, after passing the winter in the lower dungeons," whispered the gentle girl.

"Hast thou news for me, boy?—What tidings from thy mother?"

Jacopo bowed his head to conceal the anguish occasioned by this question, which he now heard for the hundredth time.

"She is happy, father—happy as one can be, who so well loves thee, when away from thy side."

"Does she speak of me often?"

"The last word that I heard from her lips was thy name."

"Holy Maria, bless her! I trust she remembers me in her prayers?"

"Doubt it not, father,—they are the prayers of an angel!"

"And thy patient sister?—thou hast not named her, son."

247

"She, too, is well, father."

"Has she ceased to blame herself for being the innocent cause of my sufferings?"

"She has."

"Then she pines no longer over a blow that cannot be helped."

The Bravo seemed to search for relief in the sympathizing eye of the pale and speechless Gelsomina.

"She has ceased to pine, father," he uttered with compelled calmness.

"Thou hast ever loved thy sister, boy, with manly tenderness. Thy heart is kind, as I have reason to know. If God has given me grief, he has blessed me in my children!"

A long pause followed, during which the parent seemed to muse on the past, while the child rejoiced in the suspension of questions which harrowed his soul, since those of whom the other spoke had long been the victims of family misfortune. The old man, for the prisoner was aged, as well as feeble, turned his look on the still kneeling Bravo, thoughtfully, and continued.

"There is little hope of thy sister marrying, for none are fond of tying themselves to the proscribed."

"She wishes it not—she wishes it not—she is happy, with my mother!"

"It is a happiness the republic will not begrudge. Is there no hope of our being able to meet soon?"

"Thou wilt meet my mother,—yes, that pleasure will come at last!"

"It is a weary time since any of my blood but thee have stood in my sight. Kneel, that I may bless thee."

Jacopo, who had arisen under his mental torture, obeyed, and bowed his head in reverence to receive the paternal benediction. The lips of the old man moved, and his eyes were turned to Heaven, but his language was of the heart, rather than that of the tongue. Gelsomina bent her head to her bosom, and seemed to unite her prayers to those of the prisoner. When the silent but solemn ceremony was ended, each made the customary sign of the cross, and Jacopo kissed the wrinkled hand of the captive.

"Hast thou hope for me?" the old man asked, this pious and grateful duty done. "Do they still promise to let me look upon the sun, again?"

"They do.—They promise fair."

"Would that their words were true! I have lived on hope, for a weary time—I have now been within these walls more than four years, methinks."

Jacopo did not answer, for he knew that his father named the period only that he himself had been permitted to see him.

"I built upon the expectation, that the doge would remember his ancient servant, and open my prison doors."

Still Jacopo was silent, for the doge of whom the other spoke had long been dead.

"And yet I should be grateful, for Maria and the saints have not forgotten me. I am not without my pleasures, in captivity."

"God be praised!" returned the Bravo. "In what manner dost thou ease thy sorrows, father?"

"Look hither, boy," exclaimed the old man, whose eye betrayed a mixture of feverish excitement, caused by the recent change in his prison, and the growing imbecility of a mind that was gradually losing its powers for want of use; "dost thou see the rent in that bit of wood? It opens with the heat, from time to time, and since I have been an inhabitant here, that fissure has doubled in length—I sometimes fancy, that when it reaches the knot, the hearts of the senators will soften, and that my doors will open. There is a satisfaction, in watching its increase, as it lengthens, inch by inch, year after year!"

"Is this all?"

"Nay, I have other pleasures. There was a spider the past year, that wove his web from yonder beam, and he was a companion, too, that I loved to see; wilt thou look, boy, if there is hope of his coming back?"

"I see him not," whispered the Bravo.

"Well, there is always the hope of its return. The flies will enter soon, and then he will be looking for his prey. They may shut me up on a false charge, and keep me weary years from my wife and daughter, but they cannot rob me of all my happiness!"

The aged captive was mute and thoughful. A childish impatience glowed in his eye, and he gazed from the rent, the companion of so many solitary summers, to the face of his son, like one who began to distrust his enjoyments.

"Well, let them take it away," he said, burying his head beneath the covering of his bed; "I will not curse them!"

"Father!"

The prisoner made no reply.

"Father!"

"Jacopo!"

In his turn the Bravo was speechless. He did not venture, even, to steal a glance towards the breathless and attentive Gelsomina, though his bosom heaved with longing to examine her guileless features.

"Dost thou hear me, son?" continued the prisoner, uncovering his head: "dost thou really think they will have the heart to chase the spider from my cell?"

"They will leave thee this pleasure, father, for it touches neither their power, nor their fame. So long as the senate can keep its foot on the neck of the people, and so long as it can keep the seemliness of a good name, it will not envy thee this."

"Blessed Maria, make me thankful!—I had my fears, child; for it is not pleasant to lose any friend in a cell!"

Jacopo then proceeded to soothe the mind of the prisoner, and he gradually led his thoughts to other subjects. He laid by the bedside a few articles of food, that he was allowed to bring with him, and again holding out the hope of eventual liberation, he proposed to take his leave.

"I will try to believe thee, son," said the old man, who had good reason to distrust assurances so often made. "I will do all I can to believe it. Thou wilt tell thy mother, that I never cease to think of her, and to pray for her; and thou wilt bless thy sister, in the name of her poor imprisoned parent."

The Bravo bowed in acquiescence, glad of any means to escape speech. At a sign from the old man he again bent his knee, and received the parting benediction. After busying himself in arranging the scanty furniture of the cell, and in trying to open one or two small fissures, with a view to admit more light and air, he quitted the place.

Neither Gelsomina nor Jacopo spoke, as they returned by the intricate passages through which they had ascended to the attic, until they were again on the Bridge of Sighs. It was seldom that human foot trod this gallery, and the former, with female quickness, selected it as a place suited to their further conference.

"Dost thou find him changed?" she asked, lingering on the arch.

"Much."

250

"Thou speakest with a frightful meaning!"

"I have not taught my countenance to lie to thee, Gelsomina."

"But there is hope.—Thou told'st him there was hope, thyself."

"Blessed Maria forgive the fraud! I could not rob the little life he has, of its only comfort."

"Carlo!—Carlo!—Why art thou so calm? I have never heard thee speak so calmly of thy father's wrongs and imprisonment."

"It is because his liberation is near."

"But this moment he was without hope, and thou speakest, now, of liberation!"

"The liberation of death. Even the anger of the senate will respect the grave."

"Dost thou think his end near? I had not seen this change."

"Thou art kind, good Gelsomina, and true to thy friends, and without suspicion of those crimes of which thou art so innocent; but to one who has seen as much evil as I, a jealous thought comes at every new event. The sufferings of my poor father are near their end, for nature is worn out; but were it not, I can foresee that means would be found to bring them to a close."

"Thou canst not suspect that any here would do him harm!"

"I suspect none that belong to thee. Both thy father and thyself, Gelsomina, are placed here by the interposition of the saints, that the fiends should not have too much power on earth."

"I do not understand thee, Carlo—but thou art often so.— Thy father used a word today that I could wish he had not, in speaking to thee."

The eye of the Bravo threw a quick, uneasy, suspicious glance at his companion, and then averted its look with haste.

"He called thee Jacopo!" continued the girl.

"Men often have glimpses of their fate, by the kindness of their patrons."

"Would'st thou say, Carlo, that thy father suspects the senate will employ the monster he named?"

"Why not?—they have employed worse men. If report says true, he is not unknown to them."

"Can this be so!—Thou art bitter against the republic, because it has done injury to thy family; but thou canst not believe it has ever dealt with the hired stiletto."

251

"I said no more than is whispered daily on the canals."

"I would thy father had not called thee by this terrible name, Carlo!"

"Thou art too wise to be moved by a word, Gelsomina. But what thinkest thou of my unhappy father?"

"This visit has not been like the others thou hast made him in my company. I know not the reason, but to me thou hast ever seemed to feel the hope with which thou hast cheered the prisoner; while now, thou seemest to have even a frightful pleasure in despair."

"Thy fears deceive thee," returned the Bravo, scarce speaking above his breath. "Thy fears deceive thee, and we will say no more. The senate mean to do us justice, at last. They are honorable Signori, of illustrious birth, and renowned names!—'Twould be madness to distrust the patricians! Dost thou not know, girl, that he who is born of gentle blood is above the weaknesses and temptations that beset us of base origin? They are men placed by birth above the weaknesses of mortals, and owing their account to none, they will be sure to do justice. This is reasonable, and who can doubt it!"

As he ended, the Bravo laughed bitterly.

"Nay, now thou triflest with me, Carlo; none are above the danger of doing wrong, but those whom the saints and kind Maria favor."

"This comes of living in a prison, and of saying thy prayers night and morning! No—no—silly girl, there are men in the world born wise, from generation to generation; born honest, virtuous, brave, incorruptible, and fit in all things to shut up and imprison those who are born base and ignoble. Where hast thou passed thy days, foolish Gelsomina, not to have felt this truth, in the very air thou breathest? 'Tis clear as the sun's light, and palpable—ay—palpable as these prison walls!"

The timid girl recoiled from his side, and there was a moment when she meditated flight; for never before, during their numberless and confidential interviews, had she ever heard so bitter a laugh, or seen so wild a gleam in the eye of her companion.

"I could almost fancy, Carlo, that thy father was right in using the name he did," she said, as recovering herself, she turned a reproachful look on his still excited features.

"It is the business of parents to name their children;—but, enough. I must leave thee, good Gelsomina, and I leave thee with a heavy heart."

252

The unsuspecting Gelsomina forgot her alarm. She knew not why, but, though the imaginary Carlo seldom quitted her that she was not sad, she felt a weight heavier than common on her spirits at this declaration.

"Thou hast thy affairs, and they must not be forgotten. Art fortunate with the gondola, of late, Carlo?"

"Gold and I are nearly strangers. The republic throws the whole charge of the venerable prisoner on my toil."

"I have little, as thou knowest, Carlo," said Gelsomina, in a half-audible voice; "but it is thine. My father is not rich, as thou canst feel, or he would not live on the sufferings of others, by holding the keys of the prison."

"He is better employed than those who set the duty. Were the choice given me, girl, to wear the horned bonnet, to feast in their halls, to rest in their palaces, to be the gayest bauble in such a pageant as that of yesterday, to plot in their secret councils, and to be the heartless judge to condemn my fellows to this misery—or to be merely the keeper of the keys and turner of the bolts—I should seize on the latter office, as not only the most innocent, but by far the most honorable!"

"Thou dost not judge as the world judges, Carlo. I had feared thou might'st feel shame at being the husband of a jailer's daughter; nay, I will not hide the secret longer, since thou speakest so calmly, I have wept that it should be so."

"Then thou hast neither understood the world nor me. Were thy father of the senate, or of the Council of Three, could the grievous fact be known, thou would'st have cause to sorrow. But Gelsomina, the canals are getting dusky, and I must leave thee."

The reluctant girl saw the truth of what he said, and applying a key, she opened the door of the covered bridge. A few turnings and a short descent brought the Bravo and his companion to the level of the quays. Here the former took a hurried leave and quitted the prison.

253

CHAPTER XX

"But they who blunder thus are raw beginners."

Don Juan

THE hour had come for the revels of the piazza, and for the movement of the gondolas. Maskers glided along the porticoes as usual; the song and cry were heard anew, and Venice was again absorbed in delusive gaiety.

When Jacopo issued from the prison on the quay, he mingled with the stream of human beings that was setting towards the squares, protected from observation by the privileged mask. While crossing the lower bridge of the canal of St. Mark, he lingered an instant, to throw a look at the glazed gallery he had just quitted, and then moved forward with the crowd—the image of the artless and confiding Gelsomina uppermost in his thoughts. As he passed slowly among the gloomy arches of the Broglio, his eye sought the person of Don Camillo Monforte. They met at the angle of the little square, and exchanging secret signs, the Bravo moved on unnoticed.

Hundreds of boats lay at the foot of the piazzetta. Among these Jacopo sought his own gondola, which he extricated from the floating mass, and urged into the stream. A few sweeps of the oar, and he lay at the side of *La Bella Sorrentina*. The padrone paced the deck, enjoying the cool of the evening, with Italian indolence, while his people sang, or rather chanted, a song of those seas, grouped on the forecastle. The greetings were blunt and brief, as is usual among men of that class. But the padrone appeared to expect the visit, for he led his guest far from the ears of his crew, to the other extremity of the felucca.

"Hast thou aught in particular, good Roderigo?" demanded the mariner, who knew the Bravo by a sign, and yet who only knew him by that fictitious name. "Thou seest we have not passed the time idly, though yesterday was a festa."

"Art though ready for the gulf?"

"For the Levant, or the pillars of Hercules, as shall please the senate. We have got our yard aloft since the sun went behind the mountains, and though we may seem careless of delay, an hour's notice will fit us for the outside of the Lido."

"Then take the notice."

"Master Roderigo, you bring your news to an overstocked market. I have already been informed that we shall be wanted tonight."

The quick movement of suspicion made by the Bravo escaped the observation of the padrone, whose eye was running over the felucca's gear, with a sailor's habitual attention to that part of his vessel, when there was question of its service.

"Thou art right, Stefano. But there is little harm in repeated caution. Preparation is the first duty in a delicate commission."

"Will you look for yourself, Signor Roderigo?" said the mariner, in a lower tone. "*La Bella Sorrentina* is not the Bucentaur, nor a galley of the Grand Master of Malta; but, for her size, better rooms are not to be had in the palace of the doge. When they told me there was a lady in the freight, the honor of Calabria was stirred in her behalf."

" 'Tis well. If they have named to thee all the particulars, thou wilt not fail to do thyself credit."

"I do not say that they have shown me half of them, good Signore," interrupted Stefano. "The secrecy of your Venetian shipments is my greatest objection to the trade. It has more than once happened to me, that I have lain weeks in the canals, with my hold as clean as a friar's conscience, when orders have come to weigh, with some such cargo as a messenger, who has got into his berth as we cleared the port, to get out of it on the coast of Dalmatia, or among the Greek islands."

"In such cases thou hast earned thy money easily."

"Diamine! Master Roderigo, if I had a friend in Venice to give timely advice, the felucca might be ballasted with articles that would bring a profit, on the other shore. Of what concern is it to the senate, when I do my duty to the nobles faithfully, that I do my duty at the same time to the good woman and her little brown children, left at home, in Calabria?"

"There is much reason in what thou sayest, Stefano; but thou knowest the republic is a hard master. An affair of this nature must be touched with a gentle hand."

"None know it better than I, for when they sent the trader with all his movables out of the city, I was obliged to throw certain casks into the sea, to make room for his worthless stuffs.

255

The senate owes me just compensation for that loss, worthy Signor Roderigo!"

"Which thou would'st be glad to repair, tonight?"

"Santissima Maria! You may be the doge himself, Signore, for anything I know of your countenance; but I could swear at the altar you ought to be of the senate for your sagacity!—If this lady will not be burthened with many effects, and there is yet time, I might humor the tastes of the Dalmatians with certain of the articles that come from the countries beyond the pillars of Hercules!"

"Thou art the judge of the probability thyself, since they told thee of the nature of thy errand."

"San Gennaro of Napoli, open my eyes!—They said not a word beyond this little fact, that a youthful lady, in whom the senate had great interest, would quit the city this night for the eastern coast. If it is at all agreeable to your conscience, Master Roderigo, I should be happy to hear who are to be her companions?"

"Of that thou shalt hear more in proper season. In the meantime I would recommend to thee a cautious tongue, for St. Mark makes no idle jokes with those who offend him. I am glad to see thee in this state of preparation, worthy padrone, and wishing thee a happy night, and a prosperous voyage, I commit thee to thy patron. But hold—ere I quit thee, I would know the hour that the land breeze will serve?"

"You are exact as a compass in your own matters, Signore, but of little charity to thy friends! With the burning sun of today we should have the air of the Alps, about the turn of the night."

"'Tis well.—My eye shall be on thee. Once more, addio."

"Cospetto! and thou hast said nothing of the cargo?"

"'Twill not be so weighty in bulk as in value," carelessly answered Jacopo, shoving his gondola from the side of the felucca. The fall of his oar into the water succeeded, and as Stefano stood, meditating the chances of his speculation on his deck, the boat glided away towards the quay, with a swift but easy movement.

Deceit, like the windings of that subtle animal the fox, often crosses its own path. It consequently throws out those by whom it is practised, as well as those who are meant to be its victims. When Jacopo parted from Don Camillo, it was with an under-

256

standing that he should adopt all the means that his native sagacity, or his experience might suggest, to ascertain in what manner the council intended to dispose of the person of Donna Violetta. They had separated on the Lido, and as none knew of their interview but him, and none would probably suspect their recent alliance, the Bravo entered on his new duty with some chances of success that might otherwise have been lost. A change of its agents, in affairs of peculiar delicacy, was one of the ordinary means taken by the republic to avoid investigation. Jacopo had often been its instrument in negotiating with the mariner, who, as has been so plainly intimated, had frequently been engaged in carrying into effect its secret, and perhaps justifiable measures of police; but in no instance had it ever been found necessary to interpose a second agent between the commencement and the consummation of its bargains, except in this. He had been ordered to see the padrone, and to keep him in preparation for immediate service; but since the examination of Antonio before the council, his employers had neglected to give him any farther instructions. The danger of leaving the bride within reach of the agents of Don Camillo was so obvious that this unusual caution had been considered necessary. It was under this disadvantage, therefore, that Jacopo entered on the discharge of his new and important duties.

That cunning, as has just been observed, is apt to overreach itself has passed into a proverb; and the case of Jacopo and his employers was one in point to prove its truth. The unusual silence of those who ordinarily sought him on similar occasions had not been lost on the agent; and the sight of the felucca, as he strayed along the quays, gave an accidental direction to his inquiries. The manner in which they were aided, by the cupidity of the Calabrian, has just been related.

Jacopo had no sooner touched the quay and secured his boat, than he hastened again to the Broglio. It was now filled by maskers and the idlers of the piazzetta. The patricians had withdrawn to the scenes of their own pleasures, or, in furtherance of that system of mysterious sway which it was their policy to maintain, they did not choose to remain exposed to the common eye, during the hours of license which were about to follow.

It would seem that Jacopo had his instructions, for no sooner did he make sure that Don Camillo had retired, than he threaded the throng with the air of a man whose course was decided.

By this time, both the squares were full, and at least half of those who spent the night in those places of amusement were masked. The step of the Bravo, though so unhesitating, was leisurely, and he found time, in passing up the piazzetta, to examine the forms, and, when circumstances permitted, the features of all he met. He proceeded, in this manner, to the point of junction between the two squares, when his elbow was touched by a light hand.

Jacopo was not accustomed, unnecessarily, to trust his voice in the square of St. Mark, and at that hour. But his look of inquiry was returned by a sign to follow. He had been stopped by one whose figure was so completely concealed by a domino as to baffle all conjecture concerning his true character. Perceiving, however, that the other wished to lead him to a part of the square that was vacant, and which was directly on the course he was about to pursue, the Bravo made a gesture of compliance and followed. No sooner were the two apart from the pressure of the crowd, and in a place where no eavesdropper could overhear their discourse without detection, than the stranger stopped. He appeared to examine the person, stature, and dress of Jacopo, from beneath his mask, with singular caution, closing the whole with a sign that meant recognition. Jacopo returned his dumb show, but maintained a rigid silence.

"Just Daniel!" muttered the stranger, when he found that his companion was not disposed to speak; "one would think, illustrious Signore, that your confessor had imposed a penance of silence, by the manner in which you refuse to speak to your servant."

"What would'st thou?"

"Here am I, sent into the piazza, among knights of industry, valets, gondoliers, and all other manner of revellers that adorn this Christian land, in search of the heir of one of the most ancient and honorable houses of Venice."

"How knowest thou I am he thou seekest?"

"Signore, there are many signs seen by a wise man that escape the unobservant. When young cavaliers have a taste for mingling with the people in honorable disguise, as in the case of a certain patrician of this republic, they are to be known by their air, if not by their voices."

"Thou art a cunning agent, Hosea; but the shrewdness of thy race is its livelihood!"

258

"It is its sole defence against the wrongs of the oppressor, young noble. We are hunted like wolves, and it is not surprising that we sometimes show the ferocity of the beasts you take us for. But why should I tell the wrongs of my people to one who believes life is a masquerade!"

"And who would not be sorry, ingenious Hosea, were it composed only of Hebrews! But, thy errand; I have no gage unredeemed, nor do I know that I owe thee gold."

"Righteous Samuel! you cavaliers of the senate are not always mindful of the past, Signore, or these are words that might have been spared. If your excellency is inclined to forget pledges, the fault is not of my seeking; but as for the account that has been so long growing between us, there is not a dealer on the Rialto that will dispute the proofs."

"Well, be it so—would'st thou dun my father's son in the face of the revellers in St. Mark?"

"I would do no discredit to any come of that illustrious race, Signore, and therefore we will say no more of the matter; always relying that, at the proper moment, you will not question your own hand and seal."

"I like thy prudence, Hebrew. It is a pledge thou comest on some errand less ungracious than common. As I am pressed for time, 'twill be a favor wert thou to name it."

Hosea examined, in a covert but very thorough manner, the vacant spot around them, and drawing nearer to the supposed noble, he continued.

"Signore, your family is in danger of meeting with a great loss! It is known to you that the senate has altogether and suddenly removed Donna Violetta, from the keeping of the faithful and illustrious senator your father."

Though Jacopo started slightly, the movement was so natural for a disappointed lover, that it rather aided than endangered his disguise.

"Compose yourself, young Signore," continued Hosea; "these disappointments attend us all in youth, as I know by severe trials. Leah was not gained without trouble, and next to success in barter, success in love is perhaps the most uncertain. Gold is a great make-weight in both, and it commonly prevails. But, you are nearer to losing the lady of your love and her possessions, than you may imagine, for I am sent expressly to say, that she is about to be removed from the city."

259

"Whither?" demanded Jacopo, so quickly as to do credit to his assumed character.

"That is the point to learn, Signore. Thy father is a sagacious senator, and is deep, at times, in the secrets of the state. But, judging from his uncertainty on this occasion, I take it he is guided more by his calculations, than by any assurance of his own knowledge. Just Daniel! I have seen the moments when I have suspected that the venerable patrician himself was a member of the Council of Three!"

"His house is ancient and his privileges well established—why should he not?"

"I say naught against it, Signore. It is a wise body, that doeth much good, and preventeth much harm. None speak evil of the secret councils on the Rialto, where men are more given to gainful industry than to wild discussions of their rulers' acts. But, Signore, be he of this or that council, or merely of the senate, a heedful hint has fallen from his lips, of the danger we are in of losing—"

"We!—Hast thou thoughts of Donna Violetta, Hosea?"

"Leah and the law forbid!—If the comely queen of Sheba, herself, were to tempt me, and a frail nature showed signs of weakness, I doubt that our rabbis would find reasons for teaching self-denial! Besides, the daughter of Levi is no favorer of polygamy, nor any other of our sex's privileges. I spoke in pluralities, Signore, because the Rialto has some stake in this marriage, as well as the house of Gradenigo."

"I understand thee. Thou hast fears for thy gold?"

"Had I been easily alarmed, Signor Giacomo, in that particular, I might not have parted with it so readily. But, though the succession of thy illustrious father will be ample to meet any loan within my humble means, that of the late Signor Tiepolo will not weaken the security."

"I admit thy sagacity, and feel the importance of thy warning. But it seems to have no other object, or warranty, than thy own fears."

"With certain obscure hints from your honored father, Signore."

"Did he say more to the point?"

"He spoke in parables, young noble, but having an oriental ear, his words were not uttered to the wind. That the rich damsel is about to be conveyed from Venice am I certain, and for the benefit of the little stake I have myself in her movements, I would give the best turquoise in my shop to know whither."

"Canst thou say with certainty, 'twill be this night."

"Giving no pledge for redemption in the event of mistake, I am so sure, young cavalier, as to have many unquiet thoughts."

"Enough—I will look to my own interests, and to thine."

Jacopo waved his hand in adieu, and pursued his walk up the piazza.

"Had I looked more sharply to the latter, as became one accustomed to deal with the accursed race," muttered the Hebrew, "it would be a matter of no concern to me if the girl married a Turk!"

"Hosea," said a mask at his ear; "a word with thee, in secret."

The jeweller started, and found that, in his zeal, he had suffered one to approach within sound of his voice unseen. The other was in a domino also, and so well enveloped as to be effectually concealed.

"What would'st thou, Signor Mask?" demanded the wary Jew.

"A word in friendship and in confidence.—Thou hast moneys to lend at usury?"

"The question had better be put to the republic's treasury! I have many stones, valued much below their weight, and would be glad to put them, with some one more lucky than myself, who will be able to keep them."

"Nay, this will not suffice—thou art known to be abounding in sequins; one of thy race and riches will never refuse a sure loan, with securities as certain as the laws of Venice. A thousand ducats in thy willing hand is no novelty."

"They who call me rich, Signor Mask, are pleased to joke with the unhappy child of a luckless race. That I might have been above want—nay, that I am not downright needy, may be true; but when they speak of a thousand ducats, they speak of affairs too weighty for my burthened shoulders. Were it your pleasure to purchase an amethyst, or a ruby, gallant Signore, there might possibly be dealings between us?"

"I have need of gold, old man, and can spare thee jewels myself, at need. My wants are urgent, at this moment, and I have little time to lose in words—name thy conditions."

"One should have good securities, Signore, to be so peremptory in a matter of money."

"Thou hast heard that the laws of Venice are not more certain. A thousand sequins, and that quickly. Thou shalt settle the usury with thine own conscience."

Hosea thought that this was giving ample room to the treaty, and he began to listen more seriously.

"Signore," he said, "a thousand ducats are not picked up at pleasure from the pavement of the great square. He who would lend them must first earn them with long and patient toil; and he who would borrow—"

"Waits at thy elbow."

"Should have a name and countenance well known on the Rialto."

"Thou lendest on sufficient pledges to masks, careful Hosea, or fame belies thy generosity."

"A sufficient pledge gives me power to see the way clearly, though the borrower should be as much hidden as those up above. But here is none forthcoming. Come to me tomorrow, masked or not, as may suit your own pleasure, for I have no impertinent desire to pry into any man's secrets, beyond what a regard to my own interests requires, and I will look into my coffers; though those of no heir apparent in Venice can be emptier."

"My necessities are too urgent to brook delay. Hast thou the gold, on condition of naming thine own usury?"

"With sufficient pledges in stones of price, I might rake together the sum, among our dispersed people, Signore. But he who goes on the island to borrow, as I shall be obliged to do, should be able to satisfy all doubts concerning the payment."

"The gold can then be had—on that point I may be easy?"

Hosea hesitated, for he had in vain endeavored to penetrate the other's disguise, and while he thought his assurance a favorable omen, with a lender's instinct he disliked his impatience.

"I have said, by the friendly aid of our people," he answered, with caution.

"This uncertainty will not answer my need. Addio, Hosea,—I must seek elsewhere."

"Signore, you could not be more hurried were the money to pay the cost of your nuptials. Could I find Isaac and Aaron within, at this late hour, I think I might be safe in saying that part of the money might be had."

"I cannot trust to this chance."

"Nay, Signore, the chance is but small, since Aaron is bed-ridden, and Isaac never fails to look into his affairs, after the toil of the day is ended. The honest Hebrew finds sufficient recreation in the employment, though I marvel at his satisfaction, since nothing but losses have come over our people the year past!"

"I tell thee, Jew, no doubt must hang over the negotiation. The money, with pledges, and thine own conscience for arbiter between us; but no equivocal dealings, to be followed by a disappointment, under the pretence that second parties are not satisfied."

"Just Daniel! to oblige you, Signore, I think I may venture!— The well-known Hebrew, Levi of Livorno, has left with me a sack, containing the very sum of which there is question, and, under the conditions named, I will convert it to my uses, and repay the good jeweller his gold, with moneys of my own, at a later day."

"I thank thee for the fact, Hosea," said the other, partially removing his mask, but as instantly replacing it. "It will greatly shorten our negotiations. Thou hast not that sack of the Jew of Livorno beneath thy domino?"

Hosea was speechless. The removal of the mask had taught him two material facts. He had been communicating his distrust of the senate's intentions concerning Donna Violetta to an unknown person, and, possibly, to an agent of the police; and he had just deprived himself of the only argument he had ever found available, in refusing the attempts of Giacomo Gradenigo to borrow, by admitting to that very inddividual that he had in his power the precise sum required.

"I trust the face of an old customer is not likely to defeat our bargain, Hosea?" demanded the profligate heir of the senator, scarce concealing the irony in which the question was put.

"Father Abraham! Had I known it had been you, Signor Giacomo, we might have greatly shortened the treaty."

"By denying that thou hadst the money, as thou hast so often done of late!"

"Nay, nay, I am not a swallower of my own words, young Signore; but my duty to Levi must not be forgotten. The careful Hebrew made me take a vow, by the name of our tribe, that I would not part with his gold to any that had not the means of placing its return beyond all chances."

"This assurance is not wanting, since thou art the borrower, thyself, to lend to me."

"Signore, you place my conscience in an awkward position. You are now my debtor some six thousand sequins, and were I to make this loan of money in trust, and were you to return it—two propositions I make on supposition—a natural love for my own might cause me to pass the payment to account, whereby I should put the assets of Levi in jeopardy."

"Settle that as thou wilt with thy conscience, Hosea—thou hast confessed to the money, and here are jewels for the pledge—I ask only the sequins."

It is probable that the appeal of Giacomo Gradenigo would not have produced much effect on the flinty nature of the Hebrew, who had all the failings of a man proscribed by opinion; but having recovered from his surprise, he began to explain to his companion his apprehensions on account of Donna Violetta, whose marriage, it will be remembered, was a secret to all but the witnesses and the Council of Three, when to his great joy he found that the gold was wanting to advance his own design of removing her to some secret place. This immediately changed the whole face of the bargain. As the pledges offered were really worth the sum to be received, Hosea thought, taking the chances of recovering back his ancient loans, from the foreign estates of the heiress, into the account, the loan would be no bad investment of the pretended sequins of his friend Levi.

As soon as the parties had come to a clear understanding, they left the square together to consummate their bargain.

CHAPTER XXI

"We'll follow Cade, we'll follow Cade."
Henry VI

THE night wore on. The strains of music again began to break through the ordinary stillness of the town, and the boats of the great were once more in motion on every canal. Hands waved timidly in recognition, from the windows of the little dark canopies, as the gondolas glided by, but few paused to greet each other in that city of mystery and suspicion. Even the refreshing air of the evening was inhaled under an appearance of restraint, which, though it might not be at the moment felt, was too much interwoven with the habits of the people, ever to be entirely thrown aside.

Among the lighter and gayer barges of the patricians, a gondola of more than usual size, but of an exterior so plain as to denote vulgar uses, came sweeping down the Great Canal. Its movement was leisurely, and the action of the gondoliers that of men either fatigued or little pressed for time. He who steered guided the boat with consummate skill, but with a single hand, while his three fellows, from time to time, suffered their oars to trail on the water in very idleness. In short, it had the ordinary listless appearance of a boat returning to the city, from an excursion on the Brenta, or to some of the more distant isles.

Suddenly, the gondola diverged from the centre of the passage, down which it rather floated than pulled, and shot into one of the least frequented canals of the city. From this moment its movement became more rapid and regular, until it reached a quarter of the town inhabited by the lowest order of the Venetians. Here it stopped by the side of a warehouse, and one of its crew ascended to a bridge. The others threw themselves on the thwarts and seemed to repose.

He who quitted the boat threaded a few narrow but public alleys, such as are to be found in every part of that confined town, and knocked lightly at a window. It was not long before the casement opened, and a female voice demanded the name of him without.

265

"It is I, Annina," returned Gino, who was not an unfrequent applicant for admission, at that private portal. "Open the door, girl, for I have come on a matter of pressing haste."

Annina complied, though not without making sure that her suitor was alone.

"Thou art come unseasonably, Gino," said the wine seller's daughter; "I was about to go to St. Mark's to breathe the evening air. My father and brothers are already departed, and I only stay to make sure of the bolts."

"Their gondola will hold a fourth?"

"They have gone by the footways."

"And thou walkest the streets alone at this hour, Annina?"

"I know not thy right to question it, if I do," returned the girl, with spirit. "San Teodoro be praised, I am not yet the slave of a Neapolitan's servitor!"

"The Neapolitan is a powerful noble, Annina, able and willing to keep his servitors in respect."

"He will have need of all his interest—but why hast thou come at this unseasonable hour? Thy visits are never too welcome, Gino, and when I have other affairs, they are disagreeable."

Had the passion of the gondolier been very deep or very sensitive, this plain dealing might have given him a shock; but Gino appeared to take the repulse as coolly as it was given.

"I am used to thy caprices, Annina," he said, throwing himself upon a bench, like one determined to remain where he was. "Some young patrician has kissed his hand to thee as thou hast crossed San Marco, or thy father has made a better day of it than common on the Lido—thy pride always mounts with thy father's purse."

"Diamine! to hear the fellow, one would think he had my troth, and that he only waited in the sacristy for the candles to be lighted to receive my vows! What art thou to me, Gino [Monaldi]* that thou takest on thee these sudden airs?"

"And what art thou to me, Annina, that thou playest off these worn-out caprices on Don Camillo's confidant?"

"Out upon thee, insolent! I have no time to waste in idleness."

* First edition reads "Tullini"; corrected in second British edition, London, 1834.

"Thou art in much haste tonight, Annina."

"To be rid of thee. Now listen to what I say, Gino, and let every word go to thy heart, for they are the last thou wilt ever hear from me. Thou servest a decayed noble, one who will shortly be chased in disgrace from the city, and with him will go all his idle servitors. I choose to remain in the city of my birth."

The gondolier laughed in real indifference at her affected scorn. But remembering his errand, he quickly assumed a graver air, and endeavored to still the resentment of his fickle mistress by a more respectful manner.

"St. Mark protect me, Annina!" he said. "If we are not to kneel before the good priore together, it is no reason we should not bargain in wines. Here have I come into the dark canals, within stone's-throw of thy very door, with a gondola of mellow lachrymae christi, such as honest Maso, thy father, has rarely dealt in, and thou treatest me as a dog that is chased from a church!"

"I have little time for thee, or thy wines, tonight, Gino. Hadst thou not stayed me, I should already have been abroad and happy."

"Close thy door, girl, and make little ceremony with an old friend," said the gondolier, officiously offering to aid her in securing the dwelling. Annina took him at his word, and as both appeared to work with good will, the house was locked, and the wilful girl and her suitor were soon in the street. Their route lay across the bridge already named. Gino pointed to the gondola, as he said, "Thou art not to be tempted, Annina?"

"Thy rashness in leading the smugglers to my father's door will bring us to harm some day, silly fellow!"

"The boldness of the act will prevent suspicion."

"Of what vineyard is the liquor?"

"It came from the foot of Vesuvius, and is ripened by the heat of the volcano. Should my friends part with it to thy enemy, old Beppo, thy father will rue the hour!"

Annina, who was much addicted to consulting her interests on all occasions, cast a longing glance at the boat. The canopy was closed, but it was large, and her willing imagination readily induced her to fancy it well fitted with skins from Naples.

"This will be the last of thy visits to our door, Gino?"

"As thou shalt please.—But go down and taste—"

Annina hesitated, and, as a woman is said always to do when she hesitates, she complied. They reached the boat, with quick steps, and without regarding the men who were still lounging on the thwarts, Annina glided immediately beneath the canopy. A fifth gondolier was lying at length on the cushions, for, unlike a boat devoted to the contraband, the canopy had the usual arrangement of a bark of the canals.

"I see nothing to turn me aside!" exclaimed the disappointed girl. "Wilt thou aught with me, Signore?"

"Thou art welcome. We shall not part so readily as before."

The stranger had arisen while speaking, and as he ended, he laid a hand on the shoulder of his visitor, who found herself confronted with Don Camillo Monforte.

Annina was too much practised in deception to indulge in any of the ordinary female symptoms, either of real or of affected alarm. Commanding her features, though in truth her limbs shook, she said, with assumed pleasantry—

"The secret trade is honored in the services of the noble Duke of St. Agata!"

"I am not here to trifle, girl, as thou wilt see in the end. Thou hast thy choice before thee, frank confession, or my just anger."

Don Camillo spoke calmly, but in a manner that plainly showed Annina she had to deal with a resolute man.

"What confession would your eccellenza have from the daughter of a poor wine seller?" she asked, her voice trembling in spite of herself.

"The truth—and remember, that this time we do not part until I am satisfied. The Venetian police and I are now fairly at issue, and thou art the first fruits of my plan."

"Signor Duca, this is a bold step to take in the heart of the canals!"

"The consequences be mine. Thy interest will teach thee to confess."

"I shall make no great merit, Signore, of doing that which is forced upon me. As it is your pleasure to know the little I can tell you, I am happy to be permitted to relate it."

"Speak, then; for time presses."

"Signore, I shall not pretend to deny you have been ill-treated. Capperi! how ill has the council treated you! A noble cavalier, of a strange country, who, the meanest gossip in Venice knows, has a just right to the honors of the senate, to be so

268

treated is a disgrace to the republic! I do not wonder that your eccellenza is out of humor with them. Blessed St. Mark himself would lose his patience to be thus treated!"

"A truce with this, girl, and to your facts."

"My facts, Signor Duca, are a thousand times clearer than the sun, and they are all at your eccellenza's service. I am sure I wish I had more of them, since they give you pleasure."

"Enough of this profession.—Speak to the facts themselves."

Annina, who, in the manner of most of her class in Italy that had been exposed to the intrigues of the towns, had been lavish of her words, now found means to cast a glance at the water, when she saw that the boat had already quitted the canals, and was rowing easily out upon the Lagunes. Perceiving how completely she was in the power of Don Camillo, she began to feel the necessity of being more explicit.

"Your eccellenza has probably suspected that the council found means to be acquainted with your intention to fly from the city with Donna Violetta?"

"All that is known to me."

"Why they chose me to be the servitor of the noble lady is beyond my powers to discover. Our Lady of Loretto! I am not the person to be sent for, when the state wishes to part two lovers!"

"I have borne with thee, Annina, because I would let the gondola get beyond the limits of the city; but now thou must throw aside thy subterfuge, and speak plainly. Where didst thou leave my wife?"

"Does your eccellenza then think the state will admit the marriage to be legal?"

"Girl, answer, or I will find means to make thee. Where didst thou leave my wife?"

"Blessed St. Theodore! Signore, the agents of the republic had little need of me, and I was put on the first bridge that the gondola passed."

"Thou strivest to deceive me in vain. Thou wast on the Lagunes till a late hour in the day, and I have notice of thy having visited the prison of St. Mark as the sun was setting; and this on thy return from the boat of Donna Violetta."

There was no acting in the wonder of Annina.

"Santissima Maria! You are better served, Signore, than the council thinks!"

"As thou wilt find to thy cost, unless the truth be spoken. From what convent didst thou come?"

"Signore, from none. If your eccellenza has discovered that the senate has shut up the Signora Tiepolo in the prison of St. Mark, for safe-keeping, it is no fault of mine."

"Thy artifice is useless, Annina," observed Don Camillo, calmly. "Thou wast in the prison, in quest of forbidden articles that thou hadst long left with thy cousin Gelsomina, the keeper's daughter, who little suspected thy errand, and on whose innocence and ignorance of the world thou hast long successfully practised. Donna Violetta is no vulgar prisoner, to be immured in a jail."

"Santissima Madre di Dio!"

Amazement confined the answer of the girl to this single, but strong, exclamation.

"Thou seest the impossibility of deception. I am acquainted with so much of thy movements as to render it impossible that thou should'st lead me far astray. Thou art not wont to visit thy cousin; but as thou entered the canals this evening—"

A shout on the water caused Don Camillo to pause. On looking out he saw a dense body of boats, sweeping towards the town as if they were all impelled by a single set of oars. A thousand voices were speaking at once, and occasionally a general and doleful cry proclaimed that the floating multitude which came on was moved by a common feeling. The singularity of the spectacle, and the fact that his own gondola lay directly in the route of the fleet, which was composed of several hundred boats, drove the examination of the girl, momentarily, from the thoughts of the noble.

"What have we here, Jacopo?" he demanded, in an undertone, of the gondolier who steered his own barge.

"They are fishermen, Signore, and by the manner in which they come down towards the canals, I doubt they are bent on some disturbance. There has been discontent among them since the refusal of the doge to liberate the boy of their companion from the galleys."

Curiosity induced the people of Don Camillo to linger a minute, and then they perceived the necessity of pulling out of the course of the floating mass, which came on like a torrent, the men sweeping their boats with that desperate stroke which is so often seen among the Italian oarsmen. A menacing hail, with a command to remain, admonished Don Camillo of the necessity of downright flight, or of obedience. He chose the latter, as the least likely to interfere with his own plans.

"Who art thou?" demanded one who had assumed the character of a leader. "If men of the Lagunes and Christians, join your friends, and away with us to St. Mark, for justice!"

"What means this tumult?" asked Don Camillo, whose dress effectually concealed his rank, a disguise that he completed by adopting the Venetian dialect. "Why are you here in these numbers, friends?"

"Behold!"

Don Camillo turned, and he beheld the withered features and glaring eyes of old Antonio, fixed in death. The explanation was made by a hundred voices, accompanied by oaths so bitter, and denunciations so deep, that had not Don Camillo been prepared by the tale of Jacopo, he would have found great difficulty in understanding what he heard.

In dragging the Lagunes for fish, the body of Antonio had been found, and the result was, first a consultation on the probable means of his death, then a collection of the men of his calling, and finally the scene described.

"Giustizia!" exclaimed fifty excited voices, as the grim visage of the fisherman was held towards the light of the moon; "Giustizia in palazzo, e pane in piazza!" *

"Ask it of the senate!" returned Jacopo, not attempting to conceal the derision of his tones.

"Thinkest thou our fellow has suffered for his boldness yesterday?"

"Stranger things have happened in Venice!"

"They forbid us to cast our nets in the Canale Orfano, lest the secrets of justice should be known, and yet they have grown bold enough to drown one of our own people in the midst of our gondolas!"

"Justice, justice!" shouted numberless hoarse throats.

"Away to St. Mark's! Lay the body at the feet of the doge— away, brethren—Antonio's blood is on their souls!"

Bent on a wild and undigested scheme of asserting their wrongs, the fishermen again plied their oars, and the whole fleet swept away, as if it were composed of a single mass.

---

* Justice in the palace and bread in the square.—Editor.

The meeting, though so short, was accompanied by cries, menaces, and all those accustomed signs of rage which mark a popular tumult among those excitable people, and it had produced a sensible effect on the nerves of Annina. Don Camillo profited by her evident terror to press his questions, for the hour no longer admitted of trifling.

The result was that while the agitated mob swept into the mouth of the Great Canal, raising hoarse shouts, the gondola of Don Camillo Monforte glided away across the wide and tranquil surface of the Lagunes.

CHAPTER XXII

"A Clifford, a Clifford! we'll follow the king and Clifford."
Henry VI

THE tranquillity of the best ordered society may be disturbed, at any time, by a sudden outbreaking of the malcontents. Against such a disaster there is no more guarding than against the commission of more vulgar crimes; but when a government trembles for its existence, before the turbulence of popular commotion, it is reasonable to infer some radical defect in its organization. Men will rally around their institutions, as freely as they rally around any other cherished interest, when they merit their care, and there can be no surer sign of their hollowness than when the rulers seriously apprehend the breath of the mob. No nation ever exhibited more of this symptomatic terror, on all occasions of internal disturbance, than the pretending republic of Venice. There was a never-ceasing and a natural tendency to dissolution, in her factious system, which was only resisted by the alertness of her aristocracy, and the political buttresses which their ingenuity had reared. Much was said of the venerable character of her polity, and of its consequent security, but it is in vain that selfishness contends with truth. Of all the fallacies with which man has attempted to gloss his expedients, there is none more evidently false than that which infers the duration of a social system, from the length of time it has already lasted. It would be quite as reasonable to affirm that the man of seventy has the same chances for life as the youth of fifteen, or that the inevitable fate of all things of mortal origin was not destruction. There is a period in human existence, when the principle of vitality has to contend with the feebleness of infancy, but this probationary state passed, the child attains the age when it has the most reasonable prospect of living. Thus the social, like any other machine which has run just long enough to prove its fitness, is at the precise period when it is least likely to fail, and although he that is young may not live to become old, it is certain that he who is old was once young. The empire of China

273

was, in its time, as youthful as our own republic, nor can we see any reason for believing that it is to outlast us, from the decrepitude which is a natural companion of its years.

At the period of our tale, Venice boasted much of her antiquity, and dreaded, in an equal degree, her end. She was still strong in her combinations, but they were combinations that had the vicious error of being formed for the benefit of the minority, and which, like the mimic fortresses and moats of a scenic representation, needed only a strong light to destroy the illusion. The alarm with which the patricians heard the shouts of the fishermen, as they swept by the different palaces, on their way to the great square, can be readily imagined. Some feared that the final consummation of their artificial condition, which had so long been anticipated by a secret political instinct, was at length arrived, and began to bethink them of the safest means of providing for their own security. Some listened in admiration, for habit had so far mastered dullness, as to have created a species of identity between the state and far more durable things, and they believed that St. Mark had gained a victory, in that decline, which was never exactly intelligible to their apathetic capacities. But a few, and these were the spirits that accumulated all the national good which was vulgarly and falsely ascribed to the system 'itself, intuitively comprehended the danger, with a just appreciation of its magnitude, as well as of the means to avoid it.

But the rioters were unequal to any estimate of their own force, and had little aptitude in measuring their accidental advantages. They acted merely on impulse. The manner in which their aged companion had triumphed on the preceding day, his cold repulse by the doge, and the scene of the Lido, which in truth led to the death of Antonio, had prepared their minds for the tumult. When the body was found, therefore, after the time necessary to collect their forces on the Lagunes, they yielded to passion, and moved away towards the palace of St. Mark, as described, without any other definite object than a simple indulgence of feeling.

On entering the canal, the narrowness of the passage compressed the boats into a mass so dense, as, in a measure, to impede the use of oars, and the progress of the crowd was necessarily slow. All were anxious to get as near as possible to the body of Antonio, and, like all mobs, they in some degree frustrated their own objects, by ill-regulated zeal. Once or twice the names of offensive senators were shouted, as if the fishermen intended to visit the crimes of the state on its agents; but these cries passed away in the violent breath that was expended. On reaching the bridge of the Rialto, more than half of the multitude landed, and took the shorter course of the streets to the point of destination, while those in front got on the faster, for being disembarrassed of the pressure in the rear. As they drew nearer to the port, the boats began to loosen, and to take something of the form of a funeral procession.

It was during this moment of change that a powerfully manned gondola swept, with strong strokes, out of a lateral passage into the Great Canal. Accident brought it directly in front of the moving phalanx of boats, that was coming down the same channel. Its crew seemed staggered by the extraordinary appearance which met their view, and for an instant its course was undecided.

"A gondola of the republic!" shouted fifty fishermen. A single voice added—"Canale Orfano!"

The bare suspicion of such an errand as was implied by the latter words, and at that moment, was sufficient to excite the mob. They raised a cry of denunciation, and some twenty boats made a furious demonstration of pursuit. The menace, however, was sufficient; for quicker far than the movements of the pursuers, the gondoliers of the republic dashed towards the shore, and leaping on one of those passages of planks which encircle so many of the palaces of Venice, they disappeared by an alley.

Encouraged by this success, the fishermen seized the boat as a waif, and towed it into their own fleet, filling the air with cries of triumph. Curiosity led a few to enter the hearse-like canopy, whence they immediately reissued, dragging forth a priest.

"Who art thou?" hoarsely demanded he who took upon himself the authority of a leader.

"A Carmelite, and a servant of God!"

"Dost thou serve St. Mark? Hast thou been to the Canale Orfano, to shrive a wretch?"

"I am here, in attendance on a young and noble lady, who has need of my council and prayers. The happy and the miserable, the free and the captive, are equally my care!"

"Ha!—Thou art not above thy office?—Thou wilt say the prayers for the dead, in behalf of a poor man's soul?"

"My son, I know no difference, in this respect, between the doge and the poorest fisherman. Still I would not willingly desert the females."

"The ladies shall receive no harm. Come into my boat, for there is need of thy holy office."

Father Anselmo—the reader will readily anticipate that it was he—entered the canopy, said a few words in explanation, to his trembling companions, and complied. He was rowed to the leading gondola, and, by a sign, directed to the dead body.

"Thou see'st that corpse, father?" continued his conductor. "It is the face of one who was an upright and pious Christian!"

"He was."

"We all knew him as the oldest and the most skilful fisherman of the Lagunes, and one ever ready to assist an unlucky companion."

"I can believe thee!"

"Thou mayest, for the holy books are not more true than my words—yesterday he came down this very canal, in triumph, for he bore away the honors of the regatta from the stoutest oars in Venice."

"I have heard of his success."

"They say that Jacopo, the Bravo—he who once held the best oar in the canals—was of the party! Santa Madonna! such a man was too precious to die!"

"It is the fate of all—rich and poor, strong and feeble, happy and miserable, must alike come to this end."

"Not to this end, reverend Carmelite, for Antonio having given offence to the republic, in the matter of a grandson that is pressed for the galleys, has been sent to purgatory without a Christian hope for his soul."

"There is an eye that watcheth on the meanest of us, son; we will believe he was not forgotten."

"Cospetto!—They say that those the senate look black upon get but little aid from the church! Wilt thou pray for him, Carmelite, and make good thy words?"

"I will," said Father Anselmo, firmly. "Make room, son, that no decency of my duty be overlooked."

The swarthy, expressive faces of the fishermen gleamed with satisfaction, for in the midst of the rude turmoil, they all retained a deep and rooted respect for the offices of the church in which they had been educated. Silence was quickly obtained, and the boats moved on with greater order than before.

276

The spectacle was now striking—In front rowed the gondola which contained the remains of the dead. The widening of the canal, as it approached the port, permitted the rays of the moon to fall upon the rigid features of old Antonio, which were set in such a look, as might be supposed to characterize the dying thoughts of a man so suddenly and so fearfully destroyed. The Carmelite, bareheaded, with clasped hands, and a devout heart, bowed his head at the feet of the body, with his white robes flowing in the light of the moon. A single gondolier guided the boat, and no other noise was audible but the plash of the water, as the oars slowly fell and rose together. This silent procession lasted a few minutes, and then the tremulous voice of the monk was heard chanting the prayers for the dead. The practised fishermen, for few in that disciplined church, and that obedient age, were ignorant of those solemn rites, took up the responses, in a manner that must be familiar to every ear that has ever listened to the sounds of Italy, the gentle washing of the element on which they glided forming a soft accompaniment. Casement after casement opened while they passed, and a thousand curious and anxious faces crowded the balconies, as the funeral cortege swept slowly on.

The gondola of the republic was towed in the centre of the moving mass by fifty lighter boats, for the fishermen still clung to their prize. In this manner the solemn procession entered the port, and touched the quay at the foot of the piazzetta. While numberless eager hands were aiding in bringing the body of Antonio to land, there arose a shout from the centre of the ducal palace, which proclaimed the presence already of the other part of their body in its court.

The squares of St. Mark now presented a novel picture. The quaint and oriental church, the rows of massive and rich architecture, the giddy pile of the Campanile, the columns of granite, the masts of triumph, and all those peculiar and remarkable fixtures which had witnessed so many scenes of violence, of rejoicing, of mourning, and of gaiety, were there, like landmarks of the earth, defying time; beautiful and venerable in despite of all those varying exhibitions of human passions that were daily acted around them.

But the song, the laugh, and the jest, had ceased. The lights of the coffeehouses had disappeared, the revellers had fled to their homes, fearful of being confounded with those who braved the anger of the senate, while the grotesque, the ballad singers, and the buffoon, had abandoned their assumed gaiety for an appearance more in unison with the true feelings of their hearts.

"Giustizia!—" cried a thousand deep voices, as the body of Antonio was borne into the court—"Illustrious Doge! Giustizia in palazzo, e pane in piazza! Give us justice! We are beggars for justice!"

The gloomy but vast court was paved with the swarthy faces and glittering eyes of the fishermen. The corpse was laid at the foot of the Giant's Stairs, while the trembling halberdier at the head of the flight scarce commanded himself sufficiently to maintain that air of firmness which was exacted by discipline and professional pride. But there was no other show of military force, for the politic power which ruled in Venice knew too well its momentary impotency to irritate when it could not quell. The mob beneath was composed of nameless rioters, whose punishment could carry no other consequences than the suppression of immediate danger, and for that, those who ruled were not prepared.

The Council of Three had been apprized of the arrival of the excited fishermen. When the mob entered the court, it was consulting in secret conclave on the probabilities of the tumult having a graver and more determined object than was apparent in the visible symptoms. The routine of office had not yet dispossessed the men, already presented to the reader, of their dangerous and despotic power.

"Are the Dalmatians apprized of this movement?" asked one of the secret tribunal whose nerves were scarcely equal to the high functions he discharged. "We may have occasion for their volleys, ere this riot is appeased."

"Confide in the ordinary authorities for that, Signore," answered the Senator Gradenigo. "I have only concern, lest some conspiracy, which may touch the fidelity of the troops, lies concealed beneath the outcry."

"The evil passions of man know no limits! What would the wretches have? For a state in the decline, Venice is to the last degree prosperous. Our ships are thriving; the bank flourishes with goodly dividends; and I do assure you, Signore, that, for many years, I have not known so ample revenues for most of our interests, as at this hour. All cannot thrive alike!"

"You are happily connected with flourishing affairs, Signore, but there are many that are less lucky. Our form of government is somewhat exclusive, and it is a penalty that we have ever paid

278

for its advantages, to be liable to sudden and malevolent accusations, for any evil turn of fortune that besets the republic."

"Can nothing satisfy these exacting spirits? Are they not free—are they not happy?"

"It would seem that they want better assurance of these facts, than our own feelings, or our words."

"Man is the creature of envy! The poor desire to be rich—the weak, powerful."

"There is an exception to your rule, at least, Signore, since the rich rarely wish to be poor, or the powerful, weak."

"You deride my sentiments, tonight, Signor Gradenigo. I speak, I hope, as becomes a senator of Venice, and in a manner that you are not unaccustomed to hear!"

"Nay, the language is not unusual. But I fear me, there is something unsuited to a falling fortune, in the exacting and narrow spirit of our laws. When a state is eminently flourishing, its subjects overlook general defects in private prosperity, but there is no more fastidious commentator on measures than your merchant of a failing trade."

"This is their gratitude! Have we not converted these muddy isles into a mart for half Christendom, and now they are dissatisfied that they cannot retain all the monopolies that the wisdom of our ancestors has accumulated."

"They complain much in your own spirit, Signore,—but you are right in saying the present riot must be looked to. Let us seek his Highness, who will go out to the people, with such patricians as may be present, and one of our number as a witness: more than that might expose our character."

The secret council withdrew to carry this resolution into effect, just as the fishermen in the court received the accession of those who arrived by water.

There is no body so sensible of an increase of its members as a mob. Without discipline, and dependent solely on animal force for its ascendency, the sentiment of physical power is blended with its very existence. When they saw the mass of living beings which had assembled within the wall of the ducal palace, the most audacious of that throng became more hardy, and even the wavering grew strong. This is the reverse of the feeling which prevails among those who are called on to repress this species of violence, who generally gain courage as its exhibition is least required.

The throng in the court was raising one of its loudest and

most menacing cries as the train of the doge appeared, approaching by one of the long open galleries of the principal floor of the edifice.

The presence of the venerable man who nominally presided over that factitious state, and the long training of the fishermen in habits of deference to authority, notwithstanding their present tone of insubordination, caused a sudden and deep silence. A feeling of awe gradually stole over the thousand dark faces that were gazing upwards, as the little cortege drew near. So profound, indeed, was the stillness caused by this sentiment, that the rustling of the ducal robes was audible, as the prince, impeded by his infirmities, and consulting the state usual to his rank, slowly advanced. The previous violence of the untutored fishermen, and their present deference to the external state that met their eyes, had its origin in the same causes;—ignorance and habit were the parents of both.

"Why are ye assembled here, my children?" asked the doge, when he had reached the summit of the Giant's Stairs,—"and most of all, why have ye come into the palace of your prince, with these unbefitting cries?"

The tremulous voice of the old man was clearly audible, for the lowest of its tones was scarcely interrupted by a breath. The fishermen gazed at each other, and all appeared to search for him who might be bold enough to answer. At length one in the centre of the crowded mass, and effectually concealed from observation, cried, "Justice!"

"Such is our object," mildly continued the prince; "and such, I will add, is our practice. Why are ye assembled here, in a manner so offensive to the state, and so disrespectful to your prince?"

Still none answered. The only spirit of their body, which had been capable of freeing itself from the trammels of usage and prejudice, had deserted the shell which lay on the lower step of the Giant's Stairs.

"Will none speak?—are ye so bold with your voices when unquestioned, and so silent when confronted?"

"Speak them fair, your Highness," whispered he of the council who was commissioned to be a secret witness of the interview;—"the Dalmatians are scarce yet apparelled."

The prince bowed to advice which he well knew must be respected, and he assumed his former tone.

"If none will acquaint me with your wants, I must command you to retire, and while my parental heart grieves—"

"Giustizia!" repeated the hidden member of the crowd.

"Name thy wants, that we may know them."

"Highness! deign to look at this!"

One bolder than the rest had turned the body of Antonio to the moon, in a manner to expose the ghastly features, and, as he spoke, he pointed towards the spectacle he had prepared. The prince started at the unexpected sight, and, slowly descending the steps, closely accompanied by his companions and his guards, he paused over the body.

"Has the assassin done this?" he asked, after looking at the dead fisherman, and crossing himself. "What could the end of one like this profit a Bravo?—haply the unfortunate man hath fallen in a broil of his class?"

"Neither, illustrious Doge! we fear that Antonio has suffered for the displeasure of St. Mark!"

"Antonio! Is this the hardy fisherman who would have taught us how to rule in the state regatta!"

"Eccellenza, it is," returned the simple laborer of the Lagunes,—"and a better hand with a net, or a truer friend in need, never rowed a gondola, to or from the Lido. Diavolo! It would have done your Highness pleasure to have seen the poor old Christian among us, on a saint's day, taking the lead in our little ceremonies, and teaching us the manner in which our fathers used to do credit to the craft!"

"Or to have been with us, illustrious Doge," cried another, for, the ice once broken, the tongues of a mob soon grow bold, "in a merrymaking, on the Lido, when old Antonio was always the foremost in the laugh, and the discreetest in knowing when to be grave."

The doge began to have a dawning of the truth, and he cast a glance aside to examine the countenance of the unknown inquisitor.

"It is far easier to understand the merits of the unfortunate man, than the manner of his death," he said, finding no explanation in the drilled members of the face he had scrutinized. "Will any of your party explain the facts?"

The principal speaker among the fishermen willingly took on himself the office, and, in the desultory manner of one of his habits, he acquainted the doge with the circumstances connected

281

with the finding of the body. When he had done, the prince again asked explanations, with his eye, from the senator at his side, for he was ignorant whether the policy of the state required an example, or simply a death.

"I see nothing in this, your Highness," observed he of the council, "but the chances of a fisherman. The unhappy old man has come to his end by accident, and it would be charity to have a few masses said for his soul."

"Noble senator!" exclaimed the fisherman, doubtingly, "St. Mark was offended!"

"Rumor tells many idle tales of the pleasure and displeasure of St. Mark. If we are to believe all that the wit of men can devise, in affairs of this nature, the criminals are not drowned in the Lagunes, but in the Canale Orfano."

"True, eccellenza, and we are forbidden to cast our nets there, on pain of sleeping with the eels at its bottom."

"So much greater reason for believing that this old man hath died by accident. Is there mark of violence on his body?—for though the state could scarcely occupy itself with such as he, some other might. Hath the condition of the body been looked to?"

"Eccellenza, it was enough to cast one of his years into the centre of the Lagunes. The stoutest arm in Venice could not save him."

"There may have been violence in some quarrel, and the proper authority should be vigilant. Here is a Carmelite!—Father, do you know aught of this?"

The monk endeavored to answer, but his voice failed. He stared wildly about him, for the whole scene resembled some frightful picture of the imagination, and then folding his arms on his bosom, he appeared to resume his prayers.

"Thou dost not answer, friar?" observed the doge, who had been as effectually deceived, by the natural and indifferent manner of the inquisitor, as any other of his auditors. "Where didst thou find this body?"

Father Anselmo briefly explained the manner in which he had been pressed into the service of the fishermen.

At the elbow of the prince there stood a young patrician, who, at the moment, filled no other office in the state, than such as belonged to his birth. Deceived, like the others, by the manner of the only one who knew the real cause of Antonio's death, he felt a humane and praiseworthy desire to make sure that no foul play had been exercised towards the victim.

"I have heard of this Antonio," said this person, who was called the Senator Soranzo, and who was gifted by nature with feelings that, in any other form of government, would have made him a philanthropist,—"and of his success in the regatta. Was it not said that Jacopo, the Bravo, was his competitor?"

A low, meaning, and common murmur ran through the throng.

"A man of his reputed passions and ferocity may well have sought to revenge defeat by violence!"

A second, and a louder murmur denoted the effect this suggestion had produced.

"Eccellenza, Jacopo deals in the stiletto!" observed the half-credulous but still doubting fisherman.

"That is as may be necessary. A man of his art and character may have recourse to other means to gratify his malice. Do you not agree with me, Signore?"

The Senator Soranzo put this question, in perfect good faith, to the unknown member of the secret council. The latter appeared struck with the probability of the truth of his companion's conjecture, but contented himself with a simple acknowledgment to that effect, by bowing.

"Jacopo!—Jacopo!" hoarsely repeated voice after voice in the crowd—"Jacopo has done this! The best gondolier in Venice has been beaten by an old fisherman, and nothing but blood could wipe out the disgrace!"

"It shall be inquired into, my children, and strict justice done," said the doge, preparing to depart. "Officers, give money for masses, that the soul of the unhappy man be not the sufferer. Reverend Carmelite, I commend the body to thy care, and thou canst do no better service than to pass the night in prayer, by its side."

A thousand caps were waved in commendation of this gracious command, and the whole throng stood in silent respect, as the prince, followed by his retinue, retired as he had approached, through the long, vaulted gallery above.

A secret order of the inquisition prevented the appearance of the Dalmatians.

A few minutes later and all was prepared. A bier and canopy were brought out of the adjoining cathedral, and the corpse was placed upon the former. Father Anselmo then headed the procession, which passed through the principal gate of the palace into the square, chanting the usual service. The piazzetta and the piazza were still empty. Here and there, indeed, a curious face, belonging to some agent of the police, or to some observer more firm than common, looked out from beneath the arches of the porticoes on the movements of the mob, though none ventured to come within its influence.

But the fishermen were no longer bent on violence. With the fickleness of men little influenced by reflection, and subject to sudden and violent emotions, a temperament which, the effect of a selfish system, is commonly tortured into the reason why it should never be improved, they had abandoned all idea of revenge on the agents of the police, and had turned their thoughts to the religious services, which, being commanded by the prince himself, were so flattering to their class.

It is true that a few of the sterner natures among them mingled menaces against the Bravo with their prayers for the dead, but these had no other effect on the matter in hand, than is commonly produced by the byplayers on the principal action of the piece.

The great portal of the venerable church was thrown open, and the solemn chant was heard issuing, in responses, from among the quaint columns and vaulted roofs within. The body of the lowly and sacrificed Antonio was borne beneath that arch which sustains the precious relics of Grecian art, and deposited in the nave. Candles glimmered before the altar and around the ghastly person of the dead, throughout the night; and the cathedral of St. Mark was pregnant with all the imposing ceremonials of the Catholic ritual, until the day once more appeared.

Priest succeeded priest in repeating the masses, while the attentive throng listened, as if each of its members felt that his own honor and importance were elevated by this concession to one of their number. In the square the maskers gradually reappeared, though the alarm had been too sudden and violent, to admit a speedy return to the levity which ordinarily was witnessed in that spot, between the setting and the rising of the sun.

CHAPTER XXIII

" 'Tis of a lady in her earliest youth,
The very last of that illustrious race."
ROGERS

WHEN the fishermen landed on the quay, they deserted the gondola of the state to a man. Donna Violetta and her governess heard the tumultuous departure of their singular captors with alarm, for they were nearly in entire ignorance of the motive which had deprived them of the protection of Father Anselmo, and which had so unexpectedly made them actors in the extraordinary scene. The monk had simply explained that his offices were required in behalf of the dead, but the apprehension of exciting unnecessary terror prevented him from adding that they were in the power of a mob. Donna Florinda, however, had ascertained sufficient, by looking from the windows of the canopy, and from the cries of those around her, to get a glimmering of the truth. Under the circumstances, she saw that the most prudent course was to keep themselves as much as possible from observation. But when the profound stillness that succeeded the landing of the rioters announced that they were alone, both she and her charge had an intuitive perception of the favorable chance which fortune had so strangely thrown in their way.

"They are gone!" whispered Donna Florinda, holding her breath in attention, as soon as she had spoken.

"And the police will be soon here to seek us!"

No further explanation passed, for Venice was a town in which even the young and innocent were taught caution. Donna Florinda stole another look without.

"They have disappeared, Heaven knows where! Let us go!"

In an instant the trembling fugitives were on the quay. The piazzetta was without a human form, except their own. A low, murmuring sound arose from the court palace, which resembled the hum of a disturbed hive; but nothing was distinct or intelligible.

"There is violence meditated," again whispered the governess; "would to God that Father Anselmo were here!"

285

A shuffling footstep caught their ears, and both turned towards a boy, in the dress of one of the Lagunes, who approached from the direction of the Broglio.

"A reverend Carmelite bid me give you this," said the youth, stealing a glance behind him, like one who dreaded detection. Then putting a small piece of paper in the hand of Donna Florinda, he turned his own swarthy palm, in which a small silver coin glittered, to the moon, and vanished.

By the aid of the same light the governess succeeded in tracing pencil marks, in a hand that had been well known to her younger days.

"Save thyself, Florinda—There is not an instant to lose. Avoid public places, and seek a shelter quickly."

"But whither?" asked the bewildered woman, when she had read aloud the scroll.

"Anywhere but here," rejoined Donna Violetta; "follow me."

Nature frequently more than supplies the advantages of training and experience, by her own gifts. Had Donna Florinda been possessed of the natural decision and firmness of her pupil, she would not now have been existing in the isolated condition which is so little congenial to female habits, nor would Father Anselmo have been a monk. Both had sacrificed inclination to what they considered to be duty, and if the ungenial life of the governess was owing to the tranquil course of her ordinary feelings, it is probable that its impunity was to be ascribed to the same respectable cause. Not so with Violetta. She was ever more ready to act than to reflect, and though, in general, the advantage might possibly be with those of a more regulated temperament, there are occasions that form exceptions to the rule. The present moment was one of those turns in the chances of life, when it is always better to do anything than to do nothing.

Donna Violetta had scarcely spoken, before her person was shadowed beneath the arches of the Broglio. Her governess clung to her side, more in affection than in compliance with the warning of the monk, or with the dictates of her own reason. A vague and romantic intention of throwing herself at the feet of the doge, who was a collateral descendant of her own ancient house, had flashed across the mind of the youthful bride, when she first fled; but no sooner had they reached the palace, than a cry from the court acquainted them with its situation, and consequently with the impossibility of penetrating to the interior.

"Let us retire, by the streets, to thy dwelling, my child," said Donna Florinda, drawing her mantle about her in womanly dignity. "None will offend females of our condition; even the senate must, in the end, respect our sex."

"This from thee, Florinda!—Thou who hast so often trembled for their anger! But go, if thou wilt—I am no longer the senate's.—Don Camillo Monforte has my duty."

Donna Florinda had no intention of disputing this point, and as the moment had now arrived when the most energetic was likely to lead, she quietly submitted herself to the superior decision of her pupil. The latter took the way along the portico, keeping always within its shadows. In passing the gateway, which opened towards the sea, the fugitives had a glimpse of what was passing in the court. The sight quickened their steps, and they now flew, rather than ran, along the arched passage. In a minute they were on the bridge which crosses the canal of St. Mark, still flying with all their force. A few mariners were looking from their feluccas and gazing in curiosity, but the sight of two terrified females, seeking refuge from a mob, had nothing in itself likely to attract notice.

At this moment, a dark mass of human bodies appeared advancing along the quay in the opposite direction. Arms glittered in the moonbeams, and the measured tread of trained men became audible. The Dalmatians were moving down from the arsenal in a body. Advance and retreat now seemed equally impossible to the breathless fugitives. As decision and self-possession are very different qualities, Donna Violetta did not understand so readily as the circumstances required, that it was more than probable the hirelings of the republic would consider the flight perfectly natural, as it had appeared to the curious gazers of the port.

Terror made them blind, and as shelter was now the sole object of the fugitives, they would probably have sought it in the chamber of doom, itself, had there been an opportunity. As it was, they turned and entered the first, and indeed the only, gate which offered. They were met by a girl, whose anxious face betrayed that singular compound of self-devotion and terror which probably has its rise in the instinct of feminine sympathies.

"Here is safety, noble ladies," said the youthful Venetian, in the soft accent of her native islands; "none will dare do you harm within these walls."

"Into whose palace have I entered?" demanded the half-breathless Violetta. "If its owner has a name in Venice, he will not refuse hospitality to a daughter of Tiepolo."

"Signora, you are welcome," returned the gentle girl, curtsying low, and still leading the way deeper within the vast edifice. "You bear the name of an illustrious house!"

"There are few in the republic of note from whom I may not claim either the kindness of ancient and near services, or that of kindred. Dost thou serve a noble master?"

"The first in Venice, lady."

"Name him, that we may demand his hospitality as befits us."

"Saint Mark."

Donna Violetta and her governess stopped short.

"Have we unconsciously entered a portal of the palace?"

"That were impossible, lady, since the canal lies between you and the residence of the doge. Still is St. Mark master here. I hope you will not esteem your safety less, because it has been obtained in the public prison, and by the aid of its keeper's daughter."

The moment for headlong decision was passed, and that of reflection had returned.

"How art thou called, child?" asked Donna Florinda, moving ahead of her pupil and taking the discourse up, where in wonder the other had permitted it to pause. "We are truly grateful for the readiness with which thou threw open the gate for our admission, in a moment of such alarm—How art thou called?"

"Gelsomina," answered the modest girl. "I am the keeper's only child—and when I saw ladies of your honorable condition, fleeing on the quay, with the Dalmatians marching on one side, and a mob shouting on the other, I bethought me that even a prison might be welcome."

"Thy goodness of heart did not mislead thee."

"Had I known it was a lady of the Tiepolo, I should have been even more ready; for there are few of that great name now left to do us honor."

Violetta curtsied to the compliment, but she seemed uneasy that haste and pride of rank had led her, so indiscreetly, to betray herself.

"Canst thou not lead us to some place less public?" she asked, observing that her conductor had stopped in a public corridor to make this explanation.

"Here you will be retired as in your own palaces, great lad-ies," answered Gelsomina, turning into a private passage, and leading the way towards the rooms of her family, from a win-dow of which she had first witnessed the embarrassment of her guests. "None enter here, without cause, but my father and myself; and my father is much occupied with his charge."

"Hast thou no domestic?"

"None, lady. A prison keeper's daughter should not be too proud to serve herself."

"Thou sayest well. One of thy discretion, good Gelsomina, must know it is not seemly for females of condition to be thrown within walls like these, even by accident, and thou wilt do us much favor, by taking more than common means, to be certain that we are unseen. We give thee much trouble, but it shall not go unrequited. Here is gold."

Gelsomina did not answer, but as she stood with her eyes cast to the floor, the color stole to her cheeks, until her usually bloodless face was in a soft glow.

"Nay, I have mistaken thy character!" said Donna Florinda, secreting the sequins, and taking the unresisting hand of the silent girl. "If I have pained thee, by my indiscretion, attribute the offer to our dread of the disgrace of being seen in this place."

The glow deepened, and the lips of the girl quivered.

"Is it then a disgrace to be innocently within these walls. lady?" she asked, still with an averted eye. "I have long suspected this, but none has ever before said it, in my hearing!"

"Holy Maria pardon me! If I have uttered a syllable to pain thee, excellent girl, it has been unwittingly and without inten-tion!"

"We are poor, lady, and the needy must submit to do that which their wishes might lead them to avoid. I understand your feelings, and will make sure of your being secret, and Blessed Maria will pardon a greater sin, than any you have committed here."

While the ladies were wondering, at witnessing such proofs of delicacy and feeling in so singular a place, the girl withdrew.

"I had not expected this in a prison!" exclaimed Violetta.

"As all is not noble, or just, in a palace, neither is all to be condemned unheard that we find in a prison. But this is, in sooth, an extraordinary girl for her condition, and we are in-debted to blessed St. Theodore (crossing herself) for putting her in our way."

"Can we do better than by making her a confidant and a friend?"

The governess was older, and less disposed than her pupil, to confide in appearances. But the more ardent mind and superior rank of the latter had given her an influence that the former did not always successfully resist. Gelsomina returned before there was time to discuss the prudence of what Violetta had proposed.

"Thou hast a father, Gelsomina?" asked the Venetian heiress, taking the hand of the gentle girl, as she put her question.

"Holy Maria be praised!—I have still that happiness."

"It is a happiness—for surely a father would not have the heart to sell his own child to ambition and mercenary hopes! And thy mother?"

"Has long been bedridden, lady. I believe we should not have been here, but we have no other place so suitable for her sufferings, as this jail."

"Gelsomina, thou art happier than I, even in thy prison. I am fatherless—motherless—I could almost say, friendless."

"And this from a lady of the Tiepolo!"

"All is not as it seems in this evil world, kind Gelsomina. We have had many doges, but we have had much suffering. Thou mayest have heard that the house of which I come is reduced to a single, youthful girl like thyself, who has been left in the senate's charge?"

"They speak little of these matters, lady, in Venice; and, of all here, none go so seldom into the square as I. Still have I heard of the beauty and riches of Donna Violetta. The last I hope is true; the first I now see is so."

The daughter of Tiepolo colored, in turn, but it was not in resentment.

"They have spoken in too much kindness for an orphan," she answered; "though that fatal wealth is perhaps not overestimated. Thou knowest that the state charges itself with the care and establishment of all noble females whom Providence has left fatherless?"

"Lady, I did not. It is kind of St. Mark to do it!"

"Thou wilt think differently, anon. Thou art young, Gelsomina, and hast passed thy time in privacy?"

"True, lady. It is seldom I go farther than my mother's room, or the cell of some suffering prisoner."

Violetta looked towards her governess, with an expression

which seemed to say that she anticipated her appeal would be made in vain, to one so little exposed to the feelings of the world.

"Thou wilt not understand then, that a noble female may have little inclination to comply with all the senate's wishes, in disposing of her duties and affections?"

Gelsomina gazed at the fair speaker, but it was evident that she did not clearly comprehend the question. Again Violetta looked at the governess as if asking aid.

"The duties of our sex are often painful," said Donna Florinda, understanding the appeal with female instinct. "Our attachments may not always follow the wishes of our friends. We may not choose, but we cannot always obey."

"I have heard that noble ladies are not suffered to see those to whom they are to be wedded, Signora, if that is what your eccellenza means, and, to me, the custom has always seemed unjust, if not cruel."

"And are females of thy class permitted to make friends among those who may become dearer at any other day?" asked Violetta.

"Lady, we have that much freedom even in the prisons."

"Then art thou happier than those of the palaces! I will trust thee, generous girl, for thou canst not be unfaithful to the weakness and wrongs of thy sex."

Gelsomina raised a hand, as if to stop the impetuous confidence of her guest, and then she listened intently.

"Few enter here," she said; "but there are many ways of learning secrets within these walls which are still unknown to me. Come deeper into the rooms, noble ladies, for here is a place that I have reason to think is safe, even from listeners."

The keeper's daughter led the way into the little room in which she was accustomed to converse with Jacopo.

"You were saying, lady, that I had a feeling for the weakness and helplessness of our sex, and surely you did me justice."

Violetta had leisure to reflect an instant, in passing from one room to the other, and she began her communications with more reserve. But the sensitive interest that a being of the gentle nature and secluded habits of Gelsomina took in her narrative won upon her own natural frankness, and, in a manner nearly imperceptible to herself, she made the keeper's daughter mistress of most of the circumstances under which she had entered the prison.

The cheek of Gelsomina became colorless as she listened, and when Donna Violetta ceased, every limb of her slight frame trembled with interest.

"The senate is a fearful power to resist!" she said, speaking so low as hardly to be audible. "Have you reflected, lady, on the chances of what you do?"

"If I have not, it is now too late to change my intentions. I am the wife of the Duke of Sant' Agata, and can never wed another."

"Gesu!—This is true.—And yet, methinks, I would choose to die a nun rather than offend the council!"

"Thou knowest not, good girl, to what courage the heart of even a young wife is equal.—Thou art still bound to thy father, in the instruction and habits of childhood, but thou mayest live to know that all thy hopes will centre in another."

Gelsomina ceased to tremble, and her mild eye brightened.

"The council is terrible," she answered, "but it must be more terrible to desert one to whom you have vowed duty and love at the altar!"

"Hast thou the means of concealing us, kind girl," interrupted Donna Florinda, "and canst thou, when this tumult shall be quieted, in any manner help us to farther secrecy or flight?"

"Lady, I have none. Even the streets and squares of Venice are nearly strangers to me. Santissima Maria! what would I give to know the ways of the town as well as my cousin Annina, who passes, at will, from her father's shop to the Lido, and from St. Mark's to the Rialto, as her pleasure suits. I will send for my cousin, who will counsel us in this fearful strait!"

"Thy cousin!—Hast thou a cousin named Annina?"

"Lady, Annina. My mother's sister's child."

"The daughter of a wine seller called Tommaso Torti?"

"Do the noble dames of the city take such heed of their inferiors!—This will charm my cousin, for she has great desires to be noted by the great."

"And does thy cousin come hither?"

"Rarely, lady—We are not of much intimacy. I suppose Annina finds a girl, simple and uninstructed as I, unworthy of her company. But she will not refuse to aid us, in a danger like this. I know she little loves the republic, for we have had words on its acts, and my cousin has been bolder of speech about them, than befits one of her years, in this prison."

"Gelsomina, thy cousin is a secret agent of the police, and unworthy of thy confidence—"

"Lady!"

"I do not speak without reason. Trust me, she is employed in duties that are unbecoming her sex, and unworthy of thy confidence."

"Noble dames, I will not say anything to do displeasure to your high rank and present distress, but you should not urge me to think thus of my mother's niece. You have been unhappy, and you may have cause to dislike the republic, and you are safe here—but I do not desire to hear Annina censured."

Both Donna Florinda and her less experienced pupil knew enough of human nature, to consider this generous incredulity as a favorable sign of the integrity of her who manifested it, and they wisely contented themselves with stipulating that Annina should, on no account, be made acquainted with their situation. After this understanding, the three discussed, more leisurely, the prospect of the fugitives being able to quit the place, when ready, without detection.

At the suggestion of the governess, a servitor of the prison was sent out by Gelsomina to observe the state of the square. He was particularly charged, though in a manner to avoid suspicion, to search for a Carmelite of the order of the barefooted friars. On his return, the menial reported that the mob had quitted the court of the palace, and was gone to the cathedral, with the body of the fisherman who had so unexpectedly gained the prize in the regatta of the preceding day.

"Repeat your aves and go to sleep, bella Gelsomina," concluded the sub-keeper, "for the fishermen have left off shouting to say their prayers. Per Diana! The bareheaded and barelegged rascals are as impudent as if St. Mark were their inheritance! The noble patricians should give them a lesson in modesty, by sending every tenth knave among them to the galleys. Miscreants! to disturb the quiet of an orderly town with their vulgar complaints!"

"But thou hast said nothing of the friar; is he with the rioters?"

"There is a Carmelite at the altar—but my blood boiled at seeing such vagabonds disturb the peace of respectable persons, and I took little note of his air or years."

"Then thou failedst to do the errand on which I sent thee.

It is now too late to repair thy fault. Thou canst return to thy charge."

"A million pardons, bellissima Gelsomina, but indignation is the uppermost feeling, when one in office sees his rights attacked by the multitude. Send me to Corfu, or to Candia, if you please, and I will bring back the color of every stone in their prisons, but do not send me among rebels. My gorge rises at the sight of villainy!"

As the keeper's daughter withdrew, while her father's assistant was making this protestation of loyalty, the latter was compelled to give vent to the rest of his indignation in a soliloquy.

One of the tendencies of oppression is to create a scale of tyranny, descending from those who rule a state, to those who domineer over a single individual. He who has been much accustomed to view men need not be told that none are so arrogant with their inferiors, as those who are oppressed by their superiors; for poor human nature has a secret longing to revenge itself on the weak for all the injuries it receives from the strong. On the other hand, no class is so willing to render that deference, when unexacted, which is the proper meed of virtue, and experience, and intelligence, as he who knows that he is fortified on every side against innovations on his natural rights. Thus it is that there is more security against popular violence and popular insults in these free states, than in any other country on earth, for there is scarcely a citizen so debased as not to feel that, in assuming the appearance of a wish to revenge the chances of fortune, he is making an undue admission of inferiority.

Though the torrent may be pent and dammed by art, it is with the constant hazard of breaking down the unnatural barriers; but left to its own course, it will become the tranquil and the deep stream, until it finally throws off its superfluous waters into the common receptacle of the ocean.

When Gelsomina returned to her visitors, it was with a report favorable to their tranquillity. The riot in the court of the palace, and the movement of the Dalmatians, had drawn all eyes in another direction; and although some errant gaze might have witnessed their entrance into the gate of the prison, it was so natural a circumstance, that no one would suspect females of their appearance of remaining there an instant longer than was necessary. The momentary absence of the few servants of the prison, who took little heed of those who entered the open parts

294

of the building, and who had been drawn away by curiosity, completed their security. The humble room they were in was exclusively devoted to the use of their gentle protector, and there was scarcely a possibility of interruption, until the council had obtained the leisure and the means of making use of those terrible means which rarely left anything it wished to know concealed.

With this explanation Donna Violetta and her companion were greatly satisfied. It left them leisure to devise means for their flight, and kindled a hope, in the former, of being speedily restored to Don Camillo. Still there existed the cruel embarrassment of not possessing the means of acquainting the latter with their situation. As the tumult ceased, they resolved to seek a boat, favored by such disguises as the means of Gelsomina could supply, and to row to his palace; but reflection convinced Donna Florinda of the danger of such a step, since the Neapolitan was known to be surrounded by the agents of the police. Accident, which is more effectual than stratagem in defeating intrigues, had thrown them into a place of momentary security, and it would be to lose the vantage ground of their situation to cast themselves, without the utmost caution, into the hazards of the public canals.

At length the governess bethought her of turning the services of the gentle creature, who had already shown so much sympathy in their behalf, to account. During the revelations of her pupil, the feminine instinct of Donna Florinda had enabled her to discover the secret springs which moved the unpractised feelings of their auditor. Gelsomina had listened to the manner in which Don Camillo had thrown himself into the canal to save the life of Violetta, with breathless admiration; her countenance was a pure reflection of her thoughts, when the daughter of Tiepolo spoke of the risks he had run to gain her love, and woman glowed in every lineament of her mild face, when the youthful bride touched on the nature of the engrossing tie which had united them, and which was far too holy to be severed by the senate's policy.

"If we had the means of getting our situation to the ears of Don Camillo," said the governess, "all might yet be saved; else will this happy refuge in the prison avail us nothing."

"Is the cavalier of too stout a heart to shrink before those up above?" demanded Gelsomina.

"He would summon the people of his confidence, and ere the dawn of day we might still be beyond their power. Those calculating senators will deal with the vows of my pupil as if they were childish oaths, and set the anger of the Holy See itself at defiance, when there is question of their interest."

"But the sacrament of marriage is not of man; that, at least, they will respect!"

"Believe it not. There is no obligation so solemn as to be respected, when their policy is concerned. What are the wishes of a girl, or what the happiness of a solitary and helpless female, to their fortunes? That my charge is young is a reason why their wisdom should interfere, though it is none to touch their hearts with the reflection that the misery, to which they would condemn her, is to last the longer. They take no account of the solemn obligations of gratitude; the ties of affection are so many means of working upon the fears of those they rule, but none for forbearance; and they laugh at the devotedness of woman's love, as a folly to amuse their leisure, or to take off the edge of disappointment in graver concerns."

"Can anything be more grave than wedlock, lady?"

"To them it is important, as it furnishes the means of perpetuating their honors and their proud names. Beyond this, the councils look little at domestic interests."

"They are fathers and husbands!"

"True, for to be legally the first, they must become the last. Marriage to them is not a tie of sacred and dear affinity, but the means of increasing their riches and of sustaining their names," continued the governess, watching the effect of her words on the countenance of the guileless girl. "They call marriages of affection children's games, and they deal with the wishes of their own daughters as they would traffic with their commodities of commerce. When a state sets up an idol of gold as its god, few will refuse to sacrifice at its altar!"

"I would I might serve the noble Donna Violetta!"

"Thou art too young, good Gelsomina, and I fear too little practised in the cunning of Venice."

"Doubt me not, lady; for I can do my duty like another, in a good cause."

"If it were possible to convey to Don Camillo Monforte a knowledge of our situation—but thou art too inexperienced for the service!"

"Believe it not, Signora," interrupted the generous Gelsomina, whose pride began to stimulate her natural sympathies with one so near her own age, and one too, like herself, subject to that passion which engrosses a female heart. "I may be apter than my appearance would give reason to think."

"I will trust thee, kind girl, and if the Sainted Virgin protects us, thy fortunes shall not be forgotten!"

The pious Gelsomina crossed herself, and, first acquainting her companions with her intentions, she went within to prepare herself, while Donna Florinda penned a note, in terms so guarded as to defy detection in the event of accident, but which might suffice to let the lord of St. Agata understand their present situation.

In a few minutes the keeper's daughter reappeared. Her ordinary attire, which was that of a modest Venetian maiden of humble condition, needed no concealment; and the mask, an article of dress which none in that city were without, effectually disguised her features. She then received the note, with the name of the street, and the palace she was to seek, a description of the person of the Neapolitan, with often-repeated cautions to be wary, and departed.

CHAPTER XXIV

"Which is the wiser here?—Justice or iniquity?"
Measure for Measure

IN the constant struggle between the innocent and the artful, the latter have the advantage, so long as they confine themselves to familiar interests. But the moment the former conquer their disgust for the study of vice, and throw themselves upon the protection of their own high principles, they are far more effectually concealed from the calculations of their adversaries, than if they practised the most refined of their subtle expedients. Nature has given to every man enough of frailty to enable him to estimate the workings of selfishness and fraud, but her truly privileged are those who can shroud their motives and intentions in a degree of justice and disinterestedness which surpass the calculations of the designing. Millions may bow to the commands of a conventional right, but few, indeed, are they who know how to choose in novel and difficult cases. There is often a mystery in virtue. While the cunning of vice is no more than a pitiful imitation of that art which endeavors to cloak its workings in the thin veil of deception, the other, in some degree, resembles the sublimity of infallible truth.

Thus men too much practised in the interests of life constantly overreach themselves when brought in contact with the simple and intelligent; and the experience of every day proves, that, as there is no fame permanent which is not founded on virtue, so there is no policy secure which is not bottomed on the good of the whole. Vulgar minds may control the concerns of a community, so long as they are limited to vulgar views; but woe to the people who confide, on great emergencies, in any but the honest, the noble, the wise, and the philanthropic; for there is no security for success when the meanly artful control the occasional and providential events which regenerate a nation. More than half the misery which has defeated, as well as disgraced, civilization proceeds from neglecting to use those great men that are always created by great occasions.

Treating, as we are, of the vices of the Venetian system, our pen has run truant with its subject, since the application of the moral must be made on the familiar scale suited to the incidents of our story. It has already been seen that Gelsomina was intrusted with certain important keys of the prison. For this trust there had been sufficient motive with the wily guardians of the jail, who had made their calculations on her serving their particular orders, without ever suspecting that she was capable of so far listening to the promptings of a generous temper, as might induce her to use them in any manner prejudicial to their own views. The service to which they were now to be applied proved that the keepers, one of which was her own father, had not fully known how to estimate the powers of the innocent and simple.

Provided with the keys in question, Gelsomina took a lamp, and passed upward from the mezzinino in which she dwelt, to the first floor of the edifice, instead of descending to its court. Door was opened after door, and many a gloomy corridor was passed by the gentle girl, with the confidence of one who knew her motive to be good. She soon crossed the Bridge of Sighs, fearless of interruption in that unfrequented gallery, and entered the palace. Here she made her way to a door that opened on the common and public vomitories of the structure. Moving with sufficient care to make impunity from detection sure, she extinguished the light, and applied the key. At the next instant she was on the vast and gloomy stairway. It required but a moment to descend it, and to reach the covered gallery which surrounded the court. A halberdier was within a few feet of her. He looked at the unknown female with interest; but as it was not his business to question those who issued from the building, nothing was said. Gelsomina walked on. A half repenting, but vindictive being was dropping an accusation in the Lion's Mouth. Gelsomina stopped involuntarily, until the secret accuser had done his treacherous work and departed. Then, when she was about to proceed, she saw that the halberdier, at the head of the Giant's Stairway, was smiling at her indecision, like one accustomed to such scenes.

"Is there danger in quitting the palace?" she asked of the rough mountaineer.

"Corpo di Bacco! There might have been, an hour since, bella donna; but the rioters are muzzled, and at their prayers!"

Gelsomina hesitated no longer. She descended the well-known flight, down which the head of Faliero had rolled, and was soon beneath the arch of the gate. Here the timid and unpractised girl again stopped, for she could not venture into the square without assuring herself, like a deer about to quit its cover, of the tranquillity of the place into which she was to enter.

The agents of the police had been too much alarmed by the rising of the fishermen, not to call their usual ingenuity and finesse into play, the moment the disturbance was appeased. Money had been given to the mountebanks and ballad singers to induce them to reappear, and groups of hirelings, some in masks and others without concealment, were ostentatiously assembled in different parts of the piazza. In short, those usual expedients were resorted to which are constantly used to restore the confidence of a people in those countries in which civilization is so new that they are not yet considered sufficiently advanced to be the guardians of their own security. There are few artifices so shallow that many will not be their dupes. The idler, the curious, the really discontented, the factious, the designing, with a suitable mixture of the unthinking, and of those who only live for the pleasure of the passing hour, a class not the least insignificant for numbers, had lent themselves to the views of the police; and when Gelsomina was ready to enter the piazzetta, she found both the squares partially filled. A few excited fishermen clustered about the doors of the cathedral, like bees swarming before their hive; but, on that side, there was no very visible cause of alarm. Unaccustomed as she was to scenes like that before her, the first glance assured the gentle girl of the real privacy which so singularly distinguishes the solitude of a crowd. Gathering her simple mantle more closely about her form, and settling her mask with care, she moved with a swift step into the centre of the piazza.

We shall not detail the progress of our heroine, as, avoiding the commonplace gallantry that assailed and offended her ear, she went her way on her errand of kindness. Young, active, and impelled by her intentions, the square was soon passed, and she reached the place of San Nico. Here was one of the landings of the public gondolas. But, at the moment, there was no boat in waiting, for curiosity or fear had induced the men to quit their usual stand. Gelsomina had ascended the bridge, and was on the crown of its arch, when a gondolier came sweeping lazily in from the direction of the Grand Canal. Her hesitation and doubting manner attracted his attention, and the man made the customary sign which conveyed the offer of his services. As she was nearly a stranger to the streets of Venice, labyrinths that offer greater embarrassment to the uninitiated, than perhaps the passages of any other town of its size, she gladly availed herself of the offer. To descend to the steps, to leap into the boat, to utter the word "Rialto," and to conceal herself in the pavilion, was the business of a minute. The boat was instantly in motion.

Gelsomina now believed herself secure of effecting her purpose, since there was little to apprehend from the knowledge, or the designs, of a common boatman. He could not know her object, and it was his interest to carry her, in safety, to the place she had commanded. But so important was success, that she could not feel secure of attaining it, while it was still unaccomplished. She soon summoned sufficient resolution to look out at the palaces and boats they were passing, and she felt the refreshing air of the canal revive her courage. Then turning, with sensitive distrust, to examine the countenance of the gondolier, she saw that his features were concealed beneath a mask that was so well designed, as not to be perceptible to a casual observer by moonlight.

Though it was common, on occasions, for the servants of the great, it was not usual for the public gondoliers, to be disguised. The circumstance itself was one justly to excite slight apprehension, though, on second thoughts, Gelsomina saw no more in it, than a return from some expedition of pleasure, or some serenade, perhaps, in which the caution of a lover had compelled his followers to resort to this species of concealment.

"Shall I put you on the public quay, Signora," demanded the gondolier, "or shall I see you to the gate of your own palace?"

The heart of Gelsomina beat high. She liked the tone of the voice, though it was necessarily smothered by the mask, but she was little accustomed to act in the affairs of others, and less still in any of so great interest, that the sounds caused her to tremble like one less worthily employed.

"Dost thou know the palace of a certain Don Camillo Monforte, a lord of Calabria, who dwells, here, in Venice?" she asked, after a moment's pause. The gondolier sensibly betrayed surprise, by the manner in which he started at the question.

"Would you be rowed there, lady?"

"If thou art certain of knowing the palazzo."

The water stirred, and the gondola glided between high walls. Gelsomina knew, by the sound, that they were in one of the smaller canals, and she augured well of the boatman's knowledge of the town. They soon stopped by the side of a water gate, and the man appeared on the step, holding an arm, to aid her in ascending, after the manner of people of his craft. Gelsomina bade him wait her return, and proceeded.

There was a marked derangement in the household of Don Camillo that one more practised than our heroine would have noted. The servants seemed undecided in the manner of performing the most ordinary duties; their looks wandered distrustfully from one to the other, and when their half-frightened visitor entered the vestibule, though all arose, none advanced to meet her. A female masked was not a rare sight, in Venice, for few of that sex went upon the canals without using the customary means of concealment; but it would seem, by their hesitating manner, that the menials of Don Camillo did not view the entrance of her who now appeared with the usual indifference.

"I am in the dwelling of the Duke of St. Agata, a Signor of Calabria?" demanded Gelsomina, who saw the necessity of being firm.

"Signora, si—"

"Is your lord in the palace?"

"Signora, he is—and he is not. What beautiful lady shall I tell him does him this honor?"

"If he be not at home, it will not be necessary to tell him anything. If he is, I could wish to see him."

The domestics, of whom there were several, put their heads together, and seemed to dispute on the propriety of receiving the visit. At this instant, a gondolier in a flowered jacket entered the vestibule. Gelsomina took courage at his good-natured eye and frank manner.

"Do you serve Don Camillo Monforte?" she asked, as he passed her, on his way to the canal.

"With the oar, bellissima donna," answered Gino, touching his cap, though scarce looking aside at the question.

"And could he be told that a female wishes earnestly to speak to him in private?—A female."

"Santa Maria! bella donna, there is no end to females who come on these errands, in Venice. You might better pay a visit to the statue of San Teodoro, in the piazza, than see my master at this moment; the stone will give you the better reception."

"And this he commands you to tell all of my sex who come!"

"Diavolo!—Lady, you are particular in your questions. Perhaps my master might, on a strait, receive one of the sex I could name, but on the honor of a gondolier he is not the most gallant cavalier of Venice, just at this moment."

"If there is one to whom he would pay this deference, you are bold for a servitor. How know you I am not that one?"

Gino started. He examined the figure of the applicant, and lifting his cap he bowed.

"Lady, I do not know anything about it," he said; "you may be his Highness the Doge, or the ambassador of the emperor. I pretend to know nothing in Venice, of late—"

The words of Gino were cut short by a tap on the shoulder from the public gondolier, who had hastily entered the vestibule. The man whispered in the ear of Don Camillo's servitor.

"This is not a moment to refuse any," he said.—"Let the stranger go up."

Gino hesitated no longer. With the decision of a favored menial, he pushed the groom of the chambers aside, and offered to conduct Gelsomina, himself, to the presence of his master. As they ascended the stairs, three of the inferior servants disappeared.

The palace of Don Camillo had an air of more than Venetian gloom. The rooms were dimly lighted, many of the walls had been stripped of the most precious of their pictures, and, in other respects a jealous eye might have detected evidence of a secret intention, on the part of its owner, not to make a permanent residence of the dwelling. But these were particulars that Gelsomina did not note, as she followed Gino through the apartments, into the more private parts of the building. Here the gondolier unlocked a door, and regarding his companion with an air, half doubting, half respectful, he made a sign for her to enter.

"My master commonly receives the ladies, here," he said, "Enter, eccellenza, while I run to tell him of his happiness."

Gelsomina did not hesitate, though she felt a violent throb at the heart, when she heard the key turning in the lock, behind her. She was in an antechamber, and, inferring from the light which shone through the door of an adjoining room, that she was to proceed, she went on. No sooner had she entered the little closet, than she found herself alone with one of her own sex.

"Annina!" burst from the lips of the unpractised prison-girl, under the impulse of surprise.

"Gelsomina!—The simple, quiet, whispering, modest Gelsomina!" returned the other.

The words of Annina admitted but of one construction. Wounded, like the bruised sensitive plant, Gelsomina withdrew her mask for air, actually gasping for breath, between offended pride and wonder.

"Thou here!" she added, scarce knowing what she uttered.

"Thou here!" repeated Annina, with such a laugh as escapes the degraded, when they believe the innocent reduced to their own level.

"Nay—I come on an errand of pity."

"Santa Maria! we are both here with the same end!"

"Annina! I know not what thou would'st say!—This is surely the palace of Don Camillo Monforte!—A noble Neapolitan, who urges claims to the honors of the senate?"

"The gayest—the handsomest—the richest, and the most inconstant cavalier in Venice! Hadst thou been here a thousand times, thou could'st not be better informed!"

Gelsomina listened in horror. Her artful cousin, who knew her character to the full extent that vice can comprehend innocence, watched her colorless cheek and contracting eye, with secret triumph. At the first moment, she had believed all that she insinuated, but second thoughts, and a view of the visible distress of the frightened girl, gave a new direction to her suspicions.

"But I tell thee nothing new," she quickly added. "I only regret thou should'st find me, where, no doubt, you expected to meet the Duca di Sant' Agata himself."

"Annina!—This from thee!"

"Thou surely didst not come to his palace to seek thy cousin!"

Gelsomina had long been familiar with grief, but until this moment she had never felt the deep humiliation of shame. Tears started from her eyes, and she sunk back into a seat, in utter inability to stand.

"I would not distress thee out of bearing," added the artful daughter of the wine seller. "But that we are both in the closet of the gayest cavalier of Venice is beyond dispute."

"I have told thee that pity for another brought me hither."

"Pity for Don Camillo."

"For a noble lady—a young, a virtuous, and a beautiful wife—a daughter of the Tiepolo—of the Tiepolo, Annina!"

"Why should a lady of the Tiepolo employ a girl of the public prisons!"

"Why!—because there has been injustice by those up above. There has been a tumult among the fishermen—and the lady with her governess were liberated by the rioters—and his Highness spoke to them in the great court—and the Dalmatians were on the quay—and the prison was a refuge for ladies of their quality, in a moment of so great terror—and the Holy Church itself has blessed their love—"

Gelsomina could utter no more, but breathless with the wish to vindicate herself, and wounded to the soul by the strange embarrassment of her situation, she sobbed aloud. Incoherent as had been her language, she had said enough to remove every doubt from the mind of Annina. Privy to the secret marriage, to the rising of the fishermen, and to the departure of the ladies from the convent on a distant island where they had been carried on quitting their own palace, the preceding night, and whither she had been compelled to conduct Don Camillo, who had ascertained the departure of those he sought without discovering their destination, the daughter of the wine seller readily comprehended, not only the errand of her cousin, but the precise situation of the fugitives.

"And thou believest this fiction, Gelsomina?" she said, affecting pity for her cousin's credulity. "The characters of thy pretended daughter of Tiepolo and her governess are no secrets to those who frequent the piazza of San Marco."

"Hadst thou seen the beauty and innocence of the lady, Annina, thou would'st not say this!"

"Blessed San Teodoro! What is more beautiful than vice! 'Tis the cheapest artifice of the devil to deceive frail sinners. This thou hast heard of thy confessor, Gelsomina, or he is of much lighter discourse than mine."

"But why should a woman of this life enter the prisons?"

"They had good reasons to dread the Dalmatians, no doubt. But, it is in my power to tell thee more of these thou hast enter-

tained, with such peril to thine own reputation. There are
women in Venice who discredit their sex in various ways, and
these, more particularly she who calls herself Florinda, is notorious for her agency in robbing St. Mark of his revenue. She has
received a largess, from the Neapolitan, of wines grown on his
Calabrian mountains, and wishing to tamper with my honesty,
she offered the liquor to me, expecting one like me to forget my
duty, and to aid her in deceiving the republic."

"Can this be true, Annina!"

"Why should I deceive thee? Are we not sisters' children,
and though affairs on the Lido keep me much from thy company, is not the love between us natural? I complained to the
authorities, and the liquors were seized, and the pretended noble
ladies were obliged to hide themselves this very day. 'Tis thought
they wish to flee the city, with their profligate Neapolitan.
Driven to take shelter, they have sent thee to acquaint him with
their hiding place, in order that he may come to their aid."

"And why art thou here, Annina?"

"I marvel that thou didst not put the question sooner. Gino,
the gondolier of Don Camillo, has long been an unfavorable
suitor of mine, and when this Florinda complained of my having, what every honest girl in Venice should do, exposed her
fraud to the authorities, he advised his master to seize me, partly
in revenge, and partly with the vain hope of making me retract
the complaint I have made. Thou hast heard of the bold violence
of these cavaliers when thwarted in their wills."

Annina then related the manner of her seizure, with sufficient
exactitude, merely concealing those facts that it was not her
interest to reveal.

"But there is a lady of the Tiepolo, Annina!"

"As sure as there are cousins like ourselves. Santa Madre di
Dio! that women so treacherous and so bold should have met
one of thy innocence! It would have been better had they fallen
in with me, who am too ignorant for their cunning, blessed
St. Anna knows!—but who has not to learn their true characters."

"They did speak of thee, Annina!"

The glance which the wine seller's daughter threw at her
cousin was such as the treacherous serpent casts at the bird;
but preserving her self-possession, she added—

"Not to my favor; it would sicken me to hear words of
favor from such as they!"

306

"They are not thy friends, Annina."

"Perhaps they told thee, child, that I was in the employment of the council?"

"Indeed they did."

"No wonder. Your dishonest people can never believe one can do an act of pure conscience. But, here comes the Neapolitan.—Note the libertine, Gelsomina, and thou wilt feel for him the same disgust as I!"

The door opened, and Don Camillo Monforte entered. There was an appearance of distrust in his manner, which proved that he did not expect to meet his bride. Gelsomina arose, and, though bewildered by the tale of her cousin, and her own previous impressions, she stood resembling a meek statue of modesty, awaiting his approach. The Neapolitan was evidently struck by her beauty, and the simplicity of her air, but his brow was fixed, like that of a man who had steeled his feelings against deceit.

"Thou would'st see me?" he said.

"I had that wish, noble Signore, but—Annina—"

"Seeing another, thy mind hath changed."

"Signore, it has."

Don Camillo looked at her earnestly, and with manly regret.

"Thou art young for thy vocation—here is gold. Retire as thou camest.—But hold—dost thou know this Annina?"

"She is my mother's sister's daughter, noble Duca."

"Per Diana! a worthy sisterhood! Depart together, for I have no need of either. But mark me," and as he spoke, Don Camillo took Annina by the arm, and led her aside, when he continued with a low but menacing voice—"Thou see'st I am to be feared, as well as thy councils. Thou canst not cross the threshold of thy father without my knowledge. If prudent, thou wilt teach thy tongue discretion. Do as thou wilt, I fear thee not; but remember, prudence,"

Annina made an humble reverence, as if in acknowledgment of the wisdom of his advice, and taking the arm of her half-unconscious cousin, she again curtsied, and hurried from the room. As the presence of their master in his closet was known to them, none of the menials presumed to stop those who issued from the privileged room. Gelsomina, who was even more impatient than her wily companion to escape from a place she believed polluted, was nearly breathless when she reached the gondola. Its owner was in waiting on the steps, and in a moment the boat whirled away from a spot which both of those it contained were, though for reasons so very different, glad to quit.

Gelsomina had forgotten her mask, in her hurry; and the gondola was no sooner in the Great Canal than she put her face at the window of the pavilion in quest of the evening air. The rays of the moon fell upon her guileless eye, and a cheek that was now glowing, partly with offended pride, and partly with joy at her escape from a situation she felt to be so degrading. Her forehead was touched with a finger, and turning she saw the gondolier making a sign of caution. He then slowly lifted his mask.

"Carlo!" had half burst from her lips, but another sign suppressed the cry.

Gelsomina withdrew her head, and, after her beating heart had ceased to throb, she bowed her face and murmured thanksgivings, at finding herself, at such a moment, under the protection of one who possessed all her confidence.

The gondolier asked no orders for his direction. The boat moved on, taking the direction of the port, which appeared perfectly natural to the two females.

Annina supposed it was returning to the square, the place she would have sought had she been alone, and Gelsomina, who believed that he whom she called Carlo toiled regularly as a gondolier for support, fancied, of course, that he was taking her to her ordinary residence.

But though the innocent can endure the scorn of the world, it is hard indeed to be suspected by those they love. All that Annina had told her of the character of Don Camillo and his associates came gradually across the mind of the gentle Gelsomina, and she felt the blood creeping to her temples, as she saw the construction her lover might put on her conduct. A dozen times did the artless girl satisfy herself with saying inwardly, "he knows me and will believe the best," and as often did her feelings prompt her to tell the truth. Suspense is far more painful, at such moments, than even vindication, which, in itself, is a humiliating duty to the virtuous. Pretending a desire to breathe the air, she left her cousin in the canopy. Annina was not sorry to be alone, for she had need to reflect on all the windings of the sinuous path on which she had entered.

Gelsomina succeeded in passing the pavilion, and in gaining the side of the gondolier.

"Carlo!"—she said, observing that he continued to row in silence.

"Gelsomina!"

"Thou hast not questioned me!"

"I know thy treacherous cousin, and can believe thou art her dupe. The moment to learn the truth will come."

"Thou didst not know me, Carlo, when I called thee from the bridge?"

"I did not—Any fare that would occupy my time was welcome."

"Why dost thou call Annina treacherous?"

"Because Venice does not hold a more wily heart, or a falser tongue."

Gelsomina remembered the warning of Donna Florinda. Possessed of the advantage of blood, and that reliance which the inexperienced always place in the integrity of their friends, until exposure comes to destroy the illusion, Annina had found it easy to persuade her cousin of the unworthiness of her guests. But here was one who had all her sympathies, who openly denounced Annina herself. In such a dilemma the bewildered girl did what nature and her feelings suggested. She recounted, in a low but rapid voice, the incidents of the evening, and Annina's construction of the conduct of the females whom she had left behind in the prison.

Jacopo listened so intently that his oar dragged in the water.

"Enough," he said, when Gelsomina, blushing with her own earnestness to stand exculpated in his eyes, had done; "I understand it all. Distrust thy cousin, for the senate itself is not more false."

The pretended Carlo spoke cautiously, but in a firm voice. Gelsomina took his meaning, though wondering at what she heard, and returned to Annina within. The gondola proceeded, as if nothing had occurred.

CHAPTER XXV

"Enough.
I could be merry now: Hubert, I love thee;
Well, I'll not say what I intend for thee:
Remember."

King John

Jacopo was deeply practised in the windings of Venetian deceit. He knew how unceasingly the eyes of the councils, through their agents, were on the movements of those in whom they took an interest, and he was far from feeling all the advantage circumstances had seemingly thrown in his way. Annina was certainly in his power, and it was not possible that she had yet communicated the intelligence, derived from Gelsomina, to any of her employers. But a gesture, a look in passing the prison gates, the appearance of duresse, or an exclamation, might give the alarm to some one of the thousand spies of the police. The disposal of Annina's person in some place of safety, therefore, became the first and the most material act. To return to the palace of Don Camillo would be to go into the midst of the hirelings of the senate; and although the Neapolitan, relying on his rank and influence, had preferred this step, when little importance was attached to the detention of the girl, and when all she knew had been revealed, the case was altered, now that she might become the connecting link in the information necessary to enable the officers to find the fugitives.

The gondola moved on. Palace after palace was passed, and the impatient Annina thrust her head from a window to note its progress. They came among the shipping of the port, and her uneasiness sensibly increased. Making a pretext similar to that of Gelsomina, the wine seller's daughter quitted the pavilion, to steal to the side of the gondolier.

"I would be landed quickly at the water gate of the doge's palace," she said, slipping a piece of silver into the hand of the boatman.

"You shall be served, bella donna. But—Diamine! I marvel

310

that a girl of thy wit should not scent the treasures in yonder felucca!"

"Dost thou mean the Sorrentine?"

"What other padrone brings as well-flavored liquors within the Lido! Quiet thy impatience to land, daughter of honest old Maso, and traffic with the padrone, for the comfort of us of the canals."

"How! Thou knowest me then?"

"To be the pretty wine seller of the Lido. Corpo di Bacco! Thou art as well known as the sea wall itself, to us gondoliers."

"Why art thou masked? thou canst not be Luigi!"

"It is little matter whether I am called Luigi, or Enrico, or Giorgio—I am thy customer, and honor the shortest hair of thy eyebrows. Thou knowest, Annina, that the young patricians have their frolics, and they swear us gondoliers to keep secret till all danger of detection is over; were any impertinent eyes following me, I might be questioned as to the manner of having passed the earlier hours."

"Methinks it would be better to have given thee gold, and to have sent thee at once to thy home."

"To be followed like a denounced Hebrew to my door. When I have confounded my boat with a thousand others, it will be time to uncover. Wilt thou to the *Bella Sorrentina?*"

"Nay, 'tis not necessary to ask, since thou takest the direction of thine own will!"

The gondolier laughed and nodded his head, as if he would give his companion to understand that he was master of her secret wishes. Annina was hesitating in what manner she should make him change his purpose, when the gondola touched the felucca's side.

"We will go up and speak to the padrone," whispered Jacopo.

"It is of no avail; he is without liquors."

"Trust him not—I know the man and his pretences."

"Thou forgettest my cousin."

"She is an innocent and unsuspecting child."

Jacopo lifted Annina, as he spoke, on the deck of the *Bella Sorrentina*, in a manner between gallantry and force, and leaped after her. Without pausing, or suffering her to rally her thoughts, he led her to the cabin stairs, which she descended, wondering at his conduct, but determined not to betray her own secret wrongs on the customs to a stranger.

311

Stefano Milano was asleep in a sail on deck. A touch aroused him, and a sign gave him to understand that the imaginary Roderigo stood before him.

"A thousand pardons, Signore," said the gaping mariner; "is the freight come?"

"In part only. I have brought thee a certain Annina Torti, the daughter of old Tommaso Torti, a wine seller of the Lido."

"Santa Madre! does the senate think it necessary to send one like her from the city in secret?"

"It does—and it lays great stress on her detention. I have come hither with her, without suspicion of my object, and she has been prevailed on to enter thy cabin, under a pretence of some secret dealings in wines. According to our former understanding, it will be thy business to make sure of her presence."

"That is easily done," returned Stefano, stepping forward and closing the cabin door, which he secured by a bolt. "She is alone, now, with the image of our Lady, and a better occasion to repeat her aves cannot offer."

"This is well, if thou canst keep her so. It is now time to lift thy anchors, and to go beyond the tiers of the vessels with the felucca."

"Signore, there wants but five minutes for that duty, since we are ready."

"Then perform it in all speed, for much depends on the management of this delicate duty. I will be with thee, anon. Hearkee, Master Stefano; take heed of thy prisoner, for the senate makes great account of her security."

The Calabrian made such a gesture, as one initiated uses, when he would express a confidence in his own shrewdness. While the pretended Roderigo re-entered his gondola, Stefano began to awaken his people. As the gondola entered the canal of San Marco, the sails of the felucca fell, and the low Calabrian vessel stole along the tiers towards the clear water beyond.

The boat quickly touched the steps of the water gate of the palace. Gelsomina entered the arch, and glided up the Giant's Stairway, the route by which she had quitted the palace. The halberdier was the same that watched as she went out. He spoke to her, in gallantry, but offered no impediment to her entrance.

"Haste, noble ladies, hasten for the love of the Holy Virgin!" exclaimed Gelsomina, as she burst into the room in which Donna Violetta and her companion awaited her appearance. "I have

312

endangered your liberty by my weakness, and there is not a moment to lose. Follow while you may, nor stop to whisper even a prayer."

"Thou art hurried and breathless," returned Donna Florinda; "hast thou seen the Duca di Sant' Agata?"

"Nay, question me not, but follow, noble dames."

Gelsomina seized the lamp, and casting a glance that appealed strongly to her visitors for tacit compliance, she led the way into the corridors. It is scarcely necessary to say that she was followed.

The prison was left in safety, the Bridge of Sighs was passed, for it will be remembered that Gelsomina was still mistress of the keys, and the party went swiftly by the great stairs of the palace into the open gallery. No obstruction was offered to their progress, and they all descended to the court, with the quiet demeanor of females who went out on their ordinary affairs.

Jacopo awaited at the water gate. In less than a minute he was driving his gondola across the port, following the course of the felucca, whose white sail was visible in the moonlight, now bellying in the breeze, and now flapping as the mariners checked her speed. Gelsomina watched their progress for a moment in breathless interest, and then she crossed the bridge of the quay, and entered the prison by its public gate.

"Hast thou made sure of the old Maso's daughter?" demanded Jacopo, on reaching the deck of the *Bella Sorrentina* again.

"She is like shifting ballast, Master Roderigo; first on one side of the cabin, and then on the other; but you see the bolt is undrawn."

" 'Tis well: here is more of thy freight—thou hast the proper passes for the galley of the guard?"

"All is in excellent order, Signore; when was Stefano Milano out of rule in a matter of haste? Diamine! let the breeze come, and though the senate should wish us back again, it might send all its sbirri* after us in vain."

"Excellent Stefano! fill thy sails, then, for our masters watch your movements, and set a value on your diligence."

While the Calabrian complied, Jacopo assisted the females to come up out of the gondola. In a moment the heavy yards swung

---

* Italian police.—Editor.

off, wing and wing, and the bubbles that appeared to glance past the sides of the *Bella Sorrentina* denoted her speed.

"Thou hast noble ladies in thy passengers," said Jacopo to the padrone, when the latter was released from the active duties of getting his vessel in motion; "and though policy requires that they should quit the city for a time, thou wilt gain favor by consulting their pleasures."

"Doubt me not, Master Roderigo; but thou forgettest that I have not yet received my sailing instructions; a felucca without a course is as badly off as an owl in the sun."

"That in good time; there will come an officer of the republic to settle this matter with thee. I would not have these noble ladies know that one like Annina is to be their fellow passenger, while they are near the port; for they might complain of disrespect. Thou understandest, Stefano?"

"Cospetto! am I a fool? a blunderer? if so, why does the senate employ me? the girl is out of hearing, and there let her stay. As long as the noble dames are willing to breathe the night air, they shall have none of her company."

"No fear of them. The dwellers of the land little relish the pent air of thy cabin. Thou wilt go without the Lido, Stefano, and await my coming. If thou should'st not see me before the hour of one, bear away for the port of Ancona, where thou wilt get further tidings."

Stefano, who had often previously received his instructions from the imaginary Roderigo, nodded assent, and they parted. It is scarcely necessary to add that the fugitives had been fully instructed in the conduct they were to maintain.

The gondola of Jacopo never flew faster than he now urged it towards the land. In the constant passage of the boats, the movements of one were not likely to be remarked; and he found, when he reached the quay of the square, that his passing and repassing had not been observed. He boldly unmasked and landed. It was near the hour when he had given Don Camillo a rendezvous in the piazza, and he walked slowly up the smaller square, towards the appointed place of meeting.

Jacopo, as has been seen in an earlier chapter, had a practice of walking near the columns of granite in the first hours of the night. It was the vulgar impression that he waited there for custom in his bloody calling, as men of more innocent lives take their stands in places of mark. When seen on his customary stand, he was avoided by all who were chary of their character, or scrupulous of appearances.

The persecuted and yet singularly tolerated Bravo was slowly pacing the flags on his way to the appointed place, unwilling to anticipate the moment, when a laquais thrust a paper into his hand, and disappeared as fast as legs would carry him. It has been seen that Jacopo could not read, for that was an age when men of his class were studiously kept in ignorance. He turned to the first passenger who had the appearance of being likely to satisfy his wishes, and desired him to do the office of interpreter.

He had addressed an honest shopkeeper of a distant quarter. The man took the scroll, and good-naturedly commenced reading its contents aloud. "I am called away, and cannot meet thee, Jacopo!" At the name of Jacopo, the tradesman dropped the paper and fled.

The Bravo walked slowly back again, towards the quay, ruminating on the awkward accident which had crossed his plans; his elbow was touched, and a masker confronted him when he turned.

"Thou art Jacopo Frontoni?" said the stranger.

"None else."

"Thou hast a hand to serve an employer, faithfully?"

"I keep my faith."

" 'Tis well,—thou wilt find a hundred sequins in this sack."

"Whose life is set against this gold?" asked Jacopo, in an undertone.

"Don Camillo Monforte."

"Don Camillo Monforte!"

"The same: dost thou know the rich noble?"

"You have well described him, Signore. He would pay his barber this for letting blood."

"Do thy job thoroughly, and the price shall be doubled."

"I want the security of a name. I know you not, Signore."

The stranger looked cautiously around him, and raising his mask for an instant, he showed the countenance of Giacomo Gradenigo.

"Is the pledge sufficient?"

"Signore, it is. When must this deed be done?"

"This night.—Nay, this hour, even."

"Shall I strike a noble of his rank in his palace—in his very pleasures?"

"Come hither, Jacopo, and thou shalt know more. Hast thou a mask?"

The Bravo signified his assent.

"Then keep thy face behind a cloud, for it is not in favor here, and seek thy boat. I will join thee."

The young patrician, whose form was effectually concealed by his attire, quitted his companion, with a view of rejoining him anew, where his person should not be known. Jacopo forced his boat from among the crowd at the quay, and having entered the open space between the tiers, he lay on his oar, well knowing that he was watched, and that he would soon be followed. His conjecture was right, for in a few moments a gondola pulled swiftly to the side of his own, and two men in masks passed from the strange boat into that of the Bravo, without speaking.

"To the Lido," said a voice, which Jacopo knew to be that of his new employer.

He was obeyed, the boat of Giacomo Gradenigo following at a little distance. When they were without the tiers, and consequently beyond the danger of being overheard, the two passengers came out of the pavilion, and made a sign to the Bravo to cease rowing.

"Thou wilt accept the service, Jacopo Frontoni?" demanded the profligate heir of the old senator.

"Shall I strike the noble in his pleasures, Signore?"

"It is not necessary. We have found means to lure him from his palace, and he is now in thy power, with no other hope than that which may come from his single arm and courage. Wilt thou take the service?"

"Gladly, Signore—It is my humor to encounter the brave."

"Thou wilt be gratified. The Neapolitan has thwarted me in my—shall I call it love, Hosea; or hast thou a better name?"

"Just Daniel! Signor Giacomo, you have no respect for reputations and surety! I see no necessity for a home thrust, Master Jacopo; but a smart wound, that may put matrimony out of the head of the duca for a time at least, and penitence into its place, would be better—"

"Strike to the heart!" interrupted Giacomo. "It is the certainty of thy blow which has caused me to seek thee."

"This is usurious vengeance, Signor Giacomo," returned the less resolute Jew. "'Twill be more than sufficient for our purposes, if we cause the Neapolitan to keep house for a month."

"Send him to his grave. Harkee, Jacopo, a hundred for thy blow—a second for insurance of its depth—a third, if the body shall be buried in the Orfano, so that the water will never give back the secret."

"If the two first must be performed, the last will be prudent caution," muttered the Jew, who was a wary villain, and who greatly preferred such secondary expedients, as might lighten the load on his conscience. "You will not trust, young Signore, to a smart wound?"

"Not a sequin. 'Twill be heating the fancy of the girl with hopes and pity. Dost thou accept the terms, Jacopo?"

"I do."

"Then row to the Lido. Among the graves of Hosea's people—why dost thou pull at my skirts, Jew! would'st thou hope to deceive a man of this character with a flimsy lie—among the graves of Hosea's people thou wilt meet Don Camillo, within the hour. He is deluded by a pretended letter from the lady of our common pursuit, and will be alone, in the hopes of flight; I trust to thee to hasten the latter, so far as the Neapolitan is concerned. Dost take my meaning?"

"Signore, it is plain."

" 'Tis enough. Thou knowest me, and can take the steps necessary for thy reward, as thou shalt serve me. Hosea, our affair is ended."

Giacomo Gradenigo made a sign for his gondola to approach, and dropping a sack which contained the retainer in this bloody business, he passed into it with the indifference of one who had been accustomed to consider such means of attaining his object lawful. Not so Hosea—he was a rogue, rather than a villain. The preservation of his money, with the temptation of a large sum which had been promised him, by both father and son, in the event of the latter's success with Violetta, were irresistible temptations to one who had lived contemned by those around him, and he found his solace for the ruthless attempt in the acquisition of those means of enjoyment which are sought equally by Christian and Jew. Still his blood curdled at the extremity to which Giacomo would push the affair, and he lingered to utter a parting word to the Bravo.

"Thou art said to carry a sure stiletto, honest Jacopo," he whispered. "A hand of thy practice must know how to maim, as well as to slay.—Strike the Neapolitan smartly, but spare his life.

317

Even the bearer of a public dagger like thine may not fare the worse, at the coming of Shilo, for having been tender of his strength, on occasion."

"Thou forgettest the gold, Hosea!"

"Father Abraham! what a memory am I getting, in my years! Thou sayest truth, mindful Jacopo; the gold shall be forthcoming, in any event—always provided that the affair is so managed as to leave my young friend a successful adventurer with the heiress."

Jacopo made an impatient gesture, for at that moment he saw a gondolier pulling rapidly towards a private part of the Lido. The Hebrew joined his companion, and the boat of the Bravo darted ahead. It was not long ere it lay on the strand of the Lido. The steps of Jacopo were rapid, as he moved towards those proscribed graves, among which he had made his confession to the very man he was now sent to slay.

"Art thou sent to meet me?" demanded one who started from behind a rising in the sands, but who took the precaution to bare his rapier as he appeared.

"Signor Duca, I am," returned the Bravo, unmasking.

"Jacopo!—This is even better than I had hoped! Hast thou tidings from my bride?"

"Follow, Don Camillo, and you shall quickly meet her."

Words were unnecessary to persuade, when there was such a promise. They were both in the gondola of Jacopo, and on their way to one of the passages through the Lido, which conducts to the gulf, before the Bravo commenced his explanation. This, however, was quickly made, not forgetting the design of Giacomo Gradenigo on the life of his auditor.

The felucca, which had been previously provided with the necessary pass by the agents of the police itself, had quitted the port under easy sail, by the very inlet through which the gondola made its way into the Adriatic. The water was smooth, the breeze fresh from the land, and in short all things were favorable to the fugitives. Donna Violetta and her governess were leaning against a mast, watching with impatient eyes the distant domes, and the midnight beauty of Venice. Occasionally, strains of music came to their ears from the canals, and then a touch of natural melancholy crossed the feelings of the former, as she feared they might be the last sounds of that nature she should ever hear from her native town. But unalloyed pleasure drove every regret from her mind when Don Camillo leaped from the gondola, and folded her in triumph to his heart.

There was little difficulty in persuading Stefano Milano to abandon, forever, the service of the senate, for that of his feudal lord. The promises and commands of the latter were sufficient of themselves to reconcile him to the change, and all were convinced there was no time to lose. The felucca soon spread her canvas to the wind, and slid away from the beach. Jacopo permitted his gondola to be towed a league to sea, before he prepared to re-enter it.

"You will steer for Ancona, Signor Don Camillo," said the Bravo, leaning on the felucca's side, still unwilling to depart, "and throw yourself, at once, under the protection of the Cardinal Secretary. If Stefano keep the sea, he may chance meet the galleys of the senate."

"Distrust us not—but thou, my excellent Jacopo—what wilt thou become, in their hands?"

"Fear not for me, Signore. God disposes of all, as he sees fit. I have told your eccellenza that I cannot yet quit Venice. If fortune favor me, I may still see your stout castle of Sant' Agata."

"And none will be more welcome within its secure walls; I have much fear for thee, Jacopo!"

"Signore, think not of it. I am used to danger—and to misery—and to hopelessness. I have known a pleasure, this night, in witnessing the happiness of two young hearts, that God, in his anger, has long denied me. Lady, the saints keep you, and God, who is above all, shield you from harm!"

He kissed the hand of Donna Violetta, who, half ignorant still of his services, listened to his words in wonder.

"Don Camillo Monforte," he continued, "distrust Venice to your dying day. Let no promises—no hopes—no desire of increasing your honors, or your riches, ever tempt you to put yourself in her power. None know the falsehood of the state, better than I, and with my parting words I warn you to be wary!"

"Thou speakest as if we were to meet no more, worthy Jacopo!"

The Bravo turned, and the action brought his features to the moon. There was a melancholy smile in which deep satisfaction at the success of the lovers was mingled with serious forebodings for himself.

"We are certain only of the past," he said, in a low voice.

Touching the hand of Don Camillo, he kissed his own and leaped hastily into his gondola. The fast was thrown loose, and the felucca glided away, leaving this extraordinary being alone in the waters. The Neapolitan ran to the taffrail, and the last he saw of Jacopo, the Bravo was rowing leisurely back towards the scene of violence and deception from which he himself was so glad to have escaped.

CHAPTER XXVI

"My limbs are bow'd, though not with toil,
   But rusted with a vile repose,
For they have been a dungeon's spoil,
   And mine hath been the fate of those
To whom the goodly earth and air
Are bann'd, and barr'd—forbidden fare."
               Prisoner of Chillon

WHEN the day dawned on the following morning, the square of St. Mark was empty. The priests still chanted their prayers for the dead, near the body of old Antonio, and a few fishermen still lingered in and near the cathedral but half persuaded of the manner in which their companion had come to his end. But, as was usual at that hour of the day, the city appeared tranquil, for though a slight alarm had passed through the canals, at the movement of the rioters, it had subsided in that specious and distrustful quiet which is, more or less, the unavoidable consequence of a system that is not substantially based on the willing support of the mass.

Jacopo was again in the attic of the doge's palace, accompanied by the gentle Gelsomina. As they threaded the windings of the building, he recounted to the eager ear of his companion, all the details connected with the escape of the lovers; omitting, as a matter of prudence, the attempt of Giacomo Gradenigo on the life of Don Camillo. The unpractised and single-hearted girl heard him in breathless attention, the color of her cheek, and the changeful eye, betraying the force of her sympathies, at each turn in their hazardous adventure.

"And dost thou think they can yet escape from those up above?" murmured Gelsomina, for few in Venice would trust their voices, by putting such a question aloud. "Thou knowest the republic hath, at all times, its galleys in the Adriatic!"

"We have had thought of that, and the Calabrian is advised to steer for the mole of Ancona. Once within the States of the Church, the influence of Don Camillo and the rights of his noble wife will protect them. Is there a place here whence we can look out upon the sea?"

Gelsomina led the Bravo into an empty room of the attic which commanded a view of the port, the Lido, and the waste of water beyond. The breeze came in strong currents, over the roofs of the town, and causing the masts of the port to rock, it lighted on the Lagunes, without the tiers of the shipping. From this point, to the barrier of sand, it was apparent, by the stooping sails and the struggles of the gondoliers who pulled towards the quay, that the air was swift. Without the Lido, itself, the element was shadowed and fitful, while farther in the distance, the troubled waters, with their crests of foam, sufficiently proved its power.

"Santa Maria be praised!" exclaimed Jacopo, when his understanding eye had run over the near and distant view—"they are already far down the coast, and with a wind like this they cannot fail to reach their haven, in a few hours.—Let us go to the cell."

Gelsomina smiled, when he assured her of the safety of the fugitives, but her look saddened when he changed the discourse. Without reply, however, she did as he desired, and in a very few moments they were standing by the side of the prisoner's pallet. The latter did not appear to observe their entrance, and Jacopo was obliged to announce himself.

"Father!" he said, with that melancholy pathos which always crept into his voice when he addressed the old man, "it is I."

The prisoner turned, and though evidently much enfeebled since the last visit, a wan smile gleamed on his wasted features.

"And thy mother, boy?" he asked, so eagerly as to cause Gelsomina to turn hastily aside.

"Happy, father—happy!"

"Happy without me?"

"She is ever with thee, in spirit, father. She thinks of thee in her prayers. Thou hast a saint for an intercessor, in my mother—father."

"And thy good sister?"

"Happy too—doubt it not, father. They are both patient and resigned."

"The senate, boy?"

"Is the same: soulless, selfish, and pretending!" answered Jacopo sternly; then turning away his face, in bitterness of heart, though without permitting the words to be audible, he cursed them.

"The noble Signori were deceived in believing me concerned

322

in the attempt to rob their revenues," returned the patient old man; "one day they will see and acknowledge their error."

Jacopo made no answer, for, unlettered as he was, and curtailed of that knowledge which should be, and is, bestowed on all, by every paternal government, the natural strength of his mind had enabled him to understand, that a system which on its face professed to be founded on the superior acquirements of a privileged few would be the least likely to admit the fallacy of its theories, by confessing it could err.

"Thou dost the nobles injustice, son; they are illustrious patricians, and have no motive in oppressing one like me."

"None, father, but the necessity of maintaining the severity of the laws which make them senators and you a prisoner."

"Nay, boy, I have known worthy gentlemen of the senate! There was the late Signor Tiepolo, who did me much favor in my youth. But for this false accusation, I might now have been one of the most thriving of my craft in Venice."

"Father, we will pray for the soul of the Tiepolo."

"Is the senator dead?"

"So says a gorgeous tomb in the church of the Redentore."

"We must all die at last," whispered the old man, crossing himself. "Doge as well as patrician—patrician as well as gondolier.—Jaco—"

"Father!" exclaimed the Bravo, so suddenly as to interrupt the coming word, then kneeling by the pallet of the prisoner he whispered in his ear, "thou forgettest there is reason why thou should'st not call me by that name. I have told thee, often, that if thus called, my visits must stop."

The prisoner looked bewildered, for the failing of nature rendered that obscure which was once so evident to his mind. After gazing long at his son, his eye wandered between him and the wall, and he smiled childishly.

"Wilt thou look, good boy, if the spider is come back?"

Jacopo groaned, but he rose to comply.

"I do not see it, father; the season is not yet warm."

"Not warm! my veins feel heated to bursting. Thou forgettest this is the attic, and that these are the leads, and then the sun—oh! the sun! The illustrious senators do not bethink them of the pain of passing the bleak winter below the canals, and the burning summers beneath hot metal."

"They think of nothing but their power," murmured

323

Jacopo—"that which is wrongfully obtained must be maintained by merciless injustice—but why should we speak of this, father; hast thou all thy body needs?"

"Air—son, air!—give me of that air which God has made for the meanest living thing."

The Bravo rushed towards those fissures in the venerable but polluted pile he had already striven to open, and with frantic force he endeavored to widen them with his hands. The material resisted, though blood flowed from the ends of his fingers, in the desperate effort.

"The door, Gelsomina, open wide the door!" he cried, turning away from the spot, exhausted with his fruitless exertions.

"Nay, I do not suffer now, my child—it is when thou hast left me, and when I am alone with my own thoughts, when I see thy weeping mother and neglected sister, that I most feel the want of air—are we not in the fervid month of August, son?"

"Father, it is not yet June."

"I shall then have more heat to bear! God's will be done, and blessed Santa Maria, his mother undefiled!—give me strength to endure it."

The eye of Jacopo gleamed with a wildness, scarcely less frightful than the ghastly look of the old man, his chest heaved, his fingers were clenched, and his breathing was audible.

"No," he said, in a low, but in so determined a voice, as to prove how fiercely his resolution was set, "thou shalt not await their torments: arise, father, and go with me. The doors are open, the ways of the palace are known to me in the darkest night, and the keys are at hand. I will find means to conceal thee until dark, and we will quit the accursed republic forever."

Hope gleamed in the eye of the old captive, as he listened to this frantic proposal, but distrust of the means immediately altered its expression.

"Thou forgettest those up above, son."

"I think only of One truly above, father."

"And this girl—how canst thou hope to deceive her?"

"She will take thy place—she is with us in heart, and will lend herself to a seeming violence. I do not promise for thee idly, kindest Gelsomina?"

The frightened girl, who had never before witnessed so plain evidence of desperation in her companion, had sunk upon an

324

article of furniture, speechless. The look of the prisoner changed from one to the other, and he made an effort to rise, but debility caused him to fall backward, and not till then did Jacopo perceive the impracticability, on many accounts, of what, in a moment of excitement, he had proposed. A long silence followed. The hard breathing of Jacopo gradually subsided, and the expression of his face changed to its customary, settled, and collected look.

"Father," he said, "I must quit thee; our misery draws near a close."

"Thou wilt come to me soon again?"

"If the saints permit—thy blessing, father."

The old man folded his hands above the head of Jacopo, and murmured a prayer. When this pious duty was performed, both the Bravo and Gelsomina busied themselves, a little time, in contributing to the bodily comforts of the prisoner, and then they departed in company.

Jacopo appeared unwilling to quit the vicinity of the cell. A melancholy presentiment seemed to possess his mind, that these stolen visits were soon to cease. After a little delay, however, they descended to the apartments below, and as Jacopo desired to quit the palace, without re-entering the prisons, Gelsomina prepared to let him out by the principal corridor.

"Thou art sadder than common, Carlo," she observed, watching with feminine assiduity his averted eye. "Methinks thou should'st rejoice in the fortunes of the Neapolitan, and of the lady of the Tiepolo."

"That escape is like a gleam of sunshine, in a wintry day. Good girl—but we are observed! why is yon spy on our movements?"

" 'Tis a menial of the palace; they constantly cross us in this part of the building: come hither, if thou art weary. The room is little used, and we may again look out upon the sea."

Jacopo followed his mild conductor into one of the neglected closets of the second floor, where, in truth, he was glad to catch a glimpse of the state of things in the piazza, before he left the palace. His first look was at the water, which was still rolling southward, before the gale from the Alps. Satisfied with this prospect, he bent his eye beneath. At the instant, an officer of the republic issued from the palace gate, preceded by a trumpeter, as was usual when there was occasion to make public proclamation of the senate's will. Gelsomina opened the casement, and both leaned forward to listen. When the little procession had reached the front of the cathedral, the trumpet sounded, and the voice of the officer was heard.

"Whereas many wicked and ruthless assassinations have of late been committed on the persons of divers good citizens of Venice,"—he proclaimed—"the senate, in its fatherly care of all whom it is charged to protect, has found reason to resort to extraordinary means of preventing the repetition of crimes so contrary to the laws of God and the security of society. The Illustrious Ten therefore offer, thus publicly, a reward of one hundred sequins to him who shall discover the perpetrator of any of these most horrible assassinations; and, whereas, during the past night, the body of a certain Antonio, a well-known fisherman, and a worthy citizen, much esteemed by the patricians, has been found in the Lagunes, and, whereas, there is but too much reason to believe that he has come to his death by the hands of a certain Jacopo Frontoni, who has the reputation of a common Bravo, but who has been long watched, in vain, by the authorities, with the hope of detecting him in the commission of some one of the aforesaid horrible assassinations; now, all good and honest citizens of the republic are enjoined to assist the authorities in seizing the person of the said Jacopo Frontoni, even though he should take sanctuary: for Venice can no longer endure the presence of one of his sanguinary habits, and for the encouragement of the same, the senate, in its paternal care, offers the reward of three hundred sequins." The usual words of prayer and sovereignty closed the proclamation.

As it was not usual for those who ruled so much in the dark to make their intentions public, all near listened, with wonder and awe, to the novel procedure. Some trembled, lest the mysterious and much-dreaded power was about to exhibit itself; while most found means of making their admiration of the fatherly interest of their rulers audible.

None heard the words of the officer with more feeling than Gelsomina. She bent her body far from the window, in order that not a syllable should escape her.

"Didst thou hear, Carlo?" demanded the eager girl, as she drew back her head; "they proclaim, at last, money for the monster who has committed so many murders!"

326

Jacopo laughed; but to the ears of his startled companion the sounds were unnatural.

"The patricians are just, and what they do is right," he said. "They are of illustrious birth, and cannot err! They will do their duty."

"But here is no other duty than that they owe to God, and to the people."

"I have heard of the duty of the people, but little is said of the senate's."

"Nay, Carlo, we will not refuse them credit when in truth they seek to keep the citizens from harm. This Jacopo is a monster, detested by all, and his bloody deeds have too long been a reproach to Venice. Thou hearest that the patricians are not niggard of their gold, when there is hope of his being taken.—Listen! they proclaim again!"

The trumpet sounded, and the proclamation was repeated between the granite columns of the piazzetta, and quite near to the window occupied by Gelsomina and her unmoved companion.

"Why dost thou mask, Carlo?" she asked, when the officer had done; "it is not usual to be disguised, in the palace, at this hour."

"They will believe it the doge, blushing to be an auditor of his own liberal justice, or they may mistake me for one of the Three, itself."

"They go by the quay to the arsenal; thence they will take boat, as is customary, for the Rialto."

"Thereby giving this redoubtable Jacopo timely notice to secrete himself! Your judges up above are mysterious when they should be open, and open when they should be secret. I must quit thee, Gelsomina; go, then, back to the room of thy father, and leave me to pass out by the court of the palace."

"It may not be, Carlo—thou knowest the permission of the authorities—I have exceeded—why should I wish to conceal it from thee—but, it was not permitted to thee to enter at this hour."

"And thou hast had the courage to transgress the leave, for my sake, Gelsomina?"

The abashed girl hung her head, and the color which glowed about her temples was like the rosy light of her own Italy.

"Thou would'st have it so," she said.

"A thousand thanks, dearest, kindest, truest Gelsomina; but doubt not my being able to leave the palace unseen. The danger was in entering. They who go forth do it with the air of having authority."

"None pass the halberdiers masked by day, Carlo, but they who have the secret word."

The Bravo appeared struck with this truth, and there was great embarrassment expressed in his manner. The terms of his admittance were so well understood to himself, that he distrusted the expediency of attempting to get upon the quays by the prison, the way he had entered, since he had little doubt that his retreat would be intercepted by those who kept the outer gate, and who were probably, by this time, in the secret of his true character. It now appeared that egress by the other route was equally hazardous. He had not been surprised so much by the substance of the proclamation, as by the publicity the senate had seen fit to give to its policy,—and he had heard himself denounced, with a severe pang, it is true, but without terror. Still he had so many means of disguise, and the practice of personal concealment was so general in Venice, that he had entertained no great distrust of the result until he now found himself in this awkward dilemma. Gelsomina read his indecision in his eye, and regretted that she should have caused him so much uneasiness.

"It is not so bad as thou seemest to think, Carlo," she observed; "they have permitted thee to visit thy father, at stated hours, and the permission is a proof that the senate is not without pity. Now that I, to oblige thy wishes, have forgotten one of their injunctions, they will not be so hard of heart as to visit the fault as a crime."

Jacopo gazed at her with pity, for well did he understand how little she knew of the real nature and wily policy of the state.

"It is time that we should part," he said, "lest thy innocence should be made to pay the price of my mistake. I am now near the public corridor, and must trust to my fortune to gain the quay."

Gelsomina hung upon his arm, unwilling to trust him to his own guidance in that fearful building.

"It will not do, Carlo; thou wilt stumble on a soldier, and thy fault will be known; perhaps they will refuse to let thee come again; perhaps altogether shut the door of thy poor father's cell."

Jacopo made a gesture for her to lead the way, and followed. With a beating but still lightened heart, Gelsomina glided along the passages, carefully locking each door, as of wont, behind her, when she had passed through it. At length they reached the well-known Bridge of Sighs. The anxious girl went on with a lighter step, when she found herself approaching her own abode, for she was busy in planning the means of concealing her companion in her father's rooms, should there be hazard in his passing out of the prison during the day.

"But a single minute, Carlo," she whispered, applying the key to the door which opened into the latter building—the lock yielded, but the hinges refused to turn. Gelsomina paled as she added—"They have drawn the bolts within!"

"No matter; I will go down by the court of the palace, and boldly pass the halberdier unmasked."

Gelsomina, after all, saw but little risk of his being known by the mercenaries who served the doge, and, anxious to relieve him from so awkward a position, she flew back to the other end of the gallery. Another key was applied to the door by which they had just entered, with the same result. Gelsomina staggered back, and sought support against the wall.

"We can neither return nor proceed!" she exclaimed, frightened she knew not why.

"I see it all," answered Jacopo, "we are prisoners on the fatal bridge."

As he spoke, the Bravo calmly removed his mask, and showed the countenance of a man whose resolution was at its height.

"Santa Madre di Dio! what can it mean?"

"That we have passed here once too often, love. The council is tender of these visits."

The bolts of both doors grated, and the hinges creaked at the same instant. An officer of the inquisition entered armed, and bearing manacles. Gelsomina shrieked, but Jacopo moved not limb or muscle, while he was fettered and chained.

"I too!" cried his frantic companion. "I am the most guilty—bind me—cast me into a cell, but let poor Carlo go."

"Carlo!" echoed an officer, laughing unfeelingly.

"Is it such a crime to seek a father in his prison! They knew of his visits—they permitted them—he has only mistaken the hour."

"Girl, dost thou know for whom thou pleadest?"

"For the kindest heart—the most faithful son in Venice! Oh! if ye had seen him weep as I have done, over the sufferings of the old captive—if ye had seen his very form shivering in agony, ye would have pity on him!"

"Listen," returned the officer, raising a finger for attention.

The trumpeter sounded on the bridge of St. Mark, immediately beneath them, and proclamation was again made, offering gold for the arrest of the Bravo.

" 'Tis the officer of the republic, bidding for the head of one who carries a common stiletto," cried the half-breathless Gelsomina, who little heeded the ceremony at that instant; "he merits his fate."

"Then why resist it?"

"Ye speak without meaning!"

"Doting girl, this is Jacopo Frontoni!"

Gelsomina would have disbelieved her ears, but for the anguished expression of Jacopo's eye. The horrible truth burst upon her mind, and she fell lifeless. At that moment the Bravo was hurried from the bridge.

CHAPTER XXVII

"Let us lift up the curtain, and observe
What passes in that chamber."
ROGERS

THERE were many rumors, uttered in the fearful and secret manner which characterized the manners of the town, in the streets of Venice that day. Hundreds passed near the granite columns, as if they expected to see the Bravo occupying his accustomed stand, in audacious defiance of the proclamation, for so long and so mysteriously had he been permitted to appear in public, that men had difficulty in persuading themselves he would quit his habits so easily. It is needless to say that the vague expectation was disappointed. Much was also said, vauntingly, in behalf of the republic's justice, for the humbled are bold enough in praising their superiors; and he who had been dumb for years on subjects of a public nature now found his voice like a fearless freeman.

But the day passed away without any new occurrence to call the citizens from their pursuits. The prayers for the dead were continued, with little intermission, and masses were said before the altars of half the churches, for the repose of the fisherman's soul. His comrades, a little distrustful but greatly gratified, watched the ceremonies with jealousy and exultation singularly blended. Ere the night set in again, they were among the most obedient of those the oligarchy habitually trod upon; for such is the effect of this species of domination, that it acquires a power to appease by its flattery, the very discontents created by its injustice. Such is the human mind: a factitious but deeply seated sentiment of respect is created by the habit of submission, which gives the subject of its influence a feeling of atonement, when he who has long played the superior comes down from his stilts and confesses the community of human frailties!

The square of St. Mark filled at the usual hour, the patricians deserted the Broglio as of wont, and the gaieties of the place were again uppermost, before the clock had struck the second

331

hour of the night. Gondolas, filled with noble dames, appeared on the canals; the blinds of the palaces were raised for the admission of the sea breeze;—and music began to be heard in the port, on the bridges, and under the balconies of the fair. The course of society was not to be arrested, merely because the wronged were unavenged, or the innocent suffered.

There stood, then, on the Grand Canal, as there stand now, many palaces of scarcely less than royal magnificence. The reader has had occasion to become acquainted with one or two of these splendid edifices, and it has now become our duty to convey him, in imagination, to another.

The peculiarity of construction, which is a consequence of the watery site of Venice, gives the same general character to all the superior dwellings of that remarkable town. The house to which the thread of the narrative now leads us, had its water gate, its vestibule, its massive marble stairs, its inner court, its magnificent suites of rooms above, its pictures, its lustres, and its floors of precious stones embedded in composition, like all those which we have already found it necessary to describe.

The hour was ten, according to our own manner of computing time. A small, but lovely family picture presented itself, deep within the walls of the patrician abode to which we have alluded. There was a father, a gentleman who had scarce attained the middle age, with an eye in which spirit, intelligence, philanthropy, and, at that moment, paternal fondness were equally glowing. He tossed in his arms, with parental pride, a laughing urchin of some three or four years, who rioted in the amusement which brought him and the author of his being, for a time, seemingly on a level. A fair Venetian dame, with golden locks, and glowing cheeks, such as Titian loved to paint her sex, reclined on a couch nigh by, following the movements of both, with the joint feelings of mother and wife, and laughing in pure sympathy with the noisy merriment of her young hope. A girl, who was the youthful image of herself, with tresses that fell to her waist, romped with a crowing infant, whose age was so tender as scarcely to admit the uncertain evidence of its intelligence. Such was the scene as the clock of the piazza told the hour. Struck with the sound, the father set down the boy, and consulted his watch.

"Dost thou use thy gondola tonight, love?" he demanded.

"With thee, Paolo?"

"Not with me, dearest; I have affairs which will employ me until twelve!"

"Nay, thou art given to cast me off, when thy caprices are wayward."

"Say not so. I have named tonight for an interview with my agent, and I know thy maternal heart too well, to doubt thy being willing to spare me for that time, while I look to the interests of these dear ones."

The Donna Giulietta rang for her mantle and attendants. The crowing infant and the noisy boy were dismissed to their beds, while the lady and the eldest child descended to the gondola. Donna Giulietta was not permitted to go unattended to her boat, for this was a family in which the inclinations had fortunately seconded the ordinary calculations of interest, when the nuptial knot was tied. Her husband kissed her hand, fondly, as he assisted her into the gondola, and the boat had glided some distance from the palace, ere he quitted the moist stones of the water gate.

"Hast thou prepared the cabinet for my friends?" demanded the Signor Soranzo, for it was the same senator who had been in company with the doge, when the latter went to meet the fishermen.

"Signore, si."

"And the quiet, and the lights—as ordered?"

"Eccellenza, all will be done."

"Thou hast placed seats for six—we shall be six."

"Signore, there are six armed chairs."

"'Tis well: when the first of my friends arrive, I will join them."

"Eccellenza, there are already two cavaliers in masks, within."

The Signor Soranzo started, again consulted his watch, and went hastily towards a distant, and very silent, part of the palace. He reached a small door unattended, and, closing it, found himself at once in the presence of those who evidently awaited his appearance.

"A thousand pardons, Signori," cried the master of the house; "this is novel duty to me, at least—I know not what may be your honorable experience—and the time stole upon me unmarked. I pray for grace, Messires; future diligence shall repair the present neglect."

Both the visitors were older men than their host, and it was quite evident by their hardened visages they were of much longer practice in the world. His excuses were received with courtesy, and, for a little time, the discourse was entirely of usage and convention.

"We are in secret here, Signore?" asked one of the guests, after some little time had been wasted in this manner.

"As the tomb. None enter here unbidden but my wife, and she has, this moment, taken boat, for better enjoyment of the evening."

"The world gives you credit, Signor Soranzo, for a happy ménage. I hope you have duly considered the necessity of shutting the door, even against the Donna Giulietta tonight?"

"Doubt me not, Signore; the affairs of St. Mark are paramount."

"I feel myself thrice happy, Signori, that in drawing a lot for the secret council, my good fortune hath given me so excellent colleagues. Believe me, I have discharged this awful trust, in my day, in less agreeable company."

This flattering speech, which the wily old senator had made regularly to all with whom chance had associated him in the inquisition, during a long life, was well received, and it was returned with equal compliments.

"It would appear that the worthy Signor Alessandro Gradenigo was one of our predecessors," he continued, looking at some papers; for though the actual three were unknown, at the time being, to all but a few secretaries and officers of the state, Venetian policy transmitted their names to their successors as a matter of course,—"a noble gentleman, and one of great devotion to the state!"

The others assented, like men accustomed to speak with caution.

"We were about to have entered on our duties at a troublesome moment, Signori," observed another. "But it would seem that this tumult of the fishermen has already subsided. I understand the knaves had some reason for their distrust of the state!"

"It is an affair happily settled," answered the senior of the three, who was long practised in the expediency of forgetting all that policy required should cease to be remembered, after the object was attained. "The galleys must be manned, else would St. Mark quickly hang his head in shame."

The Signor Soranzo, who had received some previous instruction in his new duties, looked melancholy; but he, too, was merely the creature of a system.

"Is there matter of pressing import for our reflection?" he demanded.

"Signori, there is every reason to believe that the state has just sustained a grievous loss. Ye both well know the heiress of Tiepolo, by reputation at least, though her retired manner of life may have kept you from her company."

"Donna Giulietta is eloquent in praise of her beauty," said the young husband.

"We had not a better fortune in Venice," rejoined the third inquisitor.

"Excellent in qualities, and better in riches, as she is, I fear we have lost her, Signori! Don Camillo Monforte, whom God protect until we have no future use for his influence! had come near to prevail against us; but just as the state baffled his well-laid schemes, the lady has been thrown by hazard into the hands of the rioters, since which time there is no account of her movements!"

Paolo Soranzo secretly hoped she was in the arms of the Neapolitan.

"A secretary has communicated to me the disappearance of the Duca di Sant' Agata, also," observed the third,—"nor is the felucca, usually employed in distant and delicate missions, any longer at her anchors."

The two old men regarded each other, as if the truth was beginning to dawn upon their suspicions. They saw that the case was hopeless, and as theirs was altogether a practical duty, no time was lost in useless regrets.

"We have two affairs which press," observed the elder.— "The body of the old fisherman must be laid quietly in the earth, with as little risk of future tumult, as may be—and we have this notorious Jacopo to dispose of."

"The latter must first be taken," said the Signor Soranzo.

"That has been done already. Would you think it, Sirs! he was seized in the very palace of the doge!"

"To the block with him, without delay!"

The old men again looked at each other, and it was quite apparent that, as both of them had been in previous councils, they had a secret intelligence to which their companion was yet a stranger. There was also visible in their glances, something like a design to manage his feelings, before they came more openly to the graver practices of their duties.

"For the sake of blessed St. Mark, Signori, let justice be

335

done openly in this instance!" continued the unsuspecting member of the Three. "What pity can the bearer of a common stiletto claim? And what more lovely exercise of our authority than to make public an act of severe and much-required justice?"

The old senators bowed to this sentiment of their colleague, which was uttered with the fervor of young experience, and the frankness of an upright mind; for there is a conventional acquiescence in received morals which is permitted, in semblance at least, to adorn the most tortuous.

"It may be well, Signor Soranzo, to do this homage to the right," returned the elder. "Here have been sundry charges found in different Lions' Mouths, against the Neapolitan, Signor Don Camillo Monforte. I leave it to your wisdom, my illustrious colleagues, to decide on their character."

"An excess of malice betrays its own origin," exclaimed the least-practised member of the inquisition. "My life on it, Signori, these accusations come of private spleen, and are unworthy of the state's attention. I have consorted much with the young lord of Sant' Agata, and a more worthy gentleman does not dwell among us."

"Still hath he designs on the hand of old Tiepolo's daughter!"

"Is it a crime in youth to seek beauty? He did great service to the lady in her need, and that youth should feel these sympathies is nothing strange."

"Venice hath her sympathies, as well as the youngest of us all, Signore."

"But Venice cannot wed the heiress!"

"True. St. Mark must be satisfied with playing the prudent father's part. You are yet young, Signor Soranzo, and the Donna Giulietta is of rare beauty! As life wears upon ye both, ye will see the fortunes of kingdoms, as well as families, differently. But we waste our breath uselessly in this matter, since our agents have not yet reported their success in the pursuit. The most pressing affair, just now, is the disposition of the Bravo. Hath his Highness shown you the letter of the sovereign pontiff, in the question of the intercepted dispatches, Signore?"

"He hath. A fair answer was returned by our predecessors, and it must rest there."

"We will then look freely into the matter of Jacopo Frontoni. There will be necessity of our assembling in the chamber of the inquisition, that we may have the prisoner confronted to his accusers. 'Tis a grave trial, Signori, and Venice would lose in men's estimation, were not the highest tribunal to take an interest in its decision."

"To the block with the villain!" again exclaimed the Signor Soranzo.

"He may haply meet with that fate, or even with the punishment of the wheel. A mature examination will enlighten us much on the course which policy may dictate."

"There can be but one policy when the protection of the lives of our citizens is in question. I have never before felt impatience to shorten the life of man, but in this trial I can scarce brook delay."

"Your honorable impatience shall be gratified, Signor Soranzo; for, foreseeing the urgency of the case, my colleague, the worthy senator who is joined with us in this high duty, and myself, have already issued the commands necessary to that object. The hour is near, and we will repair to the chamber of the inquisition in time to our duty."

The discourse then turned on subjects of a more general concern. This secret and extraordinary tribunal, which was obliged to confine its meetings to no particular place, which could decide on its decrees equally in the piazza, or the palace, amidst the revelries of the masquerade, or before the altar, in the assemblies of the gay, or in their own closets, had of necessity much ordinary matter submitted to its inspection. As the chances of birth entered into its original composition,—and God hath not made all alike fit for so heartless a duty,—it sometimes happened, as in the present instance, that the more worldly of its members had to overcome the generous disposition of a colleague, before the action of the terrible machine could go on.

It is worthy of remark, that communities always establish a higher standard of justice and truth than is exercised by their individual members. The reason is not to be sought for, since nature hath left to all a perception of that right which is abandoned only under the stronger impulses of personal temptation. We commend the virtue we cannot imitate. Thus it is that those countries in which public opinion has most influence are always of the purest public practice. It follows as a corollary from this proposition, that a representation should be as real as possible, for its tendency will be inevitably to elevate national morals. Miserable, indeed, is the condition of that people whose maxims and measures of public policy are below the standard of its private integrity, for the fact not only proves it is not the master of its own destinies, but the still more dangerous truth that the collective power is employed in the fatal service of undermining those very qualities which are necessary to virtue, and which have enough to do, at all times, in resisting the attacks of immediate selfishness. A strict legal representation of all its interests is far more necessary to a worldly than to a simple people, since responsibility, which is the essence of a free government, is more likely to keep the agents of a nation near to its own standard of virtue than any other means. The common opinion that a republic cannot exist without an extraordinary degree of virtue in its citizens is so flattering to our own actual condition that we seldom take the trouble to inquire into its truth; but, to us, it seems quite apparent that effect is here mistaken for the cause. It is said, as the people are virtually masters in a republic, that the people ought to be virtuous to rule well. So far as this proposition is confined to degrees, it is just as true of a republic as of any other form of government. But kings do rule, and surely all have not been virtuous; and that aristocracies have ruled with the very minimum of that quality, the subject of our tale sufficiently shows. That, other things being equal, the citizens of a republic will have a higher standard of private virtue than the subjects of any other form of government is true as an effect, we can readily believe, for responsibility to public opinion existing in all the branches of its administration, that conventional morality which characterizes the common sentiment will be left to act on the mass, and will not be perverted into a terrible engine of corruption, as is the case when factitious institutions give a false direction to its influence.

The case before us was in proof of the truth of what has here been said. The Signor Soranzo was a man of great natural excellence of character, and the charities of his domestic circle had assisted in confirming his original dispositions. Like others of his rank and expectations, he had, from time to time, made the history and polity of the self-styled republic his study, and the power of collective interests and specious necessities had made him admit sundry theories, which, presented in another form, he would have repulsed with indignation. Still the Signor Soranzo was far from understanding the full effects of that system which he was born to uphold. Even Venice paid that homage to public opinion of which there has just been question, and held forth to the world but a false picture of her true state maxims. Still many of those which were too apparent to be concealed were difficult of acceptance, with one whose mind was yet untainted with practice; and the young senator rather shut his eyes on their tendency, or, as he felt their influence in every interest which environed him, but that of poor, neglected, abstract virtue, whose rewards were so remote, he was fain to seek out some palliative, or some specious and indirect good as the excuse for his acquiescence.

In this state of mind the Signor Soranzo was unexpectedly admitted a member of the Council of Three. Often, in the daydreams of his youth, had he contemplated the possession of this very irresponsible power as the consummation of his wishes. A thousand pictures of the good he would perform had crossed his brain, and it was only as he advanced in life, and came to have a near view of the wiles which beset the best intentioned, that he could bring himself to believe most of that which he meditated was impracticable. As it was, he entered into the council with doubts and misgivings. Had he lived in a later age, under his own system modified by the knowledge which has been a consequence of the art of printing, it is probable that the Signor Soranzo would have been a noble in opposition, now supporting with ardor some measure of public benevolence, and now yielding, gracefully, to the suggestions of a sterner policy, and always influenced by the positive advantages he was born to possess, though scarcely conscious himself he was not all he professed to be. The fault, however, was not so much that of the patrician as that of circumstances, which, by placing interest in opposition to duty, lures many a benevolent mind into still greater weaknesses.

The companions of the Signor Soranzo, however, had a more difficult task to prepare him for the duties of the statesman, which were so very different from those he was accustomed to perform as a man, than they had anticipated. They were like two trained elephants of the East, possessing themselves all the finer instincts and generous qualities of the noble animal, but disciplined by a force quite foreign to their natural condition into creatures of mere convention, placed one on each side of a younger brother, fresh from the plains, and whom it was their duty to teach new services for the trunk, new affections, and haply the manner in which to carry, with dignity, the howdah of a Rajah.

With many allusions to their policy, but with no direct intimation of their own intention, the seniors of the council continued the conversation, until the hour for the meeting in the doge's palace drew nigh. They then separated, as privately as they had come together, in order that no vulgar eye might penetrate the mystery of their official character.

The most practised of the three appeared in an assembly of the patricians, which noble and beautiful dames graced with their presence, from which he disappeared in a manner to leave no clue to his motions. The other visited the deathbed of a friend, where he discoursed long and well, with a friar, of the immortality of the soul and the hopes of a Christian: when he departed, the godly man bestowing his blessing, and the family he left being loud and eloquent in his praise.

The Signor Soranzo clung to the enjoyments of his own family circle until the last moment. The Donna Giulietta had returned, fresher and more lovely than ever, from the invigorating sea breeze, and her soft voice, with the melodious laugh of his first-born, the blooming, ringlet-covered girl described, still rang in his ears, when his gondolier landed him beneath the bridge of the Rialto. Here he masked, and drawing his cloak about him, he moved with the current towards the square of St. Mark, by means of the narrow streets. Once in the crowd, there was little danger of impertinent observation. Disguise was as often useful to the oligarchy of Venice, as it was absolutely necessary to elude its despotism, and to render the town tolerable to the citizen. Paolo saw swarthy, barelegged men of the Lagunes entering occasionally into the cathedral. He followed, and found himself standing near the dimly lighted altar, at which masses were still saying for the soul of Antonio.

"This is one of thy fellows?" he asked of a fisherman, whose dark eye glittered in that light, like the organ of a basilisk.

"Signore, he was—a more honest, or a more just man, did not cast his net in the gulf."

"He has fallen a victim to his craft?"

"Cospetto di Bacco! none know in what manner he came by his end. Some say St. Mark was impatient to see him in paradise, and some pretend he has fallen by the hand of a common Bravo, named Jacopo Frontoni."

"Why should a Bravo take the life of one like this?"

"By having the goodness to answer your own question, Signore, you will spare me some trouble. Why should he, sure enough? They say Jacopo is revengeful, and that shame and anger at his defeat in the late regatta by one old as this was the reason."

"Is he so jealous of his honor with the oar?"

"Diamine! I have seen the time when Jacopo would sooner die than lose a race; but that was before he carried a stiletto. Had he kept to his oar, the thing might have happened, but once known for the hired blow, it seems unreasonable he should set his heart so strongly on the prizes of the canals."

"May not the man have fallen into the Lagunes by accident?"

"No doubt, Signore. This happens to some of us daily; but then we think it wiser to swim to the boat than to sink. Old Antonio had an arm in youth to carry him from the quay to the Lido."

"But he may have been struck in falling, and rendered unable to do himself this good office."

"There would be marks to show this, were it true, Signore!"

"Would not Jacopo have used the stiletto?"

"Perhaps not, on one like Antonio. The gondola of the old man was found in the mouth of the Grand Canal, half a league from the body, and against the wind! We note these things, Signore, for they are within our knowledge."

"A happy night to thee, fisherman."

"A most happy night, eccellenza," said the laborer of the Lagunes, gratified with having so long occupied the attention of one he rightly believed so much his superior. The disguised senator passed on. He had no difficulty in quitting the cathedral unobserved, and he had his private means of entering the palace without attracting any impertinent eye to his movements. Here he quickly joined his colleagues of the fearful tribunal.

CHAPTER XXVIII

"There the prisoners rest together; they hear not the voice of the oppressor."—*Job.*

THE manner in which the Council of Three held its more public meetings, if aught connected with that mysterious body could be called public, has already been seen. On the present occasion, there were the same robes, the same disguises, and the same officers of the inquisition, as in the scene related in a previous chapter. The only change was in the character of the judges, and in that of the accused. By a peculiar arrangement of the lamp, too, most of the light was thrown upon the spot it was intended the prisoner should occupy, while the side of the apartment on which the inquisitors sat was left in a dimness that well accorded with their gloomy and secret duties. Previously to the opening of the door by which the person to be examined was to appear, there was audible the clanking of chains. the certain evidence that the affair in hand was considered serious. The hinges turned, and the Bravo stood in presence of those unknown men who were to decide on his fate.

As Jacopo had often been before the council, though not as a prisoner, he betrayed neither surprise nor alarm at the black aspect of all his eye beheld. His features were composed though pale, his limbs immovable, and his mien decent. When the little bustle of his entrance had subsided, there reigned a stillness in the room.

"Thou art called Jacopo Frontoni?" said the secretary, who acted as the mouthpiece of the Three, on this occasion.

"I am."

"Thou art the son of a certain Ricardo* Frontoni, a man well known as having been concerned in robbing the republic's customs, and who is thought to have been banished to the distant islands, or to be otherwise punished?"

"Signore—or otherwise punished."

---

* An inconsistency; in Chapter XXX, he is named "Francesco."—Editor.

"Thou wert a gondolier in thy youth?"

"I was a gondolier."

"Thy mother is—"

"Dead," said Jacopo, perceiving the other paused to examine his notes.

The depth of the tone in which this word was uttered caused a silence that the secretary did not interrupt, until he had thrown a glance backward at the judges.

"She was not accused of thy father's crime?"

"Had she been, Signore, she is long since beyond the power of the republic."

"Shortly after thy father fell under the displeasure of the state, thou quittedst thy business of a gondolier?"

"Signore, I did."

"Thou art accused, Jacopo, of having laid aside the oar for the stiletto?"

"Signore, I am."

"For several years, the rumors of thy bloody deeds have been growing in Venice, until, of late, none have met with an untimely fate that the blow has not been attributed to thy hand?"

"This is too true, Signor Segretario—I would it were not!"

"The ears of his Highness, and of the councils, have not been closed to these reports, but they have long attended to the rumors with the earnestness which becomes a paternal and careful government. If they have suffered thee to go at large, it hath only been that there might be no hazard of sullying the ermine of justice with a premature and not sufficiently supported judgment."

Jacopo bent his head, but without speaking. A smile so wild and meaning, however, gleamed on his face at this declaration, that the permanent officer of the secret tribunal, he who served as its organ of communication, bowed nearly to the paper he held, as it might be to look deeper into his documents. Let not the reader turn back to this page in surprise, when he shall have reached the explanation of the tale, for mysticisms quite as palpable, if not of so ruthless a character, have been publicly acted by political bodies in his own times.

"There is now a specific and a frightful charge brought against thee, Jacopo Frontoni," continued the secretary; "and, in tenderness of the citizen's life, the dreaded council itself hath

343

taken the matter in hand. Didst thou know a certain Antonio Vecchio, a fisherman here in our Lagunes?"

"Signore, I knew him well of late, and much regret that it was only of late."

"Thou knowest, too, that his body hath been found, drowned in the bay?"

Jacopo shuddered, signifying his assent merely by a sign. The effect of this tacit acknowledgment on the youngest of the three was apparent, for he turned to his companions like one struck by the confession it implied. His colleagues made dignified inclinations in return, and the silent communication ceased.

"His death has excited discontent among his fellows, and its cause has become a serious subject of inquiry for the illustrious council."

"The death of the meanest man in Venice should call forth the care of the patricians, Signore."

"Dost thou know, Jacopo, that thou art accused of being his murderer?"

"Signore, I do."

"It is said that thou camest among the gondoliers in the late regatta, and that, but for this aged fisherman, thou would'st have been winner of the prize?"

"In that, rumor hath not lied, Signore."

"Thou dost not, then, deny the charge!" said the examiner, in evident surprise.

"It is certain that, but for the fisherman, I should have been the winner."

"And thou wished it, Jacopo?"

"Signore, greatly," returned the accused, with a show of emotion that had not hitherto escaped him. "I was a man condemned of his fellows, and the oar had been my pride from childhood to that hour."

Another movement of the third inquisitor betrayed, equally, his interest and his surprise.

"Dost thou confess the crime?"

Jacopo smiled, but more in derision than with any other feeling.

"If the illustrious senators here present will unmask, I may answer that question, haply, with greater confidence," he said.

"Thy request is bold and out of rule. None know the persons of the patricians who preside over the destinies of the state. Dost thou confess the crime?"

344

The entrance of an officer, in some haste, prevented a reply. The man placed a written report in the hands of the inquisitor in red and withdrew. After a short pause, the guards were ordered to retire with their prisoner.

"Great senators!" said Jacopo, advancing earnestly towards the table, as if he would seize the moment to urge what he was about to say;—"Mercy! grant me your authority to visit one in the prisons beneath the leads!—I have weighty reasons for the wish, and I pray you, as men and fathers, to grant it!"

The interest of the two who were consulting apart on the new intelligence prevented them from listening to what he urged. The other inquisitor, who was the Signor Soranzo, had drawn near the lamp, anxious to read the lineaments of one so notorious, and was gazing at his striking countenance. Touched by the pathos of his voice, and agreeably disappointed in the lineaments he studied, he took upon himself the power to grant the request.

"Humor his wish," he said to the halberdiers; "but have him in readiness to reappear."

Jacopo looked his gratitude, but, fearful that the others might still interfere to prevent his wish, he hurried from the room.

The march of the little procession, which proceeded from the chamber of the inquisition to the summer cells of its victims, was sadly characteristic of the place and the government.

It went through gloomy and secret corridors, that were hid from the vulgar eye, while thin partitions only separated it from the apartments of the doge, which, like the specious aspect of the state, concealed the nakedness and misery within by their gorgeousness and splendor! On reaching the attic, Jacopo stopped, and turned to his conductors.

"If you are beings of God's forming," he said, "take off these clanking chains, though it be but for a moment."

The keepers regarded each other in surprise, neither offering to do the charitable office.

"I go to visit, probably for the last time," continued the prisoner, "a bedridden—I may say—a dying father, who knows nothing of my situation,—will ye that he should see me thus?"

The appeal which was made, more with the voice and manner, than in the words, had its effect. A keeper removed the chains, and bade him proceed. With a cautious tread, Jacopo advanced, and when the door was opened he entered the room alone, for none there had sufficient interest in an interview

345

between a common Bravo and his father to endure the glowing warmth of the place, the while. The door was closed after him, and the room became dark.

Notwithstanding his assumed firmness, Jacopo hesitated, when he found himself so suddenly introduced to the silent misery of the forlorn captive. A hard breathing told him the situation of the pallet, but the walls, which were solid on the side of the corridor, effectually prevented the admission of light.

"Father!" said Jacopo, with gentleness.

He got no answer.

"Father!" he repeated in a stronger voice.

The breathing became more audible, and then the captive spoke.

"Holy Maria hears my prayers!" he said feebly. "God hath sent thee, son, to close my eyes!"

"Doth thy strength fail thee, father?"

"Greatly—my time is come—I had hoped to see the light of the day again; to bless thy dear mother and sister—God's will be done!"

"They pray for us both, father. They are beyond the power of the senate."

"Jacopo,—I do not understand thee!"

"My mother and sister are dead; they are saints in Heaven, father."

The old man groaned, for the tie of earth had not yet been entirely severed. Jacopo heard him murmuring a prayer, and he knelt by the side of his pallet.

"This is a sudden blow!" whispered the old man. "We depart together."

"They are long dead, father."

"Why hast thou not told me this before, Jacopo?"

"Hadst thou not sorrows enough without this!—now that thou art about to join them, it will be pleasant to know that they have so long been happy."

"And thou?—thou wilt be alone—give me thy hand,—poor Jacopo!"

The Bravo reached forth and took the feeble member of his parent; it was clammy and cold.

"Jacopo," continued the captive, whose mind still sustained the body, "I have prayed thrice within the hour—once for my own soul—once for the peace of thy mother—lastly, for thee!"

"Bless thee, father!—bless thee!—I have need of prayer!"

346

"I have asked of God—favor in thy behalf. I have bethought me—of all thy love and care—of all thy devotion to my age and sufferings. When thou wert a child, Jacopo—tenderness for thee—tempted me to acts of weakness,—I trembled lest thy manhood might bring upon me—pain and repentance. Thou hast not known the yearnings—of a parent for his offspring—but thou hast well requited them. Kneel, Jacopo—that I may ask of God—once more, to remember thee."

"I am at thy side, father."

The old man raised his feeble arms, and with a voice whose force appeared reviving, he pronounced a fervent and solemn benediction.

"The blessing of a dying parent will sweeten thy life—Jacopo," he added, after a pause, "and give peace to thy last moments."

"It will do the latter, father."

A rude summons at the door interrupted them.

"Come forth, Jacopo," said a keeper;—"the council seeks thee!"

Jacopo felt the convulsive start of his father, but he did not answer.

"Will they not leave thee—a few minutes longer?" whispered the old man—"I shall not keep thee long!"

The door opened, and a gleam from the lamp fell on the group in the cell. The keeper had the humanity to shut it again, leaving all in obscurity. The glance which Jacopo obtained, by that passing light, was the last look he had of his father's countenance. Death was fearfully on it, but the eyes were turned in unutterable affection on his own.

"The man is merciful—he will not shut thee out!" murmured the parent.

"They cannot leave thee to die alone, father!"

"Son, I am with my God—yet I would gladly have thee by my side!—Didst thou say—thy mother and thy sister were dead?"

"Dead!"

"Thy young sister, too?"

"Father, both. They are saints in Heaven."

The old man breathed thick, and there was silence. Jacopo felt a hand moving in the darkness, as if in quest of him. He aided the effort, and laid the member in reverence on his own head.

"Maria undefiled, and her Son, who is God!—bless thee,

347

Jacopo!" whispered a voice that, to the excited imagination of the kneeling Bravo, appeared to hover in the air. The solemn words were followed by a quivering sigh. Jacopo hid his face in the blanket and prayed. After which there was deep quiet.

"Father!" he asked, trembling at his own smothered voice.

He was unanswered. Stretching out a hand, it touched the features of a corpse. With a firmness that had the quality of desperation, he again bowed his head, and uttered, fervently, a prayer for the dead.

When the door of the cell opened, Jacopo appeared to the keepers, with a dignity of air that belongs only to character, and which was heightened by the scene in which he had just been an actor. He raised his hands, and stood immovable, while the manacles were replaced. This office done, they walked away together, in the direction of the secret chamber. It was not long ere all were again in their places before the Council of Three.

"Jacopo Frontoni," resumed the secretary, "thou art suspected of being privy to another dark deed that hath had place of late within our city. Hast thou any knowledge of a noble Calabrian, who hath high claim to the senate's honors, and who hath long had his abode in Venice?"

"Signore, I have."

"Hast thou had aught of concern with him?"

"Signore, yes."

A movement of common interest made itself apparent among the auditors.

"Dost thou know where the Don Camillo Monforte is, at present?"

Jacopo hesitated. He so well understood the means of intelligence possessed by the council, that he doubted how far it might be prudent to deny his connexion with the flight of the lovers. Besides, at that moment his mind was deeply impressed with a holy sentiment of truth.

"Canst thou say why the young duca is not to be found in his palace?" repeated the secretary.

"Illustrissimo, he hath quitted Venice forever."

"How canst thou know this?—Would he make a confidant of a common Bravo?"

The smile which crossed the features of Jacopo was full of superiority; it caused the conscious agent of the secret tribunal to look closely at his papers, like one who felt its power.

"Art thou his confidant—I ask again?"

"Signore, in this, I am.—I have the assurance from the mouth of Don Camillo Monforte himself, that he will not return."

"This is impossible, since it would involve a loss of all his fair hopes and illustrious fortunes."

"He consoled himself, Signore, with the possession of the heiress of Tiepolo's love, and with her riches."

Again there was a movement among the Three, which all their practised restraint, and the conventional dignity of their mysterious functions, could not prevent.

"Let the keepers withdraw," said the inquisitor of the scarlet robe. So soon as the prisoner was alone with the Three, and their permanent officer, the examination continued; the senators themselves, trusting to the effect produced by their masks, and some feints, speaking as occasion offered.

"This is important intelligence that thou hast communicated, Jacopo," continued he of the robe of flame. "It may yet redeem thy life, wert thou wise enough to turn it to account."

"What would your eccellenza, at my hands? It is plain that the council know of the flight of Don Camillo, nor will I believe, that eyes which so seldom are closed have not yet missed the daughter of the Tiepolo."

"Both are true, Jacopo; but what hast thou to say of the means? Remember, that as thou findest favor with the council, thine own fate will be decided."

The prisoner suffered another of those freezing gleams to cross his face, which invariably caused his examiners to bend their looks aside.

"The means of escape cannot be wanting to a bold lover, Signore," he replied. "Don Camillo is rich, and might employ a thousand agents, had he need of them."

"Thou art equivocating; 'twill be the worse for thee, that thou triflest with the council—who are these agents?"

"He had a generous household, eccellenza;—many hardy gondoliers, and servitors of all conditions."

"Of these we have nothing to learn. He hath escaped by other means—or art thou sure he hath escaped at all?"

"Signore, is he in Venice?"

"Nay, that we ask of thee. Here is an accusation, found in the Lion's Mouth, which charges thee with his assassination."

"And the Donna Violetta's too, eccellenza?"

"Of her, we have heard nothing. What answer dost make to the charge?"

"Signore, why should I betray my own secrets?"

"Ha! art thou equivocating and faithless? Remember that we have a prisoner beneath the leads who can extract the truth from thee."

Jacopo raised his form to such an altitude, as one might fancy to express the mounting of a liberated spirit. Still his eye was sad, and spite of an effort to the contrary, his voice melancholy.

"Senators," he said, "your prisoner beneath the leads is free."

"How! thou art trifling, in thy despair!"

"I speak truth. The liberation, so long delayed, hath come at last!"

"Thy father—"

"Is dead," interrupted Jacopo, solemnly.

The two elder members of the council looked at each other in surprise, while their junior colleague listened with the interest of one who was just entering on a noviciate of secret and embarrassing duties. The former consulted together, and then they communicated as much of their opinions to the Signor Soranzo as they deemed necessary to the occasion.

"Wilt thou consult thine own safety, Jacopo, and reveal all thou knowest of this affair of the Neapolitan?" continued the inquisitor, when this byplay was ended.

Jacopo betrayed no weakness at the menace implied by the words of the senator; but, after a moment's reflection, he answered with as much frankness as he could have used at the confessional.

"It is known to you, illustrious senator," he said, "that the state had a desire to match the heiress of Tiepolo to its own advantage; that she was beloved of the Neapolitan noble; and that, as is wont, between young and virtuous hearts, she returned his love, as became a maiden of her high condition, and tender years. Is there anything extraordinary in the circumstance that two of so illustrious hopes should struggle to prevent their own misery? Signori, the night that old Antonio died, I was alone, among the graves of the Lido, with many melancholy and bitter thoughts, and life had become a burthen to me. Had the evil spirit which was then uppermost maintained its mastery, I might have died the death of a hopeless suicide. God sent Don Camillo Monforte to my succor—praised be the immaculate Maria, and

350

her blessed Son, for the mercy! It was there I learned the wishes of the Neapolitan, and enlisted myself in his service. I swore to him, senators of Venice, to be true; to die in his cause, should it be necessary; and to help him to his bride. This pledge have I redeemed. The happy lovers are now in the States of the Church, and under the puissant protection of the Cardinal Secretary, Don Camillo's mother's brother."

"Fool! why didst thou this? Hadst thou no thought for thyself?"

"Eccellenza, but little; I thought more of finding a human bosom to pour out my sufferings to, than of your high displeasure. I have not known so sweet a moment in years, as that in which I saw the lord of Sant' Agata fold his beautiful and weeping bride to his heart!"

The inquisitors were struck with the quiet enthusiasm of the Bravo, and surprise once more held them in suspense. At length, the elder of the three resumed the examination.

"Wilt thou impart the manner of this escape, Jacopo?" he demanded. "Remember thou hast still a life to redeem!"

"Signore, it is scarce worth the trouble. But to do you pleasure, nothing shall be concealed."

Jacopo then recounted, in simple and undisguised terms, the entire means employed by Don Camillo in effecting his escape; his hopes, his disappointments, and his final success. In this narrative nothing was concealed but the place in which the ladies had temporarily taken refuge, and the name of Gelsomina. Even the attempt of Giacomo Gradenigo on the life of the Neapolitan and the agency of the Hebrew were fully exposed. None listened to this explanation so intently as the young husband. Notwithstanding his public duties, his pulses quickened as the prisoner dwelt on the different chances of the lovers, and when their final union was proclaimed, he felt his heart bound with delight. On the other hand, his more practised colleagues heard the detail of the Bravo with politic coolness. The effect of all factitious systems is to render the feelings subservient to expediency. Convention and fiction take place of passion and truth, and like the Mussulman with his doctrine of predestination, there is no one more acquiescent in defeat than he who has obtained an advantage in the face of nature and justice; his resignation being, in common, as perfect as his previous arrogance was insupportable. The two old senators perceived at once that Don Camillo, and his fair companion, were completely beyond the reach of their power, and they instantly admitted the wisdom of making a merit of necessity. Having no farther occasion for Jacopo, they summoned the keepers, and dismissed him to his cell.

"It will be seemly to send letters of congratulation, to the Cardinal Secretary on the union of his nephew with so rich an heiress of our city," said the inquisitor of the Ten, as the door closed on the retiring group. "So great an interest as that of the Neapolitan should be propitiated."

"But should he urge the state's resistance to his hopes?" returned the Signor Soranzo, in feeble objection to so bold a scheme.

"We will excuse it as the act of a former council. These misconceptions are the unavoidable consequences of the caprices of liberty, Signore. The steed that ranges the plains, in the freedom of nature, cannot be held to perfect command, like the dull beast that draws the car. This is the first of your sittings in the Three, but experience will show you, that, excellent as we are in system, we are not quite perfect in practice. This is grave matter of the young Gradenigo, Signori!"

"I have long known his unworthiness," returned his more aged colleague. "It is a thousand pities that so honorable and so noble a patrician should have produced so ignoble a child. But neither the state, nor the city, can tolerate assassination."

"Would it were less frequent!" exclaimed the Signor Soranzo, in perfect sincerity.

"Would it were, indeed! There are hints in our secret information which tend to confirm the charge of Jacopo. Though long experience has taught us to put full faith in his reports."

"How—is Jacopo, then, an agent of the police?"

"Of that more at our leisure, Signor Soranzo. At present we must look to this attempt on the life of one protected by our laws."

The Three then entered into a serious discussion of the case of the two delinquents. Venice, like all despotic governments, had the merit of great efficiency in its criminal police, when it was disposed to exert it. Justice was sure enough in those instances in which the interests of the government itself were not involved, or in which bribery could not well be used. As to the latter, through the jealousy of the state, and the constant agency of those who were removed from temptation, by being already in possession of a monopoly of benefits, it was by no means as frequent, as in some other communities in which the affluent were less interested. The Signor Soranzo had now a fair occasion for the exercise of his generous feelings. Though related to the house of Gradenigo, he was not backward in decrying the conduct of its heir. His first impulses were to make a terrible example of the accused, and to show the world that no station brought with it, in Venice, impunity for crime. From this view of the case, however, he was gradually enticed by his companions, who reminded him that the law commonly made a distinction between the intention and the execution of an offence. Driven from his first determination by the cooler heads of his colleagues, the young inquisitor next proposed that the case should be sent to the ordinary tribunals for judgment. Instances had not been wanting in which the aristocracy of Venice sacrificed one of its body to the seemliness of Justice; for when such cases were managed with discretion, they rather strengthened than weakened their ascendency. But the present crime was known to be too common to permit so lavish an expenditure of their immunities, and the old inquisitors opposed the wish of their younger colleague, with great plausibility, and with some show of reason. It was finally resolved that they should themselves decide on the case.

The next question was the degree of punishment. The wily senior of the council began by proposing a banishment for a few months, for Giacomo Gradenigo was already obnoxious to the anger of the state, on more accounts than one. But this punishment was resisted by the Signor Soranzo with the ardor of an uncorrupted and generous mind. The latter gradually prevailed, his companions taking care that their compliance should have the air of a concession to his arguments. The result of all this management was that the heir of Gradenigo was condemned to ten years' retirement in the provinces, and Hosea to banishment for life. Should the reader be of opinion that strict justice was not meted out to the offenders, he should remember that the Hebrew ought to be glad to have escaped as he did.

"We must not conceal this judgment, nor its motive," observed the inquisitor of the Ten, when the affair was concluded. "The state is never a loser for letting its justice be known."

"Nor for its exercise, I should hope," returned the Signor Soranzo. "As our affairs are ended for the night, is it your pleasures, Signori, that we return to our palaces?"

"Nay, we have this matter of Jacopo."

"Him may we, now, surely, turn over to the ordinary tribunals!"

"As you may decide, Signori; is this your pleasure?"

Both the others bowed assent, and the usual preparations were made for departure.

Ere the two seniors of the council left the palace, however, they held a long and secret conference together. The result was a private order to the criminal judge, and then they returned, each to his own abode, like men who had the approbation of their own consciences.

On the other hand, the Signor Soranzo hastened to his own luxurious and happy dwelling. For the first time in his life, he entered it with a distrust of himself. Without being conscious of the reason, he felt sad, for he had taken the first step in that tortuous and corrupting path which eventually leads to the destruction of all those generous and noble sentiments which can only flourish apart from the sophistry and fictions of selfishness. He would have rejoiced to have been as light of heart as at the moment he handed his fair-haired partner into the gondola that night; but his head had pressed the pillow for many hours before sleep drew a veil over the solemn trifling with the most serious of our duties, in which he had been an actor.

CHAPTER XXIX

"Art thou not guilty! No, indeed, I am not."
ROGERS

THE following morning brought the funeral of Antonio. The agents of the police took the precaution to circulate in the city, that the senate permitted this honor to the memory of the old fisherman, on account of his success in the regatta, and as some atonement for his unmerited and mysterious death. All the men of the Lagunes were assembled in the square at the appointed hour, in decent guise, flattered with the notice that their craft received, and more than half disposed to forget their former anger in the present favor. Thus easy is it for those who are elevated above their fellow creatures by the accident of birth, or by the opinions of a factitious social organization, to repair the wrongs they do in deeds by small concessions of their conventional superiority.

Masses were still chanted for the soul of old Antonio before the altar of St. Mark. Foremost among the priests was the good Carmelite, who had scarce known hunger or fatigue, in his pious desire to do the offices of the church, in behalf of one whose fate he might be said to have witnessed. His zeal, however, in that moment of excitement passed unnoticed by all but those whose business it was to suffer no unusual display of character, nor any unwonted circumstance to have place, without attracting their suspicion. As the Carmelite finally withdrew from the altar, previously to the removal of the body, he felt the sleeve of his robe slightly drawn aside, and yielding to the impulse, he quickly found himself among the columns of that gloomy church, alone with a stranger.

"Father, thou hast shrived many a parting soul?" observed, rather than asked, the other.

"It is the duty of my holy office, son."

"The state will note thy services; there will be need of thee when the body of this fisherman is committed to the earth."

The monk shuddered, but making the sign of the cross, he bowed his pale face, in signification of his readiness to discharge the duty. At that moment the bearers lifted the body, and the procession issued upon the great square. First marched the usual lay underlings of the cathedral, who were followed by those who chanted the offices of the occasion. Among the latter the Carmelite hastened to take his station. Next came the corpse, without a coffin, for that is a luxury of the grave even now unknown to the Italians of old Antonio's degree. The body was clad in the holiday vestments of a fisherman, the hands and feet being naked. A cross lay on the breast; the gray hairs were blowing about in the air, and, in frightful adornment of the ghastliness of death, a bouquet of flowers was placed upon the mouth. The bier was rich in gilding and carving, another melancholy evidence of the lingering wishes and false direction of human vanity.

Next to this characteristic equipage of the dead walked a lad, whose brown cheek, half-naked body, and dark, roving eye, announced the grandson of the fisherman. Venice knew when to yield gracefully, and the boy was liberated, unconditionally, from the galleys, in pity, as it was whispered, for the untimely fate of his parent. There was the aspiring look, the dauntless spirit, and the rigid honesty of Antonio, in the bearing of the lad; but these qualities were now smothered by a natural grief; and, as in the case of him whose funeral escort he followed, something obscured by the rude chances of his lot. From time to time the bosom of the generous boy heaved, as they marched along the quay, taking the route of the arsenal; and there were moments that his lips quivered, grief threatening to overcome his manhood.

Still not a tear wetted his cheek, until the body disappeared from his view. Then nature triumphed, and straying from out the circle, he took a seat apart and wept, as one of his years and simplicity would be apt to weep, at finding himself a solitary wanderer in the wilderness of the world.

Thus terminated the incident of Antonio Vecchio, the fisherman, whose name soon ceased to be mentioned in that city of mysteries, except on the Lagunes, where the men of his craft long vaunted his merit with the net, and the manner in which he bore away the prize from the best oars of Venice. His descendant lived and toiled, like others of his condition, and we will here dismiss him, by saying, that he so far inherited the native qualities of his ancestor, that he forbore to appear, a few hours later, in the crowd which curiosity and vengeance drew into the piazzetta.

Father Anselmo took boat to return to the canals, and when he landed at the quay of the smaller square, it was with the hope that he would now be permitted to seek those of whose fate he was still ignorant, but in whom he felt so deep an interest. Not so, however. The individual who had addressed him in the cathedral was, apparently, in waiting, and knowing the uselessness, as well as the danger of remonstrance, where the state was concerned, the Carmelite permitted himself to be conducted whither his guide pleased. They took a devious route, but it led them to the public prisons. Here the priest was shown into the keeper's apartment, where he was desired to wait a summons from his companion.

Our business now leads us to the cell of Jacopo. On quitting the presence of the Three, he had been remanded to his gloomy room, where he passed the night like others similarly situated. With the appearance of the dawn the Bravo had been led before those who ostensibly discharged the duties of his judges. We say ostensibly, for justice never was yet pure under a system in which the governors have an interest in the least separated from that of the governed; for in all cases which involve the ascendency of the existing authorities, the instinct of self-preservation is as certain to bias their decision, as that of life is to cause man to shun danger. If such is the fact in countries of milder sway, the reader will easily believe in its existence in a state like that of Venice. As may have been anticipated, those who sat in judgment on Jacopo had their instructions, and the trial that he sustained was rather a concession to appearances than an homage to the laws. All the records were duly made, witnesses were examined, or said to be examined, and care was had to spread the rumor in the city that the tribunals were at length occupied in deciding on the case of the extraordinary man who had so long been permitted to exercise his bloody profession with impunity, even in the centre of the canals. During the morning, the credulous tradesmen were much engaged in recounting to each other the different flagrant deeds that, in the course of the last three or four years, had been imputed to his hand. One spoke of the body of a stranger that had been found near the gaming houses, frequented by those who visited Venice. Another recalled the fate of the young noble who had fallen by the assassin's blow even on the Rialto, and another went into the details of a murder which had deprived a mother of her only son, and the daughter of a patrician of her love. In this manner, as one after another contributed to the list, a little group, assembled on the quay, enumerated no less than five-and-twenty lives which were believed to have been taken by the hand of Jacopo, without including the vindictive and useless assassination of him whose funeral rites had just been celebrated. Happily, perhaps, for his peace of mind, the subject of all these rumors, and of the maledictions which they drew upon his head, knew nothing of either. Before his judges he had made no defence whatever, firmly refusing to answer their interrogatories.

"Ye know what I have done, Messires," he said, haughtily. "And what I have not done, ye know. As for yourselves, look to your own interests."

When again in his cell, he demanded food, and ate tranquilly, though with moderation. Every instrument which could possibly be used against his life was then removed, his irons were finally and carefully examined, and he was left to his thoughts. It was in this situation that the prisoner heard the approach of footsteps to his cell. The bolts turned, and the door opened. The form of a priest appeared between him and the day. The latter, however, held a lamp, which, as the cell was again shut and secured, he placed on the low shelf that held the jug and loaf of the prisoner.

Jacopo received his visitor calmly, but with the deep respect of one who reverenced his holy office. He arose, crossed himself, and advanced as far as the chains permitted, to do him honor.

"Thou art welcome, father," he said; "in cutting me off from the earth, the council, I see, does not wish to cut me off from God."

"That would exceed their power, son. He who died for them shed His blood for thee, if thou wilt not reject His grace. But— Heaven knows I say it with reluctance! thou art not to think that one of thy sins, Jacopo, can have hope without deep and heartfelt repentance!"

"Father, have any?"

The Carmelite started, for the point of the question, and the tranquil tones of the speaker, had a strange effect in such an interview.

"Thou art not what I had supposed thee, Jacopo!" he answered. "Thy mind is not altogether obscured in darkness, and thy crimes have been committed against the consciousness of their enormity."

"I fear this is true, reverend monk."

"Thou must feel their weight in the poignancy of grief—in the—" Father Anselmo stopped, for a sob at that moment apprized them that they were not alone. Moving aside, in a little alarm, the action discovered the figure of the shrinking Gelsomina, who had entered the cell, favored by the keepers, and concealed by the robes of the Carmelite. Jacopo groaned, when he beheld her form, and, turning away, he leaned against the wall.

"Daughter, why art thou here—and who art thou?" demanded the monk.

" 'Tis the child of the principal keeper," said Jacopo, perceiving that she was unable to answer, "one known to me, in my frequent adventures in this prison."

The eye of Father Anselmo wandered from one to the other. At first its expression was severe, and then, as it saw each countenance in turn, it became less unkind, until it softened at the exhibition of their mutual agony.

"This comes of human passions!" he said, in a tone between consolation and reproof. "Such are ever the fruits of crime."

"Father," said Jacopo, with earnestness, "I may deserve the word; but the angels in Heaven are scarce purer than this weeping girl!"

"I rejoice to hear it. I will believe thee, unfortunate man, and glad am I that thy soul is relieved from the sin of having corrupted one so youthful."

The bosom of the prisoner heaved, while Gelsomina shuddered.

"Why hast thou yielded to the weakness of nature, and entered the cell?" asked the good Carmelite, endeavoring to throw into his eye a reproof that the pathos and kindness of his tones contradicted. "Didst thou know the character of the man thou loved?"

"Immaculate Maria!" exclaimed the girl—"no—no—no!"

"And now that thou hast learned the truth, surely thou art no longer the victim of wayward fancies!"

The gaze of Gelsomina was bewildered, but anguish prevailed over all other expression. She bowed her head, partly in shame, but more in sorrow, without answering.

"I know not, children, what end this interview can answer," continued the monk—"I am sent hither to receive the last confession of a Bravo, and surely one who has so much cause to condemn the deception he has practised would not wish to hear the details of such a life?"

"No—no—no—" murmured Gelsomina again, enforcing her words with a wild gesture of the hand.

"It is better, father, that she should believe me all that her fancy can imagine as monstrous," said Jacopo, in a thick voice; "she will then learn to hate my memory."

Gelsomina did not speak, but the negative gesture was repeated franticly.

"The heart of the poor child hath been sorely touched," said the Carmelite, with concern. "We must not treat so tender a flower rudely. Hearken to me, daughter, and consult thy reason more than thy weakness."

"Question her not, father;—let her curse me, and depart."

"Carlo!" shrieked Gelsomina.

A long pause succeeded. The monk perceived that human passion was superior to his art, and that the case must be left to time; while the prisoner maintained within himself, a struggle more fierce than any which it had yet been his fate to endure. The lingering desires of the world conquered, and he broke silence.

"Father," he said, advancing to the length of his chain, and speaking both solemnly, and with dignity, "I had hoped—I had prayed that this unhappy but innocent creature might have turned from her own weakness with loathing, when she came to know that the man she loved was a Bravo.—But I did injustice to the heart of woman!—Tell me, Gelsomina, and as thou valuest thy salvation, deceive me not—canst thou look at me without horror?"

Gelsomina trembled, but she raised her eyes, and smiled on him as the weeping infant returns the earnest and tender regard of its mother. The effect of that glance on Jacopo was so powerful, that his sinewy frame shook, until the wondering Carmelite heard the clanking of his chains.

"'Tis enough," he said, struggling to command himself, "Gelsomina, thou shalt hear my confession. Thou hast long been mistress of one great secret; none other shall be hid from thee."

"Antonio?" gasped the girl,—"Carlo! Carlo! what had that aged fisherman done, that thy hand should seek his life?"

"Antonio!" echoed the monk; "dost thou stand charged with his death, my son?"

"It is the crime for which I am condemned to die."

The Carmelite sunk upon the stool of the prisoner, and sat motionless, looking with an eye of horror, from the countenance of the unmoved Jacopo, to that of his trembling companion. The truth began to dawn upon him, though his mind was still enveloped in the web of Venetian mystery.

"Here is some horrible mistake!" he whispered. "I will hasten to thy judges and undeceive them."

The prisoner smiled calmly, as he reached out a hand to arrest the zealous movement of the simple Carmelite.

"'Twill be useless," he said; "it is the pleasure of the Three, that I should suffer for old Antonio's death."

"Then wilt thou die unjustly!—I am a witness that he fell by other hands."

"Father!" shrieked Gelsomina, "oh! repeat the words—say that Carlo could not do the cruel deed!"

"Of that murder, at least, is he innocent."

"Gelsomina!" said Jacopo, struggling to stretch forth his arms towards her, and yielding to a full heart, "and of every other!"

A cry of wild delight burst from the lips of the girl, who in the next instant lay senseless on his bosom.

We draw the veil before the scene that followed. Near an hour must pass before we can again remove it. The cell then exhibited a group in its centre, over which the lamp shed its feeble light, marking the countenances of the different personages with strong tints and deep shadows, in a manner to bring forth all the force of Italian expression. The Carmelite was seated on the stool, while Jacopo and Gelsomina knelt beside him. The former of the two last was speaking earnestly, while his auditors caught each syllable that issued from his lips, as if interest in his innocence were still stronger than curiosity.

"I have told you, father," he continued, "that a false accusation of having wronged the customs brought my unhappy parent under the senate's displeasure, and that he was many years an innocent inhabitant of one of these accursed cells, while we believed him in exile, among the islands. At length we succeeded in getting such proof before the council, as ought to have satisfied the patricians of their own injustice. I am afraid that when men pretend that the chosen of the earth exercise authority, they are not ready to admit their errors, for it would be proof against the merit of their system. The council delayed a weary time to do us justice—so long, that my poor mother sunk under her sufferings. My sister, a girl of Gelsomina's years, followed her soon—for the only reason given by the state, when pressed for proof, was the suspicion, that one who sought her love, was guilty of the crime for which my unhappy father perished."

"And did they refuse to repair their injustice?" exclaimed the Carmelite.

"They could not do it, father, without publishing their fallibility. The credit of certain great patricians was concerned, and I fear there is a morality in these councils which separates the deed of the man from those of the senators, putting policy before justice."

"This may be true, son; for when a community is grounded on false principles, its interests must, of necessity, be maintained by sophisms. God will view this act with a different eye!"

"Else would the world be hopeless, father! After years of prayers and interest, I was, under a solemn oath of secrecy, admitted to my father's cell. There was happiness in being able to administer to his wants—in hearing his voice—in kneeling for his blessing. Gelsomina was then a child approaching womanhood. I knew not their motive, though after thoughts left it no secret, and I was permitted to see my father through her means. When they believed that I was sufficiently caught in their toils, I was led into that fatal error which has destroyed my hopes, and brought me to this condition."

"Thou hast affirmed thy innocence, my son!"

"Innocent of shedding blood, father, but not of lending myself to their artifices. I will not weary you, holy monk, with the history of the means by which they worked upon my nature. I was sworn to serve the state, as its secret agent, for a certain time. The reward was to be my father's freedom. Had they taken me in the world, and in my senses, their arts would not have triumphed; but a daily witness of the sufferings of him who had given me life, and who was now all that was left me in the world, they were too strong for my weakness. They whispered to me of racks and wheels, and I was shown paintings of dying martyrs, that I might understand the agony they could inflict. Assassinations were frequent, and called for the care of the police—in short, father"—Jacopo hid his face in the dress of Gelsomina,—

362

"I consented to let them circulate such tales as might draw the eye of the public on me. I need not add that he who lends himself to his own infamy will soon attain his object."

"With what end was this miserable falsehood invented?"

"Father, I was applied to as to a public Bravo, and my reports, in more ways than one, answered their designs. That I saved some lives is at least a consolation for the error, or crime, into which I fell!"

"I understand thee, Jacopo. I have heard that Venice did not hesitate to use the ardent, and brave, in this manner. Holy St. Mark! can deceit like this be practised under the sanction of thy blessed name!"

"Father, it is, and more. I had other duties, connected with the interests of the republic, and of course I was practised in their discharge. The citizens marvelled that one like me should go at large, while the vindictive and revengeful took the circumstance as a proof of address. When rumor grew too strong for appearances, the Three took measures to direct it to other things; and when it grew too faint for their wishes, it was fanned. In short, for three long and bitter years did I pass the life of the damned—sustained only by the hope of liberating my father, and cheered by the love of this innocent!"

"Poor Jacopo, thou art to be pitied! I will remember thee in my prayers."

"And thou, Gelsomina?"

The keeper's daughter did not answer. Her ears had drunk in each syllable that fell from his lips, and now that the whole truth began to dawn on her mind, there was a bright radiance in her eye, that appeared almost supernatural to those who witnessed it.

"If I have failed in convincing thee, Gelsomina," continued Jacopo, "that I am not the wretch I seemed, would that I had been dumb!"

She stretched a hand towards him, and, dropping her head on his bosom, wept.

"I see all thy temptations, poor Carlo," she said, softly; "I know how strong was thy love for thy father."

"Dost thou forgive me, dearest Gelsomina, for the deception on thy innocence?"

"There was no deception—I believed thee a son ready to die for his father, and I find thee what I thought thee."

The good Carmelite regarded this scene with eyes of interest and indulgence.—Tears wetted his cheeks.

"Thy affection for each other, children," he said, "is such as angels might indulge.—Has thy intercourse been of long date?"

"It has lasted years, father."

"And thou, daughter, hast been with Jacopo in the cell of his parent?"

"I was his constant guide on these holy errands, father."

The monk mused deeply. After a silence of several minutes, he proceeded to the duties of his holy office. Receiving the spiritual confession of the prisoner, he gave the absolution, with a fervor which proved how deeply his sympathies were enlisted in behalf of the youthful pair. This duty done, he gave Gelsomina his hand, and there was a mild confidence in his countenance, as he took leave of Jacopo.

"We quit thee," he said; "but be of heart, son. I cannot think that even Venice will be deaf to a tale like thine! Trust first to thy God—and, believe that neither this faithful girl nor I will abandon thee, without an effort."

Jacopo received this assurance like one accustomed to exist in extreme jeopardy. The smile which accompanied his own adieux had in it as much of incredulity, as of melancholy. It was, however, full of the joy of a lightened heart.

CHAPTER XXX

"Your heart
Is free, and quick with virtuous wrath to accuse
Appearances; and views a criminal
In innocence's shadow."

Werner

THE Carmelite and Gelsomina found the keepers in waiting, and when they quitted the cell, its door was secured for the night. As they had no farther concerns with the jailers, they passed on unquestioned. But when the end of the corridor, which led towards the apartments of the keeper, was reached, the monk stopped.

"Art thou equal to a great effort, in order that the innocent shall not die?" he suddenly asked, though with a solemnity that denoted the influence of a high and absorbing motive.

"Father!"

"I would know if thy love for the youth can sustain thee in a trying scene; for without this effort he will surely perish!"

"I would die to save Jacopo a pang!"

"Deceive not thyself, daughter!—Canst thou forget thy habits, overstep the diffidence of thy years and condition, stand and speak fearlessly, in the presence of the great and dreaded?"

"Reverend Carmelite, I speak daily, without fear, though not without awe, to one more to be dreaded than any in Venice."

The monk looked in admiration at the gentle being, whose countenance was glowing with the mild resolution of innocence and affection, and he motioned for her to follow.

"We will go, then, before the proudest and the most fearful of earth, should there be occasion," he resumed. "We will do our duty to both parties, to the oppressor and the oppressed, that the sin of omission lie not on our souls."

Father Anselmo, without further explanation, led the obedient girl into that part of the palace which was known to be appropriated to the private uses of the titular head of the republic.

The jealousy of the Venetian patricians, on the subject of their doge, is matter of history. He was, by situation, a puppet in the hands of the nobles, who only tolerated his existence because the theory of their government required a seeming agent in the imposing ceremonies that formed part of their specious system, and in their intercourse with other states. He dwelt, in his palace, like the queen bee in the hive, pampered and honored to the eye, but in truth devoted to the objects of those who alone possess the power to injure, and perhaps we might add, like the insect named, known for consuming more than a usual portion of the fruits of the common industry.

Father Anselmo was indebted to his own decision, and to the confidence of his manner, in reaching the private apartments of a prince thus secluded and watched. He was permitted to pass by various sentinels, who imagined, from his holy calling and calm step, that he was some friar employed in his usual and privileged office. By this easy, quiet method did the Carmelite and his companion penetrate to the very antechamber of the sovereign, a spot that thousands had been defeated in attempting to reach, by means more elaborate.

There were merely two or three drowsy inferior officers of the household in waiting. One arose, quickly, at the unexpected appearance of these unknown visitors, expressing, by the surprise and the confusion of his eye, the wonder into which he was thrown by so unlooked-for guests.

"His Highness waits for us, I fear?" simply observed Father Anselmo, who had known how to quiet his concern, in a look of passive courtesy.

"Santa Maria! holy father, you should know best, but—"

"We will not lose more time in idle words, son, when there has already been this delay—show us to the closet of his Highness."

"It is forbidden to usher any, unannounced, into the presence—"

"Thou seest this is not an ordinary visit.—Go, inform the doge that the Carmelite he expects, and the youthful maiden in whom his princely bosom feels so parental an interest, await his pleasure."

"His Highness has then commanded—"

"Tell him, moreover, that time presses; for the hour is near when innocence is condemned to suffer."

The usher was deceived by the gravity and assurance of the

366

monk. He hesitated, and then throwing open a door, he showed the visitors into an inner room, where he requested them to await his return. After this, he went on the desired commission, to the closet of his master.

It has already been shown that the reigning doge, if such a title can be used of a prince who was merely a tool of the aristocracy, was a man advanced in years. He had thrown aside the cares of the day, and, in the retirement of his privacy, was endeavoring to indulge those human sympathies that had so little play in the ordinary duties of his factitious condition, by holding intercourse with the mind of one of the classics of his country. His state was laid aside for lighter ease and personal freedom. The monk could not have chosen a happier moment for his object, since the man was undefended by the usual appliances of his rank, and he was softened by communion with one who had known how to mould and temper the feelings of his readers at will. So entire was the abstraction of the doge, at the moment, that the usher entered unheeded, and had stood in respectful attention to his sovereign's pleasure, near a minute before he was seen.

"What would'st thou, Marco?" demanded the prince, when his eye rose from the page.

"Signore," returned the officer, using the familiar manner in which those nearest to the persons of princes are permitted to indulge—"here are the reverend Carmelite, and the young girl, in waiting."

"How sayest thou?—a Carmelite, and a girl!"

"Signore, the same. Those whom your Highness expects."

"What bold pretence is this!"

"Signore, I do but repeat the words of the monk. 'Tell his Highness,' said the father, 'that the Carmelite he wishes to see, and the young girl in whose happiness his princely bosom feels so parental an interest, await his pleasure.'"

There passed a glow, in which indignation was brighter than shame, over the wasted cheek of the old prince, and his eye kindled.

"And this to me—even in my palace!"

"Pardon, Signore.—This is no shameless priest, like so many that disgrace the tonsure. Both monk and girl have innocent and harmless looks, and I do suspect your Highness may have forgotten."

The bright spots disappeared from the prince's cheeks, and

his eye regained its paternal expression. But age, and experience in his delicate duties, had taught the doge of Venice caution. He well knew that memory had not failed him, and he at once saw that a hidden meaning lay concealed beneath an application so unusual. There might be a device of his enemies, who were numerous and active, or, in truth, there might be some justifiable motive to warrant the applicant in resorting to a measure so hardy.

"Did the Carmelite say more, good Marco?" he asked, after deep reflection.

"Signore, he said there was great urgency, as the hour was near when the innocent might suffer. I doubt not that he comes with a petition in behalf of some young indiscreet, for there are said to be several young nobles arrested for their follies in the carnival. The female may be a sister disguised."

"Bid one of thy companions come hither; and, when I touch my bell, do thou usher these visitors to my presence."

The attendant withdrew, taking care to pass into the ante-chamber by doors that rendered it unnecessary to show himself, too soon, to those who expected his return. The second usher quickly made his appearance, and was immediately dispatched in quest of one of the Three, who was occupied with important papers, in an adjoining closet. The senator was not slow to obey the summons, for he appeared there as a friend of the prince, having been admitted publicly, and with the customary honors.

"Here are visitors of an unusual character, Signore," said the doge, rising to receive him whom he had summoned in precaution to himself, "and I would have a witness of their requests."

"Your Highness does well to make us of the senate share your labors; though if any mistaken opinion of the necessity has led you to conceive it important to call a counsellor each time a guest enters the palace—"

"It is well, Signore," mildly interrupted the prince, touching the bell. "I hope my importunity has not deranged you. But here come those I expect."

Father Anselmo and Gelsomina entered the closet together. The first glance convinced the doge that he received strangers. He exchanged looks with the member of the secret council, and each saw in the other's eye that the surprise was mutual.

When fairly in the presence, the Carmelite threw back his cowl, entirely exposing the whole of his ascetic features, while

368

Gelsomina, awed by the rank of him who received them, shrunk abashed, partly concealed by his robes.

"What means this visit?" demanded the prince, whose finger pointed to the shrinking form of the girl, while his eye rested steadily on that of the monk, "and that unusual companion? Neither the hour, nor the mode, is customary."

Father Anselmo stood before the Venetian sovereign for the first time. Accustomed, like all of that region, and more especially in that age, to calculate his chances of success warily, before venturing to disburthen his mind, the monk fastened a penetrating look on his interrogator.

"Illustrious Prince," he said, "we come petitioners for justice. They who are thus commissioned had need be bold, lest they do their own character, and their righteous office, discredit."

"Justice is the glory of St. Mark, and the happiness of his subjects. Thy course, father, is not according to established rules, and wholesome restraints, but it may have its apology—name thy errand."

"There is one in the cells, condemned of the public tribunals, and he must die with the return of day, unless your princely authority interfere to save him."

"One condemned of the tribunals may merit his fate."

"I am the ghostly adviser of the unhappy youth, and in the execution of my sacred office, I have learned that he is innocent."

"Didst thou say, condemned of the common judges, father?"

"Sentenced to die, Highness, by a decree of the criminal tribunals."

The prince appeared relieved. So long as the affair had been public, there was at least reason to believe he might indulge his love of the species, by listening farther, without offence to the tortuous policy of the state. Glancing his eye at the motionless inquisitor, as if to seek approbation, he advanced a step nearer to the Carmelite, with increasing interest in the application.

"By what authority, reverend priest, dost thou impeach the decision of the judges?" he demanded.

"Signore, as I have just said, in virtue of knowledge gained in the exercise of my holy office. He has laid bare his soul to me, as one whose feet were in the grave; and, though offending, like all born of woman, towards his God, he is guiltless as respects the state."

"Thinkest thou, father, that the law would ever reach its

369

victim, were we to listen only to self-accusations? I am old, monk, and have long worn that troublesome cap," pointing to the horned bonnet, which lay near his hand, the symbol of his state, "and in my day, I do not recall the criminal that has not fancied himself the victim of untoward circumstances."

"That men apply this treacherous solace to their consciences, one of my vocation has not to learn. Our chief task is to show the delusion of those who, while condemning their own sins, by words of confession and self-abasement, make a merit of humility; but, Doge of Venice, there is still a virtue in the sacred rite I have this evening been required to perform which can overcome the mounting of the most exalted spirit. Many attempt to deceive themselves, at the confessional, while, by the power of God, few succeed."

"Praised be the blessed Mother and the incarnate Son, that it is so!" returned the prince, struck by the mild faith of the monk, and crossing himself, reverently. "Father, thou hast forgotten to name the condemned?"

"It is a certain Jacopo Frontoni;—a reputed Bravo."

The start, the changing color, and the glance of the prince of Venice, were full of natural surprise.

"Callest thou the bloodiest stiletto that ever disgraced the city, the weapon of a reputed Bravo! The arts of the monster have prevailed over thy experience, monk!—the true confession of such a wretch would be but a history of bloody and revolting crimes."

"I entered his cell with this opinion, but I left it convinced that the public sentiment has done him wrong. If your Highness will deign hear his tale, you will think him a fit subject for your pity, rather than for punishment."

"Of all the criminals of my reign, this is the last in whose favor I could have imagined there was aught to be said!—Speak freely, Carmelite; for curiosity is as strong as wonder."

So truly did the doge give utterance to his feelings, that he momentarily forgot the presence of the inquisitor, whose countenance might have shown him that the subject was getting to be grave.

The monk ejaculated a thanksgiving, for it was not always easy, in that city of mystery, to bring truth to the ears of the great. When men live under a system of duplicity, more or less of the quality gets interwoven with the habits of the most in-

370

genuous, although they may remain, themselves, unconscious of the taint. Thus Father Anselmo, as he proceeded with the desired explanation, touched more tenderly on the practices of the state, and used more of reserve in alluding to those usages and opinions which one of his holy calling and honest nature, under other circumstances, would have fearlessly condemned.

"It may not be known to one of your high condition, sovereign Prince," resumed the Carmelite, "that an humble, but laborious mechanic of this city, a certain Francesco Frontoni, was long since condemned for frauds against the republic's revenue. This is a crime St. Mark never fails to visit with his heavy displeasure, for when men place the goods of the world before all other considerations, they mistake the objects which have brought them together in social union."

"Father, thou wert speaking of a certain Francesco Frontoni?"

"Highness, such was his name. The unhappy man had taken into his confidence and friendship, one who, pretending to his daughter's love, might appear to be the master of his secrets. When this false suitor stood on the verge of detection, for offences against the customs, he laid a snare of deception which, while he was permitted to escape, drew the anger of the state on his too confiding friend. Francesco was condemned to the cells, until he might reveal facts which never had an existence."

"This is a hard fate, reverend friar, could it be but proved!"

" 'Tis the evil of secrecy and intrigue, great Doge, in managing the common interests!—"

"Hast thou more of this Francesco, monk?"

"His history is short, Signore; for at the age when most men are active in looking to their welfare, he was pining in a prison."

"I remember to have heard of some such accusation—but it occurred in the reign of the last doge—did it not, father?"

"And he has endured to near the close of the reign of this, Highness!"

"How! The senate, when apprized of the error of its judgment, was not slow to repair the wrong!"

The monk regarded the prince earnestly, as if he would make certain whether the surprise he witnessed was not a piece of consummate acting. He felt convinced that the affair was one of that class of acts which, however oppressive, unjust, and destructive of personal happiness, had not sufficient importance to come

371

before them who govern under systems which care more for their own preservation, than for the good of the ruled. "Signor Doge," he said, "the state is discreet in matters that touch its own reputation. There are reasons that I shall not presume to examine, why the cell of poor Francesco was kept closed, long after the death and confession of his accuser left his innocence beyond dispute."

The prince mused, and then he bethought him to consult the countenance of his companion. The marble of the pilaster against which he leaned was not more cold and unmoved than the face of the inquisitor. The man had learned to smother every natural impulse in the assumed and factitious duties of his office.

"And what has this case of Francesco to do with the execution of the Bravo?" demanded the doge, after a pause, in which he had in vain struggled to assume the indifference of his counsellor.

"That I shall leave this prison keeper's daughter to explain—stand forth, child, and relate what you know, remembering, if you speak before the prince of Venice, that you also speak before the King of Heaven!"

Gelsomina trembled, for one of her habits, however supported by her motives, could not overcome a nature so retiring without a struggle. But faithful to her promise, and sustained by her affection for the condemned, she advanced a step, and stood no longer concealed by the robes of the Carmelite.

"Thou art the daughter of the prison keeper?" asked the prince mildly, though surprise was strongly painted in his eye.

"Highness, we are poor, and we are unfortunate; we serve the state for bread."

"Ye serve a noble master, child. Dost thou know aught of this Bravo?"

"Dread Sovereign, they that call him thus know not his heart! One more true to his friends, more faithful to his word, or more suppliant with the saints, than Jacopo Frontoni, is not in Venice!"

"This is a character which art might appropriate, even to a Bravo. But we waste the moments.—What have these Frontoni, in common?"

"Highness, they are father and son. When Jacopo came to be of an age to understand the misfortunes of his family, he wearied the senators with applications in his father's behalf, until they commanded the door of the cell to be secretly opened to a child so pious. I well know, great Prince, that they who rule cannot have all-seeing eyes, else could this wrong never have happened. But Francesco wasted years in cells, chill and damp in winter, and scorching in summer, before the falsehood of the accusation was known. Then, as some relief to sufferings so little merited, Jacopo was admitted."

"With what object, girl?"

"Highness, was it not in pity? They promised too, that in good time, the service of the son should buy the father's liberty. The patricians were slow to be convinced, and they made terms with poor Jacopo, who agreed to undergo a hard service, that his father might breathe free air, before he died."

"Thou dealest in enigmas."

"I am little used, great Doge, to speak in such a presence, or on such subjects. But this I know, that for three weary years hath Jacopo been admitted to his father's cell, and that those up above consented to the visits; else would my father have denied them. I was his companion in the holy act, and will call the blessed Maria and the saints—"

"Girl, didst thou know him for a Bravo?"

"Oh! Highness, no. To me he seemed a dutiful child, fearing God and honoring his parent. I hope never to feel another pang, like that which chilled my heart when they said, he I had known as the kind Carlo was hunted in Venice as the abhorred Jacopo! But it is passed, the Mother of God be praised!"

"Thou art betrothed to this condemned man?"

The color did not deepen on the cheek of Gelsomina, at this abrupt question, for the tie between her and Jacopo had become too sacred, for the ordinary weaknesses of her sex.

"Highness, yes; we were to be married, should it have pleased God, and those great senators who have so much influence over the happiness of the poor, to permit it."

"And thou art still willing, knowing the man, to pledge thy vows to one like Jacopo!"

"It is because I do know him to be as he is, that I most reverence him, great Doge. He has sold his time and his good name to the state, in order to save his imprisoned father, and in that I see nothing to frighten one he loves."

"This affair needs explanation, Carmelite. The girl has a heated fancy, and she renders that obscure she should explain."

"Illustrious Prince, she would say that the republic was content to grant the son the indulgence of visiting the captive, with some encouragement of his release, on condition that the youth might serve the police by bearing a Bravo's reputation."

"And for this incredible tale, father, you have the word of a condemned criminal!"

"With the near view of death before his eyes. There are means of rendering truth evident, familiar to those who are often near the dying penitents, that are unknown to those of the world. In any case, Signore, the matter is worthy of investigation."

"In that thou art right. Is the hour named for the execution?"

"With the morning light, Prince."

"And the father?"

"Is dead."

"A prisoner, Carmelite!"

"A prisoner, Prince of Venice."

There was a pause.

"Hast thou heard of the death of one named Antonio?"

"Signore, yes. By the sacred nature of my holy office, do I affirm that of this crime is Jacopo innocent! I shrived the fisherman."

The doge turned away, for the truth began to dawn upon him, and the flush which glowed on his aged cheek contained a confession that might not be observed by every eye. He sought the glance of his companion, but his own expression of human feeling was met by the disciplined features of the other, as light is coldly repelled from polished stone.

"Highness!" added a tremulous voice.

"What would'st thou, child?"

"There is a God for the republic, as well as for the gondolier! Your Highness will turn this great crime from Venice?"

"Thou art of plain speech, girl!"

"The danger of Carlo has made me bold. You are much beloved by the people, and none speak of you that they do not speak of your goodness, and of your desire to serve the poor. You are the root of a rich and happy family, and you will not—nay, you cannot if you would, think it a crime for a son to devote all to a father. You are our father, and we have a right to come to you, even for mercy—but, Highness, I ask only for justice."

"Justice is the motto of Venice."

"They who live in the high favor of providence do not always know what the unhappy undergo. It has pleased God to afflict my own poor mother, who has griefs that, but for her patience and Christian faith, would have been hard to bear. The little care I had it in my power to show first caught Jacopo's eye, for his heart was then full of the duty of the child. Would your Highness consent to see poor Carlo, or to command him to be brought hither, his simple tale would give the lie to every foul slander they have dared to say against him."

"It is unnecessary—it is unnecessary. Thy faith in his innocence, girl, is more eloquent than any words of his can prove."

A gleam of joy irradiated the face of Gelsomina, who turned eagerly to the listening monk, as she continued—

"His Highness listens," she said, "and we shall prevail! Father, they menace in Venice, and alarm the timid, but they will never do the deed we feared. Is not the God of Jacopo my God, and your God?—the God of the senate, and of the doge?—of the council, and of the republic? I would the secret members of the Three could have seen poor Jacopo, as I have seen him, coming from his toil, weary with labor, and heartbroken with delay, enter the winter or the summer cell—chilling or scorching as the season might be—and struggling to be cheerful, that the falsely accused might not feel a greater weight of misery.—Oh! venerable and kind Prince, you little know the burthen that the feeble are often made to carry, for to you life has been sunshine; but there are millions who are condemned to do that they loathe, that they may not do that they dread."

"Child, thou tell'st me nothing new."

"Except in convincing you, Highness, that Jacopo is not the monster they would have him. I do not know the secret reasons of the councils for wishing the youth to lend himself to a deception that had nigh proved so fatal; but all is explained, we have naught now to fear. Come, father; we will leave the good and just doge to go to rest, as suits his years, and we will return to gladden the heart of Jacopo with our success, and thank the blessed Maria for her favor."

"Stay!" exclaimed the half-stifled old man. "Is this true that thou tellest me, girl:—Father, can it be so!"

"Signore, I have said all that truth and my conscience have prompted."

The prince seemed bewildered, turning his look from the motionless girl to the equally immovable member of the Three.

"Come hither, child," he said, his voice trembling as he spoke. "Come hither, that I may bless thee." Gelsomina sprang forward, and knelt at the feet of her sovereign. Father Anselmo never uttered a clearer or more fervent benediction than that which fell from the lips of the prince of Venice. He raised the daughter of the prison keeper, and motioned for both his visitors to withdraw. Gelsomina willingly complied, for her heart was already in the cell of Jacopo, in the eagerness to communicate her success; but the Carmelite lingered to cast a look behind, like one better acquainted with the effects of worldly policy, when connected with the interests of those who pervert governments to the advantage of the privileged. As he passed through the door, however, he felt his hopes revive, for he saw the aged prince, unable any longer to suppress his feelings, hastening towards his still silent companion, with both hands extended, eyes moistening with tears, and a look that betrayed the emotions of one anxious to find relief in human sympathies.

CHAPTER XXXI

"On—on—
It is our knell, or that of Venice.—On."
Marino Faliero

ANOTHER morning called the Venetians to their affairs. Agents of the police had been active in preparing the public mind, and as the sun rose above the narrow sea, the squares began to fill. There were present the curious citizen in his cloak and cap, barelegged laborers in wondering awe, the circumspect Hebrew in his gaberdine and beard, masked gentlemen, and many an attentive stranger from among the thousands who still frequented that declining mart. It was rumored that an act of retributive justice was about to take place, for the peace of the town and the protection of the citizen. In short, curiosity, idleness, and revenge, with all the usual train of human feelings, had drawn together a multitude eager to witness the agonies of a fellow creature.

The Dalmatians were drawn up, near the sea, in a manner to inclose the two granite columns of the piazzetta. Their grave and disciplined faces fronted inwards, towards the African pillars, those well-known landmarks of death. A few grim warriors, of higher rank, paced the flags before the troops, while a dense crowd filled the exterior space. By special favor, more than a hundred fishermen were grouped within the armed men, witnesses that their class had revenge. Between the lofty pedestals of St. Theodore and the winged lion lay the block and ax, the basket and the sawdust, the usual accompaniments of justice in that day. By their side, stood the executioner.

At length a movement in the living mass drew every eye towards the gate of the palace. A murmur arose, the multitude waved, and a small body of the sbirri came into view. Their steps were swift, like the march of destiny. The Dalmatians opened to receive these ministers of fate into their bosom, and closing their ranks again appeared to preclude the world, with its hopes, from the condemned. On reaching the block between the columns, the sbirri fell off in files, waiting at a little distance, while Jacopo was left before the engines of death, attended by his ghostly counsellor, the Carmelite. The action left them open to the gaze of the throng.

Father Anselmo was in the usual attire of a barefooted friar of his order. The cowl of the holy man was thrown back, exposing his mortified lineaments, and self-examining eye, to those around. The expression of his countenance was that of bewildered uncertainty, relieved by frequent, but fitful, glimmerings of hope. Though his lips moved constantly in prayer, his looks wandered, by an irrepressible impulse, from one window of the doge's palace to another. He took his station near the condemned, however, and thrice crossed himself, fervently.

Jacopo had tranquilly placed his person before the block. His head was bare, his cheek colorless, his throat and neck uncovered to the shoulders, his body, in its linen, and the rest of his form, was clad in the ordinary dress of a gondolier. He kneeled, with his face bowed to the block, repeated a prayer, and rising he faced the multitude, with dignity and composure. As his eye moved slowly over the array of human countenances by which he was environed, a hectic glowed on his features, for not one of them all betrayed sympathy in his sufferings. His breast heaved, and those nearest to his person thought the self-command of the miserable man was about to fail him. The result disappointed expectation. There was a shudder, and the limbs settled into repose.

"Thou hast looked in vain, among the multitude, for a friendly eye?" said the Carmelite, whose attention had been drawn to the convulsive movement.

"None here have pity for an assassin."

"Remember thy Redeemer, son. He suffered ignominy and death, for a race that denied his Godhead, and derided his sorrows."

Jacopo crossed himself, and bowed his head, in reverence.

"Hast thou more prayers to repeat, father?" demanded the chief of the sbirri, he who was particularly charged with the duty of the hour. "Though the illustrious councils are so sure in justice, they are merciful to the souls of sinners."

"Are thy orders peremptory?" asked the monk, unconsciously fixing his eye, again, on the windows of the palace. "Is it certain that the prisoner is to die?"

The officer smiled at the simplicity of the question, but with the apathy of one too much familiarized with human suffering to admit of compassion.

"Do any doubt it?" he rejoined. "It is the lot of man, reverend monk; and more especially is it the lot of those on whom the judgment of St. Mark has alighted. It were better that your penitent looked to his soul."

"Surely thou hast thy private and express commands! They have named a minute, when this bloody work is to be performed?"

"Holy Carmelite, I have. The time will not be weary, and you will do well to make the most of it, unless you have faith, already, in the prisoner's condition."

As he spoke, the officer threw a glance at the dial of the square, and walked coolly away. The action left the priest and the prisoner again alone between the columns. It was evident that the former could not yet believe in the reality of the execution.

"Hast thou no hope, Jacopo?" he asked.

"Carmelite, in my God."

"They cannot commit this wrong! I shrived Antonio—I witnessed his fate, and the prince knows it!"

"What is a prince and his justice, where the selfishness of a few rules! Father, thou art new in the senate's service."

"I shall not presume to say that God will blast those who do this deed, for we cannot trace the mysteries of His wisdom. This life, and all this world can offer, are but specks in His omniscient eye, and what to us seems evil may be pregnant with good.— Hast thou faith in thy Redeemer, Jacopo?"

The prisoner laid his hand upon his heart, and smiled, with the calm assurance that none but those who are thus sustained can feel.

"We will again pray, my son."

The Carmelite and Jacopo kneeled, side by side, the latter bowing his head to the block, while the monk uttered a final appeal to the mercy of the Deity. The former arose, but the latter continued in the suppliant attitude. The monk was so full of holy thoughts, that, forgetting his former wishes, he was nearly content the prisoner should pass into the fruition of that hope which elevated his own mind. The officer and executioner drew near, the former touching the arm of Father Anselmo, and pointing towards the distant dial.

379

"The moment is near," he whispered, more from habit, than in any tenderness to the prisoner.

The Carmelite turned instinctively towards the palace, forgetting, in the sudden impulse, all but his sense of earthly justice. There were forms at the windows, and he fancied a signal, to stay the impending blow, was about to be given.

"Hold!" he exclaimed. "For the love of Maria of most pure memory, be not too hasty!"

The exclamation was repeated by a shrill female voice, and then Gelsomina, eluding every effort to arrest her, rushed through the Dalmatians, and reached the group between the granite columns. Wonder and curiosity agitated the multitude, and a deep murmur ran through the square.

" 'Tis a maniac!" cried one.

" 'Tis a victim of his arts!" said another, for when men have a reputation for any particular vice, the world seldom fails to attribute all the rest.

Gelsomina seized the bonds of Jacopo, and endeavored, frantically, to release his arms.

"I had hoped thou would'st have been spared this sight, poor Gessina!" said the condemned.

"Be not alarmed!" she answered, gasping for breath. "They do it in mockery—'tis one of their wiles to mislead—but they cannot—no, they dare not harm a hair of thy head, Carlo!"

"Dearest Gelsomina!"

"Nay, do not hold me.—I will speak to the citizens, and tell them all. They are angry now, but when they know the truth they will love thee, Carlo, as I do."

"Bless thee—bless thee!—I would thou hadst not come!"

"Fear not for me! I am little used to such a crowd, but thou wilt see that I shall dare to speak them fair, and to make known the truth boldly. I want but breath."

"Dearest! Thou hast a mother—a father to share thy tenderness. Duty to them will make thee happy!"

"Now, I can speak, and thou shalt see how I will vindicate thy name."

She arose from the arms of her lover, who, notwithstanding his bonds, released his hold of her slight form with a reluctance greater than that with which he parted with life. The struggle in the mind of Jacopo seemed over. He bowed his head, passively, to the block, before which he was kneeling, and it is

380

probable, by the manner in which his hands were clasped, that he prayed for her who left him. Not so Gelsomina. Parting her hair, over her spotless forehead, with both hands, she advanced towards the fishermen, who were familiar to her eye, by their red caps and bare limbs. Her smile was like that which the imagination would bestow on the blessed, in their intercourse of love.

"Venetians!" she said, "I cannot blame you; ye are here to witness the death of one whom ye believe unfit to live—"

"The murderer of old Antonio!" muttered several of the group.

"Ay, even the murderer of that aged and excellent man. But, when you hear the truth, when you come to know that he whom you have believed an assassin was a pious child, a faithful servant of the republic, a gentle gondolier, and a true heart, you will change your bloody purpose, for a wish for justice."

A common murmur drowned her voice, which was so trembling and low, as to need deep stillness to render the words audible. The Carmelite had advanced to her side, and he motioned earnestly for silence.

"Hear her, men of the Lagunes!" he said; "she utters holy truth."

"This reverend and pious monk, with Heaven, is my witness. When you shall know Carlo better, and have heard his tale, ye will be the first to cry out for his release. I tell you this, that when the doge shall appear at yon window and make the signal of mercy, you need not be angry, and believe that your class has been wronged. Poor Carlo—"

"The girl raves!" interrupted the moody fishermen. "Here is no Carlo, but Jacopo Frontoni, a common Bravo."

Gelsomina smiled, in the security of the innocent, and, regaining her breath, which nervous agitation still disturbed, she resumed.

"Carlo, or Jacopo—Jacopo, or Carlo—it matters little."

"Ha! There is a sign from the palace!" shouted the Carmelite, stretching both his arms in that direction, as if to grasp a boon. The clarions sounded, and another wave stirred the multitude. Gelsomina uttered a cry of delight, and turned to throw herself upon the bosom of the reprieved. The ax glittered before her eyes, and the head of Jacopo rolled upon the stones, as if to meet her. A general movement in the living mass denoted the end.

The Dalmatians wheeled into column, the sbirri pushed aside the throng, on their way to their haunts, the water of the bay was dashed upon the flags, the clotted sawdust was gathered, the head and trunk, block, basket, ax, and executioner disappeared, and the crowd circulated around the fatal spot.

During this horrible and brief moment, neither Father Anselmo nor Gelsomina moved. All was over, and still the entire scene appeared to be delusion.

"Take away this maniac!" said an officer of the police, pointing to Gelsomina as he spoke.

He was obeyed with Venetian readiness, but his words proved prophetic, before his servitors had quitted the square. The Carmelite scarce breathed. He gazed at the moving multitude, at the windows of the palace, and at the sun which shone so gloriously in the heavens.

"Thou art lost in this crowd!" whispered one at his elbow. "Reverend Carmelite, you will do well to follow me."

The monk was too much subdued to hesitate. His conductor led him, by many secret ways, to a quay, where he instantly embarked, in a gondola, for the main. Before the sun reached the meridian, the thoughtful and trembling monk was on his journey towards the States of the Church: and ere long he became established in the castle of Sant' Agata.

At the usual hour the sun fell behind the mountains of the Tyrol, and the moon reappeared above the Lido. The narrow streets of Venice, again, poured out their thousands upon the squares. The mild light fell athwart the quaint architecture, and the giddy tower, throwing a deceptive glory on the city of islands.

The porticoes became brilliant with lamps, the gay laughed, the reckless trifled, the masker pursued his hidden purpose, the cantatrice and the grotesque acted their parts, and the million existed in that vacant enjoyment which distinguishes the pleasures of the thoughtless and the idle. Each lived for himself, while the state of Venice held its vicious sway, corrupting alike the ruler and the ruled, by its mockery of those sacred principles which are alone founded in truth and natural justice.

THE END

382